ALFRED HITCHCOCK'S
TALES TO TAKE YOUR BREATH AWAY

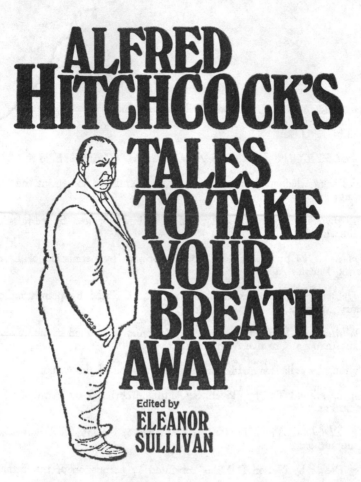

Edited by
**ELEANOR
SULLIVAN**

THE DIAL PRESS

DAVIS PUBLICATIONS, INC.
229 PARK AVE. SOUTH, NEW YORK, N.Y. 10003

COPYRIGHT NOTICES AND ACKNOWLEDGMENTS

Contents

v

Introduction

This is the second in this series of anthologies of stories from *Alfred Hitchcock's Mystery Magazine*. And starting with this anthology, the even-numbered volumes in the series will consist of stories the editors of *AHMM* believe to be the best published in the magazine the previous year.

In these pages, then, you will find the most dastardly of plots, the wittiest of contrivances, the most suspicious of circumstances, the strangest of fiction, and the direst of schemes concocted by the contributors to *AHMM* in 1976. Twenty-nine tales in all, and each of them calculated to leave you breathless—the total collection rife with the rogues and roguishness you've come to expect from *Alfred Hitchcock's Mystery Magazine*.

Alfred Hitchcock

The Arrowmont Prison Riddle

by Bill Pronzini

I first met the man who called himself by the unlikely name of Buck-master Gilloon in the late summer of 1916, my second year as warden of Arrowmont Prison. There were no living quarters within the old brick walls of the prison, which was situated on a promontory overlooking a small winding river two miles north of Arrowmont Village, so I had rented a cottage in the village proper, not far from a tavern known as Hallahan's Irish Inn. It was in this tavern, and as a result of a mutual passion for Guinness stout and the game of darts, that Gilloon and I became acquainted.

As a man he was every bit as unlikely as his name. He was in his late thirties, short and almost painfully thin; he had a glass eye and a drooping and incongruous Oriental-style mustache, wore English tweeds, gaudy Albert watch chains and plaid Scotch caps, and always carried half a dozen looseleaf notebooks in which he perpetually and secretively jotted things. He was well read and erudite, had a repertoire of bawdy stories to rival any vaudevillian in the country, and never seemed to lack ready cash. He lived in a boarding house in the center of the village and claimed to be a writer for the pulp magazines—*Argosy, Adventure, All-Story Weekly, Munsey's*. Perhaps he was, but he steadfastly refused to discuss any of his fiction, or to divulge his pseudonym or pseudonyms.

He was reticent about divulging any personal information. When personal questions arose, he deftly changed the subject. Since he did not speak with an accent, I took him to be American-born. I was able to learn, from occasional comments and observations, that he had traveled extensively throughout the world.

In my nine decades on this earth I have never encountered a more fascinating or troubling enigma than this man whose path crossed mine for a few short weeks in 1916.

Who and what was Buckmaster Gilloon? Is it possible for one enigma to be attracted and motivated by another enigma? Can that which seems natural and coincidental be the result instead of preternatural forces? These questions have plagued me in the sixty years since Gilloon and I became involved in what appeared to be an utterly enigmatic crime.

It all began on September 26, 1916—the day of the scheduled execution at Arrowmont Prison of a condemned murderer named Arthur Teasdale . . .

Shortly before noon of that day a thunderstorm struck without warning. Rain pelted down incessantly from a black sky, and lightning crackled in low jagged blazes that gave the illusion of striking unseen objects just beyond the prison walls. I was already suffering from nervous tension, as was always the case on the day of an execution, and the storm added to my discomfort. I passed the early afternoon sitting at my desk, staring out the window, listening to the inexorable ticking of my Seth Thomas, wishing the execution was done with and it was eight o'clock, when I was due to meet Gilloon at Hallahan's for Guinness and darts.

At 3:30 the two civilians who had volunteered to act as witnesses to the hanging arrived. I ushered them into a waiting room and asked them to wait until they were summoned. Then I donned a slicker and stopped by the office of Rogers, the chief guard, and asked him to accompany me to the execution shed.

The shed was relatively small, constructed of brick with a tin roof, and sat in a corner of the prison between the textile mill and the iron foundry. It was lighted by lanterns hung from the walls and the rafters and contained only a row of witness chairs and a high permanent gallows at the far end. Attached to the shed's north wall was an annex in which the death cell was located. As was customary, Teasdale had been transported there five days earlier to await due process.

He was a particularly vicious and evil man, Teasdale. He had cold-bloodedly murdered three people during an abortive robbery attempt in the state capital, and had been anything but a model prisoner during his month's confinement at Arrowmont. As a rule I had a certain compassion for those condemned to hang under my jurisdiction, and in two cases I had spoken to the governor in favor of clemency. In Teasdale's case, however, I had conceded that a continuance of his life would serve no good purpose.

When I had visited him the previous night to ask if he wished to see a clergyman or to order anything special for his last meal, he had cursed me and Rogers and the entire prison personnel with an almost maniacal intensity, vowing vengeance on us all from the grave.

I rather expected, as Rogers and I entered the death cell at ten minutes of four, to find Teasdale in much the same state. However, he had fallen instead into an acute melancholia; he lay on his cot with his knees drawn up and his eyes staring blankly at the opposite wall. The two guards assigned to him, Hollowell and Granger (Granger was also the state-appointed hangman), told us he had been like that for several hours. I spoke to him, asking again if he wished to confer with a clergyman. He did not answer, did not move. I inquired if he had any last requests, and if it was his wish to wear a hood for his final walk to the gallows and for the execution. He did not respond.

I took Hollowell aside. "Perhaps it would be better to use the hood," I said. "It will make it easier for all of us."

"Yes, sir."

Rogers and I left the annex, accompanied by Granger, for a final examination of the gallows. The rope had already been hung and the hangman's knot tied. While Granger made certain they were secure I unlocked the door beneath the platform, which opened into a short passage that ended in a narrow cubicle beneath the trap. The platform had been built eight feet off the floor, so that the death throes of the condemned man would be concealed from the witnesses—a humane gesture which was not observed by all prisons in our state, and for which I was grateful.

After I had made a routine examination of the cubicle, and relocked the door, I mounted the thirteen steps to the platform. The trap beneath the gibbet arm was operated by a lever set into the floor; when Granger threw the lever, the trap would fall open. Once we tried it and reset it, I pronounced everything in readiness and sent Rogers to summon the civilian witnesses and the prison doctor. It was then 4:35 and the execution would take place at precisely five o'clock. I had received a wire from the governor the night before, informing me that there wasn't the remotest chance of a stay being granted.

When Rogers returned with the witnesses and the doctor, we all took chairs in the row arranged some forty feet opposite the gallows. Time passed, tensely; with thunder echoing hollowly outside, a hard rain drumming against the tin roof, and eerie shadows not entirely dispelled by the lanternlight, the moments before that execution were particularly disquieting.

I held my pocket watch open on my knee, and at 4:55 I signaled to the guard at the annex door to call for the prisoner. Three more minutes crept by and then the door reopened and Granger and Hollowell brought Teasdale into the shed.

The three men made a grim procession as they crossed to the gallows steps: Granger in his black hangman's duster, Hollowell in his khaki guard uniform and peaked cap, Teasdale between them in his grey prison clothing and black hood. Teasdale's shoes dragged across the floor—he was stiffly unresisting weight until they reached the steps; then he struggled briefly and Granger and Hollowell were forced to tighten their grip and all but carry him up onto the gallows. Hollowell held him slumped on the trap while Granger solemnly fitted the noose around his neck and drew it taut.

The hands on my watch read five o'clock when, as prescribed by law, Granger intoned, "Have you any last words before the sentence imposed on you is carried out?"

Teasdale said nothing, but his body twisted with a spasm of fear.

Granger looked in my direction and I raised my hand to indicate final sanction. He backed away from Teasdale and rested his hand on the release lever. As he did so, there came from outside a long rolling peal of thunder that seemed to shake the shed roof. A chill touched the nape of my neck and I shifted uneasily in my chair.

Just as the sound of the thunder faded, Granger threw the lever and Hollowell released Teasdale and stepped back. The trap thudded open and the condemned man plummeted downward.

In that same instant I thought I saw a faint silvery glimmer above the opening, but it was so brief that I took it for an optical illusion. My attention was focused on the rope: it danced for a moment under the weight of the body, then pulled taut and became motionless. I let out a soft tired sigh and sat forward while Granger and Hollowell, both of whom were looking away from the open trap, silently counted off the passage of sixty seconds.

When the minute had elapsed, Granger turned and walked to the edge of the trap. If the body hung laxly, he would signal to me so that the prison doctor and I could enter the cubicle and officially pronounce Teasdale deceased; if the body was still thrashing, thus indicating the condemned man's neck had not been broken in the fall—grisly prospect, but I had seen it happen—more time would be allowed to pass. It sounds brutal, I know, but such was the law and it had to be obeyed without question.

But Granger's reaction was so peculiar and so violent that I came immediately to my feet. He flinched as if he had been struck in the stomach and his face twisted into an expression of disbelief. He dropped to his hands and knees at the front of the trap as Hollowell came up beside him and leaned down to peer into the passageway.

"What is it, Granger?" I called. "What's the matter?"

He straightened after a few seconds and pivoted toward me. "You better get up here, Warden Parker," he said. His voice was shrill and tremulous and he clutched at his stomach. "Quick!"

Rogers and I exchanged glances, then ran to the steps, mounted them, and hurried to the trap, the other guards and the prison doctor close behind us. As soon as I looked downward, it was my turn to stare with incredulity, to exclaim against what I saw—and what I did not see.

The hangman's noose at the end of the rope was empty.

Except for the black hood on the ground, the cubicle was empty.

Impossibly, inconceivably, the body of Arthur Teasdale had vanished.

I raced down the gallows steps and fumbled the platform door open with my key. I had the vague desperate hope that Teasdale had somehow slipped the noose and that I would see him lying within, against the door—that small section of the passageway was shrouded in darkness and not quite penetrable from above—but he wasn't there. The passageway, like the cubicle, was deserted.

While I called for a lantern Rogers hoisted up the rope to examine it and the noose. A moment later he announced that it had not been tampered with in any way. When a guard brought the lantern I embarked on a careful search of the area, but there were no loose boards in the walls of the passage or the cubicle, and the floor was of solid concrete. On the floor I discovered a thin sliver of wood about an inch long, which may or may not have been there previously. Aside from that, there was not so much as a strand of hair or a loose thread to be found. And the black hood told me nothing at all.

There simply did not seem to be any way Teasdale—or his remains—could have gotten, or been gotten, out of there.

I stood for a moment, staring at the flickering light from the lantern, listening to the distant rumbling of thunder. *Had* Teasdale died at the end of the hangman's rope? Or had he somehow managed to cheat death? I had seen him fall through the trap with my own eyes, had seen the rope dance and then pull taut with the weight of his body. He *must* have expired, I told myself.

A shiver moved along my back. I found myself remembering Teasdale's threats to wreak vengeance from the grave, and I had the irrational thought that perhaps something otherworldly had been responsible for the phenomenon we had witnessed. Teasdale had, after all, been a malignant individual. Could he have been so evil that he had managed to summon the Powers of Darkness to save him in the instant before death—or to claim him soul *and* body in the instant after it?

I refused to believe it. I am a practical man, not prone to superstition, and it has always been my nature to seek a logical explanation for even the most uncommon occurrence. Arthur Teasdale had disappeared, yes; but it could not be other than an earthly force behind the deed. Which meant that, alive or dead, Teasdale was still somewhere inside the walls of Arrowmont Prison.

I roused myself, left the passageway, and issued instructions for a thorough search of the prison guards. I ordered word sent to the guards in the watchtowers to double their normal vigilance. I noticed that Hollowell wasn't present along with the assembled guards and asked where he had gone. One of the others said he had seen Hollowell hurry out of the shed several minutes earlier.

Frowning, I pondered this information. Had Hollowell intuited something, or even seen something, and gone off unwisely to investigate on his own rather than confide in the rest of us? He had been employed at Arrowmont Prison less than two months, so I knew relatively little about him. I requested that he be found and brought to my office.

When Rogers and Granger and the other guards had departed, I escorted the two civilian witnesses to the administration building, where I asked them to remain until the mystery was explained. As I settled grimly at my desk to await Hollowell and word on the search of the grounds, I expected such an explanation within the hour.

I could not, however, have been more wrong.

The first development came after thirty minutes, and it was nearly as alarming as the disappearance of Teasdale from the gallows cubicle: one of the guards brought the news, ashen-faced, that a body had been discovered behind a stack of lumber in a lean-to between the execution shed and the iron foundry. But it was not the body of Arthur Teasdale!

It was that of Hollowell, stabbed to death with an awl.

I went immediately. As I stood beneath the rain-swept lean-to, looking down at the bloody front of poor Hollowell's uniform, a fresh set of unsettling questions tumbled through my mind. Had he been killed because, as I had first thought, he had either seen or intuited something connected with Teasdale's disappearance? If that was the case, whatever it was had died with him.

Or was it possible that he had himself been involved in the disappearance and been murdered to assure his silence? But how could he have been involved? He had been in my sight the entire time on the gallows platform. He had done nothing suspicious, could not in any way I could conceive have assisted in the deed.

Might his death have been part of Teasdale's vow to destroy us all? No. My instinct for logic fought for the upper hand.

How could Teasdale have survived the hanging?

How could he have escaped not only the gallows but the execution shed itself?

The only explanation seemed to be that it was not a live Arthur Teasdale who was carrying out his warped revenge, but a dead one who had been embraced and given earthly powers by the Forces of Evil . . .

In order to dispel the dark reflections from my mind, I personally supervised the balance of the search. Tines of lightning split the sky and thunder continued to hammer the roofs as we went from building to building. No corner of the prison compound escaped our scrutiny. No potential hiding place was overlooked. We went so far as to test for the presence of tunnels in the work areas and in the individual cells, although I had instructed just such a search only weeks before as part of my security program.

We found nothing.

Alive or dead, Arthur Teasdale was no longer within the walls of Arrowmont Prison.

I left the prison at ten o'clock that night. There was nothing more to be done, and I was filled with such depression and anxiety that I could not bear to spend another minute there. I had debated contacting the governor, of course, and, wisely or not, had decided against it for the time being. He would think me a lunatic if I requested assistance in a county or statewide search for a man who had for all intents and purposes been hanged at five o'clock that afternoon. If there were no new developments within the next twenty-four hours, I knew I would have no choice but to explain the situation to him. And I had no doubt that such an explanation unaccompanied by Teasdale or Teasdale's remains would cost me my position.

Before leaving, I swore everyone to secrecy, saying that I would have any man's job if he leaked word of the day's events to the press or to the public-at-large. The last thing I wanted was rumor-mongering and a general panic as a result of it. I warned Granger and the other guards who had come in contact with Teasdale to be especially wary and finally left word that I was to be contacted immediately if there were any further developments before morning.

I had up to that time given little thought to my own safety. But when I reached my cottage in the village I found myself imagining menace in every shadow and sound. Relaxation was impossible. After twenty minutes I felt impelled to leave, to seek out a friendly face. I told my housekeeper I would be at Hallahan's Irish Inn if anyone called for me and drove my Packard to the tavern.

The first person I saw upon entering was Buckmaster Gilloon. He was seated alone in a corner booth, writing intently in one of his notebooks, a stein of draught Guinness at his elbow.

Gilloon had always been very secretive about his notebooks and never allowed anyone to glimpse so much as a word of what he put into them. But he was so engrossed when I walked up to the booth that he did not hear me, and I happened to glance down at the open page on which he was writing. There was but a single interrogative sentence on the page, clearly legible in his bold hand. The sentence read:

If a jimbuck stands alone by the sea, on a night when the dark moon sings, how many grains of sand in a single one of his footprints?

That sentence has always haunted me, because I cannot begin to understand its significance. I have no idea what a jimbuck is, except perhaps as a fictional creation, and yet the passage was like none which ever appeared in such periodicals as *Argosy* or *Munsey's*.

Gilloon sensed my presence after a second or two, and he slammed the notebook shut. A ferocious scowl crossed his normally placid features. He said irritably, "Reading over a man's shoulder is a nasty habit, Parker."

"I'm sorry, I didn't mean to pry—"

"I'll thank you to be more respectful of my privacy in the future."

"Yes, of course." I sank wearily into the booth opposite him and called for a Guinness.

Gilloon studied me across the table. "You look haggard, Parker," he said. "What's troubling you?"

"It's . . . nothing."

"Everything is something."

"I'm not at liberty to discuss it."

"Would it have anything to do with the execution at Arrowmont Prison this afternoon?"

I blinked. "Why would you surmise that?"

"Logical assumption," Gilloon said. "You are obviously upset, and yet you are a man who lives quietly and suffers no apparent personal problems. You are warden of Arrowmont Prison and the fact of the execution is public knowledge. You customarily come to the inn at eight o'clock, and yet you didn't make your appearance tonight until after eleven."

I said, "I wish I had your mathematical mind, Gilloon."

"Indeed? Why is that?"

"Perhaps then I could find answers where none seem to exist."

"Answers to what?"

A waiter arrived with my Guinness and I took a swallow gratefully. Gilloon was looking at me with piercing interest. I avoided his one-eyed gaze, knowing I had already said too much. But there was something about Gilloon that demanded confidence. Perhaps he could shed some light on the riddle of Teasdale's disappearance.

"Come now, Parker—answers to what?" he repeated. "Has something happened at the prison?"

And of course I weakened—partly because of frustration and worry, partly because the possibility that I might never learn the secret loomed large and painful. "Yes," I said, "something has happened at the prison. Something incredible, and I mean that literally." I paused to draw a heavy breath. "If I tell you about it, do I have your word that you won't let it go beyond this table?"

"Naturally." Gilloon leaned forward and his good eye glittered with anticipation. "Go on, Parker."

More or less calmly at first, then with increasing agitation as I relived the events, I proceeded to tell Gilloon everything that had transpired at the prison. He listened with attention, not once interrupting. I had never seen him excited prior to that night, but when I had finished, he was fairly squirming. He took off his Scotch cap and ran a hand roughly through his thinning brown hair.

"Fascinating tale," he said.

"Horrifying would be a more appropriate word."

"That too, yes. No wonder you're upset."

"It simply defies explanation," I said. "And yet there has to be one. I refuse to accept the supernatural implications."

"I wouldn't be so skeptical of the supernatural if I were you, Parker. I've come across a number of things in my travels which could not be satisfactorily explained by man or science."

I stared at him. "Does that mean you believe Teasdale's disappearance was arranged by forces beyond human ken?"

"No, no. I was merely making a considered observation. Have you given me every detail of what happened?"

"I believe so."

"Think it through again—be sure."

Frowning, I reviewed the events once more. And it came to me that I had neglected to mention the brief silvery glimmer which had appeared above the trap in the instant Teasdale plunged through; I had, in fact, forgotten all about it. This time I mentioned it to Gilloon.

"Ah," he said.

"Ah? Does it have significance?"

"Perhaps. Can you be more specific about it?"

"I'm afraid not. It was so brief I took it at the time for an optical illusion."

"You saw no other such glimmers?"

"None."

"How far away from the gallows were you sitting?"

"Approximately forty feet."

"Is the shed equipped with electric lights?"

"No—lanterns."

"I see," Gilloon said meditatively. He seized one of his notebooks, opened it, shielded it from my eyes with his left arm, and began to write furiously with his pencil. He wrote without pause for a good three minutes, before I grew both irritated and anxious.

"Gilloon," I said finally, "stop that infernal scribbling and tell me what's on your mind."

He gave me no indication of having heard me. His pencil continued to scratch against the paper, filling another page. Except for the movement of his right hand and one side of his mouth gnawing at the edge of his mustache, he was as rigid as a block of stone.

"Damn it, Gilloon!"

But it was another ten seconds before the pencil became motionless. He stared at what he had written and then looked up at me. "Parker," he said, "did Arthur Teasdale have a trade?"

The question took me by surprise. "A trade?"

"Yes. What did he do for a living, if anything?"

"What bearing can that have on what's happened?"

"Perhaps a great deal," Gilloon said.

"He worked in a textile mill."

"And there is a textile mill at the prison, correct?"

"Yes."

"Does it stock quantities of silk?"

"Silk? Yes, on occasion. What—?"

I did not finish what I was about to say, for he had shut me out and resumed writing in his notebook. I repressed an oath of exasperation, took a long draught of Guinness to calm myself, and prepared to demand that he tell me what theory he had devised. Before I could do that, however, Gilloon abruptly closed the notebook, slid out of the booth, and fairly loomed over me.

"I'll need to see the execution shed," he said.

"What for?"

"Corroboration of certain facts."

"But—" I stood up hastily. "You've suspicioned a possible answer, that's clear," I said, "though I can't for the life of me see how, on the basis of the information I've given you. What is it?"

"I must see the execution shed," he said firmly. "I will not voice premature speculations."

It touched my mind that the man was a bit mad. After all, I had only known him for a few weeks, and from the first he had been decidedly eccentric in most respects. Still, I had never had cause to question his mental faculties before this, and the aura of self-assurance and confidence he projected was forceful. Because I needed so desperately to solve the riddle, I couldn't afford *not* to indulge, at least for a while, the one man who might be able to provide it.

"Very well," I said, "I'll take you to the prison."

Rain still fell in black torrents—although without thunder and lightning—when I brought my Packard around the last climbing curve onto the promontory. Lanternlight glowed fuzzily in the prison watchtowers, and the bare brick walls had an unpleasant oily sheen. At this hour of night, in the storm, the place seemed forbidding and shrouded in human despair—an atmosphere I had not previously apprehended during the two years I had been its warden. Strange how a brush with the unknown can alter one's perspective and stir the fears that lie at the bottom of one's soul.

Beside me Gilloon did not speak; he sat perfectly erect, his hands resting on the notebooks on his lap. I parked in the small lot facing the main gates, and after Gilloon had carefully tucked the notebooks inside his slicker we ran through the downpour to the gates. I gestured to the guard, who nodded beneath the hood of his oilskin, allowed us to enter, and then quickly closed the iron halves behind us and returned to the warmth of the gatehouse. I led Gilloon directly across the compound to the execution shed.

The guards I had posted inside seemed edgy and grateful for company. It was colder now, and despite the fact that all the lanterns were lit it also seemed darker and filled with more restless shadows. But the earlier aura of spiritual menace permeated the air, at least to my sensitivities. If Gilloon noticed it, he gave no indication.

He wasted no time crossing to the gallows and climbing the steps to the platform. I followed him to the trap, which still hung open. Gilloon peered into the cubicle, got onto all fours to squint at the rectangular edges of the opening, and then hoisted the hangman's rope and studied the noose. Finally, with surprising agility, he dropped down inside the cubicle, requesting a lantern which I fetched for him, and spent minutes crawling about with his nose to the floor. He located the thin splinter of wood I had noticed earlier, studied it in the lantern glow, and dropped it into the pocket of his tweed coat.

When he came out through the passageway he wore a look mixed of ferocity and satisfaction. "Stand there a minute, will you?" he said. He hurried over to where the witness chairs were arranged, then called, "In which of these chairs were you sitting during the execution?"

"Fourth one from the left."

Gilloon sat in that chair, produced his notebooks, opened one, and bent over it. I waited with mounting agitation while he committed notes to paper. When he glanced up again, the flickering lanternglow gave his face a spectral cast.

He said, "While Granger placed the noose over Teasdale's head Hollowell held the prisoner on the trap—is that correct?"

"It is."

"Stand as Hollowell was standing."

I moved to the edge of the opening, turning slightly quarter profile.

"You're certain that was the exact position?"

"Yes."

"Once the trap had been sprung, what did Hollowell do?"

"Moved a few paces away." I demonstrated.

"Did he avert his eyes from the trap?"

"Yes, he did. So did Granger. That's standard procedure."

"Which direction did he face?"

I frowned. "I'm not quite sure," I said. "My attention was on the trap and the rope."

"You're doing admirably, Parker. After Granger threw the trap lever, did he remain standing beside it?"

"Until he had counted off sixty seconds, yes."

"And then?"

"As I told you, he walked to the trap and looked into the cubicle. Again, that is standard procedure for the hangman. When he saw it was empty he uttered a shocked exclamation, went to his knees, and leaned down to see if Teasdale had somehow slipped the noose and fallen or crawled into the passageway."

"At which part of the opening did he go to his knees? Front, rear, one of the sides?"

"The front. But I don't see—"

"Would you mind illustrating?"

I grumbled but did as he asked. Some thirty seconds passed in silence. Finally I stood and turned, and of course found Gilloon again writing in his notebook. I descended the gallows steps. Gilloon closed the notebook and stood with an air of growing urgency. "Where would Granger be at this hour?" he asked. "Still here at the prison?"

"I doubt it. He came on duty at three and should have gone off again at midnight."

"It's imperative that we find him as soon as possible, Parker. Now that I'm onto the solution of this riddle, there's no time to waste."

"You have solved it?"

"I'm certain I have." He hurried me out of the shed.

I felt dazed as we crossed the rain-soaked compound, yet Gilloon's positiveness had infused in me a similar sense of urgency. We entered the administration building and I led the way to Rogers' office, where we found him preparing to depart for the night. When I asked about Granger, Rogers said that he had signed out some fifty minutes earlier, at midnight.

"Where does he live?" Gilloon asked us.

"In Hainesville, I think."

"We must go there immediately, Parker. And we had better take half a dozen well-armed men with us."

I stared at him. "Do you honestly believe that's necessary?"

"I do," Gilloon said grimly. "If we're fortunate, it will help prevent another murder."

The six-mile drive to the village of Hainesville was charged with tension, made even more acute by the muddy roads and the pelting rain. Gilloon stubbornly refused to comment on the way as to whether he believed Granger to be a culpable or innocent party, or as to whether he expected to find Teasdale—alive or dead—at Granger's home. There would be time enough later for explanations, he said.

Hunched over the wheel of the Packard, conscious of the two heavily armed prison guards in the rear seat and the headlamps of Rogers' car following closely behind, I could not help but wonder if I might be making a prize fool of myself. Suppose I had been wrong in my judgment of Gilloon, and he *was* daft after all? Or a well-meaning fool in his own right? Or worst of all, a hoaxster?

Nevertheless, there was no turning back now. I had long since committed myself. Whatever the outcome, I had placed the fate of my career firmly in the hands of Buckmaster Gilloon.

We entered the outskirts of Hainesville. One of the guards who rode with us lived there, and he directed us down the main street and into a turn just beyond the church. The lane in which Granger lived, he said, was two blocks further up and one block east.

Beside me Gilloon spoke for the first time. "I suggest we park a distance away from Granger's residence, Parker. It won't do to announce our arrival by stopping directly in front."

I nodded. When I made the turn into the lane I took the Packard onto the verge and doused its lights. Rogers' car drifted in behind, headlamps also winking out. A moment later eight of us stood in a tight group in the roadway, huddling inside our slickers as we peered up the lane.

There were four houses in the block, two on each side, spaced widely apart. The pair on our left, behind which stretched open meadowland, were dark. The furthest of the two on the right was also dark, but the closer one showed light in one of the front windows. Thick smoke curled out of its chimney and was swirled into nothingness by the howling wind. A huge oak shaded the front yard. Across the rear, a copse of swaying pine stood silhouetted against the black sky.

The guard who lived in Hainesville said, "That's Granger's place, the one showing light."

We left the road and set out laterally across the grassy flatland to the

pines, then through them toward Granger's cottage. From a point behind the house, after issuing instructions for the others to wait there,
Gilloon, Rogers, and I made our way downward past an old stone well
and through a sodden growth of weeds. The sound of the storm
muffled our approach as we proceeded single-file, Gilloon tacitly assuming leadership, along the west side of the house to the lighted window.

Gilloon put his head around the frame for the first cautious look inside. Momentarily he stepped back and motioned me to take his place.
When I had moved to where I could peer in, I saw Granger standing
relaxed before the fireplace, using a poker to prod a blazing fire not
wholly comprised of logs—something else, a blackened lump already
burned beyond recognition, was being consumed there. But he was not
alone in the room; a second man stood watching him, an expression of
concentrated malevolence on his face—and an old hammerless revolver
tucked into the waistband of his trousers.

Arthur Teasdale.

I experienced a mixture of relief, rage, and resolve as I moved away
to give Rogers his turn. It was obvious that Granger was guilty of
complicity in Teasdale's escape—and I had always liked and trusted the
man. But I supposed everyone had his price—and I may even have had
a fleeting wonder as to what my own might be.

After Rogers had his look, the three of us returned to the back yard,
where I told him to prepare the rest of the men for a front-and-rear assault on the cottage. Then Gilloon and I took up post in the shadows
behind the stone well. Now that my faith in *him*, at least, had been
vindicated, I felt an enormous gratitude—but this was hardly the time
to express it. Or to ask any of the questions that were racing through
my mind. We waited in silence.

In less than four minutes all six of my men had surrounded the
house. I could not hear it when those at the front broke in, but the
men at the back entered the rear door swiftly. Soon the sound of pistol
shots rose above the cry of the storm.

Gilloon and I hastened inside. In the parlor we found Granger sitting on the floor beside the hearth, his head buried in his hands. He
had not been injured, nor had any of the guards. Teasdale was lying
just beyond the entrance to the center hallway. The front of his shirt
was bloody, but he had merely suffered a superficial shoulder wound
and was cursing like a madman. He would live to hang again, I remember thinking, in the execution shed at Arrowmont Prison.

Sixty minutes later, after Teasdale had been placed under heavy guard in the prison infirmary and a remorsefully silent Granger had been locked in a cell, Rogers and Gilloon and I met in my office. Outside, the rain had slackened to a drizzle.

"Now then, Gilloon," I began sternly, "we owe you a great debt, and I acknowledge it here and now. But explanations are long overdue."

He smiled with the air of a man who has just been through an exhilarating experience. "Of course," he said. "Suppose we begin with Hollowell. You're quite naturally wondering if he was bribed by Teasdale—if he also assisted in the escape. The answer is no: he was an innocent pawn."

"Then why was he killed? Revenge?"

"Not at all. His life was taken—and not at the place where his body was later discovered—so that the escape trick could be worked in the first place. It was one of the primary keys to the plan's success."

"I don't understand," I said. "The escape trick had already been completed when Hollowell was stabbed."

"Ah, but it hadn't," Gilloon said. "Hollowell was murdered *before* the execution, sometime between four and five o'clock."

We stared at him. "Gilloon," I said, "Rogers and I and five other witnesses *saw* Hollowell inside the shed—"

"Did you, Parker? The execution shed is lighted by lanterns. On a dark afternoon, during a thunderstorm, visibility is not reliable. And you were some forty feet from him. You saw an average-sized man wearing a guard's uniform, with a guard's peaked cap drawn down over his forehead—a man you had no reason to assume was not Hollowell. You took his identity for granted."

"I can't dispute the logic of that," I said. "But if you're right that it wasn't Hollowell, who was it?"

"Teasdale, of course."

"Teasdale! For God's sake, man, if Teasdale assumed the identity of Hollowell, whom did we see carried in as Teasdale?"

"No one," Gilloon said.

My mouth fell open, and there was a moment of heavy silence. I broke it finally by exclaiming, "Are you saying we did not see a man hanged at five o'clock yesterday afternoon?"

"Precisely."

"Are you saying we were all victims of some sort of mass hallucination?"

"Certainly not. You saw what you believed to be Arthur Teasdale, just as you saw what you believed to be Hollowell. Again let me remind you: the lighting was poor and you had no reason at the time to suspect deception. But think back, Parker. What actually *did* you see? The shape of a man with a black hood covering his head, supported between two other men. But did you see that figure walk or hear it speak? Did you at any time discern an identifiable part of a human being, such as a hand or an exposed ankle?"

I squeezed my eyes shut for a moment, mentally re-examining the events in the shed. "No," I admitted. "I discerned nothing but the hood and the clothing and the shoes. But I *did* see him struggle at the foot of the gallows, and his body spasm on the trap. How do you explain them?"

"Simply. Like everything else, they were an illusion. At a preconceived time Granger and Teasdale had only to slow their pace and jostle the figure with their own bodies to create the impression that the figure itself was resisting them. Teasdale alone used the same method on the trap."

"If it is your contention that the figure was some sort of dummy, I can't believe it, Gilloon. How could a dummy be made to vanish any more easily than a man?"

"It was not, strictly speaking, a dummy."

"Then what the devil was it?"

Gilloon held up a hand; he appeared to be enjoying himself immensely. "Do you recall my asking if Teasdale had a trade? You responded that he had worked in a textile mill, whereupon I asked if the prison textile mill stocked silk."

"Yes, yes, I recall that."

"Come now, Parker, use your imagination. What is one of the uses of silk—varnished silk?"

"I don't know," I began, but no sooner were the words past my lips than the answer sprang into my mind. "Good Lord—balloons!"

"Exactly."

"The figure we saw was a *balloon?*"

"In effect, yes. It is not difficult to sew and tie off a large piece of silk in the rough shape of a man. When inflated to a malleable rather than a fully expanded state with helium or hydrogen, and seen in poor light from a distance of forty feet or better, while covered by clothing and a hood, and weighted down with a pair of shoes and held tightly by two men—the effect can be maintained."

I gaped.

"The handiwork would have been done by Teasdale in the relative privacy of the death cell. The material was doubtless supplied from the prison textile mill by Granger. Once the sewing and tying had been accomplished, I imagine Granger took the piece out of the prison, varnished it, and returned it later. It need not have been inflated, naturally, until just prior to the execution. As to where the gas was obtained, I would think that there would certainly be a cylinder of hydrogen in the prison foundry."

I nodded.

"In any event, between four and five o'clock, when the three of them were alone in the death annex, Teasdale murdered Hollowell with an awl Granger had given him. Granger then transported Hollowell's body behind the stack of lumber a short distance away and probably also returned the gas cylinder to the foundry. The storm would have provided all the shield necessary, though even without it the risk was one worth taking.

"Once Granger and Teasdale had brought the balloon-figure to the gallows, Granger, as hangman, placed the noose carefully around the head. You told me, Parker, that he was the last to examine the noose. While he was doing so, I expect he inserted into the fibers at the inner bottom that sharp sliver of wood you found in the trap cubicle. When he drew the noose taut, he made sure the sliver touched the balloon's surface so that when the trap was sprung and the balloon plunged downward the splinter would penetrate the silk. The sound of a balloon deflating is negligible; the storm made it more so. The dancing of the rope, of course, was caused by the escaping air.

"During the ensuing sixty seconds, the balloon completely deflated. There was nothing in the cubicle at that point except a bundle of clothing, silk, and shoes. The removal of all but the hood, to complete the trick, was a simple enough matter. You told me how it was done when you mentioned the silvery glimmer you saw above the trap.

"That glimmer was a brief reflection of lanternlight off part of a length of thin wire which had been attached to the clothing and to the balloon. Granger concealed the wire in his hand, and played out most of a seven- or eight-foot coil before he threw the trap lever.

"After he had gone to his knees with his back to the witness chairs, he merely opened the front of his duster, hauled up the bundle, and stowed it back inside the duster. No doubt it made something of a bulge, but the attention was focused on other matters. You did notice, Parker—and it was a helpful clue—that Granger appeared to be holding his stomach as if he were about to be ill. What he was actually doing was clutching the bundle so that it would not fall from beneath his duster. Later he hid the bundle among his belongings and transported it out of the prison when he went off duty. It was that bundle that we saw burning in the fireplace in his cottage."

"But how did *Teasdale* get out of the prison?"

"The most obvious way imaginable," Gilloon said. "He walked out through the front gates."

"What!"

"Yes. Remember, he was wearing a guard's uniform—supplied by Granger—and there was a storm raging. I noticed when we first arrived tonight that the gateman seemed eager to return to his gatehouse, where it was dry. He scarcely looked at you and did not question me. That being the case, it's obvious that he would not have questioned someone who wore the proper uniform and kept his face averted as he gave Hollowell's name. The guards had not yet been alerted and the gateman would have no reason to suspect trickery.

"Once out, I suspect Teasdale simply took Granger's car and drove to Hainesville. When Granger himself came off duty, I would venture to guess that he obtained a ride home with another guard, using some pretext to explain the absence of his own vehicle.

"I did not actually *know*, of course, that we would find Teasdale at Granger's place; I merely made a logical supposition in light of the other facts. Since Granger was the only other man alive who knew how the escape had been worked, I reasoned that an individual of Teasdale's stripe would not care to leave him alive and vulnerable to a confession, no matter what promises he might have made to Granger."

I sat forward.

"If Teasdale managed his actual escape that easily, why did he choose to go through all that trickery with the balloon? Why didn't he just murder Hollowell, with Granger's help, and then leave the prison *prior* to the execution, between four and five?"

"Oh, I suppose he thought that the bizarre circumstances surrounding the disappearance of an apparently hanged man would insure him enough time to get safely clear of this immediate area. If you were confused and baffled, you would not sound an instant alarm, whereas you certainly would have if he had simply disappeared from his cell. Also, I would guess that the prospect of leaving all of you a legacy of mystery and horror afforded him a warped sense of revenge."

"You're a brilliant man," I told him as I sank back in my chair.

Gilloon shrugged. "This kind of puzzle takes logic rather than brilliance, Parker. As I told you earlier tonight, it isn't always wise to discount the supernatural; but in a case where no clear evidence of the supernatural exists, the answer generally lies in some form of illusion. I've encountered a number of seemingly incredible occurrences, some of which were even more baffling than this one and most of which involved illusion. I expect I'll encounter others in the future as well."

"Why do you say that?"

"One almost seems able after a while to divine places where they will occur," he said matter-of-factly, "and therefore to make oneself available to challenge them."

I blinked at him. "Do you mean you *intuited* something like this would happen at Arrowmont Prison? That you have some sort of prevision?"

"Perhaps. Perhaps not. Perhaps I'm nothing more than a pulp writer who enjoys traveling." He gave me an enigmatic smile and got to his feet clutching his notebooks. "I can't speak for you, Parker," he said, "but I seem to have acquired an intense thirst. You wouldn't happen to know where we might obtain a Guinness at this hour, would you?"

One week later, suddenly and without notice, Gilloon left Arrowmont Village. One day he was there, the next he was not. Where he went I do not know: I neither saw him nor heard of or from him again.

Who and what was Buckmaster Gilloon? Is it possible for one enigma to be attracted and motivated by another enigma? Can that which seems natural and coincidental be the result instead of preternatural forces? Perhaps you can understand now why these questions have plagued me in the sixty years since I knew him. And why I am continually haunted by that single passage I read by accident in his notebook, the passage which may hold the key to Buckmaster Gilloon:

If a jimbuck stands alone by the sea, on a night when the dark moon sings, how many grains of sand in a single one of his footprints? . . .

End of the Line

by Edward D. Hoch

It was Saturday morning, when everything moved a bit more slowly—even the bus carrying Professor Walden Swift to his destination. Now it was the end of the line, and he got out because he knew Tommy Easton would have gotten out here too, the night before. For a time he stood silently outside the bus station, trying to see the scene the way Tommy would have seen it. He'd boarded the express bus at the University and he'd left it here in the city, less than twelve hours earlier.

But then what?

Professor Swift rubbed the mist from his glasses and focused on the line of shops across the street. The fifty-minute trip might have made Tommy hungry, or at least thirsty. He crossed the street to a greasy-windowed lunch counter with a red neon coffee cup blinking on and off above the door, circled by the words *We Never Close*.

"What'll you have?" asked a beefy counter man in a sweat-stained shirt. Stitched above his pocket was the name *Fred*.

"Coffee, black. And one of those doughnuts, please."

"Sure, Mister. Nice morning, huh?"

Walden Swift hadn't really thought about it. He rarely thought about the weather. "I suppose so."

"You down from the college?"

"How could you tell?"

"That was the express just pulled in. We get a lot of kids on weekends. You a teacher there?"

"A professor of English literature."

"Yeah? Pay pretty good?"

"Fair." Walden Swift watched while the man puttered about behind the counter, making coffee, washing dishes from the breakfast crowd, occasionally wiping off the spotted counter with a dirty damp cloth. "I'm looking for a boy," the professor said.

"Huh?"

"A boy. One of my freshman students. He left campus last evening and took a bus down here. I have to find him."

The counter man shrugged. "Lots of college kids come in here."

"This would have been last night around ten, off that same express bus. Here's a picture of him." Walden Swift opened his wallet and held out an overexposed flash photo taken at a campus political rally a few months earlier. "This boy," he said, indicating a sandy-haired youth in torn jeans and a sweatshirt.

"Yeah, maybe I seen him last night. I can't be sure." He edged away, wiping the counter. "I didn't come on till midnight."

Professor Swift returned the picture to his wallet and sat in silence, his brooding eyes scanning the fly-specked, grease-stained walls. A number of cardboard signs had been tacked up in spots, all designed to lure the college students further into the depths of the city. *Wrestling every Wednesday night! Bring your girl!* But it had been a Friday night, not a Wednesday. *Funland! No place like it!* He jotted that one down in his notebook. An amusement park was always a possibility.

Then another sign caught his eye. *Rock at Johnnie's! Every Friday night!*

"Where's Johnnie's?" he asked the counter man.

"Everybody knows where Johnnie's is."

"I don't."

"Straight down this street for five blocks, turn right and go over another block. It's on the corner."

"Many of the college crowd go there?"

"Sure. Friday nights you can't get near the place. But you're a little late. This is Saturday."

"I know." He paid for his coffee and doughnut and left a quarter tip.

Outside, the blue haze of the April morning was gradually fading before the currents of clear air off the Sound. In another hour the sun's glare would reveal the city as it truly was, spotlighting the peeled faces of the golden-haired girls on the faded soft-drink posters, sharpening the focus on the garish storefronts with their promise of instant pleasure.

On any other Saturday in April, Walden Swift might have joined in some campus activity—an impromptu picnic or even a bull session about the problems of the Third World. He liked to mingle with the young people he taught, liked the sound of their youthful laughter and the promise of their groping minds. He even liked the metallic click of a beer can being opened on a sunny afternoon, or the sweetish odor of pot being passed from hand to hand around a room.

But this Saturday was different.

Johnnie's.

The neon letters were dark. He glanced up at the sign and went in, past a lonely old lady scrubbing the lobby's tile with steaming suds, doing her part to rid the place of its mingled odors of stale cigarette smoke and perfume. The bar along one end of the dim room was cluttered with glasses and half-empty bottles. Scores of tiny tables were scattered about and covered band-instruments rested like tombstones on a raised platform by the small dance floor. The tall amplifiers at either side of the platform told him the music was loud and electrical.

"We're closed till five," a voice behind him said.

Walden Swift turned and saw a tired little man with a mustache standing in his shirtsleeves by the office doorway. "I came for some information," he told the man.

"You a food inspector or something? We keep a clean kitchen."

"On Friday nights you have rock shows."

"Sure. Nothing wrong with that." The man was on the defensive, sparring with an uncertain foe.

"Are you Johnnie?"

"That's me. Who are you?"

"Professor Walden Swift from the University."

"Walden?" Johnnie repeated with a grin.

Professor Swift returned his smile. "My father admired Thoreau." Then he turned serious. "Actually, one of my students disappeared yesterday. I've traced him as far as the city and I think he might have come here last night."

The man relaxed visibly. "The place is full of college kids on weekends. Why do you want to find him?"

"That's a long story. I think his life might be in danger." He produced the picture from his wallet once more. "Recognize him?"

Johnnie studied it for a moment, then shook his head. "They all look alike to me. I just make sure they're old enough."

"So you don't know him?"

"Never saw him."

"Is there anyone who might have? Bartenders? Waiters? Perhaps he tried to pick up a girl."

Johnnie was back on the defensive at once. "I don't run that sort of place, Professor. No drugs, no B-girls, no drinks for minors. Just good clean rock music. What they do after they leave here is no concern of mine."

Walden Swift sighed and started to turn away. He'd come to a dead end. But then, over among the tables, the cleaning woman came up with something. "Girl's purse, Johnnie," she called out, holding her prize high in the air.

"Any money in it? Identification?"

"Couple of quarters. Cigarettes. Name and address. Here!"

Johnnie accepted the cheap sequin-studded bag with obvious distaste. "She'll probably come looking for it," he said. "Jean O'Brian, 79 Fernwood Crescent. I'll give her a call."

Walden Swift cleared his throat. "I'd be happy to return it to her. It's possible she noticed this boy I'm looking for."

Johnnie thought it over, then shook his head. "No, I'd better keep it here. Sorry I can't help you."

The professor nodded. "That address was 79 Fernwood Crescent?"

"Yeah. You going to see her anyway?"

"I think so. A girl might be more likely than you to notice a boy like Tommy."

The house at 79 Fernwood Crescent was hardly the apartment of a college girl. It was in an older section of the city, a neighborhood of converted mansions which now served as oddly shaped apartments. Each one was different, having in common only the original high ceilings and high rents. Sometimes three or four working girls might take one and share the cost, but Jean O'Brian's name was alone on the mailbox.

She came to the door after the fourth ring, obviously just awakened though it was past noon, and stared at Walden Swift with a blurred uncertain look. She had the face of a sadly experienced city-dweller.

"Miss O'Brian?"

"Yes?"

"My name is Walden Swift. I'm a professor at the University. One of my students disappeared last night and I thought—"

"God!" She shook her head to clear away the fuzz of a hard night. "Not that boy I was with at Johnnie's?"

"Could I come in for a moment?"

"I'm not dressed." She bundled the blue bathrobe closer about her slim body.

"Would you look at a picture?"

"I suppose so." She took it in one hand, keeping the other arm tightly around her. "No, that's not the boy I was with."

"His name is Tommy Easton. I'm trying to find him, to retrace his route last night."

"I wonder if he's the one Sue Brady was with. He looked a little like this, with that sandy hair."

"Where can I find her?"

"I don't know. She's always around Johnnie's on Friday nights, same as me. A lot of the boys from the business college come over, but not that many from your place. That's too far away. If they come to the city at all they usually have dates lined up already."

"Tommy wouldn't have had a date lined up. He didn't know anyone here."

"No. If he's the one I remember he was sitting by himself at first, just listening to the music. I thought he might have been looking for a fix, you know?"

"Drugs? At Johnnie's?"

She blinked her eyes. "Are you kidding? Why do you think it's so popular? If you're out of your crib you can buy pot at Johnnie's, though they're careful on the hard stuff." She was warming to the subject. "It was solid rock last night, a group from Detroit that Johnnie brought in. I could see your friend Tommy liked them too, if it really was him."

"What about him? What happened?"

"Well, he sat there alone most of the night. Then finally Sue Brady came in. She was with some guy old enough to be her father, but that's not unusual. Anyway, after two drinks he went to sleep with his head on the table. Your Tommy or whoever was at the next table and he offered to take her home. They sat together for a while and then they left. That was it."

"Did Tommy get into any trouble that you saw?"

"No—everything's cool at Johnnie's."

"You don't know where she lives? Where I might find her?"

"No. Wait. My boy friend and I dropped her off once after a night at Johnnie's—one Friday when she didn't manage a date. Just a second while I check the phonebook." She disappeared inside, leaving the door a few inches ajar as a possible indication of trust.

"Here, I think this is it," she said, returning with the open telephone book. "The Parkcrest Apartments. You can write down the address."

"Thanks," he said, getting out his pad and pen. Then, writing, he said, "You left your purse at Johnnie's last night. He has it for you."

The Parkcrest was a vast U-shaped building with a center courtyard filled with early-blossoming magnolias and children at play. The building reminded Walden Swift of another like it, where he'd often visited a girl he once loved. But that had been when he was young enough to believe in a girl who told him never to get involved with people.

Sue Brady, when she answered his ring, was nothing like the other girl. Her blonde hair was caught back in a youthful ponytail, but otherwise there was a plainness about her that startled him. On the street he might have passed her without a second look.

"Miss Brady? I'm Professor Walden Swift."

"Professor?"

"I believe you were with one of my students last night—a boy named Tommy Easton."

"What do you mean, *with* him?" Her blue eyes flashed. "He brought me home from Johnnie's because my date passed out on the table. He stayed maybe ten or fifteen minutes at most and then he left."

He showed her the picture. "Was this he?"

"Yes."

"Where is he? What happened to him?"

"How should I know?"

He sighed and lowered his voice a bit. "It's very important to me. Could I come in for a moment?"

She hesitated.

"Only for a minute, please. I have to be going out."

It was a neat little apartment, marred only by an ashtray overflowing with cigarette butts.

"I'm afraid," he told her, "of what might have happened to him."

"You can search the place if you think he's hidden somewhere."

"I'm sure he's not here. I just want to know what happened to him last night."

She sat down and took out another cigarette. "I told you—he walked me home and then left me."

"Did anyone see you together, follow you, do you think?"

"Lots of people saw us together, at Johnnie's and later."

Walden Swift sighed. "Let me tell you something about Tommy

Easton. When he came to the University last September he was shy and introverted. He came from a broken home and he thought the world was against him. Maybe it was. Anyway, this first year at the University was a hard one for Tommy, and for people like me who tried to befriend him. He started smoking pot, drinking a lot, doing all the things he figured you were supposed to do."

"Like picking up girls?"

"Yes, that too. He'd come into the city on the bus and sometimes we wouldn't see him for days."

Sue Brady faced him squarely. "He went out for cigarettes," she said suddenly. "He never came back."

"Pot?"

She nodded. "I told him he could get grass at Johnnie's but it was closed by that time. He said he knew another place."

"What time was this?"

She looked away. "Around three o'clock."

"And he never came back?"

"I guess he changed his mind about me."

"He didn't change his mind. Something happened to him." He was on his feet. "Which way did he go? Can you show me?"

"I'll get my coat."

Once outside she led him to the left, down the street toward a line of stores. "He said it was down this way."

They passed a barber shop and a delicatessen, a cigar store and a beauty parlor. Presently they reached the corner and Walden Swift glanced in both directions, searching for a clue. A three-word sign caught his eyes: *We Never Close.*

"Yes," he muttered half to himself.

He walked quickly toward it with the girl trailing behind. He pushed open the door and entered, and the counter man named Fred said, "Hello again. Back for more coffee?"

"You were working this morning, weren't you? Around three o'clock?"

"What if I was?"

"Tommy Easton was in here. He came back to buy some pot."

"You're crazy."

"But you sold him something else, didn't you? Harder stuff?"

The counter man took a step backward, and Walden Swift shot a hand across the counter to grab him. "Miss Brady," he said, "call the police!"

The counter man tried to pull away, tried to reach a bread knife by the skillet, but Walden Swift held him firm with a strength he hadn't known before.

"I lied to you," he told the girl. "Tommy Easton came back to the University last night, on the last express. He'd taken a shot of heroin here and somehow managed to stagger on board. When the bus pulled in, he was dead of an overdose."

The Dettweiler Solution

by Lawrence Block

Sometimes you just can't win for losing. Business was so bad over at Dettweiler Bros. Fine Fashions for Men that Seth Dettweiler went on back to the store one Thursday night and poured out a five-gallon can of lead-free gasoline where he figured as it would do the most good. He lit a fresh Philip Morris King Size and balanced it on the edge of the counter so as it would burn for a couple of minutes and then get unbalanced enough to drop into the pool of gasoline. Then he got into an Oldsmobile that was about five days' clear of a repossession notice and drove on home.

You couldn't have had a better fire dropping napalm on a paper mill. Time it was done you could sift those ashes and not find so much as a collar button. It was far and away the most spectacularly total fire Schuyler County had ever seen, so much so that Maybrook Fidelity Insurance would have been a little tentative about settling a claim under ordinary circumstances. But the way things stood there wasn't the slightest suspicion of arson, because what kind of a dimwitted hulk goes and burns down his business establishment a full week after his fire insurance has lapsed?

No fooling.

See, it was Seth's brother Porter who took care of paying bills and such, and a little over a month ago the fire-insurance payment had been due, and Porter looked at the bill and at the bank balance and back and forth for a while and then he put the bill in a drawer. Two weeks later there was a reminder notice, and two weeks after that there was a notice that the grace period had expired and the insurance was no longer in force, and then a week after that there was one pluperfect hell of a bonfire.

Seth and Porter had always got on pretty good. (They took after each other quite a bit, folks said. Especially Porter.) Seth was forty-two years of age, and he had that long Dettweiler face topping a jutting

Van Dine jaw. (Their mother was a Van Dine hailing from just the other side of Oak Falls.) Porter was thirty-nine, equipped with the same style face and jaw. They both had black hair that lay flat on their heads like shoe polish put on in slapdash fashion. Seth had more hair left than Porter, in spite of being the older brother by three years. I could describe them in greater detail, right down to scars and warts and sundry distinguishing marks, but it's my guess that you'd enjoy reading all that about as much as I'd enjoy writing it, which is to say less than somewhat. So let's get on with it.

I was saying they got on pretty good, rarely raising their voices one to the other, rarely disagreeing seriously about anything much. Now the fire didn't entirely change the habits of a lifetime but you couldn't honestly say that it did anything to improve their relationship. You'd have to allow that it caused a definite strain.

"What I can't understand," Seth said, "is how anybody who is fool enough to let fire insurance lapse can be an even greater fool by not telling his brother about it. That in a nutshell is what I can't understand."

"What beats *me*," Porter said, "is how the same person who has the nerve to fire a place of business for the insurance also does so without consulting his partner, especially when his partner just happens to be his brother."

"Allus I was trying to do," said Seth, "was save you from the criminal culpability of being an accessory before, to, and after the fact, plus figuring you might be too chickenhearted to go along with it."

"Allus *I* was trying to do," said Porter, "was save you from worrying about financial matters you would be powerless to contend with, plus figuring it would just be an occasion for me to hear further from you on the subject of those bow ties."

"Well, you did buy one powerful lot of bow ties."

"I knew it."

"Something like a Pullman car full of bow ties, and it's not like every man and boy in Schuyler County's been getting this mad passion for bow ties of late."

"I just knew it."

"I wasn't the one brought up the subject, but since you went and mentioned those bow ties—"

"Maybe I should of mentioned the spats," Porter said.

"Oh, I don't want to hear about spats."

"No more than I wanted to hear about bow ties. Did we sell one single damn pair of spats?"

"We did."

"We did?"

"Feller bought one about fifteen months back. Had Maryland plates on his car, as I recall. Said he always wanted spats and didn't know they still made 'em."

"Well, selling one pair out of a gross isn't too bad."

"Now you leave off," Seth said.

"And you leave off of bow ties?"

"I guess."

"Anyway, the bow ties and the spats all burned up in the same damn fire," Porter said.

"You know what they say about ill winds," Seth said. "I guess there's a particle of truth in it, what they say."

While it didn't do the Dettweiler brothers much good to discuss spats and bow ties, it didn't solve their problems to leave off mentioning spats and bow ties. By the time they finished their conversation all they were back to was square one, and the view from that spot wasn't the world's best.

The only solution was bankruptcy, and it didn't look to be all that much of a solution.

"I don't mind going bankrupt," one of the brothers said. (I think it was Seth. Makes no nevermind, actually. Seth, Porter, it's all the same who said it.) "I don't mind going bankrupt, but I sure do hate the thought of being broke."

"Me too," said the other brother. (Porter, probably.)

"I've thought about bankruptcy from time to time."

"Me too."

"But there's a time and a place for bankruptcy."

"Well, the place is all right. No better place for bankruptcy than Schuyler County."

"That's true enough," said Seth. (Unless it was Porter.) "But this is surely not the time. Time to go bankrupt is in good times when you got a lot of money on hand. Only the damnedest kind of fool goes bankrupt when he's stony broke busted and there's a Depression going on."

What they were both thinking on during this conversation was a fellow name of Joe Bob Rathburton who was in the construction business over to the other end of Schuyler County. I myself don't know of a man in this part of the state with enough intelligence to bail out a leaky rowboat who doesn't respect Joe Bob Rathburton to hell and back as a man with good business sense. It was about two years ago that Joe Bob went bankrupt, and he did it the right way. First of all he did it coming off the best year's worth of business he'd ever done in his life. Then what he did was he paid off the car and the house and the boat and put them all in his wifc's name. (His wife was Mabel Washburn, but no relation to the Washburns who have the Schuyler County First National Bank. That's another family entirely.)

Once that was done, Joe Bob took out every loan and raised every dollar he possibly could, and he turned all that capital into green folding cash and sealed it in quart Mason jars which he buried out back of an old Kieffer pear tree that's sixty-plus years old and still bears fruit like crazy. And then he declared bankruptcy and sat back in his Mission rocker with a beer and a cigar and a real big-tooth smile.

"If I could think of anything worth doing," Porter Dettweiler said one night, "why, I guess I'd just go ahead and do it."

"Can't argue with that," Seth said.

"But I can't," Porter said.

"Nor I either."

"You might pass that old jug over here for a moment."

"Soon as I pour a tad for myself, if you've no objection."

"None whatsoever," said Porter.

They were over at Porter's place on the evening when this particular conversation occurred. They had taken to spending most of their evenings at Porter's on account of Seth had a wife at home, plus a daughter named Rachel who'd been working at the Ben Franklin store ever since dropping out of the junior college over at Monroe Center. Seth didn't have but the one daughter. Porter had two sons and a daughter, but they were all living with Porter's ex-wife, who had divorced him two years back and moved clear to Georgia. They were living in Valdosta now, as far as Porter knew. Least that was where he sent the check every month.

"Alimony jail," said Porter.

"How's that?"

"What I said was alimony jail. Where you go when you quit paying on your alimony."

"They got a special jug set aside for men don't pay their alimony?"

"Just an expression. I guess they put you into whatever jug's the handiest. All I got to do is quit sendin' Gert her checks and let her have them cart me away. Get my three meals a day and a roof over my head and the whole world could quit nagging me night and day for money I haven't got."

"You could never stand it. Bein' in a jail day in and day out, night in and night out."

"I know it," Porter said unhappily. "There anything left in that there jug, on the subject of jugs?"

"Some. Anyway, you haven't paid Gert a penny in how long? Three months?"

"Call it five."

"And she ain't throwed you in jail yet. Least you haven't got her close to hand so's she can talk money to you."

"Linda Mae givin' you trouble?"

"She did. Keeps a civil tongue since I beat up on her the last time."

"Lord knew what He was doin'," Porter said, "makin' men stronger than women. You ever give any thought to what life would be like if wives could beat up on their husbands instead of the other way around?"

"Now I don't even want to think about that," Seth said.

You'll notice nobody was mentioning spats or bow ties. Even with the jug of corn getting discernibly lighter every time it passed from one set of hands to the other, these two subjects did not come up. Neither did anyone speak of the shortsightedness of failing to keep up fire insurance or the myopia of incinerating a building without ascertaining that such insurance was in force. Tempers had cooled with the ashes of Dettweiler Bros. Fine Fashions for Men, and once again Seth and Porter were on the best of terms.

Which just makes what happened thereafter all the more tragic.

"What I think I got," Porter said, "is no way to turn."

(This wasn't the same evening, but if you put the two evenings side by side under a microscope you'd be hard pressed to tell them apart each from the other. They were at Porter's little house over alongside the tracks of the old spur off the Wyandotte & Southern, which I couldn't tell you the last time there was a train on that spur, and they had their feet up and their shoes off, and there was a jug of corn in the picture. Most of their evenings had come to take on this particular shade.)

"Couldn't get work if I wanted to," Porter said, "which I don't, and if I did I couldn't make enough to matter, and my debts is up to my ears and rising steady."

"It doesn't look to be gettin' better," Seth said. "On the other hand, how can it get worse?"

"I keep thinking the same."

"And?"

"And it keeps getting worse."

"I guess you know what you're talkin' about," Seth said. He scratched his bulldog chin, which hadn't been in the same room with a razor in more than a day or two. "What I been thinkin' about," he said, "is killin' myself."

"You been thinking of that?"

"Sure have."

"I think on it from time to time myself," Porter admitted. "Mostly nights when I can't sleep. It can be a powerful comfort around about three in the morning. You think of all the different ways and the next thing you know you're asleep. Beats the stuffing out of counting sheep jumping fences. You seen one sheep you seen 'em all is always been my thoughts on the subject, whereas there's any number of ways of doing away with yourself."

"I'd take a certain satisfaction in it," Seth said, more or less warming to the subject. "What I'd leave is this note tellin' Linda Mae how her and Rachel'll be taken care of with the insurance, just to get the bitch's hopes up, and then she can find out for her own self that I cashed in that insurance back in January to make the payment on the Olds-mobile. You know it's pure uncut hell gettin' along without an automobile now."

"You don't have to tell me."

"Just put a rope around my neck," said Seth, smothering a hiccup, "and my damn troubles'll be over."

"And mine in the bargain," Porter said.

"By you doin' your own self in?"

"Be no need," Porter said, "if you did *your*self in."

"How you figure that?"

"What I figure is a hundred thousand dollars," Porter said. "Lord love a duck, if I had a hundred thousand dollars I could declare bankruptcy and live like a king!"

Seth looked at him, got up, walked over to him, and took the jug away from him. He took a swig and socked the cork in place, but kept hold of the jug.

"Brother," he said, "I just guess you've had enough of this here."

"What makes you say that, brother?"

"Me killin' myself and you gettin' rich, you don't make sense. What you think you're talkin' about, anyhow?"

"Insurance," Porter said. "Insurance, that's what I think I'm talking about. Insurance."

Porter explained the whole thing. It seems there was this life insurance policy their father had taken out on them when they weren't but boys. Face amount of a hundred thousand dollars, double indemnity for accidental death. It was payable to him while they were alive, but upon his death the beneficiary changed. If Porter was to die the money went to Seth. And vice-versa.

"And you knew about this all along?"

"Sure did," Porter said.

"And never cashed it in? Not the policy on me and not the policy on you?"

"Couldn't cash 'em in," Porter said. "I guess I woulda if I coulda, but I couldn't so I didn't."

"And you didn't let these here policies lapse?" Seth said. "On account of occasionally a person can be just the least bit absent-minded and forget about keeping a policy in force. That's been known to happen," Seth said, looking off to one side, "in matters relating to fire insurance, for example, and I just thought to mention it."

(I have the feeling he wasn't the only one to worry on that score. You may have had similar thoughts yourself, figuring you know how the story's going to end, what with the insurance not valid and all. Set your mind at rest. If that was the way it had happened I'd never be taking the trouble to write it up for you. I got to select stories with some satisfaction in them if I'm going to stand a chance of selling them to the magazine, and I hope you don't figure I'm sitting here poking away at this typewriter for the sheer physical pleasure of it. If I just want to exercise my fingers I'll send them walking through the Yellow Pages if it's all the same to you.)

"Couldn't let 'em lapse," Porter said. "They're all paid up. What you call twenty-payment life, meaning you pay in it for twenty years and then you got it free and clear. And the way Pa did it, you can't borrow on it or nothing. All you can do is wait and see who dies."

"Well, I'll be."

"Except we don't have to wait to see who dies."

"Why, I guess not. I just guess a man can take matters into his own hands if he's of a mind to."

"He surely can," Porter said.

"Man wants to kill himself, that's what he can go and do."

"No law against it," Porter said.

Now you know and I know that that last is not strictly true. There's a definite no-question law against suicide in our state, and most likely in yours as well. It's harder to make it stand up than a calf with four broken legs, however, and I don't recall that anyone hereabouts was ever prosecuted for it, or likely will be. It does make you wonder some what they had in mind writing that particular law into the books.

"I'll just have another taste of that there corn," Porter said, "and why don't you have a pull on the jug your own self? You have any idea just when you might go and do it?"

"I'm studying on it," Seth said.

"There's a lot to be said for doing something soon as a man's mind's made up on the subject. Not to be hurrying you or anything of the sort, but they say that he who hesitates is last." Porter scratched his chin. "Or some such," he said.

"I just might do it tonight."

"By God," Porter said.

"Get the damn thing over with. Glory Hallelujah and my troubles is over."

"And so is mine," said Porter.

"You'll be in the money then," said Seth, "and I'll be in the bone-yard, and both of us is free and clear. You can just buy me a decent funeral and then go bankrupt in style."

"Give you Johnny Millbourne's Number One funeral," Porter promised. "Brassbound casket and all. I mean, price is no object if I'm going bankrupt anyway. Let old Johnny swing for the money."

"You a damn good man, brother."

"You the best man in the world, brother."

The jug passed back and forth a couple more times. At one point Seth announced that he was ready, and he was halfway out the door before he recollected that his car had been repossessed, which interfered with his plans to drive it off a cliff. He came back in and sat down again and had another drink on the strength of it all, and then suddenly he sat forward and stared hard at Porter.

"This policy thing," he said.

"What about it?"

"It's on both of us, is what you said."

"If I said it then must be it's the truth."

"Well then," Seth said, and sat back, arms folded on his chest.

"Well then what?"

"Well then if *you* was to kill yourself, then *I'd* get the money and *you'd* get the funeral."

"I don't see what you're getting at," Porter said slowly.

"Seems to me either one of us can go and do it," Seth said. "And here's the two of us just takin' it for granted that I'm to be the one to go and do it, and I think we should think on that a little more thoroughly."

"Why, being as you're older, Seth."

"What's that to do with anything?"

"Why, you got less years to give up."

"Still be givin' up all that's left. Older or younger don't cut no ice." Porter thought about it. "After all," he said, "it was your idea."

"That don't cut ice neither. I could mention I got a wife and child."

"I could mention I got a wife and three children."

"Ex-wife."

"All the same."

"Let's face it," Seth said. "Gert and your three don't add up to anything and neither do Linda Mae and Rachel."

"Got to agree," Porter said.

"So."

"One thing. You being the one who put us in this mess, what with firing the store, it just seems you might be the one to get us out of it."

"You bein' the one let the insurance lapse through your own stupidity, you could get us out of this mess through insurance, thus evenin' things up again."

"Now talkin' about stupidity—"

"Yes, talkin' about stupidity—"

"Spats!"

"Bow ties, damn you! *Bow ties!*"

You might have known it would come to that.

Now I've told you Seth and Porter generally got along pretty well, and here's further evidence of it. Confronted by such a stalemate, a good many people would have wrote off the whole affair and decided not to take the suicide route at all. But not even spats and bow ties could deflect Seth and Porter from the road they'd figured out as the most logical to pursue.

So what they did, one of them tossed a coin, and the other one called it while it was in the air, and they let it hit the floor and roll, and I don't recollect whether it was heads or tails, or who tossed and who called—what's significant is that Seth won.

"Well now," Seth said. "I feel I been reprieved. Just let me have that coin, I want to keep it for a luck charm."

"Two out of three."

"We already said once is as good as a million," Seth said, "so you just forget that two-out-of-three business. You got a week like we agreed but if I was you I'd get it over soon as I could."

"I got a week," Porter said.

"You'll get the brassbound casket and everything, and you can have Minnie Lucy Boxwood sing at your funeral if you want. Expense don't matter at all. What's your favorite song?"

"I suppose 'Your Cheatin' Heart.' "

"Minnie Lucy does that real pretty."

"I guess she does."

"Now you be sure and make it accidental," Seth said. "Two hundred thousand dollars goes just about twice as far as one hundred thousand dollars. Won't cost you a thing to make it accidental, just like we talked about it. What I would do is borrow Fritz Chenoweth's half-ton pickup and go up on the old Harburton Road where it takes that curve. Have yourself a belly full of corn and just keep goin' straight when the road doesn't. Lord knows I almost did that myself enough times without tryin'. Had two wheels over the edge less'n a month ago."

"That close?"

"That close."

"I'll be doggone," Porter said.

Thing is, Seth went on home after he failed to convince Porter to do it right away, and that was when things began to fall into the muck. Because Porter started thinking things over. I have a hunch it would have worked about the same way if Porter had won the flip, with Seth thinking things over. They were a whole lot alike, those two. Like two peas in a pod.

What occurred to Porter was would Seth have gone through with it if he lost, and what Porter decided was that he wouldn't. Not that there was any way for him to prove it one way or the other, but when you can't prove something you generally tend to decide on believing in what you want to believe, and Porter Dettweiler was no exception. Seth, he decided, would not have killed himself and didn't never have no intention of killing himself, which meant that for Porter to go through with killing his own self amounted to nothing more than damned foolishness.

Now it's hard to say just when he figured out what to do, but it was in the next two days, because on the third day he went over and borrowed that pickup truck off Fritz Chenoweth. "I got the back all loaded down with a couple sacks of concrete mix and a keg of nails and I don't know what all," Fritz said. "You want to unload it back of my smaller barn if you need the room."

"Oh, that's all right," Porter told him. "I guess I'll just leave it loaded and be grateful for the traction."

"Well, you keep it overnight if you have a mind," Fritz said.

"I just might do that," Porter said, and he went over to Seth's house.

"Let's you and me go for a ride," he told Seth. "Something we was talking about the other night, and I went and got me a new slant on it which the two of us ought to discuss before things go wrong altogether."

"Be right with you," Seth said, "soon as I finish this sandwich."

"Oh, just bring it along."

"I guess," said Seth.

No sooner was the pickup truck backed down and out of the driveway than Porter said, "Now will you just have a look over there, brother."

"How's that?" said Seth, and turned his head obligingly to the right, whereupon Porter gave him a good lick upside the head with a monkey wrench he'd brought along expressly for that purpose. He got him right where you have a soft spot if you're a little baby. (You also have a soft spot there if someone gets you just right with a monkey wrench.) Seth made a little sound which amounted to no more than letting his breath out, and then he went out like an icebox light when you have closed the door on it.

Now as to whether or not Seth was dead at this point I could not honestly tell you, unless I were to make up an answer knowing how slim is the likelihood of anyone presuming to contradict me. But the plain fact is that he might have been dead and he might not and even Seth could not have told you, being at the very least stone-unconscious at the time.

What Porter did was drive up the old Harburton Road, I guess figuring that he might as well stick to as much of the original plan as possible. There's a particular place where the road does a reasonably convincing imitation of a fishhook, and that spot's been described as Schuyler County's best natural brake on the population explosion since they stamped out the typhoid. A whole lot of folks fail to make that curve every year, most of them young ones with plenty of breeding years left in them. Now and then there's a movement to put up a guard rail, but the ecology people are against it so it never gets anywheres.

If you miss that curve, the next land you touch is a good five hundred feet closer to sea level.

So Porter pulls over the side of the road and then he gets out of the truck and maneuvers Seth (or Seth's body, whichever the case may have been) so he's behind the wheel. Then he stands alongside the truck working the gas pedal with one hand and the steering wheel with the other and putting the fool truck in gear and doing this and that and the other thing so he can run the truck up to the edge and over, and thinking hard every minute about those two hundred thousand pretty green dollars that is destined to make his bankruptcy considerably easier to contend with.

Well, I told you right off that sometimes you can't win for losing, which was the case for Porter and Seth both, and another way of putting it is to say that when everything goes wrong there's nothing goes right. Here's what happened. Porter slipped on a piece of loose gravel while he was pushing, and the truck had to go on its own, and where it went was halfway and no further, with its back wheel hung up on a hunk of tree limb or some such and its two front wheels hanging out over nothing and its motor stalled out deader'n smoked fish.

Porter said himself a whole mess of bad words. Then he wasted considerable time shoving the back of that truck, forgetting it was in gear and not about to budge. Then he remembered and said a few more bad words and put the thing in neutral, which involved a long reach across Seth to get to the floor shift and a lot of coordination to manipulate it and the clutch pedal at the same time. Then Porter got out of the truck and gave the door a slam, and just about then a beat-up old Chevy with Indiana plates pulls up and this fellow leaps out screaming that he's got a tow rope and he'll pull the truck to safety.

You can't hardly blame Porter for the rest of it. He wasn't the type to be great at contingency planning anyhow, and who could allow for something like this? What he did, he gave this great sob and just plain hurled himself at the back of that truck, it being in neutral now, and the truck went sailing like a kite in a tornado, and Porter, well, what he did was follow right along after it. It wasn't part of his plan but he just had himself too much momentum to manage any last-minute change of direction.

According to the fellow from Indiana, who it turned out was a veterinarian from Bloomington, Porter fell far enough to get off a couple of genuinely rank words on the way down. Last words or not, you sure wouldn't go and engrave them on any tombstone.

Speaking of which, he has the last word in tombstones, Vermont granite and all, and his brother Seth has one just like it. They had a double-barrelled funeral, the best Johnny Millbourne had to offer, and they each of them reposed in a brassbound casket, the top-of-the-line model. Minnie Lucy Boxwood sang "Your Cheatin' Heart," which was Porter's favorite song, plus she sang Seth's favorite, which was "Old Buttermilk Sky," plus she also sang free gratis "My Buddy" as a testament to brotherly love.

And Linda Mae and Rachel got themselves two hundred thousand dollars from the insurance company, which is what Gert and her kids in Valdosta, Georgia, also got. And Seth and Porter have an end to their miseries, which was all they really wanted before they got their heads turned around at the idea of all that money.

The only thing funnier than how things don't work out is how they do.

The Whitechapel Wantons

by Vincent McConnor

A door opened, the angry sound of rusty hinges echoing through the empty street, but no one heard.

And nobody saw the figure of a girl, briefly visible against a blur of candlelight that revealed a narrow hall with steep wooden stairs.

The girl closed the door and, fumbling with her key in the dark, locked it again. You couldn't be too careful, although, up to now, the Ripper had always killed in the streets. Mostly in dark alleys—some of them not far from here.

She had known all of the girls, Polly Nichols and the others.

The newspaper said that Polly was the second to die.

Hesitating on the top step, peering up and down the silent street, she returned the key to her purse and slipped it into the pocket of her jacket. Now both hands were free for any emergency she might have to face.

The ground-floor shop next door, which did a brisk trade in pickled eels during the day, was shuttered for the night.

Nobody ventured out after dark any more unless it was urgent business. It was the women who were in danger, but men stayed off the streets at night because the police were stopping them to ask who they were and where they were going. If their answers sounded suspicious they were taken in for questioning.

The pubs were suffering. There were still a few regulars every night, but a girl was afraid to speak to a stranger because he might be the Ripper. Nobody knew what he looked like.

She was probably the only one in all of London who had seen his face and she wasn't going to tell the police!

Shivering under her thin summer dress, she clutched the short velvet jacket more securely around her. The air was as sharp as a knife and it was only early October. Another week and she would need to find herself a winter coat from a pushcart in Petticoat Lane.

She glanced at the sky above the low rooftops and chimneys and saw that clouds were shoving across the stars. There was no moon.

As she came down the two splintered steps to the cobbled street, she wondered what name she ought to use tonight.

This week she had been calling herself Annie but somehow that always seemed a bit common. Maybe tonight she would use Violette again. That nice young toff last week had said it suited her when she told him her name was Violette. He had been ever so kind, paid her two whole shillings . . .

Passing a row of dark shops, heading toward the street lamp at the corner, she kept close to the buildings, hurrying her steps as she skirted the mouth of each alley.

London had been choking with smoke and fog each time the Ripper killed. Tonight, at least, there was no fog.

She had decided to tell Cora what she knew and explain about her plan. It couldn't work unless somebody helped her and Cora was her dearest friend now that Polly was dead.

Her plan. She shivered again. She had never thought she would plan to kill anybody. But Polly had been her friend since the first week she had arrived in London. They had met that rainy night near the Haymarket. What a silly innocent she was in those days, fresh from Liverpool. Only three years ago . . .

She had never seen Whitechapel until Polly brought her here, insisting she move in and share her lodgings.

That night last month when the two constables had pounded on the door waking her from a sound sleep, she couldn't believe what they told her. She had thought Polly was asleep in the other bed. Their questions had frightened her, and when they took her to identify the body she had fainted.

She still lived in Polly's room, but it was getting harder to pay the rent each week. Business was terrible because of the Ripper and it wouldn't get any better as long as he prowled the streets. She never had so much as two shillings in her purse any more—barely enough to buy a scrap of food each day. Something had to be done and the police weren't doing anything.

She reached the street lamp and turned down another dark street.

Last night in the Black Swan one of the girls said the Ripper must be a constable or he would've been caught long ago. Everybody laughed but at the same time they had wondered if the Ripper could be a policeman. Some of them were terribly nasty to a girl, cruel, and insulting. Although there was a new one—Constable Divall—who was ever so nice. In his twenties and not at all bad-looking.

There were so many extra constables on night duty in Whitechapel now that nobody could slip out to do an honest job of burglary any more, afraid they'd be picked up by the police searching the streets for the Ripper. What made it even worse was that some of the constables were not in uniform and those who were traveled in pairs. Though you couldn't blame them—the whole city of London was in a fair panic.

Now she could make out a blur of gaslight at the far end of the narrow street.

Cora should be in the Black Swan by now. It must be past midnight. The empty streets were frightening. At any moment he could appear out of the dark and come lurching toward her.

She had seen his blond hair under a black bowler, his face pale against the high collar of his black coat. She'd glimpsed his eyes when Polly took his arm and, giggling as usual, disappeared into the fog with him. Never to be seen again, at least not alive . . .

Reaching the protective circle of light from the gaslight on the corner, she paused to look in every direction, then darted across the cobbles toward the Black Swan.

A dark shape moved near her feet.

She gasped with fright, then realized it was only Old Cobbie, drunk as a lord, sprawled on the paving stones.

Grasping the wrought-iron handle, she pushed against the heavy oak door and entered the pub.

A candle in a brass lantern guttered above the bar.

Three faces turned to stare. The owner, Tom, behind the bar and two of the regulars, all three with drinks in their fists.

"Evenin', miss!"

"Seen Cora t'night, Tom?"

"Showed up ten minutes ago. She's in the back."

Violette crossed to the bar, sawdust crunching under her thin slippers. "Nobody on the street t'night."

"You girls come rushin' in like the Ripper's after ye."

"Maybe he is! He got Polly, didn't he?" She never stood close to the bar when she ordered a drink because it wasn't ladylike to lean against the polished wood the way men did. "I'll have a mild, please." She brought out her purse, selected a coin from the few she owned, and put it on the bar. "A girl can't make a livin' on these empty streets."

"If Scotland Yard don't soon catch the blighter we'll all be out of

business, every bloomin' pub in Whitechapel. Here y'are, me girl."
Tom handed her the half-pint and turned back to his cronies.

Violette carried her beer around the corner toward the back, noticing
that there was no fire on the hearth to send a flicker of warmth across
the smoke-blackened beams of the ceiling. The only light came from a
wax-encrusted candle in the mouth of a wine bottle on the table where
Cora sat—the only person in the room.

Cora waved, pushing a scarlet feather away from her eye and adjusting her velvet hat more firmly on her black curls. "I thought maybe
you wouldn' be comin' out t'night, Annie."

"I had to." She set her beer on the scrubbed wood table and sank
onto a bench, facing her friend. "Rent's due t'morrow, so I've got t'
earn a bit of money. An' I'm not Annie t'night—I'm Violette."

"Whatever you say, Vi. As I came here I saw nothin' but constables
in the streets, strips of rubber nailed t' their boots so the Ripper
wouldn' hear 'em comin'."

"I didn't see nobody." She took a first gulp of beer, observing that
Cora, as usual, was drinking gin and had been reading something on a
crumpled sheet of paper. "I have t' talk to you, luv. About Polly."

"Oh?" Cora held the sheet of paper across the table. "Did you see
this?"

As Violette took it she saw that it was a printed leaflet.

"Police 'ave spread these all over Whitechapel!"

Violette held the leaflet close to the candle so that she could read the
words.

POLICE NOTICE.

TO THE OCCUPIER.

On the mornings of Friday, 31st,
August, Saturday 8th, and Sunday,
30th of September, 1888, Women were
murdered in or near Whitechapel,
supposed by some one residing
in the immediate neighbourhood.
Should you know of any person
to whom suspicion is attached, you
are earnestly requested to com-
municate at once with the nearest

Police Station.
Metropolitan Police Office,
30th September, 1888

"Someone in the neighbourhood?" She looked at Cora. "They're bonkers! He's a toff from the West End." Handing the leaflet back across the table, she asked, "Where'd you get this?"

"Found it under me door this afternoon."

"My landlady must've gotten one but I didn't see the old girl before I came out. Been avoidin' her."

She took another gulp of beer.

"Ivy tol' me last night they're sayin' the Ripper's a famous surgeon from Harley Street! That's why he slices all his victims up so neat!"

"Ivy's a fool. Nobody knows for certain who he is—or, for that matter, how many girls he's done in."

"They're also sayin' the Ripper's a woman."

"The Ripper's a *man!* A real toff."

"Oh?" Cora folded the sheet of paper and tucked it into her purse. "How d' you know what he looks like?"

"That's what I wanted t' tell you."

"What?"

"I've seen him."

"The Ripper?"

"With me own two eyes."

"When?"

"The night he killed Polly. We was in a doorway near Swallow Court, Polly an' me, keepin' out of the cold. She seen him first, comin' down the street, an' went t' meet him—hopin' for a bit of luck, of course! I watched while they talked, standin' close t'gether in the fog, then he offered her his arm like a regular gent an' they turned back, same way he'd come. I thought, of course, they was goin' to a hotel. I had no idea it was the Ripper."

"Did he see you?"

"I never moved out of the doorway."

"But you had a good look at him?"

"I'd recognize him anywhere!"

"Have you told the police?"

"Wouldn' I be the fool t' do that! I ain't told nobody 'til this minute, not even you! An' I'm only tellin' you t'night 'cause I need your help."

Cora stared at her suspiciously. "What sort of help?"

"Well, Polly was my best friend in London. Now you're the only friend I got." She glanced toward the front of the pub to be sure the men at the bar couldn't hear what she was about to say. "The police ain't goin' t' catch the Ripper 'cause they don't know what he looks like. But I do! I've seen him! An' I'm goin' t' get rid of the blighter!"

"Get rid of him?"

"For Polly's sake! Put an end to him—once and for all. That's what I'm goin' t' do. So a girl can be safe on the streets again . . ."

"Then you *are* goin' t' tell the police what he looks like?"

"I wouldn' dare! If the Ripper found out I'd seen him—that I know what he looks like—my life wouldn' be worth a ha'penny! He'd come after me with his bloody knife! You've got t' help me, Cora. I can't do it without you. It'll take the two of us!"

"Do what, Vi? What the devil are you talkin' about?"

"I'm goin' t' kill the Ripper."

"*Kill* him?"

"Of course I have t' find him first, but . . ."

She explained her plan in a rush of words, and then arranged to meet Cora the following afternoon, to search through the nearby docks for a crate. A wooden crate large enough to hold a man's body.

Walking toward the docks late the next afternoon, they discussed the plan over and over, working out exactly what each would have to do.

Cora was dubious at first, but then she was caught up in the excitement of the idea and began to make suggestions of her own.

They located a discarded wooden crate outside one of the warehouses, which they lugged between them back to Violette's lodging. Mrs. Paddick, her landlady, watched them ease their awkward burden through the narrow hall, past her open kitchen door, with suspicious eyes. " 'Ere now! Wot's this?"

Violette winked at Cora as they set the crate down with a hollow thud.

"Cora's helping me put this in the alley, Mrs. Paddick."

"Wotever for?"

"Had t' find a large box for Polly's belongin's."

"The poor girl!"

"I'm sending her clothes an' things to her family in Birmingham. You won't mind if I leave this out in the back for a few days, will you? It's much too heavy t' carry upstairs."

"Leave it here as long as you want. Nobody'll touch it."

"It could be a week or more before I can pack everything."

"Take y'r time, luv. Let me know if there's any way I can 'elp." She moved back into the dark hole of her kitchen. "Stop by when ye finish there an' I'll 'ave a nice hot cup of tea for ye."

"That's ever so kind, Mrs. Paddick!" Cora called after her.

"She's in a right good humour t'day," Violette whispered. "I paid me rent this mornin' so she'll leave us alone. Anyway, the ol' girl's so deaf she never hears nothin' no matter how many times I come in an' out at night."

They carried their wooden box through the open back door and set it down next to the dustbin in the grimy back alley.

Violette raised the hinged lid and let it fall back down the side, then turned the crate over, with Cora's help, so that the open side, out of sight from the door, faced the dustbin.

She demonstrated how Cora could hide inside the crate until she was needed and showed her the barrow that was always propped against the wall next door, behind the eel shop. They would load the crate onto the barrow, push it down the alley to the next street, and in a matter of minutes reach the river. She also pointed to a small ax resting near a stack of firewood that was used in the eel-shop kitchen and showed her where to place the ax beside the back door so she, Vi, would be able to find it in the dark when she brought the Ripper here . . .

They went over the plan several more times in Violette's room after their tea in Mrs. Paddick's kitchen. They stretched out on the two lumpy beds and continued to discuss the plan until they fell asleep.

Later, just before midnight, they went out together.

And for the first time in many weeks they felt safer in the empty streets.

The next day they decided it would be much more practical, as well as cheaper, for both of them if Cora moved in and shared Vi's room.

Mrs. Paddick didn't suspect that she had a new tenant. She was, as Violette had said, extremely deaf and seldom came upstairs unless there was trouble with one of the lodgers.

The two girls saw to it that there was nothing to arouse her suspicions. Even when they brought visitors to their room Mrs. Paddick heard nothing and, from long experience, probably wouldn't have complained if she had.

Violette and Cora went out together each night around midnight and walked through the dark streets and alleys of Whitechapel. But Violette saw no sign of the Ripper.

The entire city of London was in a state of hysteria because any night now the Ripper was expected to kill again. It had been more than a week since the last body was found.

The newspapers printed fresh stories every day.

And, strangely, a deluge of toffs from the West End began to swarm through Whitechapel every night to see the places where Jack had slashed his victims. The pubs began to flourish again and a girl could make several shillings a night. Most of them, like Violette and Cora, took to walking in pairs—like the police—for their own protection.

The two girls went to the Black Swan every night to have a drink and catch up with the day's gossip. With the increase in business even Violette was drinking gin now.

It was crowded and noisy, every table occupied in the back room, where a new barmaid darted back and forth with trays of drinks.

Violette watched the activity, seated at her usual table with Cora, sipping at her glass of gin.

"You think he'll show up t'night?" Cora asked in a whisper.

"T'night or t'morrow night," Violette answered, feeling the warmth from the gin flowing through her body. "Whenever he shows up, we'll be ready for him."

"S'pose he never does come back?"

"He will."

"S'pose all these people keep him away. He might go to another part of London—Chelsea or Soho."

"I think, t'night, we should keep away from the busy streets—stay in the alleys, around Swallow Court, where Polly met him."

"Whatever you say."

"More gin, ladies?"

They looked up to see the blonde barmaid, smiling and eager, her apron splashed with beer.

"Not just now," Violette answered. "We'll be havin' drinks later, with some gents."

"Watch out for the Ripper." The tousled barmaid leaned closer, lowering her voice. "I heard just now, he's left-handed."

"Fancy that!" Cora exclaimed, glancing at her friend. "Left-handed."

"Who said he was?" Violette asked. "I thought nobody ain't ever seen the bloke."

"Gentleman told me it's in the newspaper t'day. Scotland Yard found out from the knife wounds in the last girl's body. Cut her up somethin' 'orrible!"

"A likely story!" Violette scoffed. "How could they tell he's left-handed from that?"

"I wouldn' know, luv. They say the Queen gave orders t' the 'ome Secretary t'day t' catch the Ripper in a hurry so the ladies of London can walk the streets in safety again." She darted away, in response to a summons from another table.

"Ladies?" Cora laughed, the feathers quivering on her hat. "That's us!"

Violette frowned. "Left-handed, is he?" She shivered suddenly.

"Drink up, luv!" Cora raised her glass. "We'd better be on our way."

Violette noticed, as they came from the Black Swan, that mist was rising between the damp cobbles and a dirty grey fog was pressing down from overhead. "The Ripper will be out t'night, I know he will . . ."

"If you say so." Cora peered up and down the narrow street but there was nobody in sight.

They turned into the first alley, choking and coughing as their lungs filled with the acrid coal smoke the fog was pushing down from nearby chimneys.

There were lanterns on the stone walls, but their light was so dim that they had to feel their way along. The rough surface dripped with moisture and, within seconds, their fingers were cold and wet. "What a filthy night!" Violette grasped Cora's arm with her hand so they wouldn't become separated. "I almost wish I was home in Liverpool."

"Do you ever think of goin' back, Vi?"

"Not really. I s'pose I could get me old job again, workin' as house-maid."

"You liked that?"

"Cleanin' an' pickin' up? I hated it!" She glimpsed a misty circle of light from a street lamp at the end of the alley. "Here's Swallow Court."

"I don't know this part of Whitechapel."

Violette wiped her damp fingers on her coat. "There's a doorway over there. We can stand out of the fog an' still see the street."

"Where you an' Polly stood that night?"

"That's right." Violette kept close to a building, looking for the remembered doorway. "We knew this street well, Polly an' me. Came here many a night." She glimpsed the dark entrance with its recessed doors through drifting veils of fog. "Here we are!" She led the way under the shallow arch and leaned back against one of the heavy oak doors.

Cora huddled beside her. "The fog's gettin' heavier."

"He'll be here t'night, I know he will." Vi motioned across the street. "You can't see it now but there's another alley over there."

"You really think he'll be out?"

"I'm sure of it!"

"Maybe we shouldn't wait . . ."

Vi turned to face Cora. "You backin' out?"

"No!"

"Do you remember what you have t' do?"

"I remember, Vi. Everything . . ."

"When I see him I'll go straight t' meet him, catch him before he can slip away. You hurry back t' Mrs. Paddick's an' through the downstairs hall t' the alley. Be sure t' put that ax where I showed you, next to the door so I can find it in the dark. Then hide inside the box until I bring him. You'll hear us but don't make a sound. An' don't show y'r face 'til I call you."

"I'm scared, Vi."

"So am I."

"He could kill us."

"We have t' do this. For Polly—for what he did t' her an' all them other poor girls."

"I know we do."

Violette froze. "Here he is!"

"You're sure?"

"It's him. You know what t' do!"

Violette stepped down from the doorway onto the wet cobblestones.

"Be careful, Vi," Cora whispered.

She hurried toward him through the swirling fog. It was the same pale face and the same blond hair under the black bowler. The same coat with the high collar. Tonight he was wearing grey gloves.

He saw her coming toward him and began to smile.

Violette slowed her steps.

"Good evening, miss . . ."

"Evenin' . . ." She listened for Cora's footsteps behind her, but there was no sound of any kind.

"Miserable evening, what?" He continued to smile.

"Yes." He wasn't a bad-looking sort. Nice smile. White teeth under a small moustache. She mustn't let him force her into Swallow Court where he had taken Polly.

"It would be much more pleasant inside somewhere, don't you think?"

"I—I've a place near here."

"Could we possibly go there, do you suppose?"

"Why not?"

"Splendid! Can you find your way in this fog?"

"Oh, yes." She trembled as she felt his gloved hand under her arm. The same hand that had killed Polly.

"It's nearby, you say?" He walked beside her, back the way she had come.

"It's a nice room where nobody will bother us. Ever so cozy . . ."

"You're not London-born, are you?"

"How'd you guess?"

"Your accent sounds like Liverpool."

"I'm not sayin' where I'm from."

He laughed. "It doesn't matter."

"We go through here." She turned with him into the side street, avoiding the alley Cora would have taken. This should give Cora time to reach the house ahead of them.

What would happen if Cora got lost in the fog? She had said she didn't know this part of Whitechapel.

Dear God! Don't let that happen . . .

"Have you been in London long?" he asked.

"Long enough t' know my way round."

"I shouldn't wonder!" He laughed again.

They saw only one person, an ancient Chinese, slinking close to the dark shopfronts.

Violette found the house without difficulty, unlocked the door, and motioned for her escort to enter. "We mustn't talk," she whispered. "The landlady lives on this floor an' she's a holy terror." She closed the door behind them and saw that he seemed taller when he removed his bowler. The only light came from a flickering candle in a niche near the stairs. "We go through the back."

"Oh? Why's that?"

"There's another house in the rear. Where I live . . ." She moved ahead of him through the narrow hall, into the shadows. The floorboards creaked underfoot but there was no other sound in the house.

Violette saw that the rear door was closed.

Had Cora gotten here ahead of them? It would be terrible if the street door flew open behind them and Cora came rushing in.

Would she be there in the back, crouched in that crate?

Violette reached the door and saw that the bolt had been pulled back.

Cora was here!

She opened the door and raised her voice as she spoke to warn Cora they had arrived. "Here we are. You go first."

"As you wish." He stepped outside, into the fog again. "I say! It's dark out here."

"Stand still for a minute. 'Til you can see where you are."

"Good idea . . . By the way, you haven't told me your name."

"Violette."

"Violette? I rather like that."

She could see his bare head now, dark against the grey fog. Bending quickly, she felt beside the step until she touched the cold wooden handle of the ax. Lifting it slowly with both hands, she had sudden aversion to what she was about to do. Never in her life had she done anything like this before. But she had to do it!

"Well, now! Which way do we go?"

The sound of his voice released her.

Violette raised the ax above her head and, with all her strength, crashed the metal head against his skull. Incredibly, as she watched, he dropped out of sight without a sound.

She had done it!

The ax slipped from her hands.

For a moment she didn't move.

The distant moan of a foghorn sounded a warning from the river.

Violette stepped down onto the hard ground and cautiously thrust her right foot out until she touched his body. She gave it a tentative kick. There was no reaction.

Only then did she find her voice. "Cora . . ."

The two girls didn't speak as, side by side, they pushed the awkward barrow through the dark streets.

Everything had worked out as they had planned.

The Ripper was dead and Violette felt no remorse. She had only paid him back for Polly and those other poor girls.

She remembered her grandmother back in Liverpool reading from the Bible. "Eye for eye, tooth for tooth, hand for hand, foot for foot . . ." Her grandmother said it really meant a life for a life.

Jack the Ripper's life for Polly's life! And for all the others.

The only noise was the creaking of the barrow as its wooden wheels bumped over the damp cobbles. No sound came from the crate, which they had covered with an old blanket, or from the silent thing that was stuffed inside.

Jack was in the box! Violette smiled at the thought . . .

She was surprised that he had died so quickly. It took so little to kill a person. She'd had no idea it was that easy.

Cora, beside her, was gasping from the effort it took to push the clumsy barrow through the fog.

Her own breathing, she realized, was becoming more difficult. Each time a wheel stuck, refused to bump over a large cobblestone, they had to lift the barrow clear before they could push on.

The foghorn sounded much louder. They must be getting close to the river. Soon they would reach the old warehouses. After that, and they would see the wharves.

She could smell the river now.

The police would fish his body out of the water, but they would find nothing to tell them who he was. They wouldn't even know he was the Ripper. She had taken all the money from his pockets and stuffed it, uncounted, into her purse. There had been no wallet. And not much money, a few pound notes and some coins.

Also, to her surprise, there had been very little blood. Early tomorrow, before Mrs. Paddick was awake, she must go down to the backyard and clean away any spots.

The barrow struck another cobblestone and wouldn't budge.

"Damn!" Cora exclaimed. "Is it much farther?"

"We're almost at the river. I can smell it." Vi released the wooden handle and circled the barrow to see what was hindering their progress.

Cora followed and bent beside her to peer underneath.

"Wot's all this?"

Cora screamed at the sound of the ominous masculine voice.

Both girls straightened as two uniformed figures appeared out of the fog.

Violette recognized one of the faces. "Constable Divall!"

"Somethin' wrong here, miss?" Divall moved closer, followed by the other constable.

"I'm helpin' me friend move," Violette answered quickly. "An' the bloomin' barrow got stuck."

"Let's see if we can help. Give me a hand, Thompson."

The girls held their breath as the other constable joined Divall to ease the wheel over the obstruction, then watched apprehensively as they lifted the barrow between them and carried it several paces before they set it down again.

"You've got somethin' right heavy here!" Divall turned to look at them again.

"It's me friend's trunk," Violette explained.

"That's right!" Cora managed to say. "Me trunk."

"All her belongin's. She's movin' t' a new lodgin' house. Thanks ever so much, Constable."

"My pleasure, miss." Divall touched his helmet as he continued on with the other constable. "Watch out for the Ripper! He could be out on a night like this."

"We'll be careful!"

Cora giggled nervously.

Violette saw now why she hadn't heard the approach of the two constables. They had thin strips of rubber—probably cut from bicycle tires—nailed to their boots. She didn't move until they had faded into the fog.

Cora sighed. "That was awful close."

"He's not a bad-lookin' sort, for a constable. C'mon, luv! Before we're caught again."

They grasped the handle of the barrow and, pushing harder than before, continued on their way. The fear of meeting other policemen strengthened their arms and quickened their steps. And they remained silent, saving their breath, until they found themselves on a wooden dock with the Thames lapping among the pilings underneath.

There were several lighted lanterns at irregular intervals along the side of the large warehouse.

They pushed the barrow to an open space at the edge of the rotting wharf.

Violette pulled the blanket away and, with Cora's help, managed to tip the crate onto the wooden planks of the wharf. Then, grasping the handle together again, they used the barrow as a ram and, pushing with all their might, shoved the crate to the edge. One final violent push and the crate scraped over the side.

It struck the water with a tremendous splash.

The two girls hurried to the edge of the wharf and looked down. In a spill of light from the nearest lantern, they saw circles of waves spreading out from the spot where the crate had entered the water.

They waited, peering down, but it didn't come to the surface again.

Without a word they turned the barrow around and, hurrying now, headed back the way they had come.

The door opened, the sound of rusty hinges muffled by the fog.

Violette came out, closing the door and locking it.

She saw that the fog was much heavier. The street lamp at the distant corner was completely blotted out.

As she came down the steps to the cobbled street she decided that it was a bit late to go back to the Black Swan. Instead she turned toward Swallow Court again. There was nothing to be afraid of there now that the Ripper was dead.

Cora was getting ready for bed when she left. It would have been impossible for her to sleep for another two or three hours—she was much too excited by what she had done . . .

Maybe she would meet a nice young toff from the West End. She couldn't take him back to her lodging because Cora would be asleep there but at least she didn't need to worry about the Ripper any more. He was at the bottom of the Thames.

When she and Cora had reached the back alley at Mrs. Paddick's, the first thing they had done was put the barrow back where it belonged behind the eel shop. Then, in the dark, she had wiped the ax clean and set it in place beside the stack of firewood.

Early tomorrow she would go down and make sure there were no other bloodstains anywhere . . .

When they went upstairs to their room, she had found several dried bloodstains on her skirt. Cold water got rid of them, but she would have to wash the skirt tomorrow . . .

The sound of her heels echoed sharply against the cobbles but that didn't matter now. She didn't care who heard them.

She had taken his money from her purse and, spreading it out on the bed, divided the pound notes and coins equally with Cora. Each of them had ended up with more than three pounds. Three whole pounds!

Apparently he had left his wallet and personal papers at home in case the police picked him up. There was nothing in his pockets that told you who he was . . .

Cora, stretched out on the other bed, had laughed. "Maybe he wasn't the Ripper!"

"Why do you say that?"

"Polly could've gone with another man first—the one you saw—then met the Ripper later."

She had continued folding the pound notes into her purse. "No, he was the Ripper all right. But we'll never know who he was—his name or nothin'."

Of course he was the Ripper! That's why his pockets were empty . . .

She sensed rather than heard that someone was following her.

As she reached the alley that led to Swallow Court she touched the damp plaster wall so she wouldn't lose her way.

The lanterns, hanging from spikes, were like small holes in the fog.

Now she could hear footsteps behind her on the cobblestones.

Maybe this would be a nice gent. Young and pleasant . . .

He was much closer now, almost at her heels.

Violette smiled as she turned to greet him.

A dark figure loomed out of the fog.

She was unable to see his face, only that he was raising an arm as though he was about to lift his hat. His left arm.

Something in his gloved hand caught a glint of light from the nearest lantern.

A knife! In his left hand!

The Ripper was left-handed . . .

Violette tried to scream, but his other gloved hand grasped her throat. She saw the arm swing down and felt the first hard thrust of the knife into her flesh.

Cora's Raid

by Isak Romun

The service station attendant opened the hood, looked in at the engine. He reached down with a hand palming a small rubber syringe and applied a quick shot of oil to the alternator.

"Gee, look, sir," the attendant said. "The alternator's shot. It's spraying oil. Once you're back on the road it'll break down in ten, fifteen miles."

The driver, a spare small man, lifted his hands to his chest, soft white palms out, as if pushing away unpleasantness. He had come off the limited-access highway to gas up and had asked the attendant to check under the hood. Bending warily over the car fender now he peeked into the darkened area below the hood. Adjusting his pince-nez, he looked unseeing at the part pointed out by the attendant. "Oh, dear," he said. "Is there anything you can do?"

"I dunno. I'll check our inventory and see if we have a replacement for it." The attendant turned and went toward a small building over which a sign, black letters on white peeling paint, proclaimed this place to be Moonstreet's Service Station and Garage. He disappeared into a gloomy, dirty car bay, its floor covered with oil-blackened sawdust, and stayed in there out of sight for a moment or two. Then he rejoined his customer outside.

"You're in luck, sir. We have one in stock. Shall I put it in?"

"Oh yes, do, please," said the car owner, his anxiety showing.

The attendant smiled encouragingly. "Don't worry, sir. I'll have your car back exactly the way it was in just a jiffy," he said as he got in to drive the vehicle into the bay. As he did, he reflected on his last statement. He had told this poor dude nothing but the exact truth.

In the bay, he switched off the engine, got out of the car, and pulled down the overhead door, shutting off the customer's view. Looking obliquely out through the small window in the door, the attendant carefully studied the customer now standing by one of the pumps looking forlornly at the garage door behind which his car had disappeared.

What the attendant saw was moderate, comfortable prosperity, a man to whom a reasonable sum was worth the price of avoiding imagined discomforts.

The attendant nodded his head decisively, strode over to the car, and flipped up its hood. He reached in and screwed off a battery cap exposing the cell's acid level. Then he took a cylindrical jar from a shelf, shook out an antacid tablet, broke the tablet into three or four small pieces, and dropped these into the battery cell. He screwed the cap back on securely and turned his attention to the alternator.

Working quickly with a solvent-dampened rag, he wiped the alternator surface clean of its oil and any foreign substance that might have clung to it. Then, after toweling the part of the last dabs of solvent, he took a can of quick-drying paint and brushed black enamel evenly across the alternator surface until it fairly sparkled, just as if it were new. A small, portable fan sped up the drying process. Finished, the attendant looked at his watch. Less than ten minutes had passed since he drove the car into the bay. Time to kill. He sat down, lit a cigarette, took up a magazine with an intriguing centerfold, and, for about the tenth time that day, hungrily surveyed its contents.

A few customers drove in for gas and as the attendant responded reluctantly to the bell summons, he flashed a friendly, confident smile at the small man waiting for his car to emerge from the garage.

"Won't be long now, sir."

"Um, yes, thank you."

At long last, after an hour and fifteen minutes, the attendant put down his magazine, snubbed out the last of many cigarettes, and got into the car. He turned the key in the ignition and heard a low whirr but, as he expected, the engine would not turn over.

He got out, opened the garage door, and beckoned to the customer. "Oh, sir, I'd like you to inspect the job," he said. With that he led the nervous car owner to the engine, indicated the painted alternator, and boasted, "Had a little trouble getting it in. This is a tough engine to work on. But it sure looks nice, don't it?"

The customer was moved to agree that the alternator did, indeed, look nice. However, any elation he might have felt at having his car at last in working order was considerably reduced by the attendant's next words.

"I'm afraid, sir, that you've got a dead battery here," he said and helpfully manipulated a hydrometer in and out of the neutralized cell to lend credence to his statement.

"I suppose this means a new battery," the little man gasped.

"Yes, sir, I think that's what we need," the attendant agreed with a joviality contrasting sharply with the car owner's downcast mood.

"Well, put it in."

The attendant did so, then labored a pencil stub over a sales slip before presenting the little man with a high three-figured bill.

"That includes tax," he said, then put in magnificently, "The boss'll kill me, but I gave you a break on the battery."

The other man took the bill and with unexpected crispness ticked off each item, totaled the figures to his satisfaction, noted the absence of a garage letterhead on the bill, and said, "Yes, everything seems to add up."

He went to his car, opened the door on the passenger side, and slid into the seat. He unlocked the glove compartment with a key that hadn't been on the same ring with the ignition key. From the compartment, he took a handy-talkie, pressed a button, and spoke briefly into the radio's receiver, "This place checks. Come on in."

He reached into the compartment once more and drew from it a pair of dark glasses and a snub-nosed revolver. The former he put on after removing his pince-nez. The latter he pointed negligently at the attendant just as a Volkswagen microbus, tires screeching, pulled into the service station.

Jake Moonstreet sat shivering in the small office of Sheriff Oscar Roche of the county in which the Moonstreet Service Station and Garage was located. Moonstreet was shivering because he was barefoot. As a matter of fact, his only covering was a thin, worn blanket that inadequately covered his large frame, the blanket's nap-free pink surface harmonizing nicely with the flesh peeking through numerous worn spots. Next to him, in a state of identical dishabille, sat his employee, Pat Challoner, also shivering.

Jake was talking to the sheriff whose attention was frequently distracted by sneezing fits brought under control only by the application of a great white handkerchief thrown full into and over the face. Beside the sheriff, a police stenographer was juggling a steno pad upon which a network of meaningless squiggles had been impressed by a usually keen and careful hand, now rendered quivering and slack-wristed by the deep drama of what Jake Moonstreet had related.

Around the walls, straining the capacity of the small office, were a number of uniformed deputies, probably every one the county employed, called in from their patrols to bear testimony first-hand on what would become known as the Moonstreet Ripoff. At any particular moment, one or another of them would be facing toward the wall, wiping eyes suddenly filled with tears, as shoulders shook in the throes of some uncontrollable emotion brought on by the narrative.

"Tell it again, please, Jake," Sheriff Roche begged, motioning toward the stenographer. "I don't think Charlie here got everything."

Jake Moonstreet sighed, shivered a little more, and told his story all over again into the handkerchief face of the sheriff.

"Well, Sheriff," Jake began, "Pat there called me up and told me there was a customer down at the station who wouldn't pay his bill until I come down personal like and talked to him. When Pat told me how much the bill was, I got into my pickup and got right down there. Well, when I got there, I saw a car, a late-model Chevy, and a Volks bus with four guys standing around it, all these guys wearing dark glasses. Pat motioned me into the office where I saw him standing with another guy, also with dark glasses on. As I go through the door, the group around the Volks breaks up. Three of them go into the garage and the other steps behind me and jams a gun in my back.

" 'What is this, a holdup?' I say. The guy with the gun almost loses it in my back and I get the idea he wants me to keep moving, so I go into the office. That's when I get a good look at the guy with Pat, a small guy with very clean hands. Uh, I notice that sort of thing in my business."

"That tells you the guy doesn't know thing one about cars. Right, Jake?" one of the deputies asked.

"*That* tells me the guy can use my station's expert help if his car's in trouble," replied Jake loftily.

He went on. "So I get a look at this guy's face, what there is of it not hidden by the glasses, and believe me, fellahs, here's a hard case, a syndicate type."

"Why do you think a syndicate type, Jake?" the sheriff asked.

"I bet they got some racket going, getting all us honest operators outa business so they can set up a chain of ripoff stations," answered Jake, raising his voice somewhat to be heard over the outburst of exuberance that greeted the word "honest."

"Has the syndicate approached you? Offered to buy you out? This is the way they usually operate."

"Well, no, Sheriff. But what else could it be?"

"I don't know, Jake. I really don't know. But go on with your story."

"Anyway, the hard type in the office with Pat says to me, 'Jacob Moonstreet?' I say, 'Yeah.' He says, 'You and your man here, Patrick Challoner, have had a good thing going. Now it's over.'

"So, the guy with the gun in my back steps around and cleans out the register. Puts everything, bills and change, even checks, into a bag with a lock trap. After he snaps the lock on the bag, he gives it to Mr. Hard Face. Just then, another one of them comes in and says, 'All set.' Hard Face asks, 'This place too?' The other guy says, 'Wired.'

"We go out then, and I notice that a guy's car we had in for a tuneup is parked across the road. They had moved it. Also moved was my pickup and Pat's Rambler, which are now in the garage bays. They manhandle Pat and I into the back of the Volks and we drive off aways, Hard Face leading in his Chevy. One guy stays behind hidden in back of an embankment and when he's sure no cars are passing on the road, he pushes down on a detonator he's got and up goes my station. Office, garage, gas pumps, the whole schmeer."

"And now tell us what happened after that," the sheriff urged.

"So, after the explosion, they drive like hell into town, through the business district, and out into that new housing subdivision."

"Warrington Heights," the sheriff clarified. "The place where all the fat bankrolls go to rest up after a hard day in town."

"Yeah, that's it. On the way there, the guy with the gun tells us to undress, like completely. He's got a good argument in his hand, so we do as he tells us. And then they put us out right there in the middle of that Heights place."

"Without a stitch on?" queried the sheriff, busily working his hand-kerchief again.

"Right. Naked as jaybirds. But you'll catch 'em, won't you, Sheriff?" Jake inquired hopefully. "I gave you their license numbers and I got another lead I didn't tell you before. A clue, like."

"What's that?"

"I think a dame runs the gang. I heard one of the guys mention her name. Cora. He knowed he said something outa school because he clammed up pronto. Maybe this Cora dame was one of them disguised." Jake Moonstreet looked eagerly at the sheriff. "You'll catch 'em, won't you?"

"I dunno," the sheriff said, suddenly sober. "We'll put out a bulletin on the cars and plates. But they'll probably have switched plates or ditched the cars by now."

Besides, the sheriff asked himself, who's the criminal here?

He was remembering the time Jake Moonstreet, some years back, did a job on the Roche family car.

The small man, once in his motel room, pulled his suitcases off the overhead rack, opened them on the room's single bed, and began packing. He packed carefully, slowly, a man who was sure of himself and what he did, and prided himself on the care and deliberation he brought to everything he did, including packing his clothes. He took a snub-nosed revolver from his pocket, hefted it briefly and then tucked it beneath some neatly folded, snow-white T-shirts.

As he went to the dresser for more clothes, he caught himself looking into the wide mirror above. He was mildly surprised to find a small smile of satisfaction creasing his normally stern features, betraying there a softness he usually exposed only to put the enemy off guard. He let the smile widen into a grin. Well, why not? he thought. It was a good operation; well planned, smoothly carried out.

A rap on the door swept the grin from his face.

"Yes. Who is it?"

"Barton, sir."

"Come in, Sergeant. It's open."

The door was pushed in and a tall bulky man wearing dark glasses let himself into the room.

The occupant looked at the newcomer, glanced up at the glasses, and said, "You can take them off, Sergeant. No need to be in uniform now."

The tall man smiled, said briskly, "Right, Lieutenant!" and removed the glasses.

"All taken care of?" the lieutenant asked.

"In the vans and on their way to Sector B. Plates'll be changed enroute. They'll be used next week by team 31 for an operation similar to the one we completed today."

"Good. Has the rest of our team departed?"

"Yes, sir, they're on their way. We'll rendezvous with them day after tomorrow at the assembly point. I have a new car outside."

"Fine. I'll pack and we'll be on our way."

"Lieutenant Valore, sir?"

"Yes?"

"What are we going up against next?"

"One of those ghetto superettes. High prices. Extends credit. Interesting accounting practices. We'll meet the research squad tomorrow and hammer out the plan with them before the operations squad arrives the next day. This will be team 17's last action before we shut down for a month with our families."

"There's precious little family life once you're in the Consumer Reaction Army."

The lieutenant turned on Sergeant Barton, his face hard as when earlier, revolver in hand, he had faced Pat Challoner, the service station attendant. "Sergeant," Valore snapped, "you don't think of personal comfort when you're fighting a war."

"Sorry, sir."

"All right. It's tough on all of us but we don't make it easier by grousing about the hardships we knew would be a part of it."

Sergeant Barton, chastened and wishing to change the subject, said, "Of course, sir. Can I help you pack?"

The lieutenant snapped a suitcase shut and replied, "I've just about got it. A few more items." His eye fell on a bottle of Irish whiskey atop the dresser. He also took in Sergeant Barton's embarrassment at being chewed out. "Relax, Barton," the lieutenant said. "Grab a couple of those plastic glasses and pour each of us a good shot of Irish."

When they raised the tumblers, the sergeant asked, "Shall we drink to our families?"

The lieutenant's mouth was a slit of disapproval. "No, the Army," he ordered.

"To CORA, then," said the sergeant.

"To CORA," said the lieutenant.

A Cup of Herbal Tea

by Robert S. Aldrich

Herbert Jenkins grumbled to himself as he drove his car up the steep, rain-splashed road to the summit of Hermitage Hill. There was a break in the storm just now but the sun was still shrouded by heavy, dark clouds. He was a fool, he thought, to respond to the old lady's invitation on a wretched day like this. If the river rose any higher, he would have a hard time getting back over the old bridge; he'd have to drive miles out of his way. There was a pile of work on his desk in his law office. She would probably keep him all afternoon with a lot of silly chatter.

Still, he reasoned, the visit had to be made. She was powerless to do anything legally now, of course, despite that young fellow she'd got hold of, fresh out of law school. Sam Cowdrey. A lot he could do for her! No, there wasn't a thing to worry about as far as the courts were concerned. But a nuisance suit would be a waste of time, and there would be the publicity. It would be better to try and get on with her. Offer her a few more token shares, perhaps.

Esther Bowen was the widow of the late Paul Bowen, an amateur and entirely self-educated inventor who called himself a chemist. Bowen had been unsuccessful most of his life. And then, past sixty, he had come up with a soft-drink formula. He had bottled it to sell locally and it had proved popular. The Brite-Joos Company had turned into a profitable bonanza—for a while, anyway. Then Bowen had overextended his credit in a flurry of reckless expansion. The bank had refused to renew his loans and had threatened foreclosure. Creditors began yammering at his door at the same time competitors were moving in, cutting sales. One mistake led to another until bankruptcy seemed the only way out.

That was when Herbert Jenkins had stepped in. Carefully sizing up Bowen's situation, he'd made his plans with his usual thoroughness. Before saying a word to Bowen, he had made a connection with Northeast Beverages, lining up a deal for them to take over Brite-Joos. He'd had to lie a little, pretending he held an interest in the firm, though at the time he didn't own a single share. Then, with a merely provisional deal in his shabby briefcase, he'd approached Bowen with an offer.

"You've got two courses open," he told the beleaguered man, after reviewing every detail of his business affairs. "Either you file for bankruptcy or you can sell out for what you can get." Then he outlined his plan. He would pay off the major creditors in return for control of the stock. Bowen would keep a minimum of shares. He had thrown in the meaningless title of board chairman as a sop to the old man's pride. Jenkins laughed to himself afterward whenever he thought about it. He'd done a real selling job. Bowen had held out for a while. Jenkins turned the screws. He hinted, without quite saying so, that the creditors were behind him, that unless Bowen gave in, they would close on him the next day.

Jenkins remembered with pleasure the moment when, with tears brimming his rheumy eyes, Bowen had at last reached for a pen and scrawled his signature on the closing agreement, his fingers pushing the pen falteringly, as if it were a great effort to sign away the business into which he had poured his life and hopes. That childlike scrawl fulfilled the dream of months for the scheming attorney.

As soon as he had ownership of the firm in his name, he had turned around and sold out to Northeast, giving him enough to pay off his loans, satisfy the creditors, and leaving himself a whopping profit. It just showed what a man could do if he understood human nature. Most men were fools. You could twist them around your finger if you knew how to handle them.

Well, he thought, the old lady is a mere detail. Still grieving, no doubt, over her dead husband. A few days after Jenkins pulled off his coup, Bowen was found in his car, inside his garage, the motor running and the door openings stuffed with rags. The note beside him didn't mention Herbert Jenkins. It held a few scrawled lines, in that childish writing, about what a failure he had been and how he hoped his poor wife would forgive him for taking his life.

The suicide caused quite a stir in the town. It was a relief to Jenkins. Saved him a lot of trouble. As he had expected, Bowen had been having second thoughts. No doubt he had begun to regret signing that agreement. It would have been most unfortunate if he had brought suit. Jenkins's part in the Northeast deal would have furnished ammunition to his enemies, even the threat of disbarment. Well, that was all over now.

The old woman didn't know anything about business. She probably figured her husband had been cheated, but there wasn't a thing she could do about it. She'd been talking to Sam Cowdrey. Well, he'd have to stroke her a little, maybe offer a few extra shares out of the Northeast stock he'd kept, though it hurt to think of being so generous. He'd see. One step at a time.

The old, two-story Victorian house looked huddled and forlorn in the rain. Jenkins pulled the collar of his raincoat around his neck and hurried up the steps. He rang the bell.

Mrs. Bowen, slender, white-haired, slightly stooped, appeared at once. "Why, Mr. Jenkins," she said, "how nice of you to come out in this storm. Do come right in."

He murmured a few polite greetings. There was a fire blazing in the living room. The doors to the dining room were closed. Heavy curtains were drawn over the windows, as if to keep out non-existent sunlight. Tiffany lamps spread pools of yellowish light on the once-rich carpets.

"Well, Mrs. Bowen, how have you been?" he asked with forced heartiness, warming his hands over the fire.

"Quite well, thank you, considering everything. My husband's passing was a terrible shock."

"Of course, I understand. Well, you seem to be living quite comfortably."

"And the manner of his death," Mrs. Bowen said. "It was so unlike him. He always spoke of people who took their own lives as weak and sinful. I have never been able to convince myself that he would do such a terrible thing."

"Yes. But you mustn't let yourself dwell on it too much, Mrs. Bowen. No doubt he was ill."

She shook her head. "He was heartbroken, Mr. Jenkins. He had poured all his energy into his business. And to lose it all so suddenly. He felt he had been betrayed."

"These things happen all the time in business," Jenkins said smoothly. "Things go wrong somewhere along the line. It wasn't your husband's fault. It just happened."

Mrs. Bowen arose from her chair and poked at the fire. "I was in a position to learn a good deal about the business, Mr. Jenkins. From what Paul told me before his death, I know it didn't 'just happen.' It's true the company was in trouble, but he was pushed into selling out for a mere fraction of its true worth." Her face was flushed, though whether from the fire or from her emotion he could not tell, as she turned to him. "You must admit that you profited very handsomely."

He smiled consolingly. "Business, Mrs. Bowen, just business. You mustn't take it as something personal. After all, you have your Northeast stock. The dividends must bring you a fair little income."

"Very little, I'm afraid. It's increasingly hard to meet my bills."

He tried to switch the subject. "Too bad about this filthy weather. I'd have liked to see your garden. I understand you have a very beautiful one."

"Yes, I have. I must show it to you one day when the weather is fine. Unfortunately, we've had trouble with moles rooting up the flowers. My gardener Amos and I have tried traps but there are too many of them."

"Moles? I know a man who got rid of moles by burying empty bottles in his garden, with the necks sticking up above the ground. He says the wind whistles through the bottles. The moles feel the vibration underground and it drives them off."

"Amos thinks there's only one sure way to get rid of them," said Mrs. Bowen. "By poisoning them. It sounds dreadful, doesn't it? I dislike killing any animal, but it seems it must be done or my lovely garden will be ruined. Saturday he went to the store and brought back a bottle of arsenic. It's in the storeroom now."

"I see."

"Amos is going to use it as soon as the ground is dry enough. Meantime, the bottle sits there. It gives me a peculiar feeling whenever I look at it." She clapped a wrinkled hand to her cheek. "Dear, I'm being a poor hostess. You would like a cup of tea, wouldn't you?"

"That would be very nice," he assured her.

"It's herbal tea," she said. "I hope you will like it. There's nothing like a good strong cup of herbal tea, especially in this weather. It has an unfamiliar taste to some people."

"I'm sure it will be fine."

Waiting for her to return from the kitchen, Jenkins wondered why she had bothered to ask him all the way out here. Probably she thought her poverty would stir his sympathy. His watch said three. He'd have to make some excuse to cut the visit short. But, first, he'd get in a few questions concerning Sam Cowdrey.

He was pondering how to put his questions when Mrs. Bowen returned. She was pushing a little wheeled cart on which were a large teapot, cups, a marbled cake, and cookies. Jenkins suppressed a sigh. "Let me help you," he said.

"In better days we had a maid to do things," Mrs. Bowen said, when they were again seated. "But since the failure of the business—well, one must make do. I can't help but recall how contented and happy Mr. Bowen and I were, looking forward to a comfortable old age together. I never foresaw being alone, with barely enough to live on."

Jenkins cleared his throat, in which a crumb had lodged. "I was thinking, Mrs. Bowen. I want you to feel satisfied with the arrangements I made with Mr. Bowen. If you have any questions, I hope you will bring them to my attention. There's no need for you to turn to anyone else for advice. Some of these young lawyers lack experience."

She was smiling vaguely. "I already have an attorney," she said. "Mr. Cowdrey gives me all the help I need. I think he may want to discuss things with you."

He tried to hide his discomfort. "Surely there's no question about the way the company's affairs were settled. Everything was done quite properly, I assure you."

"The legal fine points are over my head, Mr. Jenkins, but I gather that if it can be shown that my husband was coerced in some way, the courts might set the agreement aside."

"Coerced?" Jenkins found it hard to swallow. "There was nothing like that. All the details were put before him. His decision was made of his own free will. I am afraid you are being badly advised. A suit of that kind would stand no chance."

She looked worried. "Sam Cowdrey is a smart young man."

"A suit would only stir up unpleasant publicity, Mrs. Bowen. I'm sure you wouldn't like that."

"Yes. I've felt all along that there must be a better way."

Jenkins took another sip of tea, then did a double-take. Better way? What did she mean?

"Lawsuits are so long and dragged out," she said, sipping her own tea. "Mr. Bowen always said that if you had to settle something unpleasant, it should be done as quickly and painlessly as possible. I've thought about that a good deal." She smiled. "Do you like my tea?"

"Fine, just fine." He was puzzled. Was she hinting at something?

"Once," said Mrs. Bowen, "our old dog Rolf was very sick. It was obvious that he would have to be put out of the way. Mr. Bowen was fond of Rolf but he did not hesitate."

"What did he do?"

"He fed him some poison," said Mrs. Bowen. "Arsenic, I believe."

Jenkins nodded vaguely. "I really ought to be going," he said. "The wind seems to be getting fiercer."

"The wind is always so destructive to my garden," Mrs. Bowen said. "Whipping the heads off the flowers and scattering limbs and leaves. And the moles have been so bad this summer. Amos assures me that they will not suffer for long. Arsenic is very powerful and acts quite suddenly."

In the pause that followed he could hear the ticking of the mantel clock. She seemed obsessed with the subject of arsenic. He drained the last of his tea.

"I'm afraid it took my husband longer to die," said Mrs. Bowen. "I suppose his death was quite painless. Death by poisoning must be hard to endure. But I expect I am depressing you, talking of poison." She put her cup down. "Now, I should like to tell you something that only one or two others besides myself know. It concerns a secret that Mr. Bowen kept all his life. He . . ." She raised up. "Why, Mr. Jenkins, is anything wrong? Are you ill?"

What was wrong was that Jenkins had just had a thought, a terrible thought. Until this moment, his agile mind had not connected the two things, the odd-tasting tea in his cup and the bottle of arsenic in the storeroom. But she couldn't have!

Yes she could! *She had planned this all along.*

His hand darted to his throat. He half rose from his chair and fell back with a frightened groan. Unable to speak aloud, he uttered tormented sounds.

"You must have a bit of cake in your windpipe," Mrs. Bowen said calmly. "Take a deep breath and try to relax."

"Arsen . . . arsenic!" He tried to shout but it was only a whisper. "Help me!" But apparently Mrs. Bowen did not hear.

"As I started to say, Mr. Bowen had very little schooling. He was left an orphan and he had to make his way in the world early in life."

Jenkins did not hear her. He felt a burning in his stomach. The lights from the Tiffany lamps seemed to grow dimmer. He was badly frightened. How could she sit there, calmly talking, savoring her revenge, waiting for him to die? She must be mad. With an effort he struggled to his feet. "Please, Mrs. Bowen," he said throatily. "Telephone for a doctor! An ambulance! I must get to the hospital before it's too late!"

"Too late, Mr. Jenkins?" There was a faint smile on her lips. "It was too late for poor Mr. Bowen when he lay in his car with the motor running."

"It's not my fault that he killed himself!"

"Do you admit that you used him badly? Do you confess here and now that you tricked him, taking advantage of his ignorance?"

"All right, yes, yes! If you're dissatisfied, I'll . . . I'll make it up to you! I'll give you all my Northeast stock! Only don't waste time. Help me!"

She was getting up slowly, so slowly. She was looking down at him with no pity in her pale face. "The note the police found. You wrote it yourself. You imitated his writing, from his signature. Then you murdered him."

"No!" But every moment was precious. "Yes! I knocked him out with a wrench. I . . . I had to. He was suspicious, threatening. Yes, I'll confess everything, *only get help!*"

She had no witness. He could deny it later . . . if he lived.

"Get up, Mr. Jenkins. You look so foolish. I put nothing in your tea. You have not been poisoned."

"What?" He struggled to his feet, feeling the overwhelming shock of release, and with it anger. He had been made a fool. "You tricked me," he rasped. "I have admitted nothing . . . nothing! I will deny everything. They'll never believe you. They can prove nothing!"

"His signature, Mr. Jenkins, it was all that my husband *could* write. He never learned to read."

He stared at her. "Impossible. How could he conduct his business?"

"I helped him. I tried to warn him against your offer but he wouldn't listen. When the police showed me the note, I knew he had been murdered. I did not tell them he was illiterate. I had sworn to keep his secret. You were the only one who had anything to gain by his death."

He had regained his calm. Shrewdly he calculated his chances. No one had seen him coming here. He took a step toward her. It would take only a hard squeeze around her scrawny throat.

"It didn't matter to me that he couldn't read. We loved each other. You wouldn't understand, Mr. Jenkins, for you have never loved anyone but yourself."

Another step and it would all be over.

He whirled around as the dining-room doors slid open. Sam Cowdrey and Police Chief Bennett came toward him and halted. For one moment all four stood motionless while the rain pounded at the windows and the wind howled around the eaves.

Albion, Perfidious Albion

by Everett Greenbaum

In the summer of 1967, Mr. Mendelbright, the Beverly Hills advertising man, took his wife and young daughter on a flight from California over the Pole to England. As they flew above Greenland on a rare cloudless day, they looked down upon vast stretches of snow, crossed by rivers of solid ice which broke up the dark sea into icebergs, glistening white above the water, bottle green below. The experience seemed to augur a time of bright adventure and discovery.

A few hours later they landed in England.

Mr. Mendelbright hadn't been out of the States since his bachelor days ten years before. His wife was a soft-spoken Southern girl with an unsatisfied longing to visit foreign parts . . . especially those places where antiques were offered to the public at reasonable prices.

She was delighted with the English. "Aren't they nice?" she said. "Such nice manners. So anxious to help. So kind!"

"I told you, didn't I?" Mr. Mendelbright said. Since he had praised his old friends the British over the years, he was anxious for them to make a good impression on his family.

For several days they went from one traditional place to another. From the changing of the guards to Parliament. From the Tower of London to Old Bailey. From the British Museum to the London Museum.

Mr. Mendlebright felt that they were really absorbing culture, that his daughter was really soaking up enough history to enrich her whole life. How swiftly the cabs swept them past old grey buildings, through damp green parks from one soaking to another! The cabbies were delightful. Eager to share their London, nay, their England, with you.

As a successful author of direct-mail advertising copy, Mr. Mendelbright was, of course, anxious to visit the homes of Dr. Johnson and Charles Dickens. He almost fainted with emotion when he reached out to touch the desk where *Nicholas Nickleby* had been written. Everywhere were letters, manuscripts and mementoes in glass display cases of polished wood.

"Such nice antiques!" Mrs. Mendelbright murmured.

Evenings at the hotel, after their daughter had fallen asleep, his wife studied the currency, sorting out the florins from the half-crowns, the ten-shilling notes from the ten-pound notes.

She studied maps of London and mimeographed rules about export and import allowances.

"I'm ready to begin my shopping," she announced one night.

During the days following, Mr. Mendelbright found himself doing an unpleasant thing which he had managed to avoid after the first couple of years of marriage . . . waiting while women shopped. He found himself waiting at outdoor stands in the Portobello Road Market while little beaded things were fondled. He waited in the Camden Passage while leather and silver things were appraised. On Bond Streets, Old and New, he waited while lace was caressed and garnets were held up to the light.

Finally the absolute limit of his patience was reached. He was furious!

"I don't want to wait outside for any more shopping going on!" he said.

After ten years, Mrs. Mendlebright knew how to handle these little moods which frequently seize creative people.

"Aren't you going to buy something nice for yourself?" she asked.

What a little darling she is, Mr. Mendlebright thought, feeling like a swine for having lost his temper.

"There's a place near Cadogan Square where they sell steam engines," he said.

"Steam engines are duty free," his wife said. "Why don't you go have a look and be back in an hour?"

Mr. Mendelbright had a wonderful time at the steam engine place. These beautiful brass and steel working models had been made in an age when machinists worked long hours for little money. They couldn't possibly be duplicated in modern times.

The steam man liked Mr. Mendelbright. He invited him upstairs to see his lathe and a private collection of small pumps. Before leaving, Mr. Mendelbright bought a steam engine, not only of first quality, but one which had plenty of brass parts to be polished on Sunday afternoons during the Beverly Hills rainy season. He would put a bunch of Rodgers and Hart records on the hi-fi and polish his steam engine.

That engine was the kind of thing a person would want to keep forever.

As he was returning to the world of females, there was a screech of brakes, the stench of rubber smearing along cobblestones and the crunch of steel. In a minor bumper-to-bumper collision, Mr. Mendlebright slid onto the floor of the cab, landing on his steam engine. Quickly he untied the bundle for a look. Nothing was broken.

"I'm most sorry," the cabby said. "You all right, sir?"

"Fine," Mr. Mendlebright said.

"The reason you fell on the floor and I didn't, sir, is because I had the steering wheel to hold onto."

"I suppose so," Mr. Mendelbright said.

"If you can just brace yourself against something, you'll keep yourself from sliding on the floor," the man said.

"I see."

"It's the momentum, you see, sir. It's the momentum of your body that carries you on after the cab itself is stopped."

"I suppose so."

"What d'ya weigh, sir, about twelve stone?"

"I imagine."

"Well, there it is then, sir. You have quite a lot of momentum going for you and no wheel to hold onto."

"No wheel back here." Mr. Mendelbright forced a social chuckle, hoping that the wheel and floor talk was over.

"But I've got this wheel up here and I just took a good hold on it when I saw that bugger hit the car ahead."

Mr. Mendelbright didn't answer this time. He rubbed his leg, which hurt a little. Back at the hotel he related the incident to his family.

"I hope the driver wasn't too upset," his wife said. "They're so conscientious."

The next day he got them off to a good start at the Royal Academy. On the way to lunch, however, his wife spotted some cut glass in a store window.

"I'm only going in for one minute," she said.

At the end of an hour and a half, she had added a small cut-glass sugar bowl and a tiny silver tongs to their list of imports.

Mr. Mendelbright silently cursed the shopping instinct. Women just couldn't pass by bits of cloth, silver or glinting glass. They were magpies. And once attracted to an object, it took them forever to find out from their minds whether or not they really wanted it.

This indecision extended to food. Thirty seconds after a menu was placed in his hands, Mr. Mendelbright knew exactly what he wanted. They never knew. It broke his heart to have to send a waiter away until his ladies could decide what they wanted to eat.

Then there was the problem of getting out evenings. Either they took their daughter with them to something like Ken Dodds and his Doddikins at the Palladium or they went to the theater and arranged for a baby sitter.

He couldn't help recalling his single traveling days. Footloose and quick, he covered more museums, theaters and historical points of interest in a day than the Mendelbrights en famille did in a week. He felt tethered. He felt restless.

One evening was set aside for the washing of hair. This was always a depressing event for Mr. Mendelbright even in their large house in California. For some reason there always had to be a feeling of emergency about it.

It was "Tell me later, we're rinsing."

Or "I can't talk to you now, we're setting!"

Hair washing was going on all around him in their crowded, hot hotel room in Green Park. Mr. Mendelbright could hardly breathe through the tension.

"I think I'd like to go out for a while," he blurted.

"Well, all right," his wife said, "but don't go looking at anything we might want to see together."

Outside the air was cool. Ten years seemed to slip away from Mr. Mendelbright. The streets were full of couples walking close together, whispering and laughing. He began to walk on the balls of his feet the way he had when his waist measured thirty-two inches and his hair was bright red.

The sounds and smells of the night were delicious. Ragged measures of music threaded through the air. Sometimes the fragrance of flowers swept over him, sometimes perfume, Mr. Mendelbright thought.

The character of the neighborhood changed as he wandered. One whole street was staffed by doormen announcing that the non-stop striptease show inside was just about to start.

If it's non-stop, how did it stop in order for it to be about to start? Mr. Mendelbright mused.

Good! As long as he was capable of cold logic there was no danger that he could be foolish enough to enter one of these enticing Soho doorways.

Anyway, how would it be if he'd gone in? Stripteasers! What would the two innocents back at the hotel think if their captain in this strange land had gone in to see stripteasers?

Once he had gotten past these sirens in safety, the streets became narrower. There was more perfume, a tinkling of abandoned laughter. Miniskirts were shorter than ever.

Mr. Mendelbright felt that he had entered a whole neighborhood of Julie Christies.

Instead of walking around a large puddle, he leaped over it, landing neatly and silently on his sponge-rubber walking soles.

I bet I've lost ten pounds here, he considered. Maybe we'd better come here every summer.

A young Scotsman with a lock of blond hair over his forehead was talking to him.

"Rude movies, sir," he was saying. "Most unusual collection in the world. Two hours. Show begins in ten minutes."

"No, thank you," Mr. Mendelbright said.

"You'd surely enjoy it, sir. A rare collection, to be sure."

How friendly the fellow was! So naive, open and eager for the visitor to have a good time! More music trickled over the rooftops. He could smell sleeping roses in a nearby park.

For a forty-year-old man living in history's most corrupt century, Mr. Mendelbright had seen few rude movies. Only one, in fact—in New York at Junior Fingerhood's bachelor smoker just before he married Elaine.

This hardly counted. In the first place the picture had been blurry. Sidney Blake, who pretended to be such a great expert on cameras, didn't even know how to get a large ball of fuzz out of the lens. Once the picture started, it was the leading man's costume which provided distraction. He wore garters, black silk hose with white clocks up the sides and perforated black-and-white shoes throughout the entire performance. Mr. Mendelbright and Junior Fingerhood laughed till they cried. They missed the whole thing.

And here he was, thousands of miles from home where no one knew him, in a place where a man weighed ten pounds less and should have some kind of a wild adventure and not just shop all day . . .

The fellow's description was becoming more colorful. "Now there's one with two chaps. Then two chaps and bird. Then two birds. Then bird and mastiff in Kodachrome color."

"Is it far from here?" Mr. Mendelbright asked.

"Just a skip around the corner," the young man said quickly. "We've had nothing but good comments, sir. I'm sure you'll find it well worthwhile."

They moved together down the block and took a left turn.

The street they turned into was narrow, dark, close . . . Mr. Mendelbright stopped. A shadow of doubt. He held back for a moment.

"Ahhh, don't blame you, sir. Don't think I'd like to come in here with a stranger myself. But please keep in mind, sir, that we can't provide this kind of entertainment on Hyde Park corner. If you get my meaning." The warm laugh of his cicerone encouraged Mr. Mendelbright along to the top of a steep stairway.

After all, it's *telling* about these experiences that counts, he thought. He could see himself having lunch at Frascati's in Beverly Hills with Junior Fingerhood and Leo from the downtown office. He would hold them spellbound with his review of bird and mastiff in Kodachrome color. Then, as casually as possible, he'd order café au lait.

He would thereafter be marked in the advertising business as a man who has seen it all.

The stairway led down into a shabby brick-and-stucco structure which seemed to have several levels underneath the ground. On every landing there were crude signs reading TO THE SHOW.

Finally they came to the bottom. The Scotsman disappeared. He was replaced by a very tall young man in a crumpled brown suit. Suspicion would have returned to Mr. Mendelbright then, except for one thing: in an adjacent room, he could make out a few people on folding chairs, a projector whirring, and flickering images on a screen.

Starting into the room, he hoped to catch "bird and mastiff" from the beginning. He hated coming into the middle of a picture.

A heavy hand stopped him. It was tall brownsuit.

"You'll have to join," he said.

"Excuse me?"

"It's a film society! Private club. You can't provide this kind of entertainment on Hyde Park corner!"

All right. The fee was three pounds. Cheap enough when you considered that it provided a lifetime of luncheon conversation.

There was a place for your signature. Without a second's hesitation, Mr. Mendelbright wrote, "Vladimir Von Fleet, Chicago." Pretty neat, he thought. Most fellows would put down Joe Doe or John Smith or something trite.

Brownsuit offered him a chair. Vladimir Von Fleet, Chicago, lit the last of his American cigarettes and turned his attention to the screen.

Strange. The picture seemed to be a silent version of *Dracula.*

Clever, he thought. Any minute that bat would turn into Count Dracula and ravish the girl in the white nightgown. He was impressed by the artistic effort that had gone into the production. So much care for what could only be, at best, a limited audience. The advertising business could pick up a couple of pointers from these people!

Ten minutes of *Dracula* proved to be just *Dracula!* All the old nonsense about Transylvania, wolfbane, et cetera. Other members of the audience began to slip out of the room one by one. He could hardly blame them.

It was during the scene where Dr. Seward tells the others that he has seen Lucy sleepwalking in the garden with two strange marks on her throat when someone touched him. A thin dirty girl sitting to his right was unbuttoning his shirt.

"Want to come along with me?" she said.

Vladimir Von Fleet, Chicago, became Earl Mendelbright whose wife and daughter were washing their hair back at the hotel.

"Uh. Uh . . . no, thank you," he said.

A stocky man in the seat ahead of Mr. Mendelbright whirled around.

"What's the matter with her?" he growled. "Ain't good enough for you?"

"I'm just not interested, that's all." Mr. Mendelbright got to his feet. "I'll be running along. I'm afraid I've seen this picture be—"

The man grabbed the front of Mr. Mendelbright's J. Press summerweight jacket. Someone pinned his arms from behind. He began to struggle as the thin girl's hands began exploring his pockets.

The jacket grabber began to shout. His remarks were loud and stagey, like bad acting. They didn't seem to fit the action, past or present.

"Filthy bloody American!" he yelled. "Bloody cheek! Coming into a private club! Mauling my bird!"

The thin girl was trying desperately to get Mr. Mendelbright's wrist watch. It was a two-hundred-dollar self-winding gold watch which changed the date every midnight. It didn't understand about February or the months with thirty days in them, so several times a year he had to pull its stem on the first of the month.

He loved that watch and fought for it. He worked one arm loose, managing to clutch the watch in his fist. The girl pulled with both hands until the metal band ripped. She tried again. This time the razor-sharp torn metal cut the underside of her wrist. He still had his watch. Maddened by the sight of her own blood, the girl began to beat his head. Someone kicked his shin. The room became light purple as he lost track of things for a moment.

When he returned to the action, the girl had his watch. She was shrieking "Bloody American!" and a lot of other rotten things in a flat mean voice. She had become an ugly, wild animal.

Mr. Mendelbright had been in several fights in his lifetime. It wasn't that he always lost that bothered him. It was the way his mind would pretend it was happening to someone else, that all he had to do in the fight was to watch it.

This time, however, he was able to concentrate on trying to escape. With three people hanging onto him, he managed to reach the second landing. He could see the doorway and the lone light in the close outside.

"Help!" he yelled. "Police!"

A form darkened the narrow stairway above him. By God, someone was coming to help!

Disappointment . . . His rescuer proved to be tall brownsuit. He was holding a large cold knife, which he pressed against Mr. Mendelbright's throat.

"Your bloody armies aren't here, American," he said. "I wouldn't half mind cutting you up. Don't think I wouldn't!"

Mr. Mendelbright went limp. He thought with heart-wrenching regret about the pair back at the hotel. Now they would be sleeping softly, their sweet faces and bare arms expecting him back.

He would never see them again. Somehow, with the help of official strangers, they would return to Beverly Hills. The gentle young widow and the beautiful little girl would forget him in time . . .

"Let me go," he said.

His spectator mind heard a note of pleading in his voice. Don't give them the satisfaction, he thought.

"Listen, you people," he said, "just don't go too far. I'm an officer in the Naval Reserve." The increased pressure of the knife against his throat told him he was on a wrong tack . . .

His right leg felt oddly large. It touched the front of his trousers as though it were two legs. He knew he was hurt.

Suddenly he wailed, "I want my watch! I want my watch!" Shameful! He hated himself for that.

"Tell you what," the stocky fellow said, "give us all your ready, you can have your watch back."

Was that all they wanted! He had only ten or fifteen pounds in his wallet. Why hadn't they said so in the first place?

"All right," he said. They let him reach for his wallet. It was nice not to have a knife pressing against his windpipe.

They gave him his watch and ten shillings for cab fare. Strange. Maybe he was dying and didn't know it.

"We'll be behind you," brownsuit said. "Go to the police and we'll kill you."

Good! That meant he wasn't dying.

He could hardly believe he was free. In the close he expected hands to clutch at him again, but they didn't. Then he was in the narrow street and then a large street.

He stopped. He couldn't recognize landmarks. Where was he? What street? Someone should be told about this. Where was the opening to the close? What time was it?

He opened his fist to look at his watch. It tinkled. It had become nothing but a little gold case full of loose parts. Rage filled him. Ahead, on the street, there was a bobby.

"I've been had!" Mr. Mendelbright said, looking quickly behind.

The bobby showed some interest. He wasn't like the big, strong, handsome daytime bobbies one saw in famous public places. He was rather a nighttime bad-neighborhood bobby, even smaller than Mr. Mendelbright, with an acne condition which would surely distract from the serious study of crime control.

"Take me to them and identify them, sir," he said.

Mr. Mendelbright thought about himself and this little bobby against the stalwart staff of the rude movie management.

"We'd better get some help."

"Not at all, sir. I've got this." The bobby raised the lapel of his jacket. There was a small microphone pinned there. It resembled a rusty root-beer bottlecap with holes in it.

In a country where every telephone call is shouted against a background of loud static, Mr. Mendelbright refused to trust the ability of the bobby's root-beer cap to get through stone walls three stories underground to a wandering police car.

"Now come along, sir. We'll collar them, make the arrest and, if you'll just come along to court, the case will come up presently."

Mr. Mendelbright thought about his family waking up at dawn to view his terrifyingly empty bed.

He thought about waiting in a dingy courtroom until five in the morning and he thought about reporters and newspapers.

AMERICAN ADVERTISING SOLON IN RUDE FILM SCANDAL.

His right leg had decided not to be numb any more and throb instead. He raised his trouser leg to see a large blue knot on his shinbone.

"My God!" he said, grabbing the bobby's elbow for support.

The bobby stepped away as though he'd been clutched by a leper. On his face was an unmistakable sneer of contempt. Some sort of custom had been violated.

"The hell with you," Mr. Mendelbright said. He got into a cab.

The cabby and the hotel porter were understanding and discreet. They knew he'd been in some kind of trouble. That sort of thing is difficult to hide when your shirt is soaked with blood from a girl's wrist.

His family was asleep. Very quietly, he removed his shirt and took it to a wastebasket in the maid's hall closet. Then he bathed noiselessly, pausing from time to time to prod the three-inch blue leg bump.

He couldn't sleep for the racing, remorseful thoughts . . .

How could he keep his shame from his loved ones? It would kill them if they knew what a depraved idiot they had for husband and father. Just knowing what had happened would frighten them badly. They mustn't know, they mustn't ever . . .

It must have been just after six that he dozed off.

Around seven he was suddenly awakened.

"Oh, no!" his wife gasped. "Oh, no!"

He had kicked off his covers. His pajama pants were, as usual, hiked above the knees. She was staring at the leg bump, now reddish green.

"Just *look* at that poor little leg," she said. "That darn taxi driver should have been more careful!"

Then she began to arrange the day's activities so that they included the gourmet departments at Fortnum and Mason's as well as the Burlington Arcade, where she hoped to find a really good hairbrush.

Life or Breath

by Nelson DeMille

Martin Wallace stood in a modified parade rest position and gazed out of the twenty-third-floor hospital window. Across the thirty miles of flat suburban sprawl he could see the blazing skyscrapers of Manhattan.

They blinked, twinkled and beckoned to him.

He looked at his watch. Fifteen minutes to nine. Fifteen minutes before he could leave this oppressive room and head for the lights of that enchanted island. He rocked back and forth on the balls of his feet. His reveries were broken by a sound behind him.

He turned and looked down at the form on the bed. The limp arm was tapping the night table to get his attention. He made a slightly annoyed face as their eyes met. Who else but Myra could get herself into a fix like this? But, then, he supposed that the hospital was full of bored suburban housewives who didn't know their capacity for Valium.

He stepped up to the bed. A small green plastic box sat on its stand next to the bed. A clear accordion-type plastic hose led from the box to her throat. The box made a faint, but annoying, pneumatic sound. "Myra. I have to leave, dear. Visiting hours are over. What can I bring you?" He smiled.

She looked petulant. That was her favorite expression. Petulant. In twenty years of marriage, he had labelled every one of her expressions and voice tones.

She made small grunting sounds. She wanted to speak, but nothing came out.

"You just get a good night's rest, Myra. Rest. A nice long rest." He smiled and pulled the respirator hose out of the tracheal adaptor embedded in her throat.

Air rushed into the adaptor and made a wheezing sound. At the same time air blew out of the disconnected hose in a continuous stream. He squeezed the open end of the hose, but it was too late. The alarm went off.

Almost immediately, a big, buxom nurse charged into the room like an enraged mother hen. "Mr. Wallace! Please. I explained to you how to disconnect that. You must squeeze the hose first, before you pull it out, so that the alarm doesn't sound."

"Sorry."

She threw him a look that medical people reserve for naughty lay people. "It's like screaming wolf. You know?"

"Sorry, nurse." He looked her full figure over. Long tresses of chestnut brown hair fell onto her shoulders and framed her pretty German-Irish face. The name tag on her breast read Maureen Hesse.

She made a huff and a puff and turned around. She called back over her shoulder as she left, "Visiting hours are almost over."

"Yes, nurse." He looked down at his wife. She had placed her hand over the gaping rubber tracheal adaptor. With the hole sealed off she was able to speak in weak, aspirating sounds. Martin Wallace preferred this to the high-pitched screech he was used to.

Myra spoke. "Don't forget my magazines." She paused as air rushed into the hole. "And get them to put a different TV in here." She wheezed. "We're paying for it." She opened her mouth and tried to gulp some air. "I want one that works. Call my mother tonight." She tried taking air in through her nose. "And talk to that doctor. I want to know *exactly* how long—"

Martin Wallace gently took his wife's hand away from the tracheal adaptor. Her words faded like a slowing record. The tracheal adaptor wheezed. He began to plug the respirator hose back into her throat.

"Martin! I have more to tell you—you—" Her words were lost as the machine began pumping air back into her lungs.

"You're getting yourself excited, Myra. Now, rest. Rest. Good night." He walked around the bed and left the room.

At the nurses' station, he spotted Dr. Wasserman, the resident physician. He walked over to him. "Excuse me, Doctor."

The young resident looked up from his charts. "Oh, yes. Mr. Wallace. How is your wife doing?"

"Well, that's what I want to ask *you*, Doctor."

"Of course." Dr. Wasserman put on a look of professional concern. "Well, Mr. Wallace, it could be worse. She could be dead."

Martin Wallace did not consider that to be worse. "What's the—how do you call it—prognosis?"

"Well, it's too early to tell, really. You see, Mr. Wallace, when you take a tranquillizer, like Valium, for instance, for extended periods of time, you begin to think you're building up a resistance to it. It seems to have no clout anymore. So instead of taking, let's say, five milligrams at a time, you take maybe twenty, as your wife did. Plus that martini—"

"Manhattan."

"Yes. Whatever. So what happened is that she had a period of anoxic cardiac arrest. In other words, her breathing and heart stopped. Maybe for as long as two minutes. This may lead to residual neurological sequelae—permanent but partial damage to the nervous system."

"Meaning?"

Dr. Wasserman stroked his chin. "It's too early to tell, really."

"Come on, Doctor. What's the *worst* it can be?"

He shrugged. "She can be an invalid for the rest of her life. She may need a home respirator for a while. She may even need occasional renal dialysis. Frequent cardiac tests. There could be partial muscular paralysis. When you're dealing with the nervous system, you never know. It may take weeks to see what works and what doesn't work anymore. I mean, she was technically dead for a few minutes. How many functions come back is anybody's guess. You understand?"

"Yes."

Martin Wallace glanced back toward his wife's room. He turned back toward the doctor. "How long would she live without the respirator? I mean—you know—when she wants to speak—I'm afraid to keep the hose out too long. I don't want to—"

The doctor moved his hand in a calming gesture. "That shouldn't be a concern. When she has difficulty breathing she signals to you, doesn't she? Or she tells you."

"Yes. Yes, of course. But I was just wondering. You know. If the hose came out in her sleep, maybe."

"That's why the alarm is there, Mr. Wallace. In the event the hose comes out by accident and she can't replace it." He gave him a smile and changed his voice to a paternal scolding tone, even though he was much younger than Mr. Wallace. "You, by the way, must be more careful when you disconnect it. You can't be setting off the alarm every time. It gives the nurses a good workout, but they have enough of that anyway in the Intensive Care Unit." He smiled again. "As long as there is someone in the room or as long as the alarm system is working, there can't be any accident."

Martin Wallace smiled back, although this good news did not make him at all happy. He was asking questions with one thing in mind and the good doctor was answering him with another thing in mind. He'd have to be blunt, "Look, Doctor," he smiled again, "just out of morbid curiosity—O.K.? How long can she live without that respirator?"

Dr. Wasserman shrugged again. "Half an hour, I guess. Probably less. Hard to say. Sometimes a patient can get the voluntary muscles to work hard enough to breathe for hours and hours. But as soon as the patient gets fatigued or sleeps, the involuntary muscles, which should normally control unconscious breathing, can't do the job. I really can't give you a definite answer. But the question is academic, anyway, isn't it? The respirator breathes for her, Mr. Wallace."

"Yes. Of course. But—" He tried to put on an abashed smile. "Just one more question. I worry about these things. I'm an accountant and I have that kind of mind. You know?" He smiled a smile that tried to bespeak professional parallelism. Neurotic complicity between great minds. "I think too much, I suppose. But I was wondering, is—is there any way the alarm system can fail? You know?"

Dr. Wasserman tapped him lightly on his shoulder. "Don't worry, Mr. Wallace. As soon as that hose comes out of the tracheal adaptor and the pumped air meets no resistance, the alarm goes off here in the nurses' station. Now, I know what you're thinking. What if Mrs. Wallace pulls it loose during the night and rolls over on it." He smiled.

That's exactly what Martin Wallace was thinking. He waited, literally breathless.

"Well, it's almost impossible to pull it loose by accident, to begin with. Secondly, she'd have to roll over on it very, very quickly. Otherwise, the alarm would go off. Then she'd have to stay in that position for some time. But you see, as soon as she had difficulty breathing, she'd move or thrash. It's a normal reaction. She's not comatose. The hose, then, would be free of her body and the alarm would sound. But, anyway, in Intensive Care we check the patients regularly. Besides, you have private nurses around the clock."

Martin Wallace tried not to look glum. He nodded. Those nurses were costing him a fortune. Another one of Myra's extravagances. But there was one last glimmer of hope. Dr. Wasserman, however, had anticipated the next question and began answering it.

"And the other thing you're wondering about is the respirator itself. Well, any malfunction in the machine also triggers an alarm. There are several alarms, actually. At least three back up alarms in that model." The doctor folded his arms and glanced at his watch. "We have a dozen spare respirators standing by. Haven't lost a patient through accident yet." He smiled reassuringly.

"Power failure?" It came out with the wrong intonation. It came out as though he were begging for one.

"I beg your pardon?"

"Power failure. Power failure. You know. Blackout."

"Oh." He laughed. "You *are* a worrier, Mr. Wallace." The doctor's smile faded and his voice became impatient. "We have auxiliary generators, of course. It's the law." He looked pointedly at his watch. "I have to make my rounds. Excuse me."

"Of course."

Martin Wallace stood rooted at the nurses' station for several minutes staring straight ahead.

He walked slowly to the elevator bank. A few overstayed visitors stared wordlessly at the floor indicator. The elevator came and he stepped in. The lights blinked: 22—21—20—19—

He walked out of the hospital and into the acres of parking lot. A gentle spring breeze blew the scent of newly born flowers across the dark macadam. He walked slowly through the balmy night air as though in a trance. Invalid. Partial paralysis. Home respirator. Renal dialysis.

He had come so close to losing her for good. And now this. What a monumental mess. Myra was hard enough to take when she was well—which was almost never. Twenty years of hypochondria, and never one really good fatal illness. And now this. An invalid.

He walked up to his car and got in. He lit a cigarette and looked out the side window. Three very pretty young girls walked by. They wore jeans and T-shirts. Their long hair fell over their shoulders. Their lithe bodies and lilting voices made his chest heave. He bit his lip in suppressed desire.

Myra. Painted toenails. Painted eyes. Dyed hair. Enough jewelry to drown her in the event she ever decided to jump into the swimming pool she had insisted on having built. Myra. Ridiculous fan magazines and trashy tabloids. Does Jackie O. keep a secret picture of Jack in her snuff box? Is Robert Redford in love with Princess Grace? Who *cares?* Myra. Sitting in front of the idiot box in a crocodilian stupor. Shrieking over a game of Mah-Jongg with her bitchy friends. Sitting for hours baking her skimpy brains under a hair dryer. Myra. Barren of children. Barren of a single original thought in twenty years. Myra and Poopsie. Poopsie and Myra. Of all the dogs on God's earth, he hated poodles more than any other. Myra. Professional shopper. Myra. The last novel she read was *Love Story*. The one before that was *Valley of the Dolls.* The only time she had stirred herself in years was to join a local chapter of the women's liberation movement. The Alice Doesn't Live Here Anymore Chapter. Liberation. What a laugh. Who was freer than that lazy cow? Myra. What a dud. He laughed and slumped over the steering wheel. Tears rolled down his cheeks.

Divorce. Divorce would cost him a fortune. Her death, on the other hand, would put a hundred-thousand-dollar life insurance policy in his pocket.

Martin Wallace pulled the rear view mirror down and looked at himself in the dim light. Not bad for thirty-nine. A few weeks at a health spa. A little sun tan. New clothes. A new hair style. A new life.

He slumped back into the seat of his big, Myra-inspired Cadillac. He pictured the interior of a Porsche or a Jaguar.

He looked up at the tall, bulky, illuminated hospital. Even with his medical insurance, she was costing him two hundred a day. Even flat on her back she was draining him. Her whole life was a study in conspicuous consumption. The quintessential consumer of goods and services. She even consumed more hospital goods and services than the average patient. And she never produced one single thing in her whole life. Not even the thing she was built to produce—a child. Barren. Frigid. Worthless. In his accounting firm she would be called a continuing liability. But a liability which, if liquidated, would become an asset. Liquidated.

He started the car and wheeled out of the parking lot. Within the hour he had parked his car in a midtown garage.

He began walking up Third Avenue. It was a week night, but the streets were alive with people on this first nice spring evening. He walked into P.J. Moriarty's. At the bar were three bachelors from his office—his subordinates of sorts.

They drank there for an hour, then took taxis to each other's favorite East Side pubs. They took taxis all over town. They walked and sang and drank.

They wound up on the West Side and had a late supper at the Act I, overlooking Times Square. Down in the street the Great White Way blazed through their alcoholic haze.

They left the restaurant. To Martin Wallace, there was pure magic in the night air and in the streets of New York, as he gazed out through his clouded eyes at the lights and people swirling around him.

He separated from his friends and walked east on Central Park South and stood in front of the Plaza Hotel, overlooking the park. He fingercombed his hair and straightened his tie. Then he entered the hotel and fulfilled a long-standing recurring dream of checking in.

The marble lobby was an enchanted forest of columns and thick pile rugs. Subdued lights showed little knots of well-dressed people seated in the plush chairs and sofas. An attractive woman seemed to smile at him as the bellboy led him to the elevators.

He awoke and lay bathed in glorious late morning sunlight. He picked up the phone and ordered coffee and mixed rolls and pastry. As an afterthought—he had seen it in a movie—he ordered a pitcher of Bloody Marys.

He put his hands behind his neck and stared at the rich cream-colored ceiling. His mind wandered. On his salary, with no dependents —that is, no Myra—and with no money-sucking house in the suburbs, he reckoned that he could well afford a life style like this. A nice apartment in town. A few wild nights a week like last night. An opera or a little ballet on his easy nights. A Broadway show once in a while. Sunday brunch at the Oyster Bar downstairs. Maybe he would rent a car on weekends and get out to the hinterlands once in a while. Maybe take the train from Pennsylvania Station to the Hamptons or to Belmont Racetrack. Maybe the train from Grand Central Station to the resort hotels in the Catskills or a football game at West Point. Sunday afternoon in Central Park. Saturday in Greenwich Village. A different little restaurant every night. He would have to patronize at least one bar and one restaurant enough to become one of the regulars, though, he reminded himself. He pictured scenes he had seen in movies. The possibilities for life were unlimited in this city. No house, no car, no television, no fan magazines, no Myra. He smiled.

If he had a nice windfall of, say, a hundred thousand dollars to start with, it would be even better. And all this was only a heartbeat away. Just a single heartbeat. But it kept beating, that heart. Thump. Thump. Thump. He could hear his own heart beat heavily in his chest.

He stretched and yawned. He cleared his husky, dry throat and placed a phone call.

A woman answered. "East Park Community Hospital."

"Yes. Intensive Care Unit, please." The phone clicked.

"ICU."

"Yes. Is it still beating?"

"Sir?"

"This is Mr. Wallace. How is my darling wife, please?" He felt reckless this morning.

"Just a moment."

There was a long pause. Martin Wallace prayed.

The voice came back. "Fine, sir. Mrs. Wallace spent a comfortable night. Your private nurse is just bathing her now."

"Swell. Terrific. Thank you." He slammed the phone down and covered his face with the pillow.

There was a knock on the door.

"Come in."

The bus boy entered with a rolling cart. The cart was heaped with all manner of hotel luxury. There was even a complimentary copy of *The New York Times*. Just like in the movies. But the scene paled next to the reality of the telephone call.

He signed for the breakfast and sat down heavily on the bed. He poured a Bloody Mary into a tall glass with a coating of salt on its rim. He downed it in one long gulp.

He opened the paper as he sipped his coffee and scanned it idly. The problems of the world were minuscule compared to his own, but he had developed the defensive habit of eating breakfast behind a newspaper and it was hard to break bad habits. He read, but nothing registered. His mind was elsewhere. Myra. Thump. Thump. Thump. Her heart still beat at the rate of a couple of hundred dollars a day. Thump. Thump. It had been silent for two minutes once, but thanks to the marvels of medical science, it was thumping again. Thump. Thump. Thump. It would thump for how many more years? Twenty? Forty? Sixty?

How do you divorce an invalid, even if you are willing to pay most of your salary for the rest of your life? Why not just disappear, then? That was becoming one of the most popular track sports among men these days. The 100-yard dash into obscurity. But it was a tremendous price to pay. Loss of identity. Loss of friends. Loss of professional credentials. Why should *he* disappear? Why couldn't *she* disappear? "Die! Die, damn you! Die!" The sound of his own voice scared him.

He tossed the paper on the bed. He stared at the open pages for a long second, then picked it up again. There was a lengthy article on the question of medical life-support systems. He read it intently and discovered that he was not alone in wishing that medical science would let the dying die.

He read of cases of brain-dead patients kept alive for months and even years by artificial means. He read of cases similar to Myra's. Over-doses. Strokes. Partially destroyed nervous systems. Human beings snatched from the slashing scythe of the Grim Reaper, but not before suffering permanent life wrecking infirmities. He read of the burdens of families left with slack-jawed loved ones to care for. Left with stag-gering medical bills rendered by smiling doctors and hospitals as the price for returning these loved ones to them as vegetables.

But what interested him more was not the horror stories of misguided humanitarianism, but rather the names of individuals and organizations who opposed these extraordinary measures taken to prolong life at any cost.

He nibbled at a big cheese Danish and a smile played across his mov-ing lips.

He took the pass from the girl at the desk and stood in front of the elevator bank. The night was warm, but he wore a tan trench coat but-toned to the neck.

Swarms of visitors waited as the elevators came to collect them and carry them up into the great hospital. Martin Wallace crowded into one of the cars. He held his brown paper bag at chest level to keep it from being crushed in the press of the crowd.

In the Intensive Care Unit, he stopped at the nurses' station and ex-changed a few smiling words with Miss Hesse, then walked into Myra's private room. He nodded to the attractive private nurse he was paying for. "How's she doing, Ellen?" He smiled. She, plus the other two nurses, were costing him a fortune, he reminded himself. He also reminded himself that they were not needed, but Myra had insisted.

The petite young girl smiled at him. "Fine, Mr. Wallace. Getting better every day." She rose. "I'll just leave you two alone." She smiled at both of them and left.

Myra made a weak gesture toward her throat.

Martin Wallace nodded tiredly and reached down and grabbed the hose. He pinched before he pulled and the alarm did not sound. He placed his hand over the tracheal adaptor in her throat and the wheez-ing stopped.

Myra sucked in a big gulp of air. "I had Ellen call you all last night."

Her voice sounded stronger today, he noticed. It had some of its old screechiness back in it. "Is that so? I must have slept through the phone. Sorry."

She looked at him with expression number three. Suspicion. "I needed my nail polish and manicure kit."

The tone was accusatory. It was supposed to provoke guilt in him, even though it was barely audible and her tonal quality was hard to control. He recognized it, anyway. "Sorry."

What an incredible woman, he thought. Three days ago she was leaning heavily against death's door and today she wants her manicure kit. He stared at her for several seconds. He had an impulse to pour her bottle of skin lotion into the tracheal adaptor and watch her drown. "Sorry, Myra."

"Well, at least I see you remembered something." She pointed to the bag that he had placed on the bed. "Did you—"

He took his hand off the adaptor and air rushed in. Her words faded. "Can't have you off it too long, dear." He plugged the pinched off hose back in with his other hand and released it. The machine changed pitch and began pumping in air. It was so easy to shut her up that it was almost comical. He could see that she was furious at being cut off. She moved her hand to the hose to pull it out, but he grabbed her wrist. "Really, Myra. That's enough talking for a while."

She tried to pull her wrist free, but he held it easily. Her other hand reached out and she pushed the nurse's call buzzer.

Martin Wallace had enough for one night. He reached inside the paper bag and took out two magazines and threw them on the night table. "I could only find two."

She looked inquisitively at the still-bulging bag.

He didn't acknowledge her questioning eyes.

The private nurse, Ellen, walked in. "Yes?"

Martin Wallace smiled. "I think Mrs. Wallace wants something." He looked down at her. "I really have to go, dear. I'm sorry, Myra, darling. I have an appointment." He looked at Ellen. "Take care of my sweetheart, will you? I'll try to get over tomorrow afternoon. Otherwise I'll see you both tomorrow night." He walked to the door. "Good-bye."

Ellen smiled. "Good-bye, Mr. Wallace."

Myra shot him look number one. Pure malice with a touch of hatred and contempt.

He waved and went into the corridor.

At the elevator bank a chime sounded and a light lit up. He walked over to the open car and stepped in. There were three other early-departing visitors and one orderly. Only the lobby button was lit. Nonchalantly, he pushed B for basement.

The elevator stopped in the lobby and the doors slid open. He moved closer to the control panel and out of sight of the guards and reception desks. He frantically hit the *Door Close* button.

The elevator descended to the basement. The elevator doors opened. He stepped into a long, empty corridor. Some of the kitchens were down here and he could smell cooking. He looked around, then walked quickly up to a canvas laundry cart and shucked off his trench coat. He threw it in the cart and buried it with dirty linen. Under the trench coat he wore a white lab jacket.

Still clutching his paper bag, he paced up and down the deserted corridors, examining doors and signs.

At the end of a long, dimly lit corridor he saw it. It was marked *Sub-basement. Electrical.* He opened the steel door and descended the narrow metal staircase.

The stairwell emptied into a long, narrow corridor. He walked past the grey painted concrete walls under the harsh glow of evenly spaced naked bulbs that ran the length of the ceiling. He stopped at each of several metal doors, opening each and looking inside.

Finally, he came to a door whose stencilled sign was the announcement of the end of his search: *Electrics Room. Danger. High Voltage.* He went inside and closed the door behind him.

The dimly lit room was medium-sized and crowded with the life stuff of modern buildings. Endless tubes of wire and conduit ran across the ceiling and tracked down the grey walls. On the far side lay two huge diesel generators on raised platforms. Each had a hooded exhaust over it. To the left of the generators sat a rectangular box labelled: *Batteries—Caution: Acid.*

It would take a barrel of dynamite to completely sabotage this room. It would be necessary to blow up both generators, the storage batteries and the external city electricity source.

Every system, however, has its Achilles' heel and he did not have to be an electrical engineer to know what the soft spot in this system was. He had to find it first, though.

He walked slowly around the room. On the rear wall were about thirty black and grey painted metal panels. Plastic label tags hung from each of them. He ran his eyes over each tag.

He smiled when he found what looked like the proper one. Mounted waist high on the wall, it was the size of a deep orange-crate. It was painted a shiny, crackling black. The long switch handle on the side of the door was a sign that said: *Power Sensing and Relay Control Panel,* and *Diesel.* The switch was in the *Automatic* position.

He opened the cabinet door and it made a metallic squeak. Inside the door was a sign that said, *Power Sensing and Relay Control Panel. Disconnect Diesel Junction Connector D-3 Before Servicing.* He would disconnect more than that before he was through. This was it for sure. This was the central distribution point for the sources of the hospital's power. This box decided whether or not the city's power was normal and, if not, it would then activate the diesel generators, drawing on the storage batteries, if necessary. It all came together right here in this box. The Achilles' heel. Remove the box and you removed the whole hospital's energy supply.

From his paper bag, he removed a large number-ten fruit can. The top of the can was covered with aluminum foil. He removed the foil and shoved it into his pants pocket. Inside the can was packed the gunpowder from a box of fifty 12-gauge shotgun shells. It was a small charge by the standards of most bomb makers, but then he did not need much and it had the advantage of using an easily procured and nontraceable explosive.

Also inside the can were a simple wind-up alarm clock and two flashlight batteries attached to a switch. A cluster of the nitroglycerine primers from the shotgun shells was the detonator. The whole thing looked innocuous enough, especially in the foil covered fruit can. It looked like a container that a doting husband would use to carry homemade cookies to his ailing loved one. Even one of the rare cursory inspections by the hospital guards would have aroused no suspicion.

He put his hand into the can and set the alarm for ten o'clock. He connected the wires with alligator clips. The loud ticking seemed to fill the cryptlike room. He placed the whole thing gently inside the cabinet. He wiped it carefully for prints with a handkerchief and closed the steel door. He wiped the door, also. His face was covered with sweat as he turned from the wall of control panels.

He crossed the room and walked up to the door. From the paper bag he removed a piece of shirt cardboard and taped it to the door. He had wanted to letter the sign ahead of time, but it would be incriminating if by some rare happenstance a guard had wanted to look in the bag. He wrote in large block letters with a marking pen: *God Does Not Want People Kept Alive by Artificial Means. Let the Dying Die with Dignity.* (Signed) *The Committee to End Human Suffering.*

He heard voices outside the door. He stood motionless and breathless as the voices, two males, came abreast of the door. They walked by and he could hear their footsteps retreating down the corridor. He waited.

As he waited, he looked at the sign in the dim light. He smiled. This was enough of a red herring to throw the police off for months. And if by chance they suspected a friend or relative of one of the hospital's current patients, it would make no difference. There were at least thirty people in the Intensive Care Unit whose lives depended on one machine or another. To run down the friends and relatives of each of them would take a very long time. Eventually, they might even get around to asking him to "drop by" for questioning. But so what? There would be a few hundred others, connected with the thirty or so, they would have to question also. Then there would be all the known anti-life-support-systems groups and individuals.

It disturbed him that so many others would die also, but it could not be helped, really. To play with Myra's respirator in the hospital or to see that she had an accident when she returned home was to court life imprisonment. It was no secret to their friends and relatives that he wanted her gone.

To end all the lives hanging on the machines was to scatter the suspicion far and wide. That was the beauty of the thing.

Of course there were some people who only needed the machines for a short while before they could become self sustaining again. That was a pity. And there were even some operations scheduled at night that would never be completed. That, too, was unfortunate. But Myra had to die and he, Martin Wallace, had to live. The footsteps and voices faded away.

Slowly, he opened the door and slipped into the corridor. He walked quickly to the staircase and walked up from the subbasement into the more brightly lit corridor of the basement. He threw the paper bag into a trash barrel and walked quickly over to the laundry cart near the elevators. He ripped the white coat off and threw it in the cart, then retrieved his own trench coat and slipped it on. He hit the elevator button and waited. He noticed that his knees were shaking as he stood staring up at the floor indicator. His head felt light and his mouth was dry, but his forehead was wet.

He could hear the elevator approach. It stopped and the doors slid open. Four visitors and an orderly stood staring at him silently. He froze. They stared.

He stepped into the car quickly and faced the control panel.

The car stopped automatically in the lobby. The doors slid open.

He turned so as not to face the guard and headed for the main doors. Every step was shaky and he thought his knees might give out and he would topple over. He tried to swallow, but almost choked on the dryness. The doors got bigger and bigger and soon he was pushing on one of them. Through. The foyer. More doors. Push. Outside.

He walked, almost ran, down the path to the parking lot. His hands moved in and out of his coat and pants pockets like fluttering birds. He began tearing at the pockets. Keys. Keys. There. He nearly sprinted the remaining distance to his car.

He pulled at the door handle. It would not budge. Locked. Locked. He took a deep breath and calmed himself slightly. With a hand shaking worse than he could ever imagine, he tried to place the key in the lock. Finally, after a full minute, he got it in and twisted it.

Inside, he had difficulty finding the right key and then could not hold his hand still enough to get it in the ignition. Finally, he steadied himself and put it in. He turned the key and the engine roared to life. The sound made him jump, but then soothed him. He took a long, deep breath and fumbled for a cigarette. Within forty-five minutes he would be sitting in P.J. Moriarty's with his friends.

He threw the big Cadillac into low and shot out of the parking space —directly into the path of a huge delivery van.

"Just take it easy, Mr. Wallace. You're going to be fine. Really."

He blinked his eyes. The voice was familiar. Dr. Wasserman.

The voice spoke again, but to someone else. "It was a simple whiplash. Those headrests don't always do the job. Sometimes they even cause worse injuries if they're not set properly. I suppose you had it set downward for yourself, but it was too low for him. Hit him in the back of the neck. But it's not serious."

A weak voice to his left answered. "Yes. I did most of the driving." Myra.

Martin Wallace blinked into the overhead light. He tried to move his head, but couldn't. Something was in his mouth and he could not speak. He rolled his eyes downward as far as they would go. He could see a tube. He looked up. On the opposite wall, a television set was mounted on a high shelf. He was in Myra's room. The picture was bad and the sound was lowered so that he could not hear it. It was a commercial for Alpo. A toy poodle was being shown a can of the canine victuals by its mistress.

Another person entered the room. Martin Wallace caught a glimpse of him as he passed by. It was his family physician, Dr. Matirka. Then the face of the floor nurse, Maureen Hesse, came into view for a second, then the profile of the private nurse, Ellen.

Dr. Wasserman spoke to the others. "Whiplash. He's suffered swelling around the basal ganglia and the internal capsule above the base of the brain. Luckily, the reticular activating system was not involved. There is no loss of consciousness. He's conscious and can see and hear us. But everything from the neck down is paralyzed. He can't speak or breathe on his own. That's why I've put the intubation tube into his mouth and through the larynx, instead of into the trachea. We've given him dexamethasone to combat the swelling. The swelling and consequent paralysis didn't begin until we got him in here, so there's almost no period of anoxia. There will be no permanent damage at all once the swelling goes down in a few days."

Dr. Wasserman leaned over him and smiled. "Blink if you understood what I said, Mr. Wallace."

Martin Wallace blinked.

"So you see, as soon as the swelling at the base of the brain goes down in a few days, your nervous system will return to normal and we can take this respirator off. You'll leave here as good as you came in. Blink if you understand."

Martin Wallace blinked through eyes that were becoming misty. A tear rolled down his cheek.

"No need to be upset," said Dr. Matirka. He leaned over the bed. "In fact, I have more good news for you. Myra's breathing is returning to normal. She can get on fine without the respirator for extended periods. We're weaning her away from it a little at a time just to be safe, but I think she can go for at least an hour or two without it. In fact, she's off it now." He chuckled pleasantly and tapped Martin Wallace on the chest, but the paralyzed man felt nothing. Tears streamed down his face.

"Now, now," said Nurse Hesse, a little sternly, "getting upset will make it worse. You'll be fine in a few days. See, we didn't even have to make a tracheotomy opening for the respirator. When the swelling goes down, you can get up and walk out of here."

Ellen leaned over. "It could have been much worse. See, Mrs. Wallace is fine too. You'll both be out of here in a few days."

Only the muscles above his mouth responded to his commands. His eyes blinked furiously and tears streamed down from them. His nose twitched spasmodically and his upper lip quivered. His forehead furrowed. Even his ears wiggled just a bit.

"He does seem quite upset about something, doesn't he?" remarked Ellen.

"He'll be better when he begins to believe us," said Dr. Wasserman.

Martin Wallace fixed his blurry eyes on the television screen. The picture tube said: *Ten O'Clock News*.

Myra spoke. "Turn on *Medical Center* and raise the volume for me, Ellen. I'm not interested in the news."

The lights went out.

Someone said, "Damn it."

There was a short silence.

Dr. Wasserman's voice spoke softly. "Just a second. The auxiliary generators will kick in."

Silence.

"Just a second. They'll be on in just a half second."

Martin Wallace could hear Myra's voice in the dark as he struggled to breathe.

"I'm going to miss part of the show." Petulant.

"Just a second." Dr. Wasserman's voice sounded anxious now. "They'll be on in just a half second."

But Martin Wallace knew they would not be on ever again.

The Silver Lining

by Mick Mahoney

Even the darkest cloud has a silver lining, or so they say. And it must be true because there I was: a six-time loser, an ex-con just coming off a three to five for a two bit caper, with a smile on my face and a half million dollars as good as in my pocket.

Not that I was smiling when I went in. Not by a long shot. You don't mind spending some time in the slammer if crime is paying off for you, but I was in the red. I'd tripped up so many times I was even thinking of going legit. But just when it came down to a point where I had exactly nothing to look forward to I got the big break, the one you hardly dare dream about whether you're a thief or an office clerk. That's what I mean about a silver lining, because, believe it or not, it was being sent up the river that made it all possible.

You see, while I was in prison I met the famous Jimmy McCarthy, Jimmy Mack he was called. We worked together in the box factory at first; later we used to hang around together and got to be real pals.

Jimmy looked exactly like a vulture with those hunched shoulders, tiny eyes that peered out from little caves on each side of his big nose, and the bristles that sprouted from his bald skull. He had the sort of permanent poker face that you find on a lot of older cons. You could never tell whether he was about to snap your head off or fall asleep.

Jimmy got a lot of respect in prison and I was honored that he chose me to get friendly with. Of course he was mainly looked up to for his ability as a thief. Guys were always coming up to him with "Waddaya think about such and such a job?" or "Where did I go wrong on this or that burglary?" He either gave advice or not depending on his mood. But old Jimmy was also respected the way a madman is. There weren't too many that didn't think that Jimmy was missing a few of his marbles.

Now I suppose that some of you haven't even heard of the great Jimmy Mack. It has been a few years since he was in the limelight. Seventeen to be exact. You must remember the big armored truck robbery, though; pulled off as smoothly as a baby's bottom for a million and a half cash. That job is a legend in criminal circles. I don't know how many times we sat in the corner of the rec yard while Jimmy would go over the details in his low, phlegmy voice.

"Planning," he'd say, hitting his palm with his fist, "planning, planning, planning. I got so I knew how many sugars the guards took in their coffee. The driver, he always drank tea, with lemon."

And the planning paid off in a truly brilliant heist. But anybody that's been around even a little bit knows it's the things you don't plan on that get you in the end.

You see, Jim had recruited a top-notch stock car driver and a punchy ex-light heavyweight for the job. They did just what they were told and everything went hunky-dory. After Jimmy had stashed the loot they all laid low, as planned, to wait for things to cool off. But maybe that fighter had taken a few more shots to the head than Jimmy had figured. It turned out the slugger got plastered in a bar one night and shot his mouth off. Well, loose talk and the kind of reward the insurance company had out combined to land Jimmy in the tank real quick.

Now the standard procedure in a case like that is that when you're caught you hand over the loot in exchange for a lighter sentence. It's sort of the rules of the game. Nobody gets hurt, no hard feelings, and you get a few years free room and board to figure out where you went wrong, so you can pull off the next one without a hitch. As I say, that's what usually happens.

But with Jimmy it was different. He wouldn't give over. He was the only one who knew where the money was stashed and he clammed up. And that more than anything was why he was known to every stick-up artist and second-story man in the business as a mad genius.

The authorities really had no choice in Jimmy's case. They weren't about to let him out so he could pick up the cash and live the life of Riley. They couldn't do that; word might get out that crime really does pay. They tried every way they could think of to make him talk, offered him all kinds of deals and such. No go. Jimmy kept his mouth shut. In the end they gave him a series of maximum sentences, consecutive instead of concurrent like they usually do, so that Jimmy went up for what amounted to a life term without even the hope of parole.

"They thought I'd break," he'd say. Then he'd spit.

Of course nobody really could figure out what made Jimmy do that. What was the point in sitting on a million and a half if you were going to be locked up for the rest of your life? Some thought he had a scheme: a big break already planned, a pardon arranged, some secret deal with the insurance company, or something. Others thought of Jimmy as a real noble character, a kind of martyr who would rather die a rich man than give in to the world and go back to being a bum. In the end, though, they all came to the conclusion that he was crazy. The authorities even sent in a couple of head shrinkers. Yes, he's definitely off his rocker, they said. Not that that helped them to get back any of the loot. And I admit that I thought there was something peculiar about it myself. That is, until I found out the real reason.

Eventually Jimmy came to trust me. One day after he'd told me for the twenty thousandth time the complete story of the robbery, the planning, planning, and the driver's tea and lemon and all, I decided to come right out and ask him.

"And why didn't you give the loot back and get yourself a break?" I said.

Jimmy looked at me with that expression that was no expression. His eyes drilled holes out the back of my head. Then his face changed; it didn't move or anything, he just started looking a little more like a human and a little less like a snake.

"I got a daughter," he said real slow. "A little girl that means more to me than life."

Up until then Jimmy had only talked to me about professional matters. Now he told me of his family: his wife, a terrible nag who never once appreciated the risks Jimmy took to provide for her; and his daughter Mandy, the sweetest child God ever allowed to walk the earth despite all her mother's attempts to turn her against her own father. The little girl was a princess and, Jimmy decided, she must live the life of a queen. It was with her in mind that he planned and committed the masterpiece that got him where he was. Not only that but she was also the reason Jimmy refused to hand over the loot. His plan was to get the money to her somehow. I was fortunate enough to become part of that plan.

Of course Jimmy had not counted on getting caught. He'd figured that a few months after the robbery the coast would be clear and he could slip down to Mexico, divorce his insufferable wife, and take little Mandy on some kind of lifetime pleasure cruise. But instead the worst happened.

So for seventeen years Jimmy hung on, waiting for a chance to get word to his little girl. You see, Jimmy in his wisdom had planned on the possibility of his taking a fall. He'd hidden the cash in a spot his daughter would know about. Of course he couldn't tell her before the bust because she was only eleven at the time and he couldn't take the chance that his wife would get her hands on the loot. Besides, the cops kept a close watch on the family at first, figuring they might know where the money was stashed. Not only that but they'd sent stoolies in to try and get Jimmy to confide in them. That's why he was always so suspicious.

By the time I met him, though, almost everybody had forgotten old Jimmy. They just gave up on him as looney. But that's because they didn't know the dream that Jimmy held on to. He wasn't really any different than a lot of men. I mean, how many fathers are there that spend forty years working at a job that's not much better than prison in order to give their kids a better break?

You may be wondering why Jimmy chose me to take the information to Mandy. Why not some other short-timer and why not years before? The heat had been off for at least the last ten years. Well, first of all Jimmy needed somebody reliable; and they're just as hard to come by in prison as out. He was willing to let the messenger take a generous amount for himself, half a million to be exact; but he didn't want to send out some mug that would string poor Mandy along and then grab the bundle. Jimmy had an uncanny way of sensing the true character of a person, having lived among bluffers and con men all his life. And even if I say so myself, I'm basically an honorable type. But probably more than anything else, Jimmy was getting old. He'd lived the kind of life that saps your youth and the years had given him a real working over. He was a proud man; but hope will keep you alive a lot longer than pride and Jimmy didn't have a hope in the world. Except, that is, to get a message to his daughter that would make her a rich woman. He chose me to deliver that message and, brother, I was glad he did.

And what was a reliable, honorable fellow like me doing behind bars in the first place? I won't go into the details because it's too embarrassing. But I will give any of you potential crooks a word of advice: don't ever try to pinch a Ferris wheel.

As it turned out I served two years and two months of a three to five for grand larceny before I finally got parolled. Was I happy or what? I couldn't wait to locate Mandy and pick up an easy half million. And who knows, if she was as sweet and pretty as Jimmy claimed, plus had a million dollars . . . well, the possibilities were nothing but encouraging.

I knew about all there was to know about the family. Jimmy had gone into great detail: how Mandy's nose turned up just so, how the wife was always griping about her arthritis, everything. Still, it took a couple of weeks to find them. I had to be pretty discreet about asking around so as not to raise any suspicion. They'd moved quite a few times since Jimmy went in, but I finally traced them to a dumpy section on the outskirts of the town where they lived.

The house was small with a crooked porch and grey, peeling paint. The yard was just gravel and weeds; and there was a long wooden ramp up the front steps. I figured the old lady must have taken to a wheel chair. But when I knocked she answered the door herself. She was just like Jimmy had described her: fat, mean looking, with greasy hair and a sloppy mouth. Her eyes were just as hard as his.

"Mrs. McCarthy?" I said.

She looked at me for a minute and took a drag on her cigarette. "What the hell do you want?" she said in a voice like sandpaper.

"I have some business with your daughter Mandy," I answered. She crossed her arms and sort of squinted.

"I'm Mandy. Mrs. Nichols to you. Now what do you want?"

Let me tell you I wasn't ready for that one. She had that kind of puffy face and coarse, pocked skin that could have made her about any age. It dawned on me that the little milk and honey angel that Jimmy had in mind was an eleven-year-old girl. But seventeen years had gone under the bridge since he'd last seen her. Here she stood now, twenty-eight going on fifty-five. I swallowed my surprise. "I have a message from your father."

"So old Jimmy Mack hasn't rotted away yet, huh?" Her smile lacked a few teeth. "Sure, come on in."

The house was shabby enough, beer cans and trashy magazines all over, the ashtray overflowing with lipstick-smeared butts. I could hear a TV going somewhere and kids yelling and whining.

"I guess you must be just out of the can yourself. Don't worry, I'm used to dealing with hoods. I married one," she said, making a sweeping gesture, "and look where it got me." She tossed some newspapers off a chair and motioned for me to sit down.

I decided to get the whole thing over with as soon as possible and then write to Jimmy and say everything had gone smooth. Might as well leave the old guy his dreams.

I explained the deal Jimmy and I had agreed on, how we would go together to pick up the money and I would take my share and leave her with a million. You might have thought from the blank look on her face I was trying to sell her a vacuum cleaner. She sure took after her father in that way. Then I told her how Jimmy wanted her to be sure to know that the million was all hers and that she wasn't to let her mother have any of it. I also added something about how much her father loved her and had sacrificed for her. It was strange because I knew that Jimmy didn't have any idea that his sweet little daughter no longer fit the vision that he had of her; but I figured maybe she'd be moved by what he'd done for her. When I finished she just sat there looking at me with a sort of half-smile.

"A million dollars, huh? So that explains it. We thought he was nuts all along and we was right.

"Mister, do you know how many times I would have given a million dollars to have my old man around when I was growing up, dammit all? And poor Mama's not supposed to get any? Why, it nearly killed her when he went in. At first we hoped he would give in and tell but he never did. And Mama got sick so we couldn't even go and see him. She's been an invalid for twelve years now.

"Sure, they used to fight like a couple of tom cats. But he was a hard man and she had to be hard just to keep up with him. But in the end he destroyed her.

"Yeah, I'll take his million dollars all right; but I'll still curse his soul for leaving us. Mama married a fool and I married a fool and no million dollars is going to change that. Why, if my husband finds out I've got any cash he'll be back here in two minutes to beat it out of me and throw it away on the horses."

Poor Jimmy, I thought. All those years in the slammer and the loot winds up in the hands of an ungrateful witch like this. And I knew the last thing he wanted was for his wife to profit from any of it. Now the two of them, together with the hoodlum son-in-law, would sit around and squander Jimmy's life.

The sky was a dirty grey when we set out to collect the cash. The landmark we were looking for was a big beech tree way off in the back of a vacant lot. Jimmy used to sit under it with Mandy when she was small and tell her stories. I knew how many feet and in what direction to dig.

Mandy knew the place as soon as I mentioned it though she hadn't been back to that old neighborhood since she was a kid.

"We were real poor in those days, Mister. But let me tell you I've never been so happy since. Jimmy Mack used to sit there under that tree on long summer evenings and tell me about pirates and dragons and giants up in the clouds. I guess he knew I'd never forget that spot so that's why he stashed the stuff there. Slow down now. Right down here. Right at the bottom of this hill." Her voice betrayed the excitement that we both felt now.

A light rain was beginning to fall as we pulled up to a red light at the bottom of the hill. On the corner was a gas station, its revolving fluorescent sign bright against the murky sky. Behind it there was a huge expanse of macadam and the low, plain buildings of a shopping center. My stomach turned over. Urban renewal. I looked at Mandy. She was smiling her notched smile. "Somewhere in the area of that fried chicken joint, I'd say."

I pulled into the parking lot. The asphalt cast smeared reflections. We both got out and walked around aimlessly. Maybe there was a million and a half buried under the pavement; maybe some bulldozer operator was living it up on the French Riviera. Who knows? It hardly mattered.

We stood there under the buzzing sulphur streetlights for a while getting wet. Then Jimmy Mack's daughter started to laugh. I'd like to tell you she laughed till she cried, but she didn't. I got in the car and left her there laughing and laughing, so help me. As I drove away it began to pour. And none of those clouds up there had a lining that was anything but black as pitch, so far as I could see.

A Private Little War

by William Brittain

Jake Landis hobbled back into his classroom, hung his cane on the chalk tray, and settled himself onto the tubular steel chair at his desk. With both hands he pulled at his left leg, moving it into as comfortable a position as possible.

The stiff knee, a relic of an automobile accident five years previously, didn't pain him any more. It was just awkward sometimes. But then, a man crowding fifty, with all the dreams of becoming a sports hero or another Fred Astaire behind him, didn't need supple joints to teach freshman history. And besides, the cane added a certain style to his lessons, especially during descriptions of French swordplay or when brandished as a mock threat over the head of some lazy student. Getting up and down stairs was a tedious process, but he was usually able to find a football player to run interference for him and be there to catch him if he was in danger of falling.

He pulled the first batch of test papers from the slow class toward him and began reading: "The Boston Tea Party was wher the coloneal daims planed ther part in the Revelushin." Oh, boy! It was going to be a long two hours until five o'clock.

There was a knock at the classroom door, and Jake looked up. The door opened, and Harvey Cassidy of the math department stuck his head in. "Got a minute, Jake?" he asked.

"Sure. Come on in, Harv. But if it's about math, I'm telling you right now, I always figured you guys worked by magic, not logic. Just apply the right spell, and the volume of a pyramid is yours for the asking."

"At least it's better than reviewing a couple of centuries of man's inhumanity to man," replied Cassidy with a grin. He leaned against one of the student desks, and suddenly the grin disappeared.

"Jake, you've got Alec Whitnine in one of your classes, haven't you?" he asked in a flat voice.

"Sure. Third period. He sits over there by the window. Why?"

"Tell me what you think of him, will you? Never mind the test scores. What's he like as a person?"

Jake considered the question for a moment. "To tell the truth, I don't really know that much about him," he said. "A pretty quiet kid most of the time. About the only time he speaks out is to ask some question designed to embarrass me in front of the class. He's something of a pain in the neck, but not really all that bad. And Mabel Fuchs considers him the darling of her science classes." He adjusted his leg to a more comfortable angle. "Why do you ask?"

Cassidy's gaze was piercing. "Because," said the math teacher, "earlier today, I think Alec Whitnine deliberately tried to kill me."

"What?" Jake's head shook in disbelief. "Alec's a little squirt of a freshman, Harv. You must weigh close to two hundred pounds. He couldn't take you on with anything less than a cannon. And besides, what do you mean you 'think' he tried to kill you? Don't you know?"

Cassidy held up a hand. "Let me tell you what happened. It was seventh period. I'd covered the lesson faster than usual, so I gave the class the last ten minutes to begin their homework. And since the weather's been so hot lately, I had all the windows up as far as they'd go."

"But what's the weather got to do with . . ."

"My room's back in the new wing of the building, remember? The windows there come down to within a couple of feet of the floor. You know how the administration's always warning us to be careful around them. Anyway, the kids were working on their own like a bunch of Einsteins, so I leaned out the window to get a breath of air. My back was to the class, but I didn't figure there'd be any trouble. I heard one or two of 'em walking around the room, but that was all right—they're allowed to get paper or go to the pencil sharpener any time they like."

"Harv, will you get to the point of this cockamamie story?"

"I don't know what it was that made me turn around. But when I did, there was Alec, holding the window pole up over his shoulder like it was a spear. He let it fly just as I turned. The thing missed me by a couple of inches and went right out through the open window. Made an awful clatter when it hit the sidewalk below."

"Look, my students play with the window pole in here too. Either they're Little John fighting Robin Hood or Knights of the Round Table at a jousting tournament."

Cassidy slapped his fist angrily against the top of the wooden desk. "Dammit, this wasn't done in fun! I was kind of off balance leaning out that window, and it's two stories down to the sidewalk. If I hadn't turned at just that moment they'd have been scraping me up with a putty knife!"

"Take it easy, Harv," said Jake soothingly. "All right, Alec was out of line. But he didn't mean any harm. Probably the whole thing scared him a lot more than it did you."

Cassidy shook his head. "With ten years in this business, I figure I can read human reactions as well as the next guy. He wasn't scared. He acted more like he was . . . was . . ."

"Was what?"

"Disappointed," said Cassidy softly.

There was a silence in the room, and the clock clicked off another minute. "Oh, come on," said Jake. "What reason would Alec have to do a thing like that?"

"He got a fifty on a class quiz the other day. First failing mark for him in math all year."

Jake almost laughed out loud. "Now are you going to be scared of any kid you have to fail?"

"I tell you, Alec is—well—different. He's had it in for me since he got the paper back."

"What makes you think so?"

"It's nothing you can put your finger on. Just something I can sense. The way he looks at me. You know how it is. The wise-guy way he phrases his questions. And I'm not the only one who thinks Alec Whitnine is creepy."

"Who else?"

"Manny Shelberg. He's coaching freshman baseball this year. Last week was tryouts, and Alec got cut from the squad. That day, after the practice was over, the kid came into the exercise room to ask Manny to reconsider. Manny was down on the floor looking for one of his contact lenses that had fallen out, and he told Alec to beat it. Five minutes later one of the barbells rolled off its rack when Manny was right beneath it. The way he tells it, if he hadn't done a fast somersault, the thing would have come down on his spine. Have you got any idea how much damage a two-hundred-pound weight falling three feet can do, Jake?"

Jake shrugged. "An accident."

"But there's no way the barbell could have jumped out of the grooves in the rack. Unless it was helped. And Manny remembers he never heard Alec leave the locker room. He could have slipped up on the other side of those racks and . . ."

"And maybe Manny hit the rack with his shoulders while he was crawling around. Maybe a hundred other things. Come on, Harv, you're being silly. You say Alec's got it in for you because of a failing paper. Mabel Fuchs had to flunk him on a few tests, and the two of 'em still get along like a couple of mice in a corn crib. If he's the monster you seem to think, why hasn't he tried anything with her?"

"I don't know, Jake. But from now on I'm going to be on my guard. And I suggest you do the same. That kid'll kill somebody yet. And he'll take the greatest of pleasure in doing it."

Four days later, Alec Whitnine failed his first quiz in Mr. Landis's history class.

At the dismissal bell, Alec chose to remain for what Jake liked to call the inquest. Alec stood before the teacher's desk, a small figure with a vestigial layer of baby fat that made his body resemble an overripe peach. Unlike most of the boys, who wore their hair at collar length and elaborately styled, Alec's was cropped in a short, military manner, one step away from a completely shaved head.

"Mr. Landis," said the boy, "I should have gotten more than a sixty-one on my essay."

Just like that, thought Jake. Shape up, Mr. Landis, and give me the mark I feel I deserve.

"Alec," he began, "you did a fine job on your analysis of the Stamp Act, but the question did say to discuss three causes of the American Revolution. You completely left out the other two."

"I thought, Mr. Landis, that an in-depth discussion of a single cause would be more to your liking." The boy's voice dripped syrupy sarcasm.

"Well, you thought wrong. The question was quite clear."

"Another four points would be sufficient," said the boy. "Simply a passing mark."

It wasn't a request; it was a command. Jake hadn't been talked to that way since boot camp. "You'd better leave, Alec," he said firmly.

Alec merely hunched his shoulders and stared at the floor.

"Look, young fella," the teacher went on. "In about thirty seconds a class of students will be coming through that door. And unless you're out of here by then, they're going to meet you flying low in the opposite direction off the toe of my shoe. Clear?" Jake grinned to make a joke of the threat.

The expression on Alec's face changed, and Jake felt as if he'd been drenched with a pail of ice water. The concentrated malevolence in the young eyes was something all his years of teaching hadn't prepared him for. The boy's twisted features were fanatic—almost inhuman. In the face of this naked hatred, sweat began trickling down Jake's neck, and suddenly Cassidy's story about Alec's attempt to kill him seemed all too possible.

Without a word, Alec pivoted and stalked out of the room.

Jake got through the rest of the day, both ashamed and afraid of the thoughts going through his brain. Alec had to be like all the other students, probably angrier at himself for failing than at the teacher, and yet the awful menace of that single moment before the boy had left made Jake's skin crawl every time he thought about it.

The dismissal bell finally rang, and five minutes later Jake was at work on his homework corrections. He worked his way through the papers in record time and was halfway finished with the last one when he heard the sound out in the hall.

A door opening.

It couldn't be a custodian. Cal Stettner had finished cleaning this section of the building more than an hour ago.

"Hello!" Jake called.

No answer.

Jake hauled himself to his feet, gripped the cane, and hobbled out into the hall. It was empty. He peered around the corner.

The hydraulic device on the door to the boys' lavatory was slowly pulling it closed.

Jake walked into the lavatory, his shoes making shuffling noises on the white tile floor. Nothing. Whoever it was must have been leaving when the teacher had heard him. And it was clear that the unknown person didn't want to be discovered.

As Jake went out into the hall again, the silence was an almost solid thing, broken only by the gentle hissing of air as the lavatory door closed.

And then something else.

A soft, guarded sound of steps on the stairwell beyond Jake's room. He lurched to the top step.

"Who's there?" he called. "Come on, speak up. You know students aren't allowed to walk around the building after school." He looked downward, wishing he could see beyond the landing.

From the floor below came a single low whistle that lasted less than a second.

"Games, huh?" Jake snorted. "O.K., let's find out who in blazes you are."

Bracing himself with the cane, he set his left foot slowly and laboriously down onto the first step and gripped the railing tightly as he brought his right foot down beside it. That's one, he thought. Only twenty-three more to go. He'd never catch the kid, of course, but with a little perseverance, maybe he could chase whoever it was out of the building.

Two steps.

Three.

And then, on the fourth step, as he leaned forward to shift his weight to the cane, its tip squirted off the flat surface as if the rubber tip had grown wheels. Overbalanced, Jake instinctively thrust out his injured leg, but it skidded and slid as if the stairs had turned to ice.

He was falling! He crashed down on one hip, and pain streaked along his side. He gripped at the steps, but all friction between his hands and the terrazzo surface seemed to have vanished. As he rolled over and over, trying to protect his face with his arms, he was aware of a strange odor, musky and somewhat sweet.

Then he tumbled heavily to the landing, banging the side of his head against the radiator.

For a moment he was dazed, and flashes of bright light danced before his eyes. Then, ignoring his pounding head and ringing ears, he gingerly moved first his arms and then his good leg. Finally, the stiff leg, which ached dully but seemed to be in reasonably good condition.

A series of jerky movements brought him to his feet, and he looked upward at the dozen steps down which he had fallen. Lucky, he thought to himself. A broken arm or leg was a distinct possibility from a fall like that, a snapped neck or spine not completely out of the question. What could have caused . . .

He rubbed the thumb and forefinger of his left hand together, feeling a slimy something against his fingertips. Then he brought the hand to his nose and sniffed.

Soap!

Both his palms were covered with the slippery liquid soap used in the school lavatories. One shoe also had traces of the stuff, as did the tip of his cane. Wiping it off with a handkerchief, Jake torturously made his way back up the stairs until he reached the fourth from the top.

The surface of the step had been liberally coated with the soap.

The noises outside his room had been deliberate. He'd been lured into the hall by someone who was bent on killing him.

Someone?

Alec Whitnine?

At home that evening, soaking his aches in a steaming tub, Jake pondered the problem of how to handle the situation with Alec. Tell someone? But who? He remembered how he'd scoffed at Harv Cassidy's story just last week. No, he couldn't mention it to anyone at school.

The police? They'd want proof, and he had no proof. Just a step with soap on it, which could be looked on as accidental, and the expression on a boy's face. But how, Mr. Landis, do you go about getting a facial expression into police records?

And yet a potential murder victim couldn't be expected to wait idly by to give his prospective killer a second chance.

The following day, Jake used his free period to look up Alec Whitnine's record in the guidance office. Not much there. Alec's mother had been dead for ten years, and Alec lived with his father on Derby Avenue. The old man had to be loaded to afford a house in that section. Alec's grade school had been Chindale Park, the newest and best in the whole district. Average marks through the first six years, with only a few D's and F's.

Seventh grade had been a different matter. The low marks became more numerous, with three F's in English alone. Jake smiled. It took more than a cute smile and a polite manner to impress old Sadie Treska. The absentee card for that year showed a total of twenty-five days Alec had been absent.

The teacher thumbed back through the earlier cards. Strange. In all his first six years put together, Alec had only been absent seventeen days. And it couldn't have been a major illness or an accident. The days were too widely spaced for that.

Eighth grade showed much the same pattern. Lower marks and increased absences. But the teacher, Bob Hausermann, had added some comments of his own:

10/17—"Alec's a loner. Quiet. Perhaps too quiet for his own good."

1/29—"Usually a peaceful boy. But sometimes becomes belligerent with classmates at little or no provocation."

2/27—"Moody and unapproachable since midyear marks."

The final comment, dated 4/15, had been heavily crossed out. Jake peered closely at the network of lines on the back of the report card. The first letter was, he thought, a T.

Finally he was able to make out more letters. "To—y Ale-tri— –o . . ."

And then Jake had it.

"Today Alec tried to . . ." There was no more. And Bob Hausermann had done his best to see that no one would read the message.

Jake ducked into an unused guidance office. He picked up the telephone on the desk and dialed the extension for the Chindale Park School. He asked to speak to Mr. Hausermann and listened to a three-minute lecture from the secretary about phoning a teacher during classes. Jake was finally able to convince her of the importance of the call, and she grudgingly got the eighth grade teacher on the line.

"Hi, Jake! Say, I haven't seen much of you this year. Why don't we . . ."

"Listen, Bob, I've got no time for the niceties. Give me a fast rundown on Alec Whitnine, a kid you had last year. I've been reviewing his record. I'm particularly interested in your last comment—the one you crossed out. Do you remember it?"

A long silence. Then: "Yeah, Jake. I remember it. But now that the records are open to the parents, I'm not sure I want to get my head handed to me by . . ."

"Bob, this is me—Jake. Nothing you tell me will go any further. That's a promise. Now give."

"The kid's got problems, Jake. The father's a big bull of a man. Expects his kid to produce just the way all those companies he owns are supposed to. I can't prove it, but I think that during the last year or so he attended here, Alec got slapped around when he brought home low marks. Any time he had a bad time with a test, he'd be out the next day or two. And when he came back, there were the bruises. I saw them."

"Well, that's a start on what I need. But about the report card and your comment . . ."

"Jake, I'll call you a liar if you tell another soul. But I'm sure Alec Whitnine tried to kill me. Don't laugh. It's true."

"I'm not laughing, Bob. How'd it happen?"

"We were getting an assembly program ready. Alec had a lead part. Y'know, that kid's really something. He can mimic anybody. I caught him in front of the class one day doing me, and I couldn't get mad because he was really good."

"What's that got to do with . . ."

"I'm getting to that. Three days before the show, I caught Alec cheating on a grammar test. I took the part away from him. The next day he was absent. I guess you can figure out why."

"His father again?"

"Sure. Anyway, the day he came back I had a practice after school. Naturally Alec wasn't included. I was on the stage, talking to the cast. I finished what I was saying and moved to the front of the stage to hop down to the floor. Just when I moved, a curtain counterweight fell and caved in two boards right where I'd been standing. Later on, when I'd gotten myself and the kids calmed down, I looked at the rope on the weight. It'd been cut. And a janitor told me he thought he'd seen Alec sneaking around in the loft above the stage. Naturally he denied it. There wasn't any real action I could take, but I did start to put a note on his report card. Then I got to thinking of what the legal consequences might be, and I thought better of it."

Slowly Jake settled the telephone receiver onto its cradle, his mind spinning from what he'd just heard. Bob Hausermann . . . Manny Shelberg . . . Harv Cassidy . . . and now his own "accident" on the stairs. Alec Whitnine, it seemed, was prepared to kill whenever the prospect of failure arose.

No, that wasn't really true. His science teacher, Mabel Fuchs, hadn't had any trouble. And Sadie Treska, back in seventh grade, had noticed nothing unusual.

And then Jake understood the pattern.

Until Bob Hausermann in eighth grade, Alec had had only women teachers. And there'd been no trouble. Even now, the boy couldn't consider women among his victims.

But men! When men attacked Alec's image of himself and caused dire consequences at home, the attack had to be repulsed. In the surest and most permanent way possible.

Murder.

Jake wondered whether Alec looked upon all men as surrogate fathers who were there only to punish him unfairly. Or perhaps there was something in his twisted code of honor that made women immune from retaliation, regardless of the provocation. Whatever the case, it was clear that Alec was carrying on his own private little war against any male teacher who implied that he wasn't measuring up to some nebulous standard the boy had set for himself.

But it was done so cleverly that only those attacked even knew that the war existed. And they couldn't do anything about it.

The bell rang for the beginning of the next period.

That evening, Jake deliberately waited until seven o'clock to telephone the Whitnine house. He wanted to be sure to talk to Mr. Whitnine, and he decided that if Alec answered he'd hang up and try again.

"Sam Whitnine here." The voice sounded as if it was coming from inside a bass drum. "Who's calling?"

"My name's Landis," Jake began.

"Landis? Oh, yes. Alec's teacher. What can I do for you, Mr. Landis?"

In for a penny, in for a pound, thought Jake. Taking a deep breath, he poured out the whole story. Events, comments, suspicions. All he left out were the names of the other teachers involved. "So I think your boy's in trouble," he concluded, "and frankly, Mr. Whitnine, I don't know how to handle it."

He leaned back in his chair and waited for the blast. You don't tell a parent point-blank that his child has homicidal tendencies and expect to escape unscarred. What, he wondered, would he be threatened with first? Dismissal? A lawsuit?

"Mr. Landis," said the deep voice, "I must say you make a mighty convincing case. Matter of fact, I've been noticing some things about Alec I'm not too happy about either. I wonder if you'd do me the favor of dropping by sometime so we can discuss what's to be done?"

Jake stared at the phone in disbelief.

"Would tonight be O.K.?" he asked.

"Fine. Alec's out to a movie or something. In about an hour, say?"

The Whitnine house was a colonial with a fieldstone facade, and it looked big enough to park the Hindenberg zeppelin. Jake limped up the brick steps and rang the bell. A little metal box beside the door showed a red light, and Mr. Whitnine's voice came from it.

"That you, Landis?"

"It's me, Mr. Whitnine."

"The door's unlocked. Come on in. I'm in my study, just to the right beyond the living room."

Jake opened the door and stepped inside. The living room, about the size of a basketball court, was done in pseudo-Japanese with low chairs and tables, bamboolike wallpaper, an exotic chandelier right out of Fu Manchu, and even a samurai sword hung in its sheath on the far wall.

Jake looked about. There were two tiny lights on, but they didn't begin to dispel the shadows. Then, at the far end of the room he noticed a brighter glow.

He made his way across a rug deep enough to drown in and finally reached the open door to Mr. Whitnine's study. It was a Civil War buff's dream, filled with relics that ranged from cap-and-ball pistols to canteens and Confederate flags. And in the center, at a flat desk that Lincoln himself might well have used, sat Samuel Whitnine.

His lined face seemed sculpted from marble, and the set of his mouth indicated that here was a man who stood for no nonsense. His arms were outstretched on the desk, and his hands were pressed flat against its surface. In spite of the warmth of the evening he wore a wool robe of brilliant colors which seemed to accentuate the man's aggressiveness.

Jake stepped into the room. He coughed gently, preparing to speak.

But then the cane slipped from shaking fingers, and he struggled to retain mental control over himself. His mind refused to accept what his eyes told him had to be true:

The teacup on the corner of the desk, with no liquid in it but only a thick layer of white powder at its bottom.

The man's staring eyes and uncanny lack of movement.

The thin layer of dust on his sleeves and the backs of his hands.

And finally—horribly—the single strand of spider web that extended from one corner of his half-open mouth down to the edge of the desk.

Alec Whitnine's private little war had claimed its first and most logical victim.

"Welcome to my house, Mr. Landis." The booming voice behind him was the same one the teacher had heard on the telephone an hour earlier.

That kid's really something, Bob Hausermann had told him. *"He can mimic anybody."*

There was a metallic slithering sound as the samurai sword was removed from its sheath.

And Jake Landis, helpless without the cane now lying on the floor, bowed his head and waited for Alec Whitnine to claim his second victory.

Superscam

by Francis M. Nevins, Jr.

Every afternoon a segment of the St. Francis Hotel's ornate lobby is transformed into an elegant little tearoom. Waitresses in low-cut velvet minidresses wheel carts full of creamy pastries and gleaming silver urns into the alcove, where they dispense coffee, tea, and glimpses of their cleavage. During my few months' stay in San Francisco I had grown to savor the ritual, preferably with a companion of the opposite sex and as a quiet prelude to more passionate activity a bit later in the day. On this particular rainy afternoon, however, I nibbled alone. I ate and drank in an unobtrusive but precise manner, two bites of a finger-shaped eclair and then a sip of tea, two more bites and another sip. That was the signal so the young man would know me.

A tall thirtyish man in a three-piece Italian silk suit and with an off-white trenchcoat draped over his arm crossed the lobby slowly and made a casual survey of the alcove. He was Lincoln-lanky, tanned by the sun or a first-rate lamp, thick and dark of hair and sporting an Errol Flynn mustache. He cast an appreciative glance at a particularly scrumptious waitress, sauntered into the alcove and seated himself in the empty red plush armchair next to me and ordered a cup of decaffeinated black coffee. That was the signal so I would know the young man.

"Roy Cogan," he said barely above a whisper, eyes focused straight ahead on the coffee urn. "The word was that Milo Turner might have a job for me."

"Word from where?"

"The Jock," he said.

Eight days ago, when I had finished working out all the details, I'd called Jock Schultz in L.A., and asked him to find me a young man of a certain description. I was too old to pull this scam alone, and besides I don't look Greek. Jock had called back yesterday to set up this meeting. "Background?" I asked the young man.

"Drama school, came out west to break into movies or TV. Rotten luck. Movies are dead and TV's dying. I drifted into the life and discovered I was good at it." He named a few recent scams in which he'd taken part, and gave me the distinct impression that with a few more years of practice he could develop into one of the luminaries of our profession. We finished our beverages and cabbed to my apartment on Geary, where an hour of private conversation with him completed the task of satisfying me. His age was right, his looks wcrc right, and he had enough skill as an actor to put on a touch of Greek accent if needed. "You're hired," I said. "I've got a part for you to play." His eyes glittered with interest.

What had generated the scam had been the death of a very rich and very silly man. Eighteen months ago Nikos Alexiou, the Greek immigrant boy who'd grown up to become the founder of the fifth largest aircraft manufacturing company in America, had died at his lavish manor on the edge of St. Louis County. A series of strokes had partially paralyzed him and confined him to his forty-two-room mansion for the last two years of his life. He had died a sixty-eight-year-old widower, leaving behind him a grown son, Stavros, known as Buddy, and a will that was a masterpiece of ethnic chauvinism. What was left of his $13,000,000 estate after taxes and expenses had been placed in trust for the benefit of his son, who would receive the income until he turned forty and the principal on his fortieth birthday. But there was a catch. He had to marry by the time he was twenty-eight, and remain married until he was forty, to—and I quote from the will—"a woman of true Greek blood and orthodox religion."

If he didn't comply, he forfeited all rights under the trust and the money was to be turned over to the Alexiou Aircraft Corporation employees' pension fund. The problem was that no one knew whether Buddy had complied with the condition or not, since he had dropped out of sight five years ago, at age twenty-four, into the drug culture according to rumor. And therein lay the scam.

"You," I told Cogan, "are going to turn up as Buddy. I've got some pictures of the way he looked before he dropped out, and we can get you to look just like him with the help of an out-of-work movie makeup man I know."

"Ah, I get it. We find me a Greek belly dancer, go through a quickie marriage, and I claim the trust." A look of apprehension crept into his features. "But isn't that a hell of a risky game? Suppose the real Buddy shows up with a Greek broad of his own? And how do we backdate the marriage certificate to before the real Buddy's twenty-eighth birthday?"

I bestowed on him a glance of towering disdain. "It's been a year and a half since old Nikos left us," I pointed out. "It's safe to assume that if Buddy were going to come back he'd have done it by now. And we don't backdate marriage certificates, because you're not going to get married and you're not going to claim your share directly. We're going to get a lawyer and file suit to set aside that true-Greek-blood clause and give you your share free and clear of the condition. Then we wait for Alexiou Aircraft and the trustee to settle with us out of court for around twenty percent of the estate, which gives us a nice profit and the pension fund a juicy shot in the arm too. We collect one-fifth of the income from the trust till you turn forty—rather till Buddy does—then we take twenty percent of the principal."

Cogan let out a piercing whistle of awe. "Wow, what a socko scam! But wait, that means you need a lawyer in the picture too, right?"

"We'll get one in St. Louis," I said. "That's where the old man died and where Alexiou Aircraft and the trustee who's handling the estate have their main offices. I'll call the Jock tonight and get a name, then call the lawyer and hire him by phone to start the wheels turning. From the lawyer's point of view it's just a suit to knock out part of a bigoted will."

"You've planned this pretty carefully," Cogan remarked.

"Milo's Maxim #42," I said. "Work it out in your head first and you don't wind up on your butt later."

For the ladies and gentlemen of my profession, Jock Schultz was a human supermarket. He charged outrageously for his services but he earned his money. It has been conservatively estimated that without him half the major scams of the last decade would never have been pulled off. One might say to the Jock, as I did that night: "Jock, I need a lawyer, in the St. Louis area, a solo practitioner, not a member of a big firm. He has to be honest and a crackerjack negotiator, but not a huge financial success. He has to be naive enough so that when I hand him a case he'll look very closely at the legal issue and not too closely at me. I need him by Tuesday." Then the computers in Jock's head would start blipping and in a few days or less he would call back with the answer.

In this case his answer was: "Spencer Bennell. He's close to eighty but still in good shape, plays golf and squash every weekend. Hangs his hat in Clayton which is right outside St. Louis, and ye can twist him around your pinky if ye've a mind to without even breathing hard."

My next request of Ma Bell was for a line to Clayton, Missouri. "Mr. Bennell? Mr. Spencer Bennell?" I gave my voice a querulous rasp which he would remember when we met in person. "This is J. Dennison Dent from San Francisco. I'm with the Institute for Human Dignity. Are you, ah, familiar with the Institute?" I expected a negative answer, even though I had taken the pains several years ago to have it legally established as a not-for-profit corporation. "The Institute is concerned with maintaining the freedom and dignity of the individual against the pressures of a conformist society. We've been asked by a young man named Stavros Alexiou to defend his freedom and dignity against the will of his late father, Nikos Alexiou, the aircraft manufacturer." I quoted the ethnic restriction in the old bigot's will and orated thunderously on every person's right to marry or not marry as he or she chooses. "Mr. Alexiou is single and wishes to remain so. The Institute does not feel he should therefore have to give up his patrimony and has decided on the basis of your professional reputation to retain you for whatever litigation is needed to overturn that clause in the will." It was one of my noblest speeches, and I barely resisted the urge to pat myself approvingly on the shoulder. Bennell agreed to take the case and I agreed to send him an Institute check that day for his retainer. He would proceed to do the necessary research and Buddy Alexiou and I would fly in for a conference a week from Wednesday.

There were dozens of details to clean up before we flew east. I deposited Cogan in the San Francisco Public Library with instructions to memorize every known fact about the Alexiou family. Each evening I quizzed him intensively and was amazed at his retentive memory. "I was always a quick study," he said modestly. I lined up the make-up man to revise Cogan's face, built a superb file of phony proofs of identity courtesy of my friendly neighborhood document forger, and devoted my spare moments to reading the financial statements of Alexiou Aircraft Corporation, which I learned did a booming business selling planes to foreign governments as well as to the U. S. Air Force and our major domestic airlines.

The four-hour flight on Continental from San Francisco to Lambert International Airport was smooth as a sheet of glass. Our plane, I noticed, had been built by Alexiou. I killed time reading Xerox copies of old newspaper clippings describing how Buddy had stormed out of the Alexiou home in a rage five years ago after a violent quarrel with his father. A friend of the family by the name of Lang had driven him to the airport and no mortal eye had seen him again from that day forward. We rented a Vega at Lambert, took it east along Interstate 70 and settled in at the Chase-Park Plaza in the central west end of St. Louis. That afternoon at 3:30 as per appointment we entered the trim brick office building at the corner of Brentwood and Carondelet in the suburb of Clayton and elevatored ourselves to the third-floor office labelled SPENCER BENNELL, ESQ., COUNSELOR AT LAW.

There I received a rude but delightful shock. Whoever sat behind the paper-littered desk to which we were ushered most assuredly was not Spencer Bennell.

"Hi," the young lady greeted us cheerily. "I'm Gael Irwin. I work with Spencer. One of his clients had an emergency and Spencer had to go to court so he asked me to see you." She had long dark flowing hair, a perky face and a figure of Playboy-bunny delectability hidden inside one of those expensive pants suits that are tailored to look like a laborer's jeans and work shirt. It took me a few moments before I thought to glance at the framed documents on the wall above her desk and confirm that this bird-bright young lovely actually was a member of the bar. I handed her my Institute for Human Dignity card with "J. Dennison Dent, Assistant Director" printed discreetly in the lower left corner. "You are familiar with the facts of the case?" I asked, practicing my querulous rasp.

Ms. Irwin clapped her hands together in a burst of glee. "They're *great* facts!" she squealed delightedly. "I *love* human dignity cases and I've spent hours and *hours* doing the research for Spencer on your problem." She opened one of the dozens of file folders strewn across her desk top and dug out a sheaf of typed papers. "Here's the memorandum I did. I'll make a copy for you before you go but would you like me to give you a summary?" The eagerness in her voice told me she had become positively entranced with the case, and I decided to make an ally of her by listening attentively to whatever she had to say.

"Well, first off, the Constitution is useless. There's nothing in the Bill of Rights that says it's illegal to put a condition in a will that restricts someone's freedom to marry. The courts in Virginia and Pennsylvania have knocked out certain kinds of religious restrictions in wills on grounds of public policy. But the really *neat* argument on your side comes from a line of English cases that hold you can't draft that kind of restriction without making it so vague the courts will refuse to figure out what it means."

"Superb argument," I murmured appreciatively, and Cogan nodded in agreement.

"There's only one thing wrong with it," Ms. Irwin went on. "No American court has bought the argument yet. I want our case to be the one that establishes a great new principle!" She handed Cogan and me thick sheaves of Xerox paper stapled together. "These are copies of a *fantastic* law journal article called 'Testamentary Conditions: The Principle of Uncertainty and Religion.' They'll tell you everything you ever wanted to know about bigots who write wills."

A quick skimming of the article sent an attack of second thoughts about this scam running through my system, and Cogan in the chair next to me was chewing the end of his mustache diffidently. Without a strong legal theory to attack that restriction, I had no way of forcing the trustee and the Alexiou Aircraft Corporation to the bargaining table. But we were already so deeply committed that I decided we couldn't turn back. And when I remembered how many times I had heard that refrain from defenders of our little adventure in Southeast Asia, I felt more disheartened than ever.

"What do you think we should do?" Cogan asked our attorney in a tone that indicated he didn't think it made much difference what we did.

"Well," she said brightly, "Spencer and I will draw up a petition to set aside the restriction, but before we file suit we'll call the trustee and have a meeting to see if we can settle out of court. If they won't settle we sue and strike a blow for Human Dignity!" Her enthusiasm was infectious, and I would have hired her on the spot as a litigator for the IHD if such an institute had more than a paper existence. Cogan and I left her office assured that our legal destiny was in capable hands.

Now we had to wait, but not for long. The next afternoon Cogan and I returned from lunch to find a note in my message box to call Spencer Bennell. I dashed to the nearest pay phone in the lobby and complied. "Bennell here. Yes, Mr. Dent, sorry I missed you too, but we're making progress. Yes indeed, sir. A meeting has been arranged for 10:00 A.M. Monday at the trustee's office, that's Mr. Lang, in the Boatmen's Bank Building downtown on North Broadway. Edgar Lang Associates."

Which turned out to be a firm of International Business Consultants occupying half the nineteenth floor. From the brochure I read in the discreetly luxurious waiting room I learned that the firm specialized in arranging deals between U.S. corporations and foreign governments, and that Alexiou Aircraft was one of the firm's biggest clients. Edgar Lang's corner suite faced east, with a grand view of the six-hundred-foot-tall Gateway Arch. Edgar Lang himself sat behind his polished walnut fortress of a desk, sporting a pot belly and muttonchop side-whiskers that made him look like a villain in a Dickens novel. My seat was one end of a green leather couch, with Gael Irwin nestled delightfully between me and Spencer Bennell, who looked incredibly vigorous for a man pushing eighty. Across the room Cogan was leaning forward in his straight chair, carrying on an animated low conversation with the man who ran Alexiou Aircraft, President Basil Johnson, who was tall and pale, and showed streaks of grey at the temples and in his trim little Van Dyke, and twitched a lot. Cogan spun reminiscences about the collegiate vacations he'd spent working for the company, and did it with superb aplomb considering that he'd never seen the other man before in his life. Most of Cogan's patter came, of course, from the dossier on Buddy I had assembled, spiced up with some wild tales of his supposed life after his departure from home five years earlier. The small talk died when Edgar Lang gave a throat-clearing bark like a judge calling for order in the court. In no uncertain terms he told us that his duty was to enforce the trust as his dear old friend Nikos Alexiou had intended and that he would not authorize release of one cent of the accrued income to Nikos' son since that son had chosen to turn twenty-eight without marrying a proper wife. "The trust is clear," Lang harrumphed. "A woman of true Greek blood and orthodox religion."

"That is about as clear as the muddy Mississippi!" Gael sprang off the couch and into the fray. "Who knows the difference between true Greek blood and false Greek blood? How much does it take to be *of* true Greek blood? And what's orthodox religion? The will doesn't say Greek Orthodox, it says orthodox. And even if we knew what it meant, who is *of* that religion? Just the people that believe it all literally? Suppose I take some of it as poetry, am I *of* that religion or not? And do you really want a *court* to decide questions like that? For God's sake!" She gave a magnificent performance, mouth wide open, head tossing violently, glaring at the dumbfounded trustee as if never in the history of American law had Right so clearly opposed Wrong.

"It was Mr. Alexiou's property to dispose of as he wished." Dumbfounded Lang may have been, but defeated he was not. "Your client should have found himself a proper wife."

"N-now wait a minute here." Basil Johnson aimed a trembling finger at the walnut fortress. "I thought about this b-before I came here and I agree with B-B-Buddy. The fact that he didn't happen to f-find a Greek wife who satisfied him doesn't mean he should lose *all* the money. I think he and the corporation can work out a reasonable compromise as to who gets how much."

Lang glared at the stuttering president with icy disregard. "The decision is not yours to make, sir," he said sternly.

"Then he can g-get his lawyer to sue to t-terminate the entire trust. He's entitled to the principal when he turns f-forty but I think he can get it s-sooner. And if he wins, there go your trustees' c-commissions."

This new development scared the socks off me for a moment, but then I realized that if it worked it would actually be an improvement on my original plan, so I beamed contentedly.

"You can all waste your funds as you see fit," Edgar Lang blustered. "You will learn that the courts of this state still respect property rights." And on that sour note Bennell and Gael and Johnson and Cogan and I said perfunctory farewells to Lang and adjourned for lunch and a strategy session at Papa Tosca's, where Cogan continued to pour out a veritable Niagara of completely impromptu tales of his wanderings across America in the past five years. God, he was good. He made me wonder why he'd taken to my profession instead of remaining in the performing arts. He made me just a little envious.

And suddenly, just after Spencer Bennell had agreed to start a lawsuit to terminate the trust, I felt a monstrous twinge inside me, and it wasn't heartburn from the linguini. It was the realization that more than one scam might be in progress around the happy table.

I kept as straight a face as possible and continued my utterly fictitious explanation of IHD's inner workings to an excited Gael Irwin. Finally the party broke up and Cogan and I rode back to the Chase in the rented Vega. Once in the privacy of my room I picked up the phone and put in a feverish call to the Jock, who promised to get back to me in a day or two.

Which from my point of view was a hell of a long wait.

Cogan wanted to find himself a woman the next evening, so I called Bennell's office and invited Gael out to dinner. We tackled the London broil and the superb salad bar at The Leather Bottle in Clayton, and over a succession of after-dinner drinks—myself favoring brandy while she sipped Velvet Hammers—she treated me to a lecture on the premature termination of trusts.

"In England we'd win in a walk. The English courts hold that when you put property in trust for somebody till he's X years old and he gets the principal on his Xth birthday, the beneficiary is really the owner of the property and he can terminate the trust before he turns X and take the property outright. But most American courts take the position that the dead man was the owner of the property and his restrictions have to be respected so the beneficiary can't terminate the trust before the trust instrument says he can. There are a few cases here that follow the English view and I think we have some chance of winning."

"A most instructive exshpo—er, account," I said, "and would you like another Velvet Monkeywrench?"

She made a gracefully clownish face at me. "Oh dear, this doesn't seem to be the night for Human Dignity, does it?"

It certainly didn't. When the phone on my night table at the Chase screamed at me the next morning, it was all I could do to roll to the edge of the bed and grope for the receiver and mutter gibberish into it.

"Mr. Dent?" a voice assaulted my tender ear. "Mr. J. Dennison Dent of the Institute for Human Dignity? The gentleman who came to St. Louis with Buddy Alexiou?"

"Speaking," I snarled.

"You will want to see me," the voice assured me. "I just flew in from Boston and am calling from the airport. The limo will take me about half an hour to get to the Chase."

"Now wait just a minute!" I yelled. "Who the hell do you think you are anyway?"

A knowing chuckle traveled over the wire. "Why, that's an easy one. I'm the real Buddy Alexiou! Thirty minutes." And he hung up with a click that nearly deafened me. The old twinge started bouncing around my innards again, and I forced myself into the hottest followed by the coldest shower I could stand and then into a suit, thinking frantically every second. I grabbed the phone and dialed Cogan's room.

"Milo. Do well last night? Glad to hear it. Now listen carefully. Get dressed, get out of this hotel and stay out all day. Call me before you come back. Go downtown, visit the Arch or take the ride up the river on the *Huck Finn* or something, but don't come near me till further notice. Understood? I'll explain later." That was to insure that the two putative Buddy Alexious didn't accidentally encounter each other. I had enough catastrophes on my hands already.

Forty minutes later, with the second self-styled Buddy sitting in the wing chair across from me, ankles crossed indolently, I looked up from the papers he had offered me to prove his identity. An old driver's license, social security card, a wallet-sized photo of a younger version of himself and a teen-aged girl standing arm-in-arm on the lawn of what was clearly old Nikos Alexiou's lordly manor—if these were fakes he had a better document forger than my man, and they don't come any better than my man.

"Convinced?" he asked. "Since I'm the real Buddy, Mr. Dent, that means you've been taken in by some con artist posing as me."

"It would seem possible," I replied, cradling my chin judiciously. "I suppose the Institute could have been hoodwinked by an impostor, but we do make careful checks, you know, and we can't be responsible if . . ."

He waved an impatient and well-manicured hand at me. "No, no, I'm not going to make trouble for your Institute. I don't even want to make trouble for the guy who's impersonating me. All I want is for the two of you to keep on with what you're doing, trying to break that trust. If you win, I'll take 75 percent of the proceeds and let the other guy keep the rest."

Bewilderment socked me in the solar plexus, and I clutched the arms of my chair as if the room were swaying. "You just lost me. Are you saying you don't want to appear personally in the case—you want, er, the other claimant to be a sort of proxy for you?"

"That's it." He laughed bitterly for a moment. "I don't want so much as a look at the damned airplane factory. I would have come back sooner to fight Pop's trust but I didn't think the risk was worth it until a contact I still have at the factory called me the other day and said he'd heard Johnson and one of the vice-presidents talking about my being back here and how the company was supporting me in a suit to end the trust. Then I knew I had to come back. You see, that restriction in the trust was why I vanished five years ago. Pop had found out about me."

"I'm lost again. Your father tried to make you marry a woman of true Greek blood and . . ."

"No, no, that blood and religion stuff was just camouflage to keep the real reason hidden. My father tried to make me marry a *woman*."

Sunlight was now beginning to dispel the fog in my head, so that his next statement wasn't necessary.

"I'm gay, you see," he said simply.

It was an eminently believable story, even to the point that he had a high-paying job in Boston under another name which he stood to lose if he came back to St. Louis to fight his father's trust. By the time Buddy Two departed from my princely chamber, my brain seemed to be falling apart. I pulled notepaper out of a bureau drawer, jotted down the hotel and the assumed name my visitor said he would use while in town—Rodeway Inn, James Gilbert—and then just sat there, trying to devise a way to handle this insane situation.

When I'd begun this scam the real Buddy Alexiou had been gone for five years—dead or an amnesia victim for all I knew—and the only contender for the title had been Roy Cogan, who of course was a fake. Then, over luncheon at Papa Tosca's, when I'd realized what a consummate job Cogan was doing as Buddy, it had crossed my mind that maybe, just maybe, my phony wasn't a phony at all but the real thing. Could the genuine Buddy Alexiou have somehow gotten the word from the Jock that Milo Turner was looking for a young man of his precise description, and have made the contract with me for the purpose of finding out what I was up to? It sounded absurd, but Cogan had struck me as just too good in the role of Buddy, although I still had no idea what labyrinthine scam of his own he had in mind. The appearance of Buddy Two, however, threw all my theories into chaos, because if he *was* genuine then my man was indeed nothing but the simple fake I'd first thought he was. But if Buddy Two was a phony then Cogan still might be the genuine Buddy Alexiou.

Like a doctor whose patient's symptoms squared with no known disease, I needed a second opinion. Not Cogan's; he was part of the symptoms. Certainly not the opinion of the blustering Edgar Lang nor of the stuttering Basil Johnson. That seemed to leave only Spencer Bennell, and in desperation I dialed his office, confident that I could give him all the facts without revealing my own identity.

"I'm sorry, Mr. Dent," the receptionist said, "but Mr. Bennell had to go to Cape Girardeau to try a case and won't be back till the end of the week. Would you care to speak to Miss Irwin?"

An hour later, on the edge of the client's chair in her file-littered office, I was describing to her my encounter with Buddy Two. When I had finished my account she played with a strand of her lustrous dark hair and nibbled on her lower lip. Finally she looked me square in the eyeballs and gave her diagnosis.

"It's very simple. There can't be two genuine Buddies. So if Buddy Two is real, the Buddy that went to your Institute for help is a fake. And if your Buddy is genuine, Buddy Two is a fake!"

I nodded at these observations as if they had dropped from the mouth of Socrates.

"So all you have to do is put both of them together in a locked room with two or three people who knew the real Buddy best and have them quiz both the guys until one or the other gives himself away!"

I could imagine no more horrendous suggestion, because just in case Cogan *was* playing the game straight with me, both he and my original scam would be blown clear out of the water in such a confrontation. But how to veto it without giving myself away? "I'm afraid that is just too likely to be inconclusive," I objected, shaking my head thoughtfully. "Suppose some quizzers wound up backing one claimant and others the other?"

"Fingerprints!" Gael shrieked excitedly.

Of course, I had made sure before ever committing myself to the scam that the real Buddy's prints were nowhere spread upon the public record. "I don't think there are any records of Buddy's prints before he left St. Louis," I said, feigning uncertainty.

We sat in silence for a bit, and then she spread out her hands on the desk top. "I'm bankrupt of ideas," she confessed. "I'm sorry, but I can't think of any other way we can tell who's real and who isn't. And when Spencer comes back from Cape Girardeau I'm going to have to tell him that someone's attempting a fraud and I think he's going to have to tell the cops and let them figure it out."

"Hooray for legal ethics," I mumbled, not daring to try and stop her for fear it would blow my cover. I thanked her for her invaluable help, sped back to the Chase and made plans to retrieve Cogan and get us both out of town before we began hearing official knocks on our doors.

There was a message in my box to call Los Angeles. I tore up to my room as if a demon were breathing down the back of my neck and snatched up the phone and dialed. "Jock? Milo. You've got it?"

"I have indeed," Jock said. "And did ye really think I'd send ye a lad that wasn't what he seemed?" He reeled off a litany of names, dates and places, including several summer stock productions Cogan had played in and two or three jails he'd done time in, a whole spectrum of life experiences that established beyond dispute that Roy Cogan was exactly what he had told me he was, a small-time actor turned con man. I whooshed out a breath of relief that could have broken a window.

"Jock," I said, "you don't know what a favor you've just done me."

"Oh, ye don't think so?" he replied in a tone that left no doubt his bill would be steep. I thanked him profusely, wished the wind at his back on all his journeys, and hung up.

Scratch one irrational suspicion. Roy Cogan was genuine—a genuine fake Buddy Alexiou, that is. He was just so much better at the game than even I had been at his age that subconsciously I must have been resenting him like hell and building up an insane theory against him.

Now I had to get hold of him in a hurry and hustle both of us out of St. Louis; but having no idea where he'd gone when I'd called him this morning and told him to dematerialize, I could do little but sit by the phone and wait for him to call. I had to save his skin as well as my own. I owed him that much.

I waited and waited some more, and then when I'd begun to think something had gone wrong with the phone, it rang, and I snatched at it. "Cogan? I . . ."

"No, sweetie, it's me. Who's Cogan?" There was no mistaking the tinkletones of my least favorite kooky woman lawyer. "I called you because a minute ago something just struck me about your two Buddies problem."

"I'm all ears," I lied, wishing she'd get the hell off the line and clear it for Cogan's call.

"Just because one of them has to be a phony," she said, enunciating each word precisely, "that doesn't mean the other one has to be the real thing! Why couldn't they *both* be fakes?"

And as if on cue, I suddenly had what my Zen Buddhist friends would call a *satori,* an overpoweringly enlightening intuitive understanding of the whole ball of wax. It was like that moment in one of my favorite Hitchcock films, *Vertigo,* where James Stewart fastens the necklace around Kim Novak's neck and suddenly understands everything that has happened to him in the picture. I recalled the clippings I'd read on the plane about the circumstances of Buddy's disappearance, and those damnably genuine-looking papers Buddy Two had shown me, and the way he'd known my assumed name and where I was staying when he'd phoned me this morning. And when I put all the pieces together I saw how a second superscam had been going on parallel to my own, and I knew what to do about it.

"Are you still there?" Gael asked in alarm. "And you still haven't told me who Cogan is!"

"Oh, ah, Cogan's the head of the private detective agency the Institute uses to check out people who come to us with cases. I was expecting him to call me so we could go over the check he ran on Buddy One and see if there could have been a slip-up. Thanks for your thought, Gael, I appreciate it more than I can tell you."

The second the call ended I twirled the dial and made one of my own, back to the Jock's human supermarket. "I need a man quick," I said, "and the hell with the cost. Someone here in St. Louis who can tap a phone on short notice with no questions asked." I didn't really need the confirmation the tap would provide but thought it might be useful to have some physical evidence in my back pocket. The Jock gave me a name, telling me the man was an ex-CIA spook who'd been caught with his hand in the till. I called the man and drove out to his office. By the cocktail hour the bug was in place.

I was lucky. My man called me back at 8:30 that night and played me a most revealing conversation he'd picked up, a dialogue that confirmed my intuition of what the caper was all about. "O.K.," I told him. "Make me a copy of that and get me a battery recorder to go with it. I'll be over for it in an hour. Kill the tap and have your bill ready. I'll pay in cash." I slammed the phone down, picked it up again and dialed Cogan's room. He'd come in at suppertime and was watching TV now, waiting for action. "Get packed," I told him. "Then get up here and pack my bags, pay our bills, take a cab to the airport and wait. If I'm not there by 2:00 A.M., grab the first flight out and drop a note to the I.H.D. post office address telling me where you've holed up. Got it?"

"Milo, what the hell has been going on around here today?" Cogan demanded irritably.

"Explanations afterward," I promised. "Now move it, unless you want the lead in the next production at the Jefferson City pen . . ."

An hour and a half later, I braked the Vega in the graveled driveway beside one of the largest houses in the posh and snobby suburb of Crevecoeur, and a few minutes after my arrival I was deep in private conversation with the rather astonished master of the establishment.

"You can't use that in court," Edgar Lang chattered, his teeth tapping against each other in his fright. "Tapes aren't admissible . . ."

"We're not in court. This is just between us." The battery-powered cassette recorder in my lap gave a little click as the tape rewound to its starting point. "Even without the tape it had to be you. Who was the last person to see Buddy alive five years ago? You, who supposedly drove him to the airport. Who had Buddy's genuine ID? Your boy, Buddy Two. You killed your best friend's son five years ago, took his ID, and just waited for old Nikos to die and enough time to pass so that a fake Buddy would pass muster here in St. Louis. Your ringer would come here, sue to end the trust, and you'd wind up with the whole fund minus whatever your Buddy Two's cut was. Nice deal. I have to admit your ringer's a good man; he had me fooled for a few minutes. I may use him myself someday. You must have felt as if the top of your head were coming off at that meeting at your office; you knew the man playing Buddy was a phony, because you'd killed the genuine article five years ago, but you had to go along with the game because your own phony Buddy was waiting in the wings, just about to make his appearance. So you simply had your man make his pitch to me. The fact that Buddy Two knew who I was and where I was staying was another thing that gave you away; only the people at the meeting knew those things. And by the way, where did you bury Buddy's body? If the cops started digging up the gardens around old Alexiou's house, would they find some bones that didn't belong?"

A good shot, that last speculation. Lang fell back in his chair.

"O.K., so what do you want?" he demanded. "You're not a cop . . ."

"Money," I said. "Lots of it, because you've cost me a bunch. Forty thousand would be a reasonable figure, I should think." He turned pale as a daiquiri. "And in cash, and tonight. That shouldn't give you any trouble. As the head of a firm that arranges big business deals with foreign governments, you've got to have a slush fund around."

"I can't get it for you tonight," he protested feebly.

"The police station is always open," I pointed out, fingering my cassette recorder pointedly, "and your conversation with Mr. James Gilbert of the Rodeway Inn would be instructive to the bunco squad."

We paid a visit to his squirrel hole that night.

It was a little after 1:30 A.M. when I slid the Vega into one of the return slots for rented cars at Lambert Airport and made tracks for the central lounge. Cogan was waiting in a scooped-out seat. I slipped into the seat beside him and gave him a quick rundown of the action. We decided it would be safe enough to take a direct flight back to California, using one of the credit cards in false names I always carry to pay for our tickets. I had to get back to dismantle the I.H.D. office before the cops began checking into the nonexistent crusader for human dignity known as J. Dennison Dent. I could reorganize the Institute later, under another name and in another state, when the heat died down.

That bright and kooky law lady had cost me one of my best covers, at least temporarily, but somehow I couldn't work up any resentment against her. I wished she were on my side of society's fence; we'd make a great team on a scam. I passed through the security checkpoint with forty thousand dollars spread around various portions of my anatomy, and Cogan and I flew the friendly skies back to safety.

Have You Ever Seen This Woman?

by John Lutz

David Hastings awoke slowly, painfully, not really wanting to lose the oblivion of sleep. As he opened his eyes to slits he raised a hand gingerly to his throbbing head and touched his fingertips to just below his hairline. His hand came away with blood on it, and his eyes opened all the way.

He was in the bedroom, he realized, lying on his back on the made bed. Every beat of his heart echoed with pain in his head. It was morning, judging by the softly angled rays of light filtering through the curtains, the bark of a faraway dog, the distant clanging of a trash can. Hastings' mind was blank to everything but an unexplainable dread, a terrible fact just beyond consciousness that he knew he would soon have to face.

With great effort Hastings raised himself and supported his upper body on the bed with his elbows. Summoning even more strength, he twisted and sat on the edge of the mattress, noticing that his white shirtfront was covered with scarlet-brown splotches. He saw, too, that there were several stains on his wrinkled checked sport coat and his tie. Hastings stood, took a few heavy steps, and leaned on his dresser to look at himself in the mirror.

Vacant, frightened eyes stared out of a face stained with blood from a long deep gash high on his forehead. There was another deep cut on his left cheekbone. Quickly, Hastings turned away from the mirror. He was hot, his body suddenly burning. He peeled off his coat and tie and hung them in the closet, then he unbuttoned the top two buttons on his shirt.

The door to the living room was half open. For a reason he couldn't fathom Hastings knew he didn't want to go through that door, but he also knew he must. He began moving toward the door with uneven groping steps, realizing for the first time that he was wearing only one shoe. As he pushed the door all the way open and stepped into the living room he shuddered, his disbelieving eyes narrowed.

There were slivers of clear glass scattered over the dark green carpet, as if a crystal bomb had exploded in the room. Hastings' left shoe was lying on its side, still tied, near the armchair. On the other side of the room, where the shattered pieces of crystal were the heaviest, the carpet was soaked by a huge reddish stain. And in the center of that stain, near the television with its wildly rolling and distorted silent picture, lay the still, the unbelievably still body of Agnes.

In horrible fascination Hastings extended his outstretched hands before him, as if pushing something away, and stepped slowly over and gazed down at his dead wife.

Agnes's nightgown was torn and wrapped about her neck and shoulders. Her face, framed in a tangle of auburn hair, was completely crusted with dried blood, and the head had been unmercifully battered, unmercifully and brutally mutilated.

Hastings' breathing was abnormally loud, like steam hissing in the small room. He began backing away from the body, cutting his stockinged foot on a piece of broken crystal. Then he slumped down and sat on the floor, his back against the wall. His mind was a revolving, horror-filled maze, a jumble of terrible puzzle pieces that would not fit together no matter how they were turned. With dazed eyes he looked slowly about the living room, and he knew then where the shattered crystal had come from.

The swan. The glass swan that Agnes's mother had sent them from Mexico last summer. Probably it was a typical tourist item, but Agnes had liked it and placed it on the bookcase in the living room. Hastings had also rather liked the swan. It seemed to be made of a very delicate clear crystal that had a prismlike effect so the shapes and colors reflected within the rounded body and long graceful neck were dismembered and twisted to fit the graceful lines of the sculpting. And now it had been used . . . for this.

Hastings closed his eyes and rested the back of his head against the living room wall, and with a pain that was both physical and mental he began trying to re-create in his mind the horror of last night.

He remembered parking his car in front of his small brick home on Lime Avenue, he remembered that clearly enough. He had worked late at the office and hadn't left until almost nine o'clock.

The house was lighted, the glow of the living room swag-lamp shining through the drawn drapes. Hastings walked up the winding cement path onto the porch and turned the doorknob. But the front door was locked. That hadn't seemed normal to Hastings. Agnes seldom locked doors of any kind. He drew his house key from his pocket, unlocked the front door and entered the house.

Here Hastings bowed his head and rested it painfully on his drawnup knees. He didn't want to remember the rest—his mind recoiled from it. But he made himself fit the pieces together.

Agnes had been at the opposite end of the living room, near the turned-on television set, and she was struggling with a man, a tall man dressed in dark clothes, a man who had his gloved hand pressed to Agnes's mouth.

What had the man looked like? His features were blurred—as if he had a nylon stocking pulled down over his face.

The man saw Hastings and was motionless for a second, then he felled Agnes with a chopping blow across the back of her neck and came at Hastings.

The man was bigger than Hastings, and stronger, so the struggle didn't last long. Hastings remembered being shoved back toward the bedroom door, remembered seeing the man's gloved fingers curl around the natural handle of the crystal swan's neck. And then the swan smashed into his head. The man pushed him violently against the closed bedroom door, breaking the latch and springing it open as Hastings staggered back into the bedroom. Again the swan smashed into his head, and Hastings fell backward across the bed. He remembered feeling the welcome softness of the mattress before losing consciousness.

Hastings raised his head from his knees and looked at the bedroom doorframe, at the splintered wood near the latch. Then he looked again, for just a second, at the still body of his wife.

After knocking him unconscious, Hastings thought, the man must have gone back into the living room and continued his attack on Agnes. Somehow Hastings knew that the object was rape from the beginning. Agnes must have regained consciousness, must have begun to fight or scream, or attempted to run, and the man with the stockinged face must have used the swan to beat her to the silence and submissiveness of death.

Slowly Hastings raised himself to his feet and stood unsteadily, leaning against the wall. Then he made his way into the bathroom and splashed cold water on his face. For a long time he stood slumped over the washbasin, watching the red tinted water swirl counterclockwise down the drain. When he was finally ready, he went back into the bedroom and picked up the phone.

The police converged on Hastings' house in great numbers, photographing, dusting for fingerprints, examining, discussing. And then Agnes was taken away by two men in white uniforms, and Hastings was left with a Lieutenant Sam Newell, a crewcut heavy-browed man who had been personally assigned to the case. Hastings' neighbor and good friend Philip Barrett also remained in the house after all the other policemen but Newell had departed. The three men sat in the living room drinking coffee that Barrett had been thoughtful enough to brew.

Agnes's murder had occurred in Plainton, the community in which they lived a scant few miles from the city, and while the larger and more efficient Metropolitan Police Department would give some assistance, solving the crime was the responsibility only of the Plainton Police Department, for everything had happened within their jurisdiction. A murder investigation was not the sort of task Lieutenant Newell undertook very often.

"How old was Agnes, Mr. Hastings?" he asked, flipping the leather cover of his notebook.

"Thirty-six, the same as me," Hastings replied, watching Newell make quick jabbing motions at his notepaper with a short pencil.

"And did she have any enemies that you knew of?"

"Agnes was well liked by everyone," Phil Barrett said in a sad voice. "It's impossible to believe this has happened."

Lieutenant Newell glared at him over the rim of his coffee cup. "If you don't mind, Mr. Barrett, we'll get to your statement in the course of the investigation."

Barrett said nothing, raising his own steaming coffee cup to his lips as if he hadn't heard the lieutenant.

"Phil's right," Hastings said. "Agnes didn't have any enemies that I knew of."

"Somebody didn't like her," Newell said. "That swan was shattered into such small pieces we couldn't fit it together." He made a short notation in his book. "Understand now, Mr. Hastings, this next question is simply part of the routine. Did your wife Agnes have any . . . extramarital affairs? Had you heard any rumors of her running around?"

Hastings couldn't keep the agitation out of his voice. "We were happily married, Lieutenant."

"You know what they say about who's the last to know," Newell said. He glanced at Phil Barrett.

"Agnes wasn't the type to go out on her husband," Barrett said.

"What kind of activities was she interested in?" Newell asked.

"As I told you," Hastings said, "we never had any children. Agnes contented herself pretty much with staying home, watching TV, and she worked hard keeping the house neat." He looked around at the blood-stained disarray of the living room and put his head down.

Lieutenant Newell flipped his leather notebook shut and stood slowly, betraying what he was, a policeman with sore feet. "In all honesty there's not much here to work with. The description of the man you struggled with—tall, average weight, dark clothes, stocking mask—it's a phantom. We'll be in touch with you, Mr. Hastings, and I'll let you know about the coroner's report on your wife." He nodded. "I'm sorry," he said and left.

"Don't pay too much attention to his questions, Dave," Phil Barrett told Hastings when they were alone. "They're routine."

"I don't mind the questions," Hastings said, "if they'll help catch Agnes's killer."

Barrett stood and drained the last of his coffee. "Why don't you go in and get some rest?" he said. "I'll clean this place up—the police said it'd be O.K."

Hastings nodded, feeling suddenly as tired as he'd ever felt. "That's nice of you, Phil."

Barrett shrugged. "Listen," he said in a concerned voice, "if you'd rather spend tonight at our place, Myra and I would be glad to have you . . ."

"Thanks anyway," Hastings said, "but with a shower and some sleep I think I can face things here." He rose to go to the bedroom, and the hurt and anger seemed to rise with him. "Dammit, Phil! Why would anybody want to kill Agnes? Why did this maniac have to choose her for a victim?"

"Who knows?" Barrett said in a sympathetic voice. "He might have just seen her somewhere and followed her to find out where she lived. I guess the husband of any victim would be asking himself the same questions you are."

"I guess so," Hastings said wearily. He touched the bandage on his forehead over the wound that the police surgeon had stitched, as if to assure himself of its reality, and, sidestepping the broken glass, he walked from the living room.

The next afternoon Lieutenant Newell telephoned Hastings to inform him of the coroner's report. Agnes had been sexually molested. Newell then asked Hastings about any men who had expressed interest in Agnes, any rejected suitors. But Hastings could think of no one. He and Agnes had been married fourteen years. The murderer might have been a psycho, Newell speculated, a maniac who had chosen Agnes by chance out of millions without even knowing her name and struck her as lightning might strike. He assured Hastings that the police would keep working on the case and hung up . . .

A week passed, and as far as Hastings was concerned the Plainton Police Department wasn't working hard enough. They had come up with nothing.

The desire to see Agnes's killer apprehended had grown in Hastings, causing him agonizing days and sleepless nights. And the feeling persisted that there was something he should know, something that skirted the outer edges of his mind and that, try as he may, he could never grasp.

Hastings began to telephone Lieutenant Newell regularly, asking him about progress on the case, about what the Plainton Police Department was doing to bring about progress. But there was never any news. He always got a polite brushoff. He came to realize that the Plainton Police Department had finished digging, that they would never apprehend Agnes's killer.

It was then Hastings decided to take action himself. Lying awake nights he worked out a general plan of investigation. The first thing he did was to go next door and talk to his neighbor, Phil Barrett. Here Hastings possessed an advantage over the police, for he knew that Barrett would talk to him confidentially and with complete honesty.

Barrett was in his long narrow back yard, spraying his rose bushes. As Hastings approached him he stooped to spread the aerosol mist on the bottom side of some perforated leaves and smiled up at Hastings.

"Morning, Dave."

Hastings stood, watching some of the spray drift up and past him.

"Haven't seen you," Barrett said. "How are you getting along?"

Hastings smiled and shrugged.

Barrett straightened and wiped his hands on the paint-stained trousers he was wearing. "Have the police found out anything?"

"No," Hastings said, "and it looks now like they won't. That's what I wanted to talk to you about, Phil. I need some honest answers to some questions."

Barrett looked at him with a vague puzzled frown. "I wouldn't lie to you, Dave."

"Not unless you thought you were doing me a favor," Hastings said. "I want to know about Agnes."

Barrett grinned and shook his head. "She was your wife. You know more about her than I do."

"But you might have heard some things. Things a woman's husband wouldn't hear." The breeze mussed Hastings' combed brown hair, causing a lock to fall over the red scar on his forehead. "Did you hear anything, Phil?"

The aerosol can hissed as Barrett loosed some spray in the general direction of one of his rose bushes, then he stood staring at the ground. "I heard a few things, Dave. They didn't mean anything, they were none of my business."

"They're my business now," Hastings said quietly.

Barrett continued to stare at the newly mowed grass for a while before speaking. "I heard she'd been seen a few places around town," he said, "restaurants, taverns, places like that. That's all I heard . . ."

"Seen with men?" Hastings asked, holding back the sudden flow of anger and disbelief that he should have expected.

"Yes, Dave." Barrett raised his head to look Hastings in the eye. "With men, different men, but like I said all I ever heard was second or third hand. It could be that none of it was true, just the kind of loose talk that sometimes follows an attractive woman."

"Did you believe what you heard?" Hastings asked.

Barrett looked at him with an agonized expression as he squinted into the sun. "That's not a fair question, Dave. I didn't know whether to believe the stories or not. You know how Agnes was—she just didn't seem the type."

No, Hastings thought, by all outward appearances Agnes wasn't the type. Auburn-haired, dark-eyed Agnes, slender, pretty in her plain dress or modest slacks, smiling as she worked about the house . . .

"I'm sorry, Dave."

Hastings felt sick. Lately someone was always sorry for him. He nodded to Barrett, said his thanks and walked back to his empty house.

The bottle of bourbon he'd bought a month ago was in the kitchen cupboard above the sink, still over half full. He got it down, sat at the table and poured himself a drink. He couldn't imagine Agnes having affairs with other men. That was another side of her that he couldn't believe existed. But there had been stories, rumors that had never reached his ears. It could be that they were false, and yet who knew what happened on the dark side of a person's mind?

Hastings stood and replaced the bottle in the cupboard, setting the empty glass in the sink. Then he went into the living room and began to rummage through the desk drawers for a clear and recent photograph of Agnes. Finally he settled on one, a color snapshot of his dead wife wearing a pink blouse, staring out of the photo directly at the camera with a tender and somewhat embarrassed smile.

As Hastings slipped the photo into his wallet he found its exact duplicate, another print, behind his identification card. He slid the second photo in the cellophane pocket on top of the first.

That evening he began. He shaved for the first time that day, put on a suit, and drove toward town.

The first place he stopped was on the outskirts of the city, a lounge and restaurant named Tony's. He went to the bar and showed the bartender Agnes's photograph.

"Do you recognize her?" Hastings asked. "Have you seen this woman in the past few months?"

"You the police?" the bartender asked.

"No," Hastings said, "I'm her husband."

The bartender looked at Hastings, then squinted at the photograph. He shook his head. He hadn't seen her, he told Hastings. At least if he had he couldn't recall. There were a lot of women who came in here with men. There were a lot who came in alone and left with men. It was impossible to remember them all.

Hastings thanked the bartender, bought him a beer and left.

He drove to three more places, and none of the people there remembered Agnes. Though at a place called The Lion's Mane a red-vested bartender had stared at Hastings in a peculiar fashion as if he were about to say something, then a customer had called him away.

Hastings' last stop was at The Purple Bottle on Wilton Avenue. The bartender was a round-faced man with a mustache who reminded Hastings of somebody. He approached Hastings and smiled at him.

"Bourbon and water," Hastings said. He was sitting toward the end of the long bar, away from the other customers, and when the bartender returned with his drink he opened his wallet and showed him the photograph.

"Do you recognize her?" he asked. "Do you remember ever seeing her in here?"

The round-faced bartender set the glass on a coaster and stared down at the snapshot.

"She's pretty," he said, "but I don't ever remember her coming in here. Of course, I could have forgotten." He turned and beckoned to a younger bartender who was working at the other end of the bar, a slender young man with long black hair.

"Billy," he asked the young bartender, "have you ever seen this woman?"

Billy stared at the photograph curiously, then looked at Hastings.

"No," he said, "but I think I remember her picture."

Hastings' hand began to tremble as he raised his glass to his lips.

"Sure," Billy said, "somebody came in here—must have been about a month ago—showed me a photograph and asked me if I'd seen the girl."

"Are you positive?" Hastings asked.

"I don't know. I seen her picture before somewhere."

"Could it have been the newspapers?" Hastings asked.

Billy's lean face brightened. "Maybe. Maybe the paper. Why? She do something?"

"No," Hastings said, "nothing."

The round-faced bartender's eyes moved to convey a look to his companion, and the younger bartender moved away toward the other end of the bar.

Hastings left without finishing his drink and drove home.

He shut his front door behind him and stood leaning against it, breathing as if he'd been running hard. The nerve of that young punk, saying he'd seen Agnes's picture before! The nerve of him!

Hastings wiped his forehead, got undressed and took a shower. Wearing pajamas and a bathrobe, he walked into the kitchen to prepare something to eat. He couldn't get the young bartender's words out of his mind, the sincere expression in the eyes.

There was nothing in the refrigerator, only frozen food that would have to thaw, and Hastings was hungry. He decided to get dressed and go out someplace to eat, someplace that stayed open late. He would treat himself to a steak dinner and forget about the rest of the evening. Slamming the refrigerator door shut, he turned and walked into the bedroom.

He dressed in dark slacks and a white shirt, then walked to the closet and absently pulled out his checked sport coat, not realizing until after he'd put it on that it was the one he'd worn the night of the murder. It was still wrinkled and blood-spattered. Unconsciously he slipped his hand into the right side pocket, and his body stiffened as if a thrown switch had sent electricity through him.

Hastings withdrew his hand from the pocket, staring at it as if it belonged to someone else. Clutched firmly in his grip was the graceful head and jaggedly broken neck of the glass swan.

He stood staring at the crystal head, felt the heft of the smooth glass in his hand. He remembered now. *He had to remember! He* had been in that tavern before, asking the young bartender about Agnes. Lately she had been cold to him, and Hastings had heard the rumors about her and had simply wanted to check. And no one had recognized the photograph—in the half dozen likely places he'd gone to that night no one had recognized the photograph.

Still, that hadn't been enough for Hastings. He had gone home at nine that evening after his inquiries at the various night spots, and he had tried to force her to make love. Agnes had refused his advances and he had confronted her with the ugly rumors he had been unable to substantiate. She had said he was crazy, that they were only rumors and he could believe them if he liked. Then she had screamed that she no longer loved him, that she wanted a divorce. He had grabbed her then, and she had struggled. He could see her now as he pushed her toward the bedroom, her slender hand closing on the crystal swan neck.

Then she had struck him twice, brutally, on the head.

Hastings shuddered as he remembered his rage, as he remembered wresting the swan from Agnes and smashing it against her head until she was dead, walking her about the living room in a grotesque dance, striking her over and over until her face and head were a horrible bloody mass among glittering pieces of broken crystal.

And then . . .

He refused to remember what had happened then. He remembered only stumbling to the bedroom, kicking open the door, falling dizzily onto the mattress.

Hastings stood in trembling horror, staring down at what he'd pulled from his pocket. Then, as if a sudden soothing hand had passed over him, he stopped trembling.

He walked into the kitchen and laid the neck and head of the broken swan in the sink. Trancelike, he opened a drawer and brought out a metal meat-tenderizer mallet. Then rhythmically he brought the mallet down again and again, shattering what was left of the swan into tiny crystals that he washed down the drain in a swirl of water. After replacing the mallet in the drawer, he opened the cupboard above the sink and got down the bottle of bourbon. With a slow and clumsy rhythm, he walked back into the bedroom.

He awoke slowly, painfully, not really wanting to lose the oblivion of sleep. It was morning, judging by the softly angled rays of light filtering through the curtains, the bark of a faraway dog, the distant clanging of a trash can. He struggled to a sitting position on the edge of the mattress, knocking the empty bottle onto the floor. Too much to drink last night, he told himself reproachfully, wondering why he had been so foolish. Looking down at his wrinkled and blood-stained sport coat, he remembered it was the one he'd been wearing the night of Agnes's murder.

Drawing a deep breath, he stood. He peeled off the sport coat and hung it in the closet, then he removed the rest of his clothes and stumbled into the bathroom to shower.

After a breakfast of eggs and toast, he picked up the telephone and called Lieutenant Newell to see if there was any news on Agnes's case. There was none, the lieutenant said in an officially sympathetic voice. He assured Hastings that the Plainton Police Department had done everything possible.

Hastings thanked him and hung up.

That evening he drove into the city and at random chose a neon-lighted tavern. Benny's was the name of the place. Hastings stared straight ahead as he walked across the parking lot, entered and sat at the bar. When the bartender came he ordered a beer and as his drink was set before him he withdrew his wallet and showed the bartender the picture of Agnes.

"Has she ever been in here?" he asked. "Have you ever seen this woman?"

Joe Cutter's Game

by Brian Garfield

Myerson looked up from the desk. "Hello, Ross."

Ross shut the door. "Where's Joe?"

"Late. As usual."

As far as Ross remembered there'd been only one time when Joe Cutter had been late arriving in this office and that had been the result of a bomb scare that had grounded everything for three hours at Templehof. Myerson's acidulous remark had been a cheap shot. But then that was Myerson.

Myerson pretended to read a report in a manila file. The silence began to rag Ross' nerves. "What's the flap?"

"We'll wait for Joe." Myerson didn't look up from the file.

The room was stale with Myerson's illegal Havana smoke. It was a room that always unnerved Ross because Myerson's varied indeterminate functions were that of hatchet man. Any audience with him might turn out to be one's last: fall into disfavor with anyone on the Fourth Floor and one could have a can tied to one's tail at any time, Civil Service or no Civil Service; and as very junior staff Ross had no illusions about his right to tenure.

But Myerson didn't seem to be in a savage mood right now. The rudeness was all right—that was what passed for amiability with Myerson.

Finally Joe Cutter walked in, lean and dark with his actorish good looks and the cold eyes that concealed his spectacular shrewdness.

"You're late."

"O.K." Joe Cutter glanced at Ross and tossed his travel coat across a chair. Not hat; Cutter seldom wore a hat.

Myerson folded the file shut. "That's all you've got to say to me?"

"Would you like a note from my mother explaining my tardiness?"

"Your sarcasms seldom amuse me, Joe."

"Then don't provoke them. We were in the holding pattern over Dulles International." Cutter sat down. "What's on?"

"We have a signal from Arbuckle." Myerson tapped the file with a fingertip.

"Where's Arbuckle?"

"East Africa. You really ought to try and keep up on the postings in your own department, Joe." Myerson lit a cigar, making a smug ritualistic show of it.

Cutter's amused glance bounced off Ross. Myerson, puffing smoke, said, "In Dar-es-Salaam."

Ross' impatience burst its confines. "What's the flap, then?"

"I do wish you'd learn not to repeat yourself, Ross. And it distresses me that you're the only drone in this department who doesn't realize that words like 'flap' became obsolete long ago."

Cutter said, "If you're through amusing yourself maybe you could answer Ross' question."

Myerson squinted through the smoke and after a moment evidently decided not to be affronted. "As you may know, affairs in Tanzania remain sensitive. The balance is precarious between our influence and that of the Chinese. It would require only a slight upheaval to tip the bal—"

"Can't you spare us the tiresome diplomatic summaries and get down to it?"

"Contain your childish eagerness, Joe."

"I assumed you hadn't summoned me all the way from Belgrade to chew the rag about Tanzanian politics."

Ross marveled that their sparring always seemed to produce satisfactory results in the end. Their antipathy wasn't an act—the mutual contempt was genuine enough.

Along the Fourth Floor they called Cutter "007"—he was one of the last of the adventurers, the ones who'd come into the game for excitement and challenge back in the days when you could still tell the good guys from the bad guys. Myerson naturally regarded him as a hopeless romantic, incurable sentimentalist, obsolete relic.

And Cutter held Myerson in equal scorn: saw Myerson as a pale slug gone soft where he sat and soft where he did his thinking—clever enough of course but comfortable in his bureaucratic web. Cutter detested comfortable people.

On the surface they were equally cold but Ross knew the difference: Myerson's coldness was genuine and Cutter's was not. The bitterness between them masked a mutual respect neither of them would admit on pain of torture. Myerson was without peer as a strategist and Cutter was equally brilliant as a tactician in the field and Myerson knew that or he wouldn't have kept assigning Joe Cutter to the toughest ones.

And me?

Leonard Ross is just along for the ride to hold everybody's coat.

But Ross didn't mind. He'd never have a better pair of teachers. And despite all Cutter's efforts to keep him at a rigid distance Ross liked him. If you knew you had Cutter at your back you never had to worry about what might be creeping up on you.

Myerson reopened the file. He selected a photograph and held it up on display. "Recognize the woman?"

To Ross it was only a badly focused black-and-white of a thin woman with attractive and vaguely Oriental features, age indeterminate. But Cutter said immediately, "Marie Lapautre."

"Indeed."

Ross leaned forward for a closer look. It was the first time he'd seen a likeness of the dragon lady, whose reputation in the shadow world was something like that of John Wesley Hardin in the days of the gunslingers.

"The signal from Arbuckle reports she's been seen in the lobby of the Kilimanjaro in Dar. Buying a picture postcard," Myerson added drily.

"Could be she's out for a good time," Cutter said. "Spending some of the blood money on travel like any other well-heeled tourist. She's never worked that part of the world, you know."

"Which is precisely why Peking might select her if they had a sensitive job to be done there."

"That's all you've got? Just the one sighting? No confirmation from Arbuckle, no evidence of a caper in progress?"

"Joe, if we wait for evidence it could arrive in a pine box. We'd prefer not to have that sort of confirmation." The cigar had grown a substantial ash and Myerson tapped it into the big glass tray. "The triumvirate in Dar is fairly balanced. The President—Nyerere—is a confirmed neutralist and an honest one. I'm explaining this for your benefit, Ross, since it's not your usual territory. Of Nyerere's two partners in leadership one leans toward the West and the other toward the Communists. The tension keeps things in equilibrium and it's produced good results over a span of years. We have every reason to wish that the status remain quo. That's both the official line and the under-the-counter reality."

Ross was perfectly well aware of all that but Myerson enjoyed exposition and it would have annoyed him to be interrupted by a junior. An annoyed Myerson was something Ross preferred not to have to deal with. Cutter could get away with insulting Myerson because Cutter knew he was not expendable.

"The Chinese are not as charitable as we are toward neutralists," Myerson went on. "Particularly in view of the Russian meddling in Angola. The Chinese have been discussing the idea of increasing their own influence in Africa. I have that confirmed in recent signals from Hong Kong station. Add to this background the presence of Marie Lapautre in Dar-es-Salaam and I believe we must face the likelihood of an explosive event. Possibly you can forecast the nature of it as well as I can?"

It was an obvious challenge and Ross was pleased to see Cutter rise to meet it without effort: "Assuming you're right, I'd guess Lapautre's job would be to assassinate one of the three leaders."

"Which one?"

"The one who leans toward the Communists."

Ross said, "What?"

Cutter said, "The assassination would look like an American plot."

Myerson, his head obscured in a grey cloud, said, "It would take no more than that to tilt the balance over toward the East."

"Deal and double deal," Cutter said under his breath.

Myerson said, "You two are booked on the afternoon flight by way of Zurich. The assignment is to prevent Lapautre from embarrassing us."

"All right." That was the sum of Cutter's response. He asked no questions; he turned toward the door.

Ross said, "Wait one. Why not warn the Tanzanians? Wouldn't that get us off the hook if anything did happen?"

"Hardly," Myerson said. "It would make it worse. Don't explain it to him, Joe—let him reason it out for himself. It should be a useful exercise for him. On your way now—you've hardly time to make your plane."

By the time they were belted into their seats he thought he had it worked out. "If we threw them a warning and then the assassination actually took place later, it would look like we'd done it ourselves and tried to alibi it in advance. Is that what Myerson meant?"

"Go to the head of the class." Cutter fed him the sliver of a smile. "Things are touchy—there's an excess of suspicion of *auslanders* over there—they're xenophobes, you can't tell them things for their own good. Our only option is to neutralize the dragon lady without anyone knowing about it."

"Can we pin down exactly what we mean by that word 'neutralize?'"

"I'll put it this way," Cutter said. "Have you ever killed a woman, Ross?"

"No. Nor a man for that matter."

"Neither have I. And I intend to keep it that way. I've got enough on my conscience."

"Then how can we possibly handle it? We can't just ask her to go away."

"Let's see how things size up first." Cutter tipped his head back against the paper antimacassar and closed his eyes.

It was obvious from Cutter's complacency that he had a scheme in mind. If he hadn't he'd have made more of a show of arrogant confidence.

The flight was interminable. They had to change planes in Zurich and from there it was another nine hours. Ross tried to sleep but he'd never been able to relax on airplanes. He spent the hours trying to predict Cutter's plan. How did you deal with an assassin who had never been known to botch an assignment?

He reviewed what he knew about Marie Lapautre—fact, rumor and legend garnered from various briefings and shop-talk along the corridors in Langley.

French father, Vietnamese mother. Born 1934 on a plantation west of Saigon. Served as a sniper in the Viet Minh forces at Dienbienphu. Ran with the Cong in the late 1960s with assignments ranging from commando infiltration to assassinations of village leaders and then South Vietnamese officials. Seconded to Peking in 1969 for specialized terrorist instruction. Detached from the Viet Cong, inducted into the Chinese Army and assigned to the Seventh Bureau—a rare honor. Seconded as training cadre to the Japanese Red Army. It was rumored Lapautre had planned the tactics for the bombings of Tel Aviv Airport. During the past few years Lapautre's name had come across Ross' desk at least five times in reports dealing with unsolved assassinations in Laos, Syria, Turkey, Libya and West Germany.

Marie Lapautre's weapon was the rifle. Four of the five unsolved assassinations had been effected with long-range fire from Kashkalnikov sniper rifles—the model known to be Lapautre's choice.

Lapautre was forty-two years old, five feet four, one hundred and five pounds, black hair and eyes, mottled burn scar on back of right hand. Spoke five languages including English. Ate red meat barely cooked when the choice was open. She lived between jobs in a 17th century villa on the Italian Riviera—a home she had bought with funds reportedly acquired from hire-contract jobs as a free-lance. Three of the five suspected assassinations had been bounty jobs and the other two had been unpaid because she still held a commission in Peking's Seventh Bureau.

That was the sum of Ross' knowledge and it told him nothing except that Lapautre was a professional with a preference for the 7.62-mm. Kashkalnikov and the reputation for never missing a score. By implication it told him one other thing: if Lapautre became aware of the fact that two Americans were moving in to prevent her from completing her present assignment then she would not hesitate to kill them and she naturally would kill them with proficient dispatch.

He was having trouble keeping his eyes open by the time they checked into the New Africa Hotel. It had been built by the Germans when Tanganyika had been one of the Kaiser's colonies and it had been rebuilt by Africans to encourage business travel; it was comfortable enough and Cutter had picked it because it was within easy walking distance along the harborfront to the Kilimanjaro where Lapautre had been spotted. Also, unlike the Hiltonized Kilimanjaro, the New Africa emulated the middle-class businessmen's hotels of Europe and one didn't need to waste energy trying to look like a tourist.

The change in time zones was bewildering; it was the same time of afternoon in Dar as it had been at Dulles Airport when they'd boarded the 747 but to Ross it was the wee hours of the morning and he stumbled groggily when he went along with Cutter to the shabby export office that housed the front organization for Arbuckle's soporific East Africa station.

It wasn't as steamy as he'd anticipated. A fresh breeze came off the water and he had to concede he'd never seen a more beautiful harbor, ringed by palm-shaded beaches and colorful expensive houses on the slopes. Some of the older buildings bespoke a dusty Mexican sort of poverty but the city was more modern and energetic than anything he'd expected to find near the Equator on the short of the Indian Ocean. There were jams of hooting traffic on the main boulevards; on the sidewalks business-suited pedestrians mingled with turbaned Arabs and dark-eyed Asians and black Africans in proud tribal costumes. Here and there a 4x4 lorry growled by with a squad of armed soldiers in it but they all seemed bound for some innocent destination and there was no police-state tension on the streets. There was a proliferation of cubbyhole curio shops selling African carvings and cloth but the main shop windows were well dressed out with sophisticated displays of European fashions. It occurred to Ross after they reached Arbuckle's office that he hadn't been accosted by a single beggar.

Arbuckle was a tall man, thin and bald and somewhat nervous; inescapably he was known in the Agency as Fatty. He had one item to add to the information Myerson had already provided: Lapautre was still in Dar.

"We've been keeping her under informal surveillance. She's in four-eleven at the Kilimanjaro but she takes most of her dinners in the dining room at the New Africa. They've got better steaks. Watch out you don't bump into her there. She knows your face, I suppose."

"She's probably seen dossiers on me," Cutter said. "I doubt she'd know Ross by sight."

Ross said, "Sometimes it pays to be unimportant."

"Hang onto that thought," Cutter told him. When they left the office he added, "You'd better go back to the room and catch up on your jet-lag."

"What about you?"

"Chores and snooping. Department of dirty tricks and all that. Catch you for breakfast—seven o'clock."

"You going to tell me what the program is?"

He saw Cutter wince. "I see no point discussing anything at all with you until you've had sixteen hours' sleep."

"Don't *you* ever sleep?"

"When I haven't got anything better to do."

Ross watched him walk away under the palms.

He came famished down to the second-floor dining room and found Cutter there nibbling on a mango. The breakfast layout was a fabulous array of fruits and juices and breads and coldcuts. He heaped a plate full and began to devour it unabashedly.

The room wasn't crowded but there was a sprinkling of businessmen from Europe and the Far East, African officials, tourist couples, a table of Englishmen who probably were engineers on hire to Tanzanian industries, a trio of overweight Americans in safari costumes that appeared to have been tailored in Hollywood. Cutter said mildly, "I picked the table at random," by which he meant that it probably wasn't bugged.

Ross said, "Then we're free to discuss sensitive state secrets."

"Do you have to talk in alliterative sibilants at this hour of the morning?" Cutter tasted his coffee and made a face. "You'd think they could make it better. After all, they grow the stuff here." He put the cup down. "All right. We've got to play her cagy and careful. If anything blows loose there won't be any cavalry to rescue us."

"Us?"

"Did you think you were here just to feed me straight lines, Ross? It's a two-man job. Actually it's a six-man job but the two of us have got to carry it."

"Wonderful. Should I start practicing my quick-draw?"

"If you'd stop asking droll questions we'd get along a little faster."

"All right. Proceed, my general."

"First the backgrounding. We're jumping to a number of conclusions based on flimsy evidence but it can't be helped." Cutter ticked them off on his fingers. "We assume, one, that she's here on a job and not just to take pictures of elephants. Two, that it's a Seventh Bureau assignment. Three, that the job is to assassinate somebody. Four, that the target is a government leader here. We don't know the timetable so we have to assume. Five, that it could happen at any moment. Therefore we must act immediately. Are you with me so far?"

"So far, sure."

"We assume, six, that the local Chinese station is unaware of her mission."

"Why do we assume that?"

"Because they're bugging her room."

Ross gawked at him.

Cutter made a show of patience.

"I didn't waste the night sleeping."

"All right, you went through the dragon lady's room, you found a bug. But how do you know it's a Chinese bug?"

"Because I found not one bug but three. One was ours—up-to-date equipment and I checked it out with Arbuckle. Had to get him out of bed, he wasn't happy but he admitted it's our bug. The second was American-made but obsolescent. Presumably the Tanzanian secret service placed it there. We sold a batch of that model to them some years back. The third mike was made in Sinkiang Province, one of those square little numbers they must have shown you in tech briefings back in school. Satisfied?"

"O.K. No Soviet agent worth his vodka would stoop to using a bug of Chinese manufacture, so that leaves the Chinese. So the local Chinese station is bugging her room and that means they don't know why she's here. Go on."

"They're bugging her because she's been known to free-lance. Naturally they're nervous. They want to find out who she's working for and who she's gunning for. Peking hasn't told them because of interservice rivalry and need-to-know and all that nonsense—they're paranoid by definition, the Seventh Bureau never tells anybody anything. They feel a secret has the best chance of remaining a secret only so long as the number of people who know it is kept to a minimum. The thing is, Ross, as far as the local Chinese are concerned she could just as easily be down here on a job for Warsaw or East Berlin or London or Washington or some Arab oil sheik. They just don't know—so they're keeping an eye on her."

"Go on."

"Now the Tanzanians are bugging her as well and they don't bug just any tourist who checks into a first-class hotel. That means they know who she is. They're not sure enough to take action but they're suspicious. So whatever we do we handle it very quietly. We don't make waves that might splash up against the presidential palace. That's another reason we can't have a termination-with-extreme-prejudice on the record of this caper. When we leave here we leave everything exactly as we found it. That's the cardinal rule. Corpses don't figure in the equation—not Lapautre's corpse and certainly not yours or mine."

"I'll vote for that."

"More assumptions. We assume, seven, that Lapautre isn't a hip-shooter. If she were she wouldn't have lasted this long. She's careful, she finds out what the situation is before she steps into it. We can use that caution of hers. And finally—crucially—we assume, eight, that she's not very well versed in surveillance technology."

"We do? How?"

"She's never been an intelligence gatherer. Her experience is in violence. She's a basic sort of creature—a carnivore. I don't see her as a scientific whiz. She uses an old-fashioned sniper rifle because she's comfortable with it—she's not an experimenter. She'd know the rudiments of electronic eavesdropping but when it comes to sophisticated devices I doubt she's got much interest. Apparently she either doesn't know her room is bugged or knows it but doesn't care. Either way it indicates the whole area is outside her field of interest. Likely there are types of equipment she doesn't even know about."

"Types like for instance?"

"Parabolic reflectors. Long-range directionals."

"Those are hardly ultrasophisticated. They date back to World War Two."

"But not in the Indochinese jungles. They wouldn't be a normal part of her experience."

"Does it matter?"

"I'm not briefing you just to listen to the sound of my dulcet voice, Ross. The local Chinese station is equipped with parabolics and directionals."

"Now I begin to get the idea." Ross felt overstuffed. Forewarned by Cutter's reaction he eschewed the coffee and pushed his chair back.

Cutter said, "Good breakfast?"

"Best I ever ate."

"You've got to memorize your lines now and play the part perfectly the first time out. You're well fed and you look spry enough but are you awake?"

"Go ahead. I'm awake," Ross said dismally . . .

According to plan Ross made the phone call at nine in the morning from a coin telephone in the cable office. A clerk answered and Ross asked to be connected to extension four-eleven. It rang three times and was picked up: the woman's voice was low and smoky. *"Oui?"*

"Two hundred thousand dollars, deposited to a Swiss account." That was the opening line because it was unlikely she'd hang up until she found out what it was about. "Are you interested?"

"Is this a crank?"

"Not a crank, Mademoiselle, but clearly one does not mention names or details on an open telephone line. I think we should arrange a meeting. It's an urgent matter."

Beside him Joe Cutter watched without expression. Ross gripped the receiver with a palm gone damp and clammy.

"Are you speaking for yourself, M'sieur?"

"I represent certain principals." Because she wouldn't deal directly with anyone fool enough to act as his own front man. Ross said, "You've been waiting to hear from me, *n'est-ce-pas?*" That was for the benefit of those who were bugging her phone; he went on quickly before she could deny it: "At noon today I'll be on the beach just north of the fishing village at the head of the bay. I'll be wearing a white shirt, short sleeves, khaki trousers and white plimsolls. I'll be alone and of course without weapons." He had to swallow quickly.

The line seemed dead for a while but he resisted the urge to test it. Finally the woman spoke. "Perhaps."

Click.

"Perhaps," he repeated for Cutter's benefit and Cutter shrugged—in any case there was nothing they could do about it now. He would have to be on the beach at noon and hope she showed.

Driving north in the rent-a-car he said to Cutter, "She didn't sound enthusiastic. I doubt she'll come."

"She'll come."

"What makes you so confident?"

"Without phone calls like that she wouldn't be able to maintain her standard of living. She can't afford to turn down an offer of two hundred thousand American. She'll come."

"Armed to the teeth, no doubt," Ross muttered.

"No. She's a pro. A pro never carries a gun when he doesn't have to —a gun can get you in too much trouble if it's discovered. But she's probably capable of dismantling you by hand in any one of a dozen methods so try not to provoke her suspicions until we've sprung the trap."

"You have a way of being incredibly comforting sometimes, you know that?"

"You're green, Ross, and you have a tendency to be flip when you shouldn't be. This isn't a matter for frivolous heroics. You're not without courage and it's silly to pretend otherwise. But it's a mistake to treat this kind of thing with childish bravado. There's a serious risk of ending up in the surf face-down if you don't treat the woman with all the caution in the world. Your job's simple and straightforward and there's nothing funny about it—just keep her interested and steer her to the right place. And remember your lines, for God's sake."

They parked the car on the verge of the road and walked through the palms to the edge of the water. The beach was a narrow white strip of perfect sand curving away in a crescent. At the far end was a scatter of thatched huts and a few sagging docks to which was tethered a small fleet of primitive catamaran fishing boats. It was pleasantly warm and the air was surprisingly clear and dry. Two small black children ran up and down the distant sand laughing; their voices carried weakly to Ross' ears. The half mile of beach between was empty of visible life. A tourist-poster scene, Ross thought, but a feeling of menace put the taste of brass on his tongue.

A few small wretched boats floated at anchor and farther out on the open water a pair of junks drifted south with the mild wind in their square sails. A dazzling white sport fisherman with a flying bridge rode the swells in a lazy figure-eight pattern about four hundred yards offshore; two men in floppy white hats sat in the stern chairs, trolling their lines. A few miles out toward the horizon a tramp prowled northward, following the coast, steaming from port to port—Tanga next, then Mombasa, and so forth. And there was a faint spiral of smoke even farther out—probably the Zanzibar ferry.

Cutter put his back to the ocean and spoke in a voice calculated to reach no farther than Ross' ears. "Spot them?"

Ross was searching the beach, running his glance along the belt of palms that shaded the sand. "Not a soul. Maybe they didn't get the hint."

"The sport fisherman, Ross. Use your head. They've got telescopes and long-range microphones focused on this beach right now and if I were facing them they'd hear every word I'm saying."

That was why they'd given it three hours lead-time after making the phone call. To give the Chinese time to get in position to monitor the meet. In a way Ross felt relieved; at least they'd taken the bait. It remained to be seen whether the dragon lady would prove equally gullible.

He turned to say something to Cutter but found he was alone at the edge of the trees: Cutter had disappeared without a sound. Discomfited, Ross began to walk along the beach toward the village, kicking sand with his toes. He put his hands in his pockets and then thought better of that and took them out again so that it was obvious they were empty. He twisted his wrist to look at his watch and found it was eleven fifty-five. He walked to the middle of the crescent of sand and stood there looking inland, trying to ignore the fishing boat a quarter of a mile behind him, trying to talk himself out of the acute feeling that a rifle's telescopic crosshairs were centered between his shoulderblades. He discovered that his back muscles had gone tense against an awaited bullet.

He started walking around in an aimless little circle, spurred by the vague theory that they'd have a harder time hitting a moving target. He realized how ridiculous it was: they had no reason to take potshots at him—they'd be curious, not murderous—but he was no longer in a state of mind where logic was the ruling factor.

He heard the putt-putt of an engine and turned with casual curiosity and watched a little outboard come in sight around the headland and beat its way forward, its bow slapping the water. Then he looked away, looked back up into the palm trees wondering when the woman would show up. He did a slow take and turned on his heel again and watched the outboard come straight toward him.

It was the dragon lady and she was alone at the tiller. She ran the boat up onto the beach, tipped the engine up across the transom, jumped overside and came nimbly ashore. She dragged the boat forward and then turned to look at Ross across the intervening fifty yards of sand. He tried to meet her stare without cringing. Her eyes left him and began to explore the trees and she made a thorough job of it before she stirred, coming toward him with lithe graceful strides.

She was not a big woman but there was nothing fragile or petite about the way she held herself. The unlined face was harder than the photograph had suggested; it was something in the eyes, as if her pupils were chipped out of brittle obsidian stone. She wore an *ao dai*, the simple form-fitting dress of Indochina; it was painted to her skin and there was no possibility she could have concealed any sort of weapon under it. Perhaps she wore it for that reason.

Ross didn't move; he let her come to him. It was in his instructions. "Well then, M'sieur."

"The money," he began, and then he stopped, tongue-tied.

He'd forgotten his lines.

The obsidian eyes drilled into him. *"Oui?"*

In the corner of his vision he saw the white sport boat bobbing on a swell. Somehow it galvanized him. He cleared his throat. "The money's already on deposit and we have the receipt. If you do the job you'll be given both the receipt and the number of the account. Two hundred thousand in American dollars. That works out to something over half a million Swiss francs at the current rate."

Her lip curled a bit—an exquisitely subtle expression. "I would need a bit more information than that, M'sieur."

"The name of the target, of course. The deadline date by which the assignment must be completed. More than that you don't get." He kept his face straight and feverishly rehearsed the rest of his lines.

"But of course there is one item you've left out," she said.

"I don't think there is, Mlle. Lapautre."

"I must know the nature of my employers."

"Not included in the price of your ticket, I'm afraid."

"Then we have wasted our morning, both of us."

"For two hundred thousand dollars we expected a higher class of discretion than you seemed inclined to exercise." It was a line Cutter had drilled into him and it went against his usual mode of expression but Cutter had insisted on the precise wording. And it was amazing the way she responded: as if Cutter had somehow written her dialogue as well as Ross'. His predictions had been uncanny.

She said, "Discretion costs a little more, M'sieur, especially if it concerns those whom I might regard as my natural enemies."

"Capitalists, you mean."

"You *are* American?"

"I am," Ross said. "That's not to say my principals are Americans." *The thing is, Ross, you want to keep her talking, you don't want to close the door and send her skittering away. And at the same time you don't want to get her mad at you. String her along, get her curiosity whetted. She'll insist on having more information. Stretch it out. Stall her. Edge her away. Don't give her the name of the target until she's in position.*

Casually he put his hands in his pockets and turned away from her and strolled very slowly toward the palms. He didn't look back to see if she was following him. He spoke in a normal tone so that she'd have trouble hearing him if she let him get too far ahead of her. "My principals are willing to discuss the matter more directly with you if you agree to take the job on. Not a face-to-face meeting of course, none of us could afford that. But they'll speak to you on safe lines. Coin telephones at both ends—I'm sure you know the drill, you're not an amateur." The words tasted sour on his tongue: if anyone in this game was an amateur it was himself.

But it was working. She was trailing along, moving as casually as he was. He threw his head back and stared at the sky. "The target isn't a difficult one. The security measures aren't severe."

"But he's an important one. A visible figure. Otherwise the price would not be so high," she said. It was something Cutter hadn't forecast and Ross wasn't quite sure how to answer it.

So he made no reply at all. He kept drifting toward the palms, moving in aimless half circles. After a moment he said, "Of course you weren't followed here?" It was in the script.

"Why do you think I chose to come by open boat, M'sieur? No one followed me. Can you say the same?"

Position.

He turned and watched her move alongside. She had, as Cutter had predicted, followed his lead. It was Indochinese courtesy, inbred and unconscious—the residue of a servile upbringing.

She stood beside him now a few feet to his right; like Ross she was facing the palm trees.

Ross dropped his voice and spoke without turning his head; there was no possibility the microphones would hear him. "Don't speak for a moment now. Look slightly to your right—the palm tree with the thick bole."

He stepped back a pace as he spoke. He watched her head turn slowly. Saw her stiffen when she spotted Cutter, indistinct in the shadows. Cutter stirred then and it was enough to make the sun ripple along the barrel of his rifle.

In the same guarded low voice Ross said, "It's a Mannlicher bolt action with high-speed ammunition. Hollowpoint bullets and a 'scope sight calibrated to anything up to eight hundred yards. You wouldn't stand a chance if you tried to run for it." He kept stepping back because he didn't want her close enough to him to jump him and use him for a shield. Yet he had to stay within voice range of her because if he lifted his tone or turned his head more than a quarter-inch the finely focused directional mike on the sport fisherman would pick up his words immediately.

He saw her shoulders drop half an inch and felt the beginnings of a swell of triumph. *If she doesn't break for it in the first five seconds she won't break at all. She's a pro, Ross, remember that. A pro doesn't fight the drop. Not when it's dead clear to her what the situation is.*

"You're in a box, Mlle. Lapautre, and you've only got one way to get out of it alive. Are you listening to me?"

"Certainly."

"Don't try to figure everything out because it would take you too long and there are parts of it you'll never know. We're playing out a charade, that's all you need to keep in mind. If you play your part as required, nobody gets hurt."

"What is it you want, then?"

Her cool aplomb amazed him even though Cutter had told him to expect it. Again: *She's a pro.* She had sized up the situation and that was that.

Cutter was motionless in the shadows, too far away for Lapautre to recognize his features; because of the angle he was hidden from the view of those on board the sport fisherman. All they'd be able to tell was that Ross and Marie Lapautre were having a conversation in tones too low for their eavesdropping equipment to record. They'd be frustrated and angry but there wouldn't be anything they could do about it. They'd hang on station hoping to pick up scraps of words that they could later edit together and make some sense out of.

Ross answered her, *sotto voce.* "I want you to obey my instructions. In a moment I'm going to step around in front of you and face you. The man in the trees will keep his rifle aimed at you at all times. If you make any sudden move he'll kill you. But he's too far away to hear us unless we speak up. I'm going to start talking to you in a loud voice. The things I say may not make much sense to you. I don't care what you say by way of response. But whatever it is I want you to say it very softly so that nobody hears your answers. And I want you to look as if you're agreeing with whatever proposition I make to you. Understand?"

"No," she said, "I do not understand but I'll do as you wish."

"That's good enough. Take it easy now."

Then he stepped off to the left and made a careful circle around her, keeping his distance, looking as casual as he knew how. He stopped when he was facing her from her port bow: off to the right he could see the sport fisherman and if he turned his head to the left he could see Cutter. She would have to cross fifteen feet of sand to interpose Ross between herself and the rifle and she knew there wouldn't be time for that. She didn't speak: she only watched Ross.

He cleared his throat and spoke as if in continuation of a conversation already begun. He enunciated the words clearly, mindful of the shotgun microphone that was focused on his lips from four hundred yards offshore.

"Then we've got a deal. I'm glad you agreed to take it on—you're the best in the business, I think everyone knows that."

Her lip curled again, ever so slightly; she murmured in confounding amusement, "And just what is it I'm supposed to have agreed to, M'sieur?"

Ross nodded vigorously. "Exactly. When you talk to my principals you'll realize immediately that their accents are Russian—Ukrainian to be precise—but I hope that won't deter you from putting your best effort into the assignment."

"This is absurd." But she kept her voice down when she said it.

"That's right," Ross said cheerfully. "There will be no official Soviet record of the transaction. If they're confronted with any accusation, naturally they'll deny it and the world will have only your word to the contrary. I needn't remind you what your word would be worth on the open market—a woman of your reputation? So you can see that it's in your own best interests to keep absolutely silent about the matter."

"This is pointless. Who can possibly benefit from this ridiculous performance?"

"I think they'll find that acceptable," Ross said. "Now then, to get down to the matter at hand."

He saw her eyes flick briefly toward the palms. He didn't look over his shoulder; he knew Cutter was still there. He went on in his overconfident voice:

"The target must be taken out within the next twelve days because that's the deadline for a particular international maneuver the details of which needn't concern you. The target is here in Dar-es-Salaam, so you should have plenty of time to set up the assassination. Do you recognize the name Chiang Hsien?"

She laughed then. She actually laughed. "Incredible."

He forced himself to smile. "Yes. The chief of the China station in Dar. Now there's just one more detail."

"Is that all? Thank goodness for that."

Ross nodded pleasantly. "Yes, that's right. You must make it appear that the assassination is the work of Americans. I'd suggest, for example, that you use an American rifle. I leave the other details in your hands, but the circumstantial evidence must be crystal clear that the assassination was the result of an American plot against the Chinese people's representative in East Africa."

The woman rolled her eyes expressively. "Is that all?"

Ross smiled again. "If you still want confirmation I'll arrange for the telephone contact between you and my principals. In the meantime the receipt and the account number on the Swiss bank will be delivered to your hotel. As soon as we receive confirmation of the death of Chiang Hsien, we'll issue instructions to the bank to transfer ownership of the numbered account and honor your applications for withdrawals. I think that covers everything. It's been pleasant doing business with you, Mlle. Lapautre." With a courtly bow Ross turned briskly on his heel and marched away toward the trees without looking back.

He entered the palms about forty feet to Cutter's right and kept going until he was certain he was out of sight of the lenses on the sport fishing boat. Then he curled behind a tree and had his look around.

Cutter was still there, holding the rifle and looking menacing; Cutter winked at him.

The woman was walking back down the beach toward her open boat. The junks had disappeared past the point of land to the south; the catamarans were still tied up on the water by the village; the coastal steamer was plowing north, the ferryboat's smoke had disappeared, the sport fisherman was still figure-eighting on the water but now the two white-hatted men in the stern were packing up their rods and getting out of their swivel chairs.

Ross stood without moving for a stretching interval while the dragon lady pushed her boat out into the surf, climbed over the gunwale, made her way aft and hooked the outboard engine over the transom. She yanked the cord several times until it sputtered into life and then she went chugging out in a wide circle toward the open water, angling to starboard to clear the headland at the end of the bay.

When she'd gone a couple of hundred yards Cutter came through the trees slinging his rifle. "Beautiful job, Ross. You didn't miff a line."

"What happens now?"

"Watch."

The sport fisherman was moving now, its engines whining, planing the water—collision course. Near the headland it intercepted Marie Lapautre's little boat. She tried to turn away but the big white boat leaped ahead of her and skidded athwart her course.

"That skipper knows how to handle her," Cutter commented.

With no choice in the matter the woman allowed her boat to be drawn alongside by a long-armed man with a boathook. One of the white-hatted men came along the deck and gave Marie Lapautre a hand aboard.

The last Ross saw of them the two boats, one towing the other, were disappearing around the headland.

Cutter walked him back to the car. "They'll milk her, of course. But they won't believe a word of it. They've got the evidence on tape—how can she deny it? They wouldn't buy the truth in a thousand years and it's all she's got to offer."

"I feel queasy as hell, Joe. You know what they're going to do to her after they squeeze her dry."

"It'll happen a long way from here and nobody will ever know about it."

"And that makes it right?"

"No. It adds another load to what we've already got on our consciences. You may survive this but if she does she'll never get another job. They'll never trust her again."

They got into the car. Cutter tossed the rifle in the back seat; they'd drop it off at Arbuckle's office to go back into the safe.

Ross said, "It hasn't solved a thing." He gave Cutter a petulant look. "They'll send somebody to take her place. Next week or next month."

"Maybe yes, maybe no. If they do we'll have to deal with it when it happens. You may as well get used to it, Ross. You play one game, you finish it, you add up the score and then you start the next game. That's all there is to it—and that's the fun of it."

Ross stared at him. "I guess it is," he said reluctantly.

He turned the key. Cutter smiled briefly. The starter meshed and Ross put it in gear. He said with sudden savagery, "But it's not all that much fun for the loser, is it?" And fishtailed the car angrily out into the road.

A Cabin in the Woods

by John Coyne

Michael remembered clearly the first piece of fungus: a thin, irregular patch twelve inches wide, greyish, like the color of candle grease, growing on the new pine wall of the bathroom. He reached up gingerly to touch it. The crust was lumpy and the edges serrated. He pulled the resinous flesh from the wood, like removing a scab, tossed the fungus into the waste can and finished shaving.

He had come up from the city late the night before, driving the last few hours through the mountain roads in heavy fog and rain and arriving at his new cabin in the woods after midnight. It was his first trip to the lake that spring.

Michael had come early in the week to work, bringing with him the galleys of his latest novel. He needed to spend several more days making corrections. It was the only task of writing that he really enjoyed, the final step when the book was still part of him. Once it appeared between covers, it belonged to others.

He was in no hurry to read the galleys. That could be done at leisure over the next few days. Barbara wasn't arriving until Friday and their guests weren't due until Saturday morning. It was a weekend they had planned for several months to celebrate the completion of the new house.

So while shaving that first morning at the cabin, Michael found himself relaxed and smiling. He was pleased about the house. It was bigger and more attractive than even the blueprints had suggested.

It had been designed by a young architect from the nearby village. Local carpenters had built it, using lumber cut from the pine and oak and walnut woods behind the lake. They had left the lumber rough hewed and unfinished.

The cabin was built into the side of the mountain, with a spectacular view of the lake. Only a few trees had been cut to accommodate the construction; so from a distance, and through the trees, the building looked like a large boulder that had been unearthed and tumbled into the sun to dry.

"I want the ambience *rustic*," Barbara explained to the architect. "A sense of the *wilderness*." She whispered the words, as if to suggest the mysterious.

"Don't make it too austere," Michael instructed. "I don't want the feeling we're camping out. This is a cabin we want to escape to from the city; we want some conveniences. I want a place that can sleep eight or ten if need be." He paced the small office of the architect as he listed his requirements, banging his new boots on the wooden floor. Michael liked the authoritative sound, the suggestion to this kid that here was someone who knew what he wanted out of life.

"And cozy!" Barbara leaned forward to catch the architect's attention. She had a round pretty face with saucer-sized blue eyes. She flirted with the young man to make her point. "And a stone fireplace the length of one wall. We may want to come up here with our friends during skiing season." She beamed.

The architect looked from one to the other and said nothing.

"He's not one of your great talkers, is he?" Barbara remarked as they left the village.

"That's the way of these mountain people. They come cheap and they give you a full day's work. It's O.K. with me. I'd rather deal with locals than someone from the city."

Still, the cabin cost $10,000 more than Michael had expected. The price of supplies, he was told, had tripled. However, they had land-scaped the lawn to the lake and put in a gravel drive to the county road. Michael said he wanted only to turn the key and find the place livable. "I'm no handyman," he had told the architect.

While the second home in the mountains was costly, Michael was no longer worried about money. When he had finished the new novel and submitted it to the publisher it was picked up immediately with an advance of $50,000, more than he had made on any of his other books. The next week it had sold to the movies for $200,000, and a percentage of the gross. Then just before driving to the mountains, his agent telephoned with the news that the paperback rights had gone for half a million.

"Everything I touch is turning to gold," Michael bragged to Barbara. "I told you I'd make it big."

What he did not tell Barbara was that this was his worst book, written only to make money. He had used all the clichés of plot and situation and it had paid off.

He finished dressing and made plans for the day. The station wagon was still packed with bags of groceries. The night before he had been too tired after the drive to do more than build a fire and pour himself a drink. Then, carrying his drink, he had toured through the empty rooms—his boots echoing on the oak floors—and admired the craftsmanship of the mountain carpenters. The cabin was sturdy and well built; the joints fit together like giant Lincoln logs.

The three bedrooms of the house were upstairs in the back and they were connected by an open walk that overlooked the livingroom, which was the height and width of the front of the cabin. The facade was nearly all windows, long panels that reached the roof.

One full wall was Barbara's stone fireplace, made from boulders quarried in the mountains and trucked to the lake site. The foundation was made from the same rocks. As Barbara bragged to friends with newly acquired chauvinism, "All that's not from the mountains are the kitchen appliances and ourselves."

Michael moved the station wagon behind the house and unpacked the groceries, carrying the bundles in through the back door and stacking the bags on the butcher-block table. He filled the refrigerator first with perishables and the several bottles of white wine he planned to have evenings with his meals. His own special present to himself at the success of the book.

Packing the refrigerator gave Michael a sense of belonging. With that simple chore, he had taken possession of the place and the cabin felt like home.

He had thought of leaving the staples until Barbara arrived—she would have her own notion of where everything should go—but after the satisfaction of filling the refrigerator, Michael decided to put the staples away, beginning with the liquor.

He carried the box into the livingroom and knelt down behind the bar and opened the cabinet doors. Inside, growing along the two empty plain wooden shelves, was grey fungus. It grew thick, covering the whole interior of the cabinet, and the discovery frightened Michael, like finding an abnormality.

"My God!" A shiver ran along his spine.

He filled several of the empty grocery bags with the fungus. It pulled easily off the shelves and was removed in minutes. Then he scrubbed the hard pine boards with soap and water and put away the bottles of liquor.

It was the dampness of the house, he guessed, that had caused the growth. The house had stood empty and without heat since it had been finished. He knew fungus grew rapidly in damp weather, but still the spread of the candle-grey patch was alarming.

He returned to the kitchen and apprehensively opened the knotty pine cupboards over the counter. The insides were clean, with the smell about them of sawdust. He ran his hand across the shelves and picked up shavings. Michael closed the door and sighed.

Barbara had given him a list of chores to do in the house before the weekend. The beds in the guest rooms should be made, the windows needed washing, and the whole house, from top to bottom, had to be swept. Also, the livingroom rug had arrived and was rolled up in the corner. It had to be put down and vacuumed.

First, however, Michael decided to have breakfast. On Sundays in the city he always made breakfast, grand ones of Eggs Doremus, crepes, or Swedish pancakes with lingonberry. Lately Barbara had begun to invite friends over for brunch. His cooking had become well known among their friends and his editor had suggested that he might write a cookbook about Sunday breakfasts.

Michael unpacked the skillet, and turning on the front burner melted a slice of butter into the pan. He took a bottle of white wine, one of the inexpensive California Chablis, uncorked it, and added a half cup to the skillet. The butter and wine sizzled over the flame and the rich smell made Michael hungry.

He broke two eggs into the skillet, seasoned them with salt and pepper, and then searched the shopping bags for cayenne, but Barbara hadn't packed the spices. He could do without but made a mental note to pick up cayenne and more spices when he drove to the village later that morning.

Michael moved easily around the kitchen, enjoying the space to maneuver. In their apartment in the city, only one of them could cook at a time. Here, they had put in two stoves and two sinks, and enough counter space for both to work at once.

Michael glanced at the eggs. The whites were nearly firm. He took the toaster and plugged it in, noticing with satisfaction that the electrical outlets worked. That was one less problem to worry about. He dropped two pieces of bread into the toaster and then, going back to the bar, took the vodka, opened a can of tomato juice, and made himself a Bloody Mary.

He was working quickly now, sure of the kitchen. He cut the flame under the skillet, crumbled Roquefort cheese and sprinkled it on the eggs; then he buttered the toast and unpacked a dish and silverware. He smiled, pleased. He was going to enjoy cooking in this kitchen.

Perhaps, he thought, he should move full time to the mountains. He could write more, he knew, if he lived by the lake, away from interruptions and distractions. He fantasized a moment. He could see himself going down on cool, misty mornings to the lake. He could smell the pine trees and the water as he crossed the flat lake to bass fish before sunup. He could see the boat gracefully arching through the calm water as behind it a small wave rippled to the shore. He sipped the Bloody Mary and let the pleasant thought relax him.

Then he remembered the eggs and he slipped them from the skillet onto the buttered toast, and carrying the plate and his drink walked out onto the oak deck. The deck was a dozen feet wide and built along the length of the east wall to catch the early morning sun. It was Barbara's idea that they could have breakfast on the deck.

The sun had cleared the mountains and touched the house. It had dried the puddles of rain water and warmed the deck so Michael was comfortable in shirt sleeves.

They had not yet purchased deck furniture, so he perched himself on the wide banister and finished the eggs. He could see the length of the front lawn from where he sat. It sloped gracefully down to the shore and the new pier.

The pier he had built himself during the winter. One weekend he had come up to the village, bought 300 feet of lumber, hired two men from a construction firm, and driven out to the lake in four-wheel-drive jeeps. Along the shore of the lake they found twelve sassafras trees that they cut and trimmed and pulled across the ice to Michael's property. They chopped holes in the thick ice and sledgehammered the poles into place to make the foundation. Then they cut two-by-eights into four-foot lengths and nailed them between the poles to make the pier.

Michael's hands blistered and his back ached for a week, but he was proud of his hard labor, and proud, too, of the pier which went forty feet into the water and could easily handle his two boats.

At first he could not see the pier because a late morning mist clung to the shore. It rolled against the bank like a range of low clouds. But as he sat finishing his eggs and drink, the rising sun burned away the mist and the thin slice of pier jutting into the mountain lake came slowly into view like a strange gothic phenomenon.

"What the . . ."

Michael stood abruptly and the dish and his drink tumbled off the railing. He peered down, confused. The whole length of the pier was covered with grey fungus. He looked around for more fungus, expecting to see it everywhere. He scanned the landscaped lawn, the pine trees which grew thick to the edge of his property. He spun about and ran the length of the oak deck, leaned over the railing and searched the high rear wall of the cabin. He glanced at the trash heap of construction materials left by the builders. No sign of more mold.

Next he ran into the house and taking the steps two at a time raced to the second floor. He turned into the bathroom and flipped on the light. No fungus grew on the pine wall. He turned immediately and ran downstairs, boots stomping on the wooden stairs, and opened the cabinet doors below the bar. The bottles of liquor were stacked as he had arranged them.

Michael calmed down, gained control. He kept walking, however, through the house, opening closet doors, checking cabinets. He went again to the kitchen and looked through all the cupboards. He opened the basement door and peered into the dark downstairs. The basement had been left unfinished, a damp cellar. Still no fungus.

When he was satisfied there was no fungus in the house, he left the cabin and walked across the lawn to the tool shed and found a shovel. He began where the pier touched the shore, scraping away the fungus and dumping the growth into the water, where it plopped and floated away. He shoveled quickly. The flat tenacious flesh of the fungus ripped easily off the wood. It was oddly exhilarating work. In a matter of minutes he had cleaned the length of the pier.

He stuck the shovel into the turf and went again to the house where he found a mop and bucket, poured detergent into the bucket, filled it with hot water, and returned to the pier to mop the planks. The pier sparkled in the morning sun.

Then Michael locked the cabin, backed the station wagon out of the drive, and drove into the village.

The village was only a few streets where the interstate crossed the mountains. It had grown up on both sides of a white river, and adjacent to railroad tracks. The tracks were now defunct and the river polluted. The few buildings were weather weary and old. The only new construction was the service station at the interstate, and a few drive-ins. When Barbara first saw the town, she wouldn't let him stop.

But the hills and valleys beyond the place were spectacular and unspoiled and when they found five acres of woods overlooking the lake they decided that in spite of the town, they'd buy.

"I looked down at the pier and the whole goddamn thing was covered with fungus. It's a grey color, like someone's puke." Michael paced the architect's office. He had already told the young man about the fungus in the bathroom and beneath the bar. And without saying so, implied it was the architect's fault.

"I'm not a biologist." The young man spoke carefully. He was unnerved by Michael. The man had barged into his office shouting about fungus. It had taken him several minutes to comprehend what the problem was.

"You're from these hills. You grew up here, right? You should know about fungus. What's all this mountain folklore we keep hearing about?" Michael quit pacing and sat down across from the architect. He was suddenly tired. The anxiety and anger over the fungus had worn him out. "That's a new house out there. I sunk $50,000 into it and you can't tell me why there's fungus growing on the bathroom walls? Goddammit! What kind of wood did you use?"

"The lumber was green, true, but I told you we'd have problems. It was your idea to build the place with pine off your land. Well, pine needs time to dry. Still . . ." The architect shook his head. The growth of fungus confused him. He had never heard of such a thing. But the man might be exaggerating. He glanced at Michael.

Michael was short and plump with a round, soft face, and brown eyes that kept widening with alarm. He wore new Levi pants and jacket, and cowboy boots that gave him an extra inch of height. Around his neck he had fastened a blue bandanna into an ascot. He looked, the architect thought, slightly ridiculous.

"Who knows about this fungus?" Michael asked. He had taken out another blue bandanna to wipe the sweat off his face. In his exasperated state, the sweat poured.

"I guess someone at the college . . ."

"And you don't think it's any of your concern? You stuck me for $10,000 over the original estimate and now that you've got your money, you don't give a damn."

"I told you before we started construction that we'd get hit by inflation. We could have held the costs close to that first estimate if your wife hadn't wanted all the custom cabinets, those wardrobes, and items like bathroom fixtures from Italy . . ."

Michael waved away the architect's explanation. He was mad at the kid for not solving the problem of the fungus. "Where's this college?" he asked.

"Brailey. It's across the mountain."

"How many miles?" Michael stood. He had his car keys out and was spinning them impatiently.

"Maybe thirty, but these are mountain roads. It will take an hour's drive. Why not telephone? You're welcome to use my phone." He pushed the telephone across the desk.

Michael fidgeted with his keys. He didn't want to let the architect do him any favors, but he also didn't want to spend the morning driving through the mountains.

"O.K. You might be right." He sat down again and, picking up the receiver, dialed information.

It took him several calls and the help of the college switchboard operator before he reached a Doctor Clyde Bessey, an associate professor at the state university. Dr. Bessey had a thin, raspy voice, as if someone had a hand to his throat. He said he was a mycologist in the Department of Plant Pathology.

"Do you know anything about fungus?" Michael asked.

"Why, yes." The doctor spoke carefully, as if his words were under examination. "Mycology is the study of fungi."

"Then you're the person I want," Michael replied quickly. Then, without asking if the man had time, he described the events of the morning.

"*Peniophora gigantea*," Doctor Bessey replied.

"What?"

"The species of fungi you've described sounds like *Peniophora gigantea*. It's more commonly called resin fungus. A rather dull-colored species that spreads out like a crust on the wood. You say the edges are serrated?"

"And it's lumpy . . ."

"Rightly so! *Peniophora gigantea*. Sometimes laymen mistake this species of crust fungi for a resinous secretion of the conifer."

"Does it grow like that? That fast?"

"No, what you've described is odd." He sounded thoughtful. "Fungi won't grow that extensively, unless, of course, a house has been abandoned. And certainly not that fast. We did have a damp winter and spring, still . . . you said the cabin was built with green lumber?"

"Yes, I'm afraid so." Michael glanced at the architect.

"Still . . ."

"Well, how in the hell do I stop it?" Michael was sharp, because the laborious manner of the professor was irritating.

"I don't know exactly what to tell you. Your situation sounds a bit unusual. Fungi doesn't grow as rapidly as you've described. In laboratory conditions, we've had fungus cover the surface of a three-inch-wide culture dish in two days. But that's ideal conditions. Without competition from other fungi or bacteria. But, generally speaking, fungi does thrive better than any other organism on earth." He said that with a flourish of pride.

"Doctor, I'm sure this is all just wonderful, but it doesn't help me, you see. I'm infested with the crap!"

"Yes, of course . . . If you don't mind, I'd like to drive over and take some cultures. I'll be able to tell more once I've had the opportunity to study some samples."

"You can have all you want."

"You've cleaned up the fungi, I presume . . ."

"With soap and water."

"Well, that should destroy any mycelium, but then we never can be sure. One germinating spore and the process begins again. Rather amazing, actually."

"Let's hope you're wrong. It's a $50,000 house."

"Oh, I'm sure there's no permanent problem, just a biological phenomenon. Fungi are harmless, really, when they're kept in control. Your home will suffer no lasting effects." He sounded confident.

"Maybe you're right." Michael was cautious. Still, Doctor Bessey had eased his mind. Michael hung up feeling better.

"Do you mind if I make another call?" he asked the architect. "Our phone hasn't been installed at the cabin . . ." The young man gestured for Michael to go ahead. Actually, he wasn't that bad, Michael thought, dialing Barbara in the city.

"I'm sure it's nothing serious," Barbara said when Michael told her about the fungus. "The wet weather and all . . ." Her mind was elsewhere, planning for the weekend. "Did you have time to make the beds?"

"The whole pier was covered, like a tropical jungle. *Peniophora gigantea* . . . that's what the mycologist called it."

"The who?"

"Dr. Bessey. He studies fungi."

"Well, if it's that well known, then it can't be any problem . . . Have you had a chance to wash the windows? Perhaps I should come up earlier . . ."

"Don't worry about getting the cabin clean. I'll do that!" Michael snapped at her. He was upset that she hadn't responded. Barbara had a frustrating habit of not caring about a household problem unless it affected her directly. "I'll clean the windows, make the beds, and sweep the goddamn floors once I get rid of this fungus!"

"And the rugs . . ."

"And the rugs!"

"Michael dear, there's no need to be upset with me. I have nothing to do with your fungus."

"Yes, dear, but you wanted the place built from our lumber, our *green* lumber."

"And you said it would make the place look more authentic."

"The lumber's green!"

"I don't see where that's my fault!"

"It might mean that we'll have to live with this goddamn fungus!" Michael knew he was being unreasonable, but he couldn't stop himself. He was mad at her for not taking the fungus seriously.

"I'm sure you'll think of something," Barbara pampered him and then dismissed the whole issue. "You'll remember the windows . . . ?" She sounded like a recording.

Before leaving the village, Michael went to the general store and shopped for the week. He did not want to leave the lake again for errands. He bought Windex, the spices Barbara had forgotten, a new mop, a second broom. He bought two five-gallon cans of gas for the boats and more fishing tackle. He bought a box of lures; good, he was told by the store owner, for mountain lakes. He picked up a minnow box, a fish net and a filet knife. He would need them if he planned to do any serious fishing.

But he understood himself enough to realize also that this impulse buying was only a compensation for the upsetting morning. Now that he had the money, he spent it quickly, filling the station wagon like a sled with toys. And driving back to the cabin, his good mood returned.

He would not clean the cabin that morning, he decided, nor would he make the beds. Instead, he'd take out the flat-bottom boat and fish for bass in the small lagoon of the lake. And he'd pan fry the catch that evening for dinner. He'd just have the fish and some fresh vegetables, asparagus or sliced cucumbers, and a bottle of the Pinot Noir.

Michael pictured himself on the deck frying the bass. The cloud of smoke from the coals drifting off into the trees, the late sun catching the glass of wine, the pale yellow color like tarnished gold. He'd cover the fish a moment, stop to sip the wine, and look out over the lake as the trees darkened on the other shore, and a mist formed. He'd get a thick ski sweater and put it on. When the darkness spread up the lawn to the house, he'd be the last object visible, moving on the deck like a lingering shadow.

Michael turned the station wagon off the county road and onto his drive and the crunch of gravel under the wheels snapped him from his daydream. He touched the accelerator and the big car spun over the loose stones. On that side of the property the trees grew thick and close and kept the house from view until Michael had swung the car into the parking space and stopped. Then he saw the fungus, a wide spread growing across the rock foundation like prehistoric ivy.

He ran from the car to the wall and grabbed the fungus. The mold tore away in large chunks. With both hands, frantically, he kept ripping away. Now it was wet and clammy, like the soft underbelly of fish.

Michael left the fungus on the ground, left his new fishing tackle and other supplies in the car, and ran into the house. He pulled open the cabinet doors. The grey growth had spread again across the two shelves. It covered the liquor, grew thick among the bottles like cob-webs.

In the bathroom upstairs the patch of mold was the width of the wall. It stretched from floor to ceiling and had crept around the mirror, grown into the wash bowl, and smothered the toilet. He reached out and pulled a dozen inches away in his fingers. The waxy flesh of the fungus clung to his hand. Michael fell back exhausted against the bathroom door and wiped the sweat off his face with his sleeve.

It was hot in the cabin. Michael took off his jacket and pulled off the blue bandanna ascot, then he started on the bathroom fungus. He filled five paper bags with fungus and dumped them into the trash heap behind the house. He went to the bar and removed the liquor and scraped the shelves clean again. He took the fungus to the trash pile and going back to the car got one of the cans of gas, poured it on the fungus, and started a blaze.

The wet fungus produced a heavy fog and a nasty odor, like the burning of manure. Michael watched it burn with pleasure, but when he returned to the kitchen to put away the supplies, he found that the fungus had spread, was growing extensively in all the cupboards and beneath the sink. It even lined the insides of the oven and grew up the back of the refrigerator.

Michael needed to stand on a kitchen chair to reach the fungus that grew at the rear of the cupboards, but he had learned now how to rip the mold away in large pieces, like pulling off old, wet wallpaper. Still, it took him longer; the fungus was more extensive and nestled in all the corners of the custom-made cupboards.

He went outside and found the wheelbarrow and carted away the fungus, dumping it into the fire behind the house. The grey smoke billowed into the trees. The mountain air stank. He swept the kitchen clean and washed the cupboards, the bathroom, and the cabinets beneath the bar. It was late afternoon when he had the house finally in order and he went upstairs and flopped into bed, feeling as if he hadn't slept in weeks.

He woke after seven o'clock. It was still daylight, but the sun was low in the sky and the bedroom was shaded by trees and dark.

He had been deeply asleep and came awake slowly so it was several minutes before he remembered where he was and what had happened. When he did remember, he realized at the same time that the fungus would have returned, that it was growing again in the bathroom, beneath the bar, and in all the cupboards of the kitchen.

But he did not know that now the fungus had spread further and was growing along the green pine walls of the bedroom, had spread over the bare oak floors, and even started down the stairs, like an organic carpet. Michael sat up and swung his bare feet off the bed and onto the floor. His feet touched the lumpy wet fungus. It was as if he had been swimming in the lake and had tried to stand on the mucky bottom. His toes dug into the slime.

He shoveled the fungus off the floor and threw it out the bedroom window. The shovel tore into the rough hewed floor, caught between the planks, and he had ruined the floor when he was done. He took a rake from the shed and used it to pull the fungus off the walls. He cleaned the bathroom again and shoveled the fungus off the stairs. Repeatedly, he filled the wheelbarrow and dumped it outside. The fire burned steadily.

It took Michael three hours to clean the cabin and only when he was done, resting in the kitchen, sitting at the butcher-block table and drinking a bottle of beer, did he first see the fungus seeping under the cellar door. It grew rapidly before his eyes, twisting and turning, slipping across the tile floor like a snake. Michael grabbed the shovel and cut through the fungus at the door. The dismembered end continued across the tile with a life of its own.

He jerked open the cellar door to beat back the growth, but the grey fungus had filled the cellar, was jammed against the door, and when he opened the door it smothered him in an avalanche of mold.

Now it was everywhere. The cupboards burst open and the fungus flopped out and onto the counter. A tide of it pushed aside the food and shoved cans to the floor.

In the livingroom it grew along the rock fireplace and tumbled down the stairs. It spread across the floor, came up between the cracks in the oak floors. It grew around the tables and chairs and covered all the furniture with a grey dustcover of mold. It oozed from the center of the rolled-up rug, like pus from a sore. There was fungus on the ceiling, crawling towards the peak of the cabin. It was under foot. Michael slipped and slid as he ran from the house.

The fungus crawled along the rock foundation. It filled the deck, and under its weight the wooden supports gave way and the deck crashed to the ground. The pier again was covered and the grey mold came off the wood and across the new lawn, ripping the sod as it moved. It raced towards Michael like a tide.

Michael got the other can of gas from the station wagon. He went inside the house again and poured gas through the livingroom, splashing it against the wooden stairs, the pine walls. He ran into the kitchen and threw gas in a long, yellow spray at the cupboards, emptying the last of the can on the butcher-block table. When he dropped the can to the floor it sank into the thick fungus with a thud.

He was breathless, panting. His fingers shook and fumbled as he found matches, struck and tossed them at the gas-soaked mold. Flame roared up, ate away at the fungus, caught hold of the pine and oak and walnut with a blaze. In the livingroom he tossed matches into the liquor cabinet and set fire to the bar. He lit up the stairs and the flame ran along the steps. He tore through the fungus covering the furniture and ignited the couch.

The fungus had grown deep and billowy. It was as if Michael was trying to stand on top of a deflating parachute. He kept slipping and falling as the lumpy surface changed directions and expanded. The floor was a sea of mold. The front door was almost blocked from view. Grey smoke began to choke him. He tumbled towards the door and fungus swelled under foot and knocked him aside.

Michael found the shovel and used it to rip through the layers of wet mold. He cut a path, like digging a trench, to the outside. He ran for the station wagon. The fungus had reached the parking space and lapped at the wheels of the car.

Behind him the cabin blazed. Flames reached the shingled roof and leaped up the frame siding. The house burned like a bonfire. He spun the car around. The wheels slid over the slick mold like the car was caught on a field of ice, but he kept the station wagon on the gravel and tromped on the gas. The car fishtailed down the drive and onto the safety of the county road. Michael drove for his life.

"It's a total loss?" Barbara asked again, still confused by Michael's tale. Her blue saucer eyes looked puzzled.

Michael nodded. "In the rearview mirror I could see most of it in flames. I didn't have the courage to go back and check." He spoke with a new honesty and sense of awe.

"But to burn down our own home! Wasn't there some other way . . . ?" She stared at Michael. It was unbelievable. He had arrived at the apartment after midnight, trembling and incoherent. She had wanted to call a doctor, but he raged and struck her when she said he needed help. She cowed in the corner of the couch, shaking, as he paced the room and told her about the fungus and the fire.

"I tried to keep cleaning it with soap and water, but it kept . . ." He began to cry, deep, chest-rending sobs. She went quickly to him and smothered him against her breasts. She could smell the smoke in his hair, the bitter smell of wood that had smoldered in the rain.

"A smoke?" Barbara suggested. "It will calm you down." She rolled them a joint. Her hands were trembling with excitement. It was the first time in years that he had hit her, and the blow had both frightened and excited her. Her skin tingled.

They passed the joint back and forth as they sat huddled on the couch, like two lone survivors. Michael, again, and in great detail, told about the fungus, and why he had to burn the cabin.

"I know you were absolutely right," Barbara kept saying to reassure him, but in the back of her mind, growing like a cancer, was her doubt. To stop her own suspicious thoughts and his now insistent explanations, she interrupted, "Darling . . ." And she reached to unbutton his shirt.

They did not make it to the bedroom. Michael slipped his hands inside her blouse, then he pulled her to the floor and took his revenge and defeat out on her. It was brief and violent and cathartic.

Michael held her tenderly, arms wrapped around her, hugging her to him. He turned her head and kissed her eyes. It was all right, she whispered. He was home and safe and she would take care of him.

Yes, Michael thought, everything was all right. He was home in the city and they would forget the mountains and the second home on the lake. He had his writing and he had her, and that was all that mattered. And then his lips touched the candle-grey fungus that grew in a thin, irregular patch more than twelve inches wide across her breasts like a bra.

Crook of the Month

by Robert Bloch

Edison was right.

Genius is one percent inspiration and ninety-nine percent perspiration.

Jerry Cribbs started sweating long before the plane touched down in the Rio dawn and continued all through Customs inspection. But the black bag preserved its secret, and he hugged it in his lap during the long taxi ride to his Copacabana hotel. Anyone who survives a cab trip through Rio de Janeiro traffic is entitled to feel relieved, but by the time Jerry checked into his room he was still perspiring. And a shower didn't help even though he took the bag into the stall with him.

Jerry dried off, only to find himself wringing wet again in the few moments it took him to dress and shave. Then he sat soaking and waiting for the phone to ring. He held the black bag on his lap, hugging his secret—and his genius—to him for reassurance.

Why didn't the call come?

A knock on the door answered his question. Of course they'd never risk using the telephone; they'd rely on personal contact.

Or would they?

Jerry shoved the bag under the bed and moved to the door.

A soft voice from the hall outside murmured, "Mr. Cribbs?"

Jerry flinched. He'd registered downstairs as Mr. Brown, figuring that any alias good enough for the late Al Capone should be good enough for him. And yet the stranger beyond the door knew his name. In a way it was reassuring, but he had to make certain.

"Who sent you?" he whispered.

"The Big Bird."

With a sigh of relief, Jerry opened the door.

A baldheaded black giant entered, nodding curtly. He was dressed in the ornate uniform of a Brazilian general or chauffeur—it didn't matter which, because the Big Bird could have sent either if he chose.

"Come with me, please," said the giant.

Jerry turned and started out, but a hand gripped his shoulder.

"Aren't you forgetting something?" the giant asked.

"Sorry." Jerry stopped and retrieved the black bag from its hiding-place beneath the bed. The giant reached for it but Jerry shook his head.

"I'll carry it," he said.

The giant shrugged. "As you wish." He followed Jerry through the doorway and down the hall. He didn't speak in the elevator or in the lobby below, and his silence continued as he led Jerry to the huge limousine parked insolently on the sidewalk outside the entrance.

Jerry slid into the back seat and his escort got behind the wheel.

If Jerry had any doubts about the black giant being a chauffeur, they were quickly dispelled as the car weaved through Rio's noonday traffic —from the way he drove, he was obviously a general.

Once aboard the waiting launch at the wharf the man proved himself to be an admiral too. The boat raced off across the harbor and out into the open sea while Jerry crouched in the bow with the black bag between his trembling knees.

The long sleek lines of the yacht loomed ahead, bobbing in the swell. As they pulled astern Jerry looked up at the gold-leaf lettering which identified the vessel as *The Water Closet*.

The black giant killed the engine and rose, cupping his hands. "Ahoy there!" he called.

A bearded seaman peered down from the deck above.

"Let down the ladder," the black man muttered.

Climbing a rope-ladder while holding the handle of the black bag in his teeth wasn't easy, but Jerry managed it. Once on deck he followed the giant along the deck, past an elegant array of staterooms, a sauna, a private projection-room, a bowling-alley. They stopped just beyond an outdoor bar, at an Olympic-sized swimming pool.

"He's expecting you," said the black man.

Jerry squinted at the pool. Over the stereophonic screech of raucous rock shrill shrieks rose from the pool, where a half dozen figures splashed and sported, stark naked in the sunlight.

Jerry had no trouble recognizing his host; he was the only male.

"Mr. Buzzard?" he murmured.

The scrawny balding little man climbed out of the water, scowling against the sun as a waiting attendant instantly draped a gold lamé robe over his shoulders.

The Big Bird nodded. "I'm Al Buzzard," he said. "You've met my wife." He gestured vaguely towards the naiades in the pool.

"Oh—sure."

"Come on then." Buzzard held out both hands. The alert attendant placed a frosted full triple-martini glass in one of the hands and a lighted Upmann in the other, then Buzzard turned and led Jerry aft.

From the appearance of the stateroom they entered, with its mirrored walls and ceiling and king-sized circular bed covered with leopardskin, Jerry decided he was in the Captain's cabin.

The scrawny man closed the door. With a lightning-fast gesture he swallowed his drink, then set the empty glass on the mink carpet. He sprawled back on the bed, puffing his cigar and staring moodily at his visitor.

"Did you ever have one of those days when nothing goes right?" he sighed. "Just look at that!" He gestured toward the empty glass. "A triple martini with only two olives in it! As soon as we get out into international waters, remind me to have the bartender keelhauled."

"Really, Mr. Buzzard, it isn't all that bad—"

"Hah!" Buzzard snorted and sat up. "You sound just like Barabass."

"Barabass?"

"My publisher. He was out here last week. We got into a conversation during the orgy and he said to me, 'Why don't you look on the bright side of things for a change? After all, you're the world's most popular author, next to Conway Mann, that is. Ten all-time best sellers, eight blockbuster movies, a hit television series that lasted almost an entire season—what more do you want? Why, your name is a household word—like Drāno and Sani-flush.' That's what he told me."

"Well, it's true, isn't it?"

"No—it's a damnable lie! I'm much more popular than Con Mann. Him and his sexy romances—"

"But you're rich and famous." Jerry gestured at the mirrored walls. "You live on this big yacht, you have a lovely wife—"

Buzzard shrugged. "Boats make me seasick. I have to stay on board because the minute I set foot on land the I.R.S. will lay a suit on me for thirty-three million dollars in back taxes. And my wife isn't all that lovely—the first nine were much more attractive. Trouble is, none of them could understand me. This one doesn't understand me, nor do any of my mistresses. The shrinks all tell me we don't have the right chemistry. So what am I supposed to do about that?"

Sighing wearily, Buzzard rose and threw his cigar out of a porthole.

When he turned back he was a different man; his shoulders straightened beneath the gold robe and his beady eyes matched its glitter. "Now, to business," he said. "Have you got it?"

"It's in the bag."

Jerry held out the black bag and Buzzard's twitching fingers closed around the handle. He carried it to the bed and scrabbled at the lock.

"The key!" he panted. "Where's the key?"

Jerry rolled up his trouser leg and ripped the adhesive tape from his right ankle. He handed the key to Buzzard, who inserted it in the lock with a vicious twisting motion. The bag sprang open and its contents tumbled out onto the leopardskin coverlet.

Buzzard stared down at the bed, rubbing his hands together.

"How many pages?" he whispered.

"Three hundred."

"It's all there then?"

"All but the last chapter. I expected to finish by the end of next week, but then your wire came—"

"You can knock off the ending when you get back," Buzzard said. "Just so's I get the whole thing to the publisher by the end of the month. We gotta hit the fall list before Conway Mann beats us to it. I hear he's got a big one coming up, but we'll show him." He paused, eying Jerry suspiciously. "It *is* a goodie, isn't it?"

"I think so."

"Think? I'm not paying you to think—I'm paying you to write." Buzzard made a face. "It better be good. After all, I've got a reputation to live down to."

"Don't worry, Mr. Buzzard. Just read it and you'll see for yourself."

"Yeah, yeah—later sometime." Al Buzzard gathered up the pages, hefting them. "Feels nice and thick, anyhow. Barabass likes them that way." He frowned. "Where's the carbon?"

"Home, in the safe."

"Good." Buzzard nodded. "Speaking of home, we better get you on the next flight out of here. I'd invite you to stay for lunch, but seeing as how you still have a chapter to go there's no sense wasting time. Besides, you can grab a sannich or something on the plane, right?"

"Uh—aren't you forgetting something, Mr. Buzzard?"

Buzzard scowled. "I know. That's the difference between guys like you and a creative artist like I am. All you writers ever think about is money."

Sighing, he reached under the bed and pulled out a locked metal box. "O.K., if that's the way you want it."

He fiddled with the combination until the box flew open, cascading a heap of glittering objects over the bed.

"Damn!" he muttered. "I told you this wasn't my day. Wrong box—I got the diamonds by mistake!"

Buzzard stooped and fumbled until he found a second metal container identical with the first. When its tumblers clicked and the lid rose, Jerry stared down at the stacks of currency.

"Petty cash," Buzzard explained. "Only fifties and hundreds." He extracted a wad of bills and began to count. "Let's see now. Three hundred pages at ten dollars a page—"

"You promised me fifteen this time, Mr. Buzzard."

"Oh, yeah—fifteen times three hundred—"

"Forty-five hundred," said Jerry.

"What's the matter, don't you think I know how to count?" Scowling, Buzzard thrust a sheaf of currency into Jerry's hands. "That's a lot of loot, fella. If you ask me, you're being overpaid."

"But it took me almost six months to write the book, Mr. Buzzard. Nowadays a plumber can make that much in three weeks."

"So take the money and study plumbing," Buzzard told him. "Just so you finish up that last chapter first. If you got a pencil and paper, maybe you can write it on the plane."

But Jerry Cribbs did no writing on the return flight. He brooded.

The plane slipped between the crowded peaks, plunged into a few air pockets above Latin America, then sped like a thief up the Atlantic Coast. When it landed at Kennedy, Jerry was still brooding.

"Darling—what's the matter?"

Jerry halted at the terminal exit and stared at Ann Remington's troubled face. Then he kissed it. "I'll tell you later," he said.

Thanks to the marvels of modern technology Jerry got through Customs, into Ann's car, out of the airport, and through the city traffic in less time than it had taken him to fly from South America.

In the car he unburdened himself. "Don't you see?" he sighed. "It's the same old story."

"But it's a *good* story," Ann said. "I was reading one of your carbons just last night. I like that hero of yours, Lance Pustule. And having him murder his parents at the age of eight—it's going to win a lot of reader sympathy. Everybody has a kindly feeling for orphans."

"Ann, please—"

"That scene where he's raped by his grandmother is terrific! And all those killings and tortures he uses to get control of the television network—you really tell it like it is! The drugs and violence and kinky sex are dynamite. By the way, what's the title of the book?"

"*The Aristocrats.*"

"Perfect!"

Jerry shook his head. "Al Buzzard pays me forty-five hundred dollars for ghostwriting a book that will make him millions. What's so perfect about that? All he does is sit on his big fat yacht, divorcing wives and having affairs with movie stars and throwing fashion models overboard—"

"But that's why he gets all the money," Ann said. "Doing those things makes him a celebrity. His life style is front-page news, so when he writes a book that's news too."

"Only he doesn't write books. *I* do, and I can't even earn enough for us to get married." Jerry sighed. "If I could just write my own book, under my own name—"

"Why don't you?"

"Because I can't find the time, or the money."

Ann smiled. "We could manage. There's my secretarial job at the travel agency."

"I'm not going to live off your salary."

Ann's smile faded as she gripped the steering-wheel and swung the car toward the curb in front of the dingy rundown apartment building where Jerry spent his dingy rundown life.

"I don't understand you," she murmured. "How can a man who writes such trendy modern porn have such old-fashioned ideas?"

"Because I *am* old-fashioned." Jerry lugged his bags out of the car. "And when I do write my book, it isn't going to be trendy either. A good novel doesn't need all that cheap sensationalism." Ann started to get out of the car, but he checked her with a gesture. "Sorry, you'd better not come up with me. I have to get to work on the last chapter right away. The big identity-crisis scene when Lance finally discovers where his head is at—he gets rid of his wife and girl friend and becomes a child-molester."

"When will I see you?"

"I should have everything wrapped up by tomorrow night. Come around and we'll have dinner together. Make it about seven."

They clung together for a moment, then Ann drove away and Jerry hastened upstairs to commit a statutory offense on paper.

Neither of them noticed the little man crouching behind the pillars before the apartment-house entryway. "Seven o'clock," the little man whispered. "Tomorrow night."

It had been a good day's work, Jerry decided. Three thousand words, many of which were four-letter; twelve pages of solid hardcore sex and violence. Al Buzzard and his readers would be happy, and Jerry was satisfied with a dishonest job, well done.

He showered, shaved and dressed, and when the doorbell rang shortly before seven he was ready.

He lifted the latch and the door swung open.

"Ann—" he said.

"Wrong." The little man stood in the doorway, staring him up and down.

Jerry frowned, perplexed. "Who are you?"

"Sorry, no time for introductions." The little man moved past him into the apartment. "You're coming with me."

"Now wait a minute—"

"I don't have a minute." The intruder crooked a commanding finger. "Let's go."

"No way," said Jerry, eying the stranger. Whoever he was and whatever he wanted, Jerry had no intention of being pushed around by this little character.

He turned, and that was his mistake.

Because a big man loomed up in the doorway behind him, raising a rubber truncheon.

As the weapon descended on Jerry's skull, the little man looked at his wristwatch and nodded approvingly.

"Six forty-nine," he said. "Right on schedule."

"Yah," said the big man, who was preoccupied with the task of stuffing Jerry into a large gunnysack. Grunting, he swung the sack over his shoulder and carried it down the hall to the backstairs exit of the building.

The little man followed and they descended the steps together.

The big man scowled at him apprehensively. "*Mach schnell*," he panted. "Maybe somebody sees us."

"Don't worry." The little man nodded. "It's in the bag."

In the bag was no place to be, and when Jerry recovered consciousness he wanted out.

Voicing these sentiments through a mouthful of burlap he was conscious of a shuddering drone and a sound like faroff thunder, gradually fading.

Then a knife slashed through the cloth above his head, the gunnysack shredded and fell in folds about his shoulders, and Jerry emerged. He wobbled to his feet, blinking at his surroundings.

He stood in the capacious cabin of a private plane—a Lear jet, from the looks of it. Only a man wealthy enough to own such an aircraft could afford to decorate its interior with the original artwork exhibited on the walls.

Jerry recognized a Renoir, a Picasso, a Modigliani. And then, turning toward the far end of the cabin, he recognized the owner of the paintings.

There was no mistaking the identity of the bearded figure seated behind the ornate Chippendale desk, wearing an incongruously crumpled hat and peering at him through tinted glasses. The face would be instantly familiar to anyone who had ever watched a television interview program or *Bowling for Dollars*.

"Conway Mann!" gasped Jerry.

The bearded author nodded. He smiled and beckoned Jerry to the Heppelwhite chair before the desk.

"Welcome to my humble digs," he said. "I trust you'll excuse the crudity of my invitation, but I had to see you, Mr. Gibbs."

"Cribbs."

"Exactly." The pudgy hand investigated the contents of a desk drawer, emerging with a fistful of yellow pills which disappeared between his bearded lips. He gulped and nodded. "I suppose you're wondering what brought you here."

"I already know," said Jerry. "Two goons and a gunnysack."

"My dear Hibbs—"

"Cribbs."

"Ah, yes." The hand fumbled in the drawer once more, then rose to extend a crumpled sheet of paper. "Please be good enough to read this proof of an advertisement scheduled to appear in *Publishers Weekly*. I think it may interest you."

Jerry stared down at the bold lettering of the full-page ad.

SHOCKING! SCANDALOUS!
SENSATIONAL!
Searing sex . . . vicious violence . . . raw and raunchy . . . a novel

that rips aside the last shreds of convention to reveal the hidden world of secret passions and unbridled lusts behind the locked doors of America's power-mad masters . . . as they move from boardroom to bedroom in their savage search for forbidden pleasures! Don't miss

THE TASTE-MAKERS

by

CONWAY MANN

The best-selling blockbuster of the year from

SCRIBBLER'S & SONS

Jerry put the ad down on the desktop. "Your new novel?"

"Precisely so."

"Is it good?"

Conway Mann shrugged. "That's up to you. You're going to write it."

"Now hold on—"

"I'm holding on, Mr. Dribbs. But I can't hold on much longer. The manuscript is due at the publisher's office by the end of the month."

"Let me get this straight. You mean to say you don't write your own books?"

"Why should that surprise you? That wretched Al Buzzard doesn't write his novels either."

"Then you know?"

"Of course. Why else would I bring you here?" Conway Mann shook his head. "Don't get me wrong. I'm perfectly capable of doing the job myself, but lately I've suffered from writer's block."

"When did it start?"

"In 1959." The pudgy hand popped red capsules into its owner's mouth. "I have a full schedule of commitments ahead of me—Johnny Carson, Merv Griffin, *Hollywood Squares*—best-selling authors must live up to their responsibilities, even at the sacrifice of the creative impulse. And that's where you come in."

"That's where I get out," Jerry told him.

"At forty thousand feet in the air?" Conway Mann shrugged again. "Very well, suit yourself."

"Now see here," Jerry cried, "you kidnapped me! That's a federal offense. I can push charges."

"You'll push up daisies if you refuse."

"But why me?" Jerry said. "Surely you must have a regular ghostwriter. What happened to him?"

"He refused," Conway Mann murmured. "Would you like to see where he's buried?"

Conway Mann, with his royalties and reputation at stake, wasn't conning. When his hand again descended to the desk drawer, Jerry expected it to reappear holding a revolver.

Instead it clutched a bundle of bills.

"Six thousand," said the bearded man. "In advance."

"Six thousand?"

"That's more than you get from that chintzy Buzzard, if my spies are correct." The pudgy hand extended. "Now take it and get out—you've got a deadline to meet."

"But I couldn't possibly write an entire novel by the end of the month," Jerry said.

"You can and you will," Conway Mann told him. "Unless you're awfully fond of daisies."

Jerry pocketed the bills, not an easy task for trembling hands. "I'll try," he said. "Only you haven't told me what the book will be about."

"Ninety thousand words, that's what it's about." Conway Mann gestured at the proof-sheet on the desktop. "This ad doesn't mention much about a plot, so you can suit yourself. You know what readers expect. Behind the scenes in politics and big business, and the further behind the better. Maybe a touch of necrophilia in San Francisco, a Black Mass at the U.N., orgies in the White House—I leave it to your discretion."

Jerry took a deep breath. "I'll do my best."

"Your best isn't good enough," Conway Mann said. "I want your worst."

He rose and came around the desk, glancing at his watch. "I'll tell the pilot to take us down, and the boys will see to it that you get home safely."

"That's not necessary."

"I think it is." Conway Mann's eyes narrowed behind the tinted lenses. "They're going to be keeping tabs on you until the book is finished."

"And if it isn't?"

"Then they'll finish you."

"I'm not afraid of your threats," Jerry said. "I can call the police—"

"That's already been taken care of. Your phone is dead. And unless you want to follow its example, you'll stay in your apartment from tonight until the manuscript is in the hands of my publishers." Conway

Mann put his hand on Jerry's shoulder and smiled. "If you want to stay healthy, learn a lesson from the flowers. Daisies don't tell."

It was good advice, but Jerry couldn't take it. Not when he found Ann waiting for him outside the apartment door.

"It's after nine o'clock!" she told him. "I've been waiting here for two hours. Where on earth have you been?"

"I wasn't exactly on earth," Jerry said, looking toward the car from which he'd emerged. The headlights glared, the motor growled, and its sleek black length crouched at the curb like a panther waiting to spring.

Ann followed his gaze, noting the big man behind the wheel and his small companion beside him.

"Please, darling, come inside." Jerry gripped her arm and drew her through the doorway. "I can explain everything."

"It better be good."

But once inside the apartment, it wasn't good.

"Not good at all," Ann said, after she'd listened to Jerry's account of the evening. "It took you months to knock out the novel for Buzzard, and now Mann expects you to do one in a couple of weeks!"

"It's impossible." Jerry nodded. "But there's no way out."

"Not for *you*," Ann said. "But *I'm* free to come and go."

"Meaning?"

"It's simple." Ann smiled. "I'm going to leave now. The minute I get home I'll put through a call to the police. They'll get over here, you tell them what happened, and you're home free."

"Dynamite!"

Ann smiled reassuringly as she moved to the door and opened it. Then her smile faded. The little man stood in the doorway, his eyes bulging. There was another ominous bulge where his hand rested in his pocket.

"I heard what you just said, lady. Nobody's calling the fuzz."

Ann stared at him. "You mean you intend to keep me locked up here with Jerry?"

The man shook his head. "I didn't say that. Somebody's got to go for groceries and it might as well be you. But whenever you cut out, I go with you. And my buddy downstairs keeps an eye on your boy friend. Boss's orders."

Jerry faced him, frowning. "He thinks of everything, doesn't he?"

"You better believe it." The little man gave him a crooked smile. "Time for you to start thinking too, fella. You got a book to write."

The days that followed moved in a blinding blur. Ann spent most of her time in the living room, while Jerry's typewriter pounded away behind the bedroom door. Sometimes she read, sometimes she watched television, sometimes she just stood at the window and stared down at the black limousine. On occasion she took brief walks or shopped at the supermarket, but always under escort. She didn't talk to the little man and he didn't talk to her. She scarcely talked to Jerry when he came out of the bedroom for meals.

One look at his haggard face told the story. He was racing the deadline, racing for his life, and she resolved not to nag him with questions.

But as the end of the month inched closer there came a moment when she could keep silent no longer.

They were seated at the kitchen table over coffee, and the sight of Jerry's gaunt features and glassy stare was too much for her to bear. From her lips burst the age-old question, the question every writer dreads.

"How's it going?" she asked.

Jerry shook his head. "It isn't," he muttered.

"You mean you won't finish in time?"

"I haven't started."

"Haven't started?" Ann frowned. "But you've been in there typing night and day."

"I type at night because I can't sleep. And I can't sleep because of what I type during the day. Page after page of new beginnings—none of them making sense, all of them going into the wastebasket. I'm afraid it's finally happened, just the way it did to Al Buzzard and Conway Mann."

"What are you talking about?"

"When they started, they wrote their own stuff. Then gradually it got to them. No man can stand such a pace forever—a daily diet of corruption, brutality, mayhem, incest, voyeurism, sado-masochistic satyriasis, all of it so hard to spell. So they hired ghostwriters, people like myself. The trouble is, now the same thing is happening to me." Jerry raised his anguished face. "All those rapes and murders—it's too much! Even Jack the Ripper had to quit in the end."

Ann rose and moved to the stricken man. "Listen to me," she said softly. "It's not that bad. All you have to do is get Buzzard's last chapter to the publisher. If you can only go on a little longer, until you do Conway Mann's novel—"

"Don't you understand?" Jerry slammed a clenched fist on the table. "It's too late now. Even if I stay at the typewriter twenty-four hours a day, I'll never beat the deadline. There isn't time."

Ann sighed, and walked to the living room. Jerry followed. Together they stared out of the window, down at the black car crouched and waiting. Neither of them said a word. Words wouldn't help now—unless Jerry could put ninety thousand of them onto paper within the next three days.

It was Ann who broke the silence, her face and voice thoughtful.

"Maybe it's all for the best," she said.

"What do you mean?"

"Even if you could have finished on time, it wouldn't help. At first I hoped this would be a blessing in disguise. Forty-five hundred from Al Buzzard and six thousand from Conway Mann—that's ten thousand five hundred dollars in cash, enough to live on until you realized your ambition. With that much money you could finally write a novel of your own. But it doesn't matter now, does it? If you say you can't write any more—"

"I never said that!" Jerry gripped her hands tightly in his own. "I said I couldn't turn out any more sex and violence. The novel I want to write is different. No sensationalism, no cheap anti-heroes, no ripoff of celebrities disguised under other names. My book would be about ordinary people, coping with everyday problems that all of us have to face."

"But would such a book sell?"

There was doubt in Ann's voice, but none in Jerry's. "Why not? At least I'd give the readers some reality, something to think about and remember. Those porno fairy-tales Buzzard and Mann are credited with are just the same thing repeated over and over again—you can't tell one from another in the long run. I'm talking about real literature."

Ann eyed him dubiously. "How would you promote it?"

"An honest book doesn't need promotion," Jerry told her. "A good writer doesn't need notoriety. Think about it—did Thackeray have a yacht? Did Henry James wear a funny hat and fly around in a Lear jet? Did Jane Austen sleep around? Did Shakespeare ever appear on a late-night talk show?"

"I am thinking about it," Ann told him. An odd note crept into her voice. "Jerry, do me a favor. Come into the bedroom with me for a minute. I want you to show me where you keep your files."

Together they went to the bedroom. "Right here in this cabinet," Jerry said.

"I see." But Ann's glance strayed from the filing-cabinet to Jerry's desk—the typewriter, the paper, the carbons resting under a heavy paperweight. Her eyes narrowed. "Jerry—about this book of yours. Do you really want to write it?"

"More than anything in the world."

"And you're sure it could sell?"

Jerry nodded, then turned away. "If I'm wrong, may I be struck dead on the spot."

It was then that Ann hit him with the paperweight . . .

"Dead," Jerry mumbled. "Well, I asked for it—"

"Wake up." Ann was shaking him by the shoulders. "You're not dead."

Jerry opened his eyes. The room was dark and he could just make out Ann's shadowy face peering anxiously over him.

"Why did you do it?" he said, sitting up and rubbing the lump on the side of his left temple.

"I'll explain later. Right now there isn't time. We've got to get out of here."

"What about the goon squad?"

"See for yourself."

Legs shaking, Jerry allowed her to lead him back into the living room and over to the window.

He stared down.

The black limousine was gone. Ann's car stood in its place.

"Come on," Ann said. "We've got to get to the airport. Your bags are packed and in the car."

"Where are we going?"

"Costa Rica."

Jerry frowned. "I don't get it."

"You will."

And once the plane took off, he did.

"What you said about writing your own novel convinced me," Ann told him. "That's when I got the idea. I'm sorry about knocking you out, but I knew you'd never agree to go through with it on your own."

"Agree to what?"

"Delivering Conway Mann's new novel to his publisher."

"But there is no new novel!"

"There is now. I took one of the carbons of Al Buzzard's manuscript. All I did was go through it and change the names of the characters."

"You mean you gave both publishers the same book?"

"Including the last chapter." Ann nodded. "You said yourself that these things are all alike."

"So that's why Conway Mann's goons let us go."

"Right. Once the manuscript got to the office of Scribbler's and Sons, they took off. And so have we."

"But why Costa Rica?"

"They don't have an extradition law. Even if Mann and Buzzard find out, you can't be touched. You've got the cash, enough to keep us going for a year, and you can write your book." Ann smiled. "Besides, darling, if what you say is true, nobody will find out. Not Buzzard, or Mann, or the publishers, and certainly not the readers."

Jerry groaned. "I hope you're right," he whispered.

Ann patted his hand. "I know I am," she said.

And she was.

In the months that followed, *The Aristocrats* hit the best-seller lists with such force that Al Buzzard bought a new yacht, with two swimming pools, one of which he kept filled with champagne. If anything, *The Taste-Makers* was an even bigger success. Conway Mann was able to purchase a Jackson Pollock, a Van Gogh, a Rembrandt, and another hat.

Best of all, Jerry Cribbs finally wrote his own novel, which was duly published under his own name. You may have read it.

Then again, you may not. It sold 148 copies.

Death of a Peruke-Maker

by Clayton Matthews

Williamsburg
23 April, 1773

My Dear Wife:

Temperature on arising at 6 o'clock 54°.

Friend Patrick, who is sharing bed with me at the Raleigh, sports me for washing my feet in cold water on arising, even while he himself suffers from the ague.

After my morning meal, I sallied forth along Duke of Gloucester Street bound for the Capitol Building. It was a gray day and bespoke foul weather. Gloucester was ajostle with carriages, wheels striking sparks from the worn cobblestones. Tradesmen and hucksters were all about plying their wares. More so than on a normal day, since 23 April, as you know, dear wife, is St. George's Day, the day of the yearly town fair.

On this day I did not reach the Capitol Building. The House of Burgesses was not graced by my presence.

As I started past Thomas Devereaux's wigmaking shop, a lad of 12 or thereabouts came out pellmell. Twas young John Lyons, Devereaux's apprentice. He had horrifying news to convey.

He gasped out, "Murder, sire! Murder most foul!"

He made as if to scurry on. I seized his arm and shook him. "Who, lad? Who is the victim of the deed?"

"Tis Master Carpenter, sire."

You may recall, dear wife, that Andrew Carpenter is Thomas Devereaux's journeyman. He, I believe, tended to your wig when you were in Williamsburg this autumn past, residing with Friend George Wythe.

Journeyman Carpenter was a dandy, something of a womanizer and a toper, I understand. I have never cared for the man. That, I will grant, may be an unwonted prejudice on my part. Wigmaking does not seem to me a profession befitting a man. I do not care much for the wearing of a wig, yet it does seem a necessity for a man in Public Life.

To young John Lyons, I said, "On your way to the Courthouse and fetch Constable Turner. Away with you now."

Young Lyons hastened on his errand and I went into the shop of the peruke-maker. With great reluctance, since I have an abhorrence of violent deeds.

The day outside being so dark and no lamps lighted inside, at first I could see little. Like all wigmaking shops, it was a bewildering clutter. To my left was the high work bench on which sat a miscellany of wig blocks, so like human skulls they are I always get a chill. And toward the rear, on my right, was that instrument of medieval torture, the Satan-blessed barber chair. Well do I recall this winter past when I suffered the agonies of the damned with an abscessed tooth and came to Thomas Devereaux to have it lanced in that same chair. The infamous rack of the Inquisition could not compare.

Still, I did not see anything untoward. Thinking that young Lyons must be suffering from vaporous imaginings, I ventured around the high bench and saw him there. Journeyman Carpenter on his face in death's grip, a pair of barber shears buried to the hilt between his shoulder blades.

I knelt and felt his flesh. It was cold. It was plain to me that he had been long dead, perhaps as long as last eventide.

His own wig had fallen awry, revealing his shaven skull. I mused upon tales I had heard of wigmakers ofttimes making their wigs from their own sheared locks.

That recalled to me something I had once read in Diderot's *Encyclopedia*. In general the hair of persons not given to excesses lasts a long time, while that of men who live in sexual debauchery, or of women who give themselves to the uses of men, has less sap, dries out, and loses its quality.

If the veracity of all the tales told of Journeyman Carpenter's debauchery is to be believed, the quality of his own hair was not of the best quality.

Then I took note of something mystifying. The wig awry on his head was not his own, at least not one I had seen him wear. This wig was a brown dress bob much like my own, much like most men of substance in Williamsburg wear, whereas on all the prior occasions that I had seen Journeyman Carpenter he had been adorned with a cadogan wig, that elaborate affair so much beloved by the young fops of England who affect to call themselves "macaronis."

At the sounds of a commotion in the doorway, I got to my feet to see Constable Turner bustling in. I saw a number of villagers gathered outside. I reflected that young Lyons had served effectively as the town crier.

Constable Turner is short, red of face, hard of breath, and as plump as a market-day shoat.

"Constable, I would counsel closing the door against the curious."

"Good counsel, sir, good counsel."

He touched his forelock, his own hair I daresay, and puffed over to close the door. Constable Turner has been in office for some years, but I am sure he has yet to be involved in a crime as violent as murder. A debtor to lock in the Gaol, a drunkard pilloried in the Stocks, a thief to be investigated, a tradesmen dispute to be arbitrated, perhaps roisterers to be quelled, have thus far been the extent of his duties.

This judgement was confirmed when he came around the bench and had his first glimpse of the dead man.

He went pale as wig powder. He swayed, as though from an attack of the vapors.

"Oh, this is a dreadful business, sir, a dreadful business."

"Indeed it is, Constable," I said with some dryness.

I let him go about his affairs, which consisted of little more than staring at the corpse, insofar as I could see, and continued my perusal of the shop. I was searching for nothing in particular, but I have learned from my study of the law that it is of great value to catalogue every item present on the premises later to be in debate in a legal proceedings. Not that I had any intentions of being engaged in such a debate, but I was there. No person will have occasion to complain about the want of time who never loses any.

I could see nothing untoward.

I did note Thomas Devereaux's account book open on the bench, which struck me as a queer place for it. I stepped up to inspect it. You are well aware, my dear wife, how addicted I am to account books.

By some happenchance the account-book pages open for inspection included those of my own and one Richard Jones. I noted that so far this year past I had purchased from Thomas Devereaux two brown dress wigs, a pair of curls, a pound of wig powder, one dressing, and had been charged with the aforementioned lancing. Total, one pound, four shillings.

I turned my attention to the account of Richard Jones. I was not personally acquainted with the man, but I knew him to be a local tobacco planter, with a small plantation a few miles distant from Williamsburg.

The amount due from Richard Jones was considerable, a sum in excess of ten pounds. It dated back two years, with no payments on the principal. Much can be told about a man from a look at the account sheets of his creditors. Richard Jones had a rather large family and several slaves. Thomas Devereaux had charged him for a number of wigs, both male and female, several dressings and shavings, as well as numerous bleedings and teeth pullings for his slaves.

There is nothing at all unusual for a wigmaker's customers to be a year or so in arrears. The cursed Crown forbids us here in the Colonies to mint our own coins. Almost all accounts are settled yearly, most often in tender instead of coin of the realm. Warehouse receipts for varying amounts of stored tobacco are universally acceptable for payment of debts. This year past the tobacco crop had fared poorly. Richard Jones had my sympathy.

A knocking came at the door. I looked in that direction. It was Thomas Devereaux himself. Constable Turner hastened to allow him entrance.

Thomas Devereaux is rather portly and not too young in years, being a man for strong drink and gambling, yet a fellow of uncommon good nature. I have always liked him.

He gave me a rather distracted greeting, and said to the constable, "What are these bad tidings I hear?"

"Bad tidings indeed, Master Devereaux. A dreadful business."

So saying, the constable showed him the mortal remains of Journeyman Carpenter.

Thomas Devereaux blanched and removed his brown dress wig to mop at his pink scalp. "Distressing. Oh, yes, distressing. But I cautioned him that such could happen."

"And why is that, sir?" I said, rather sharply I am afraid.

Thomas Devereaux turned his gaze on me. "He had a liking for the ladies, did young Carpenter. And he cared not if they were wed. He did much dressing and fitting of wigs for ladies who wished not to venture forth to my shop. And many a husband has complained to me about his undue attention to their spouses. With some I fear it went beyond that."

"You are saying then that some cuckolded husband has committed this deed?"

His faded eyes shifted away from mine. "All I am saying, sir, is that my journeyman was too free and easy with the ladies."

Was the peruke-maker being evasive or was he belatedly becoming precautionary about blackening the good name of a dead man? Or was there a reason for Devereaux himself to wish his journeyman dead?

I was pondering these questions when a loud voice spoke from the doorway. "Your journeyman was indeed free with the ladies, Thomas Devereaux. Just inquire of Silas Marlowe." The voice now turned into braying laughter.

I looked in the direction of the voice and saw that the constable's opening the door to Thomas Devereaux had, in effect, opened Pandora's Box. The entrance was crowded with the curious. In the forefront was a slat of a man with the red nose of a toper, and I had the conviction that there was the man with the donkey's braying laugh.

I took a step forward. "And just what should we inquire of Silas Marlowe, sir?"

"Inquire of him about his spouse and Journeyman Carpenter. Just last eve he conversed with me over several pints. Gone in drink he was, mumbling about being cuckolded by young Carpenter yonder. He swore to me that he would venge himself, as any proper husband would."

Voices behind him murmured agreement, several averring they had heard these selfsame words from the lips of Silas Marlowe.

I said, "Who is this Silas Marlowe?"

The response came from Thomas Devereaux. "Silas Marlowe, the silversmith. His shop is on Nickolson Street."

Cries came from the doorway.

"To the Gaol with him!"

"A murderer must know the hangman's rope!"

"It is our duty to see that he pays the penalty!"

The slat of a man with the red nose looked about him with a startled manner.

To him, I said, "And who might you be, sir?"

"Richard Jones." He bent a knee. "At your service, sir."

It was now clear to me why he was in debt to Thomas Devereaux so heavily. Idling away time in taverns instead of seeing to the industry of his plantation.

I raised my voice above the hubbub. "It would be advisable if you fetch this silversmith from his shop, Constable. Escort him to the Apollo Room at the Raleigh posthaste and we shall thereupon inquire into the truth of this matter."

It was nigh onto the noon hour when I crossed Gloucester to the

Raleigh Tavern. So occupied had been my thoughts with the murder that I had not measured the passage of time. I had long since missed roll call in the House of Burgesses, but since there were no pressing matters on the agenda, I assumed in all good conscience that my presence would not be sorely missed.

The carriage and foot traffic had quickened along Gloucester, and people were thick as flies on syrup. Tradesmen were hurrying toward Market Square toting their wares to display at the fair.

I was delighted to escape the street noise and into the Raleigh. Unfortunately, the tavern was equally boisterous. The tap room and the game room rang with loud voices. And even the Apollo Room, where so many times we had repaired from the Capitol Building to decide matters we could not settle on the floor of the House of Burgesses, was also full. It was even fuller by the time Constable Turner arrived with Silas Marlowe.

As you very well know, dear wife, I have an abhorrence of mobs. If I could not get to Heaven but with a party, I would not go there at all. It came to mind to instruct Constable Turner to insure us privacy, but I curbed my tongue. It was not within my province. Besides, rumors would fly enough. Who can hazard what rumors might gain currency if our proceedings were conducted in privy council, as it were?

The silversmith, I was surprised to see, was an elder. Not in his dotage but far beyond the years where a man's spouse would normally cuckold him.

Seized by a sudden suspicion, I leaned to the ear of Thomas Devereaux. "How old a wife has this silversmith?"

"Oh, young, sir," said Thomas Devereaux with a bawdy grin. "Little more than a maid."

That, of course, explained it. I do not look with favor upon a man taking for wife a woman so tender of age, thus making him the likely victim for barnyard humor.

This Silas Marlowe was a brawny fellow, for all his years, with sturdy forearms from years of working a smith's bellows. He could have driven the shears into Journeyman Carpenter's back with ease.

With a pewter plate I pounded on the table for quiet. When the bedlam died, I said, "What say you, silversmith? Rumor has it that you, sir, while in your cups, did voice threats against the life of Journeyman Carpenter. What truth to the charge?"

"The threats I did make, sir. But I was indeed in my cups," he said in anguished tones. "It was an empty threat, on God's oath I swear! 'Tis not in me to slay a man, though he did make free with my wife." The poor man wrung his hands in despair.

Loud voices were raised, and the villagers crowded close. I was troubled, fearing that my judgement in not excluding them might have been a grave error. A motley crowd can be fickle, changing from good humor to rancor in a twinkling.

The poor wretch of a silversmith, frightened out of his wits, fell to his knees, hands clasped together, face upturned in prayer. The crowd jostled, closing in, smelling rancid as a swine's breath. So unruly did they become that Thomas Devereaux, standing by my side, was sent staggering, wig falling to the table. In an agony of embarrassment he snatched it up again to cover his bald pate.

In a distemper I pounded the pewter plate on the table and roared, "Silence and order! Be you men of good will or barnyard animals brawling at the feeding trough? If I do not have silence and decorum, Constable Turner shall clear this room!"

To my astonishment the room fell quiet at once. What a blessing it would be if the House of Burgesses could be brought to order so easily during one of our not infrequent heated debates.

To the silversmith, I said, "Get to your feet, man. It is not seemly that a man should shame himself so before his peers."

All a-tremble, Silas Marlowe got to his feet. He glanced in terror at the glower of faces surrounding him.

"Stand back and let the silversmith breathe!"

"Sir, he might take flight," said Jones. "The wretch is a murderer!"

"Is he indeed?" To Thomas Devereaux, I said, "This journeyman of yours . . . Was it his custom to wear wigs other than his own?"

Thomas Devereaux's face puckered in worriment. "Not to my knowledge, sir. Tis not sanitary."

"Yet the wig he was wearing at the moment he was struck down was not his own. It was much like yours."

"Oh, that I can explain." The wigmaker's face broadened in a smile. "He was engaged in making a new dress bob for me. Although not of my wishing, he ofttimes used his own head instead of a wig block. Our skulls, strange as it may strike you, were identical in size and shape."

"Are they indeed?" I observed the wigmaker closely. "He could, in fact, be taken for you, in poor light. You are of identical height."

Thomas Devereaux looked startled. "True. Except for . . ." He patted his ample girth, that protuberance so much like a woman quick with child.

"Yet from behind that would not be so easily observed."

Thomas Devereaux's eyes widened. "What are you suggesting?"

"I am suggesting that the murderer made a grave error. He mistook Journeyman Carpenter for you. You, sir, were the intended victim."

A concerted gasp came from the onlookers, and the wigmaker blanched. "But who would wish to slay me?"

"A man in mortal fear of debtor's prison."

I had not taken my gaze from Richard Jones. Now I saw him slipping smooth as an eel toward the door. "Stop that man, Constable!"

Constable Turner followed the direction of my pointing finger, gaping in befuddlement. Had not there been so many men present, Richard Jones would have made good his escape. But the crowd, now alerted, closed in around him and in a twinkling he was brought to stand before me, arms held in a vise at his sides.

He did not cringe, not this Richard Jones. "What is this calumny, sir? I have dawdled overlong here and was taking my leave to oversee the affairs of my plantation."

"Better you should have concerned yourself heretofore. Else you would not be in your present straits. Wigmaker, have you not been pressing Richard Jones for payment of his account? Have you threatened him with debtor's prison?"

The wigmaker's round face flushed with indignation. "I have indeed! His account is long overdue. He pled inability to pay. My patience was at an end."

"And so you, Richard Jones, thinking to cancel your debt, crept like a thief into the wigmaking shop last eve," I said. "Mistaking Journeyman Carpenter, in poor light, for Thomas Devereaux, you drove barber shears into his back, thus slaying him!"

His head went back, black eyes flashing defiance.

"What was even more reprehensible, you endeavored to then place the guilt on the silversmith. Do you deny the charges, sir?"

"I deny nothing! I admit nothing!"

I stared at him with some sorrow. In our present state, the Colonies need men of such fire and spirit. It is indeed sad that economic repression by the Crown should drive men to such desperate deeds.

It is not that I hold a brief for his act. The rule of law must be observed. And whenever you do a thing, though it can never be known but to yourself, ask yourself how you would act were all the world looking at you. "Murder will out." Thus did Cervantes say it.

I sighed and gestured. "Take him to the Gaol keeper, Constable, for safekeeping. A week or so to ponder and he will be amenable to confessing the deed, I wager."

As the constable took Richard Jones out, the villagers melted away like butter in a hot skillet. Soon, I was alone in the Apollo Room with Thomas Devereaux.

"I am grateful to you, sir, for unveiling our murderer. To think that he had selected me as his victim." His face creased in thought. "But now that he is in Gaol, how do I collect for his overdue account?"

"Mayhap the silversmith will, in gratitude, assume his debt."

Leaving him gaping after me in wonderment, I repaired to my quarters upstairs.

I am presently writing this letter to you, dear wife, from the desk at the window overlooking Gloucester. The weather has turned fair. All bodes well for the fair in Market Square.

It will shortly be time to sup. And Patrick Henry will soon come roaring in, demanding from me the reason for my absence from the House of Burgesses. Knowing his appetite for adventure, I can anticipate his relish for the tale I have to relate.

Yours affectionately,
Th: Jefferson

The Forever Duel

by James McKimmey

Charles Kinniger sat in the front passenger seat of the small, expensive sports car as Alex Tolbert drove expertly up the grade toward the target of the Sierra Nevada Mountains and their streams and lakes. Kinniger, a medium-sized man with a face easily forgotten, felt his hands tensing on his thighs—he was wearing an old poplin fishing jacket and twill trousers he'd owned for over half of his 42 years. An assortment of dry flies, used in his fishing, was affixed to the sheepskin band of his venerable narrow-brimmed hat. You've done it, Tolbert, he thought. Any minute now, a cat toying with a defeated mouse, you'll tell me what and how.

He looked at Tolbert, steering easily with thin-gloved hands and smiling faintly. Nearly the same age as Kinniger, Tolbert was a strikingly handsome man, slimly built almost to the point of delicacy. Both earned similar incomes as professors of criminology at separate Bay Area institutions of higher learning. But, in contrast to Kinniger's careful conservation of funds, Tolbert bought only the finest. His was a corduroy car coat purchased at one of San Francisco's expensive sportswear stores. His matching hat and gabardine slacks came from the same store.

"You seem remote, Charles," Tolbert said cheerfully, glancing at Kinniger. "Unhappy. Tense."

"I'm fine, Alex," Kinniger said grimly.

"Fishing should be excellent."

"The streams'll be low—they always are in the fall. I like the conditions of deeper water."

"You're a pessimist," Tolbert said. "As always. But why should that bother a fly fisherman? The fish have to surface for your flies, don't they? And, anyway, the art of doing it is all that counts, isn't it?"

Listening to Tolbert laughing softly, Kinniger felt an underlying anger.

It had always irritated him that Tolbert failed to understand anything of the true sport of fishing. Fly fishing *was* an art, one Kinniger had worked at assiduously for much of his life. It was the pleasure of standing in a stream, in wading boots, making the cast, surely, accurately, then watching the fly float, waiting for the strike, using needle-sharp reflexes when the fish did, then setting the hook and working the fish to exhaustion and the net. He wasn't always successful, but that didn't matter—it was the proper doing of it that mattered.

Tolbert, on the other hand, didn't care how he caught fish. His usual method was simply using a spinning rod and salmon eggs on the hook, or *worms*, for God's sake! He would spear them, if he could. He would dive into the water and catch them with his teeth if that were possible! All that mattered was the accumulation of as much fish as possible, no matter what the method, no matter what the legal limit.

Creep, Kinniger thought, realizing how much he'd come to hate and resent the man.

"I love this country," Tolbert said with relish.

They had reached one of the higher elevations where winter winds had bent stands of pine trees into permanent curves. Some of the top limbs had been wrenched away so that the trunks pointed jaggedly to a sky now floating small fluffy white clouds. Below was a lake backed by rugged mountains, an azure circle with a wooden pier running outward. Beside it, small boats rocked gently. At this time of morning you would have to troll for the fish, Kinniger knew, and trolling was not acceptable to him. Only fly fishing, on a good rushing trout stream. But he could find no anticipation even in that today.

"You *do* seem preoccupied," Tolbert said.

"*Tell* me," Kinniger demanded forcefully.

"Tell you?" There was a lilt of pleasure in Tolbert's voice, a voice honed to vibrating resonance after years of classroom delivery. "Tell you what, pray, Charles?"

"You've done it, haven't you?"

Again Tolbert looked at Kinniger, his eyes flashing with suppressed mirth. "You're taking a terribly circuitous route, my man."

"You know what I mean."

Once more Tolbert was laughing softly, but he failed to respond otherwise.

Kinniger found himself thinking back to when it had started, in the excellent seaside restaurant where they had gone for lunch one Sunday weeks ago . . .

The interior was not overly crowded, and they had obtained a table with a window view of the waves crashing against a thick rock retaining wall. Tolbert studied the menu written in Italian with infuriating slowness as a black-suited waiter stood impatiently beside them. Kinniger had always enjoyed eating here, but the waiters intimidated him.

"Signore?" the waiter asked, staring at Tolbert with dark angry eyes.

"Ah, well," Tolbert said. *"Calamari con pomodoro,* I think."

The waiter scribbled swiftly.

"And a simple salad for two. Just please bring the lettuce, the oil, vinegar, and condiments. I'll mix it myself. Oh, yes, and a decent Chianti, of course. Charles?"

"Spaghetti," Kinniger said simply, as he always did.

The waiter turned his resentment upon Kinniger now, as he waited for his selection of sauce. Tolbert refused to assist, knowing full well that Kinniger could not read the menu nor remember what he'd had before.

"Con salsa semplice di pomodoro?" the waiter barked at last. *"Con salsa di vongoli? Con salsa di carne?"*

Tolbert chuckled and said, "With plain tomato sauce, Charles? With clam sauce? Or with meat sauce?"

"Meat sauce," Kinniger said, feeling his face warming. The waiter scribbled again, and moved off. Tolbert smiled at Kinniger. "You could have *said* meat sauce. One mustn't be afraid to be honest about one's shortcomings, Charles."

The condescension bothered Kinniger. He knew Tolbert had no fluency with the Italian language. He simply had taken a menu from this restaurant, as he had from other foreign restaurants, looked up the listings in a book, and memorized the translations and pronunciations.

"Be of good cheer, Charles. Please don't think of Lucille."

Kinniger looked away from him and studied the water breaking against the stone, his face flushing again. Lucille, he thought. The only woman he'd ever wanted enough to marry, with her outgoing warmth that had made Kinniger feel more secure and protected than ever before in his life. He'd brought her here several evenings and had glowed in her warmth. It was at this table, in fact, that Kinniger had proposed marriage: she had accepted in the very chair Tolbert was sitting in now.

Days later, Tolbert, to whom he'd introduced her—reluctantly, sensing he should not do it, doing it just the same to show off—had seduced her. And when he had had his fill, he'd informed Kinniger of the fact and dropped her—as, of course, had Kinniger.

It was not only the loss of Lucille that continued to upset Kinniger, it was the way in which it had been done. Tolbert always won everything at which they competed—chess, golf, fishing . . . The list was endless. But losing Lucille to him, who had cared nothing for her, was the most bitter forfeiture.

"Stop thinking of her," Tolbert said gently. "She wasn't worth a jot."

"I'm not thinking of her!" Kinniger said explosively.

The waiter arrived with the wine and salad, glaring at Kinniger.

"We mustn't bother the other diners, Charles," Tolbert smiled.

Kinniger fell silent, knowing that he could not hold his voice down until he regained control. He waited in that silence as Tolbert mixed their salads. He did not like a salad made only with oil and vinegar; he liked lettuce with avocado topped with blue-cheese dressing.

"There we are," Tolbert said politely, handing a plate to Kinniger. "Dig in."

Kinniger did so in silence.

"Now we're pouting, aren't we, Charles?" Tolbert said at last.

"I am not pouting!"

"Now, Charles."

"I'm trying to enjoy this!"

"I should hope so. It's well made, isn't it?"

When the salad had been consumed, the entrees were brought. Kinniger, as was his pleasure, spooned a generous amount of Parmesan cheese over his spaghetti, then began eating, feeling more in control. He looked across at Tolbert, who was tasting his food and sipping his wine with obvious appreciation. "What is that you ordered, anyway?" Kinniger asked.

"Squid," Tolbert said.

Kinniger's appetite faltered for a moment, then he resumed eating, averting his eyes from Tolbert's plate.

Finally, over a small Marsala custard he had selected for dessert, Tolbert said, "Well, Professor, I've been thinking."

"What have you been thinking?"

"That while we study and teach criminology, that while we're considered experts at the business of crime, the fact is that we are merely observers at the edge of it, aren't we?"

"I don't know what you're talking about."

"Then I'll be more specific. What I'm saying is that we are merely ivory-tower academicians. We've had no taste of the real thing. And I suggest we should."

Kinniger put down his spoon and looked at Tolbert. "In what fashion?"

"In whatever fashion either of us individually selects—in whatever fashion we can successfully accomplish."

"The wine's gone to your head, Alex."

"I think not. I've been considering this for some time. I believe, personally, that I'm ready. How about you, Charles?" There was challenge in his voice. "Charles?"

"Am I supposed to steal pencils out of a blind man's cap? Thieve someone's morning newspaper from his porch?"

"*Charles.* Not such petty wrongs. I'm talking about committing true crime!"

"But why?"

"To get to know the criminal mentality, not simply theorize on it as we've *been* doing. Get into the water and *swim.*"

"I still don't understand—"

"I'm suggesting you commit a crime you believe yourself to be capable of, and bringing it off undetected. I shall do the same."

Another contest, Kinniger thought with apprehension. One he would be quite foolish to get into. Yet . . . could he refuse? Allowing Tolbert one more victory without so much as an effort on his part? *Damn* the man!

"What do you say, Charles?"

"How far do we go?"

Tolbert motioned with a fragile hand. "I set no limits. We should each simply choose, plan, do, and then inform the other, once it has been done. I should imagine the greater crime accomplished would decide the victor. Are you game, Charles? Do you have the mettle, do you think?"

Kinniger struck a fist against the table. "I can do anything you can do, Alex!" He tried to make the statement emphatic, tried to believe in the words.

That was weeks ago, he thought now, driving the mountain road with Tolbert. His words had *not* been valid. He'd done nothing whatever about Tolbert's contest. He'd dreamed up a half-dozen criminal actions and planned them in precise detail. But when it came to the doing he'd failed. Tolbert had not, he knew. The man's manner today indicated that he had indeed committed his crime, and won another contest.

"I demand that you tell me, Alex," Kinniger said angrily. "What did you *do?*"

Tolbert's expression reflected extraordinary self-satisfaction. "Do you recall a recent San Francisco incident concerning the Hiviana Bank?"

Kinniger suddenly felt ill. He read avidly about all crimes and he'd certainly read of that one—a simple but effective robbery that had netted the thieves just a little over one-hundred-thousand dollars. "You're not going to tell me you had anything to do with that!"

"Oh, but yes," Tolbert said with relish.

"You manipulated that from behind the scenes? Is that what you're going to try to foist off on me? No good, Alex. The man who got the money went into the bank accompanied by a woman carrying an automatic weapon. He was an ex-con and was found later on the beach shot to death, apparently by that same weapon. He was absolutely identified as the robber, because he'd worn no disguise in the bank. There was no evidence of the money on him. It's assumed the woman did the killing and ran off with it. You had nothing to do with that heist!"

"But I did, Charles. I've been using that bank for nearly twenty years and I know the operation down to every small detail. I've made friends there and I know where the vulnerabilities are. I planned everything, including gaining the assistance of that ex-convict. I knew he'd just gotten out of San Quentin—and I knew, just as you know, the unconscious predilection of such people wishing to return to their cells by immediately committing a fresh crime. So—I telephoned him, disguising my voice, and made the proposal. He accepted."

"Poppycock!" Kinniger said.

"I did not give him the name of the institution, told him only that it was a bank. He met me at the appointed place of rendezvous, where I had ready a stolen car—the simplest of accomplishments, my man. I carefully outlined what we were to do and how. We carried out the caper most successfully."

"There was a woman with him!"

"It was I, Charles."

Kinniger stared at the other man, feeling his pulse pounding. *That* he could believe—Tolbert would be capable of a convincing masquerade as a woman—but had he actually done anything so bizarre as dress-

ing as a woman and helping an ex-con rob a bank? Then had he actually *murdered* the man?

"When we went to the beach to divide the money," Tolbert said, "I
shot him to death. He was a stupid individual, as most criminals are.
But not *this* criminal, Charles—I got away with it."

Grand theft, and murder as well! Kinniger thought furiously.

"There's no way to trace anything to me, Charles. I threw the gun
from the Golden Gate Bridge. The gentleman who actually collected
the money from the bank, as I held that weapon, never knew who I
was or, in fact, that I was not a female. He knew nothing of the identity of the bank we intended to rob until we were prepared to walk
into it—so he could have told no one about that prior to the robbery. I
was with him during the robbery and after—until his demise."

Kinniger's hands knotted into fists. "Where did you get a gun?" He
had to find a hole somewhere, anywhere.

"I stole it from the library of a gun collector I've known for years."

"In drag, I suspect."

"You suspect correctly."

Kinniger sat in cold silence. Finally he said, "I reject it all, out of
hand."

"My creel on the back seat," Tolbert said. "Lift it forward."

Kinniger turned and looked at the large monogrammed wicker container with the leather harness attached; Tolbert usually caught so
many fish that its large size was essential. "What about the damned
creel?"

"The money's inside."

"If it is, which I doubt, I'm not putting my fingerprints anywhere
near it."

Tolbert peeled off one driving glove, then the other. He handed
them to Kinniger.

Kinniger put them on and yanked the creel forward, feeling instinctively that the money was there. He lifted the cover and made a hurried count that revealed Tolbert's story to be absolutely true.

"When we return to the Bay Area," Tolbert said, enjoying himself,
"I shall drop you off, then deposit that currency where it shall never be
found by anyone but me. A nice little ace in the hole, eh? Plus the satisfaction of actually having done what I did. Now, my man, what
magnificent crime have you committed to outdo me? Let's hear it."

"Go to hell, Tolbert!" Kinniger raged.

Tolbert used a little-known trail to get to a secluded section. He maneuvered his car expertly through the woods and parked on a rock plateau beside a stream.

He gathered his tackle eagerly from the trunk of the car. Kinniger was listless as he began his own preparations. He watched Tolbert don waders and a fishing vest, then fit into the harness of the wicker creel—he knew he would wear the creel constantly here, now that its contents had been revealed. For collecting fish, Tolbert would use the metal stringer he had attached to his belt.

Kinniger shook his head, tasting bitterness. Also wearing a fishing vest, with a small net creel attached, he put together his 8-foot fly rod. He fitted the heavy fly line through the lead guards of the rod and tied on a light 10-foot leader. He estimated the time of day and year, the condition of the water, their location, then selected a McGinty fly to approximate the yellow jackets buzzing over the water.

Tolbert, standing at the edge of a pool just upstream, caught his first trout even before Kinniger had attached the McGinty to his leader. He bellowed with joy and victory as he always did. Kinniger trudged downstream around a bend and to the bottom of a falls, then started working up and down the stream, from pools to white-water riffles, trying everything: black gnats, royal coachmen, hackles, mosquitoes, quills, pink ladies, red ants. Almost every fly he owned.

Nothing worked. There was not the slightest evidence that fish even existed in these waters.

Yet he kept hearing Tolbert's infuriating shouts as he continued to draw fish from a stream that refused Kinniger the same privilege.

Then Tolbert was directly above him, working carefully along a rock ledge at the lower side of a pool where water spilled over and came down in a flashing roar to where Kinniger cast into the rapids in front of him.

Tolbert shouted again, and held a wriggling trout of impressive size for Kinniger to see. Kinniger swore silently, then blinked as the idea came to him, full-blown.

He did not think more about it—he simply acted, as fury seethed within him.

He found in his vest a very large hook he'd used on a one-time saltwater excursion in the Pacific Ocean. He cut the leader line from the heavier fly line to which it had been attached, then swiftly tied the large hook to the fly line and pinched on split shot for added distance and control. He made several quick false casts, the large hook flying back and forth over his head.

Then he looked up to see that Tolbert was still on the ledge at the top of the falls, perhaps fifty feet above where Kinniger stood with the water churning around jagged rocks.

Kinniger made his real cast now, sending the line upward, straight at Tolbert, his accuracy unerring. The hook bit into Tolbert's vest. Kinniger yanked his line, fixing the hook, and pulling Tolbert off the ledge. Tolbert shouted as he came down—then he struck the rocks. Kinniger let his catch be pushed along by the rapids a distance. Finally, when Tolbert reached quieter waters, Kinniger worked him in.

When he had beached him on the bank, he examined him and knew that Tolbert was quite dead.

He removed the harness of the creel from Tolbert's body, then opened the cover. The money had gotten a bit wet, but it would soon dry. Kinniger closed the cover and wrapped the harness around the creel. He had done it! No planning, no plotting, just the action itself! He'd not only murdered, he'd murdered Tolbert himself! And he had Tolbert's stolen money. All he had to do now was hide the money to retrieve later, then drive Tolbert's car to the nearest phone to report the accident.

He knelt beside Tolbert and took his car keys. As he did, he smiled at the stringer hooked to Tolbert's belt where some of the fish were still flopping. He would simply leave them secured, proof that Tolbert had not needed a creel.

He stood up with the creel and started up along the bank toward the sports car. He could hide the creel anywhere nearby. Who would be likely to find it even if they should search for it? Why should anyone search for *anything*?

Then it came to him, as he climbed, that perhaps there was the faintest possibility that someone *would* think of foul play. It was unreasonable—he and Tolbert had been outwardly regarded as the best of friends. Yet the lawman's mind was constantly honed by suspicion, wasn't it? The creel, if it were found with the money in it, could be identified as Tolbert's. And the money would constitute a motive. Someone had dashed Tolbert to the rocks and taken his creel with the money in it . . .

Kinniger stopped, feeling his heart racing as hard as it had when he'd pulled Tolbert off the ledge. A small chipmunk scurried in front of him so that Kinniger actually jumped. A jay sounded a bitter tirade at him from a pine branch above. Kinniger's nerves sang in response.

Go back to the body, he thought, turning and hurrying down toward it. Put the harness of the creel back on Tolbert, remove the money and transfer the fish from the stringer to the creel. Find some other container to put the money in, so that it's safe here for a time, in the wilderness . . .

No, he thought. Foolish thinking. He was overreacting. Everything was fine. All he had to do was hide the creel as it was, somewhere, anywhere, remembering its location, then go ahead and report the accidental death.

He climbed upward again, trying to remain calm. As he neared the car, it came to him: what if Tolbert had not committed the perfect crime, after all? What if the man Tolbert had killed, the ex-con with whom he'd committed the bank robbery, had somehow found out Tolbert's real identity—had left evidence of the fact in some way, telling someone, writing it down where it could still be found . . .

Or something else: what if the bank had a record of some of the serial numbers on the currency!

Kinniger turned and plunged back down the bank, thinking: forget the money! Put the harness and creel back on Tolbert and leave the currency in the creel, and drive off to phone in the report. Who could accuse Kinniger of foul play if that kind of money remained in Tolbert's possession?

As he neared the body he stopped, thinking: leave a hundred thousand dollars? All of the security he'd always wanted and needed? Leave it? Just like that?

He couldn't do it!

He whirled and went upward again. He'd been so certain that he had at last beaten Tolbert, beaten him all the way, once and for all. But now another thought rushed at him, a vicious, stupendous thought!

What if Tolbert, knowing that he was going to reveal to Kinniger the fact that he'd robbed a bank and murdered a man, using the money to prove the fact, had also left a document behind? "In case of my untoward death, gentlemen, look to Mr. Charles Kinniger, who was informed of my crimes and knew of the stolen money . . ."

He stopped and turned and went downward again. Give the money back to Tolbert, he thought wildly—let him have it, even in death! . . .

But, no, he thought, his mind whirling as he reversed himself and started back up the incline, he couldn't give it up—he couldn't! Yet . . .

And he found, with maddening realization, that he was simply running back and forth over the same path, unable to make a decision. The peaks surrounded him in primeval grandeur. The stream sounded its sweet free-spirited tumbling. But he felt as trapped, as defeated, as any animal caught in an unrelenting cage.

"*Damn you!*" he shouted down toward the dead man. "*Damn you, Tolbert!*" he screamed, knowing that his condemnation was as useless as it had always been.

The Challenge

by Carroll Mayers

On a bright May morning, at age forty-three, Mrs. Margate committed a successful crime. Not that she regarded her act as a felony; it was, rather, a bold spur-of-the-moment impulse which, once completed, left her breathless and deliciously exhilarated.

Her prize—a silvered brooch on sale at Hansen's Department Store for $12.95—was nothing she truly needed. But fondling the shiny pin at home, Mrs. Margate again shivered with pleasure. What would the girls at the bridge club say if they knew what she'd done! For that matter, what would her husband George say! Stolid stuffy old George, who essentially was only a clerk in a brokerage house and who hadn't done or said anything exciting in fifteen years.

Mrs. Margate hummed gaily as she prepared dinner that night. It was simply unbelievable she'd never tried anything like that before. A challenge was what it represented. Something to buoy her and change her very existence.

And *fun!*

On ensuing days, Mrs. Margate visited Hansen's three more times. Coincident with her visits, her collection of trophies grew: a lovely golden compact, fortuitously monogrammed *M*, a tiny phial of expensive French perfume, a lady's scarf . . .

Never had her days been so pleasurable. She could scarcely wait for each successful foray. Her pride of accomplishment surged. Could she dare hint of her activity to the bridge club? Mrs. Margate could just hear their incredulous gasps.

Unfortunately, such speculation was premature. On an afternoon of the following week, an unobtrusive little man in a conservative grey business suit quietly followed Mrs. Margate as she left Hansen's. He touched her arm.

"One moment, ma'am."

She turned and regarded her accoster. "Yes?"

"I must ask you to step back into the store with me."

Mrs. Margate bridled. "I most certainly will not," she rejoined.

There was a glint in the little man's gaze which belied his mild manner. "After you, ma'am," he said. At the same time, his touch on her arm firmed.

A spate of uneasiness washed over Mrs. Margate, but she steeled herself against it. No one could have seen her. She'd been too clever, too deft—

"Very well," she said, mustering haughty distaste. She permitted the little man to take her back inside Hansen's and escort her to an office on the second floor. The office door was inscribed *Manager*.

"My name is Castle, madam," the heavy-set man occupying the office said soberly, rising and indicating a chair beside his desk. "This is most unpleasant."

Mrs. Margate seated herself, aware that her disquietude was growing slightly, but still feeling in command of the situation. "I have no idea what you're implying," she said. "I've been brought up here—"

The little man who'd done so cut her short. "There's a pair of ladies' evening gloves in her purse, Mr. Castle," he said simply. "Not paid for."

A chill traced Mrs. Margate's spine. So she *had* been seen . . .

Manager Castle smoothed an incipient bald spot. "Would you care to open your purse?" he said.

How could she refuse the request? Indignation, perhaps. Mrs. Margate tossed her head.

"I see no need to."

The manager sighed. "As I said, this is most unpleasant. The police could make it more so."

The police! Dismay flooded Mrs. Margate. Until that moment she had not fully credited that possibility. They *could* make her open her purse.

Her mind raced. Perhaps if she temporized a bit—

Mrs. Margate allowed her shoulders to slump. She unsnapped her purse and withdrew the ladies' evening gloves. "I don't know what came over me," she said, her lips trembling. "I've never done anything like this before."

Manager Castle shook his head. "I'm sorry, but Mr. Barrand here has been watching you, madam . . ."

His words trailed off. "May I have your name?"

She could lie, of course. But such a tactic might only intensify her predicament. A lie could be exposed.

"Mrs. Margate," she acknowledged. "Mrs. Arlene Margate."

Manager Castle made a notation on a scratch pad. When he resumed, a thread of regret laced his speech. "You're clearly a refined cultured woman, Mrs. Margate," he told her. "But shoplifting is a crime, a serious problem that's sweeping the country. Merchants are losing millions of dollars every year and it's getting worse."

He paused, trading a brief glance with his security man. "Here at Hansen's, we've been reluctant to prosecute, but we simply cannot continue to absorb these losses."

Mrs. Margate's dismay eased a bit. The rueful note of the manager's mini-sermon was not lost on her; patently he had no relish for prosecution. He'd said that calling in the police could make the incident more unpleasant. *Could.* Not *would.*

His next words confirmed his aversion to precipitate action. "Perhaps you'd care to phone your husband?"

She seized upon the offer. The very stolidity and stuffiness she deplored in George nonetheless suggested the impeccable respectability that might tip the scale and firm the manager's obvious reluctance, provided satisfactory restitution was forthcoming.

Mrs. Margate permitted her lips to tremble once more. "Yes, I would," she murmured.

George arrived on the scene in twenty minutes. Having assimilated but a smattering of the situation over the phone, he reacted with stunned disbelief when Manager Castle and Mr. Barrand documented his worst fears.

"But this is incredible!" he protested. "There must be some mistake. My wife is no shoplifter!"

The manager shook his head. "We have to disagree, sir. There have been at least four instances—"

George gaped at Mrs. Margate, who in turn calculatedly dropped her gaze.

"You're positive?" George queried the manager.

"Quite."

George drew a breath. He was a pudgy individual, almost roly-poly, with plump cheeks. "Have you notified the police?"

Manager Castle sighed in turn.

"Not yet, Mr. Margate. As I told your wife, Hansen's finds these occurrences most unpleasant but—"

"I appreciate your position," George interrupted, "but certainly you can allow for a temporary aberration on my wife's part. I assure you, you'll receive full reimbursement."

Mr. Barrand started to say something but his employer interrupted. "I'm not fully convinced the store should not bring charges, sir," he said slowly, "but on the other hand . . ." He hesitated, fingers drumming the desk top. Finally, he capitulated. "Very well. But I must insist that Mrs. Margate does not enter these premises again."

At the pronouncement, the lady in question remained discreetly silent.

George built a tight smile.

"She won't, Mr. Castle," he said firmly. "And thank you. Now—what is the amount of your losses? I will personally bring you a check in the morning."

Once home, George sought a full explanation. "In heaven's name, Arlene, whatever made you do such a thing?" he protested. "Think of my position!"

Now that the crisis was past, Mrs. Margate saw no reason for excessive repentance.

"Think of *my* position," she countered. "You're colorless, George. You're stolid and dull. We never do anything exciting. I wanted some fun! I wanted a little spice in my life—"

He blinked in total astonishment. "Good Lord! Shoplifting? Spice?"

It was not a compatible evening. In the morning, George wrote a check for the amount Mr. Castle had mentioned, then stopped by Hansen's on his way to the brokerage office to deliver the check personally as he'd promised.

Early as it was, the aisles were crowded with shoppers. Threading his way through, George noted that the countertops were littered with merchandise. He frowned. Damn it, no wonder Arlene had been tempted!

That evening Mrs. Margate went to her bridge club.

Alone, George settled down with the afternoon paper but found concentration difficult. In bed the night before and all day today he'd been nagged by his wife's disparaging characterization of him. Perhaps he *was* stolid and colorless. Perhaps he *had* allowed himself to settle into a rut. That was wrong, at any age. A man should guard against that.

Turning a page, George plucked a cigarette from a pack on the coffee table, then withdrew a lighter from his pocket. The lighter was new, heavily chromed, shafting warm highlights.

He regarded it appreciatively as he fired his cigarette, then returned the gadget to his pocket. If a man *were* to change, George reflected, he had to start somewhere.

Extra Work

by Robert W. Wells

The tall, greying man got out of his car and walked across the yard to the door of the white-clapboard farmhouse. He stood on the porch for a moment, his shoulders a little stooped, his sunburned face thoughtful. Then he rapped just once on the screen door. He took off his hat quickly when the young woman opened it.

"Can I step in, Mrs. Fram?"

His voice was soft. It would have seemed shy in a younger man.

"You're from the sheriff's? I don't know what questions you've got I haven't already answered."

He smiled reassuringly at her and followed her into the kitchen. It was a large bare room. There was a cooking stove in one corner and next to it an old-fashioned icebox.

The linoleum on the floor was cracked and darkened with long wear, but it was clean. So were the cheap cotton curtains at the windows. The panes of glass themselves were spotless.

The tall man's eyes took in these details approvingly. He sat down at the plastic-covered kitchen table. The woman remained standing, her arms folded defiantly.

"Set down." The way he said it, it was not an order but a suggestion. "This might take awhile. Don't pay to be in a hurry when it's murder you're dealing with. Anyway, so they tell me."

She eased herself into one of the plain wooden chairs across the table from him. She was a tall woman, in her early twenties. Her chestnut hair was combed back severely from her oval face, which was entirely free of makeup. There were the beginnings of dark circles under her brown eyes, but none of the redness that comes with weeping.

"Have they caught the tramp yet?" she asked.

"No. Funny thing about that. A town like Marsburg, a stranger stands out. Seems like nobody saw the fellow you described at all." He pulled a battered briar from his pocket, filled it with tobacco from a can he carried in his hip pocket, tamped it down carefully and lit it. "That is, nobody but you. And Sam. Only, of course, Sam ain't around to tell us."

She watched him warily, her lips pressed tightly together. He pushed himself back in the chair and exhaled a cloud of smoke toward the ceiling.

"Guess I ought to introduce myself," he said. "My name's Vaughan. My ma called me Horace, but it wasn't long before folks changed it to plain Horse. Don't know why exactly, but my wife claims it's on account of I look a little like one. I don't hold to that myself. I always tell her it's a tribute to my horse sense."

He looked over at the young woman quickly to see if she was smiling but she wasn't and he sighed and tipped his chair back a little further, balancing himself with his knees on the underside of the table.

"Now let's see, Mrs. Fram," he said. "I know you told old Keezey, the sheriff, how it happened when we was out here yesterday and I was supposed to be listening, but I wonder if you'd just go over the whole thing once more? I got kind of a poor memory."

She jumped to her feet and walked over to a small mirror that hung over the cast-iron sink. It was slightly crooked and she straightened it and walked back to where he was sitting.

"You're trying to trap me. That's it, isn't it?"

Vaughan's surprise seemed genuine. "Now why'd I want to do that? Like I told you, I'm a fellow who forgets things easy."

"All right," she said. "I'll go through it again. We was sitting right here having supper and—"

"That would be Sam and you?"

"Who else?" she demanded. She looked at him suspiciously but his expression was bland. "He was sitting in that chair you're in and I was just getting up to go to the stove to get him some more pork chops when he must of seen something out the window because he jumped up and ran out. I took the skillet off the fire and went out on the back porch to see what was going on. Sam was out by the barn arguing with this tramp."

"You hear what they was saying?"

"Not the words, but I could see Sam swinging his arms around like he was excited. The tramp was just standing there, not saying much. I figured Sam was ordering him off the place, only he didn't look like he was going, so I went to the closet and got the shotgun."

"You check to see it was loaded?"

"I knew it wasn't. I don't allow loaded guns around my house. I put a shell in. Sam kept them in a dresser drawer. I figured I'd take the gun out and give it to Sam in case he needed it to get the tramp to leave."

"This tramp, now. Seems like I recollect you said he was a sawed-off little runt, hardly five foot high. That right?"

"Yes. He had a day's growth of beard. I'd judge he was maybe in his forties. An ugly little man."

"About the same age as Sam and me."

"Just about. Husky too. Huskier than Sam, even if he was a lot shorter. Dirty clothes. Smelly, like they hadn't been washed in weeks. Sam was always so clean."

She sat down quickly in the chair and put her hands over her face. After a few moments Vaughan leaned forward and touched her gently.

"Hate to be a nuisance, Mrs. Fram," he said, "but when you get hold of yourself I'd like to hear what happened next."

She put down her hands.

"What are they saying in the village, Mr. Vaughan? Don't believe all you hear. They never liked me here. Said I was stuck-up on account of I never mixed much."

He leaned back in his chair again. His voice was apologetic. He rubbed his chin with one heavy hand in apparent embarrassment.

"Folks always say lots of things, Mrs. Fram. They think it's funny nobody saw this tramp but you. They even say you and Sam didn't get along so good. Anything to that?"

"We argued sometimes. Everybody argues."

"They say old Sam was such a bug on keeping everything clean it might of made him pretty hard to live with. They say on account of him being a bachelor so long, not getting married 'til he was past forty-five, he didn't know how to treat a young girl. They say you didn't like it much, after living in the city, being stuck off here on a side road on this rundown farm. I'm just telling you what they say, now."

She leaned toward him and gripped his arm with both her hands.

"They think I done it, don't they? That's what they been telling you. How do they know what it was like living with Sam? None of them ever come around to see how I was getting along, not one. Not a single one. Maybe we was happy together and maybe we wasn't, but nobody in Marsburg would know one way or the other."

"Well now, Mrs. Fram. Folks in the village are about like those anyplace else. You ever go out of your way to be friendly?"

"I didn't know how!" she cried. "I would have but I didn't know how!"

She rubbed a hand wearily across her forehead and her voice died down almost to a whisper.

"Besides, Sam didn't want me to be mixing. He didn't want me to talk to people. He didn't want me to do lots of things—like wearing lipstick or putting my hair up nice. All he wanted was for me to scrub the place clean—scrub and scrub and scrub! He acted like he was scared of dirt, somehow—and him a farmer all his life. Well, I did like he said. I scrubbed 'til my hands was raw. And now look at what's happened."

Vaughan acted as though he had scarcely heard her. He was looking up at the ceiling, watching the smoke rise toward it, his eyes half closed and his hands clasped comfortably across his tan shirt.

"To get back to when you took out the shotgun," he suggested apologetically. "As I recall what you told us yesterday, Sam got shot right where we found him, out next to the barn."

She nodded. "That's right. I took the gun, like I said, and ran out toward the barn, intending to give it to Sam. But this tramp fellow heard me coming. He grabbed it out of my hand before I knew what he was about. Then Sam wrestled with him and got a hold of the gun and the thing went off."

"And Sam right in front of it, I take it. So it was more like an accident, then. That'd make it second degree, I guess."

"That all the questions? I got work to do. I got to wash down the back steps before dark."

Vaughan brought his chair down with a crash. The sound seemed to startle him and he stood up, his red face flushing.

"You don't have to no more, you know," he told her. "Sam's dead now. You don't need to scrub 'em unless you want to."

She looked up at him warily.

"No, I guess I don't," she said. "I forgot."

"Habit's a funny thing," he said. He sauntered over to the window and looked out. "There's still a couple of points puzzle me, Mrs. Fram. 'Course, I puzzle easy. Maybe you can straighten me out. Right at first, I got to admit, it looked like an easy job and that made me feel good on account of I got some work to do around home, fixing up the yard for my old woman. But then I noticed something that got me to wondering."

"Mind telling me what it was?"

Her tone seemed as casual as his. He glanced at her quickly, but she didn't look up. She was polishing the plastic tablecloth with a crumpled paper napkin, her arm making wider and wider circles as she rubbed.

"Well, now, we'll get to that," he said. "But first I guess I ought to mention that we got some help from the crime lab in the city. We don't usually bother—Keezey don't hold much with that scientific stuff. But this time we did. The boys there tell me they found only one set of fingerprints on the gun. They wasn't yours, Mrs. Fram, and they wasn't Sam's. Seems like they belong to a fellow with a record. His name's Carson—Herman Carson, nicknamed Kit. He did time down at Columbus a couple of years back. Ever hear of him?"

She was still rubbing the tablecloth, her eyes focused on the task.

"Maybe that was the tramp's name," she said. "How should I know?"

"Could be. Funny thing, though. The description they got of Carson don't jibe worth a cent with the one you give us. Seems like Carson's a big fellow, over six feet, and a lot younger than you said the tramp was. Good looking, too, judging from his pictures, if you like the kind of looks that goes with slicked-back hair. Matter of fact, he sounds like just about the opposite of the bird you told us about. Makes it hard to figure exactly what to think."

"I bet you tried," the woman said bitterly. "I bet you tried real hard. And you come out here, soft spoken and all, acting like you're so friendly."

Vaughan walked over, not hurrying, and looked down at her, his long face as innocent of guile as a colt's.

"I'm as friendly a fellow as you're likely to meet," he said. "Can't say I enjoy this, but old Keezey talked me into taking this deputy's job a few years back and there are things I got to do to earn my pay." For the first time something hard and implacable came into his tone. "Like asking you to stop telling fibs, Mrs. Fram."

She jumped to her feet and hurried to the back porch. Grabbing a broom that was hanging there, suspended by a string through its handle, she began brushing the steps vigorously. Vaughan came to her and took the broom out of her hand and motioned to her to sit down. She dropped to the top step and cradled her chin in her hand, looking out across the distant fields, her expression sullen.

"I told you all I'm going to," she said.

The tall man looked down at her, his face sad.

"Suppose I tell you what I think happened, Mrs. Fram. Then you say where I slipped up, if I'm wrong."

She didn't answer. He shook his head regretfully.

"You're a good-looking woman. Don't know how you got mixed up with Sam. Not that he wasn't a good man, in his way, but he ought to of married somebody nearer his own age. Anyway, that part's none of my business." He pulled his pipe from his pocket and lit it, savoring the smoke for a moment, reluctant to begin. "This Carson fellow," he said. "The way I got it figured, maybe you knew him in the city. According to the stuff the boys there sent us, he used to have a wife about your age. About your build too. Same color hair and all. She divorced him while he was in the pen. I don't say it was you, but it could of been, couldn't it?"

He eased his massive frame down on the step beside her, grunting softly with the effort. His eyes moved casually toward her and studied her face briefly, but when she gave no sign he resumed talking.

"Say for the sake of argument it was you. Nothing wrong in that. Girls get mixed up with the wrong fellows sometimes. Now just suppose it was you and after you got the divorce you decided to start all over and you started looking for a place to disappear. Let's say you met a fellow from the country, a fellow like Sam, and you figured if you married him and moved out in the sticks Carson couldn't find you and you could forget about him. So you did and you found out pretty soon you'd bought yourself no bed of roses. But you tried to make the best of things. You did like old Sam told you. You quit wearing lipstick and you learned how to swing a scrub brush. You kept the place nice and clean like he wanted and you stayed away from the folks in the village, maybe partly because Sam was jealous, him having a young wife and all, but maybe partly so's there'd be less chance of running into somebody you knew from the old days."

"You've got it all wrong," she said.

She wasn't looking at him. Her hands were clasping and unclasping themselves in her lap nervously, as though anxious to be about some task. Her mouth was sullen but there was something desperate and frightened in her eyes. Vaughan's placid voice droned on.

"Maybe. Maybe not. Anyhow, let's suppose that some way or other this Kit Carson fellow found out you was here and he come around on the sly yesterday, making sure nobody seen him, and hid out until Sam changed his clothes and left to take that load of feed to town. Then maybe this Carson come up to the house. Maybe Sam come home while he was here. Maybe he didn't like it, seeing the two of you together. Maybe that's when Sam got shot. It could've happened like that."

"It could have," she said, her voice flat and hard. "Only it didn't."

"Some of it was right, though, wasn't it?"

She didn't answer. Her face was calm, but her eyes darted from side to side, desperate with their need to get away from Vaughan's soft approach. He leaned back, his elbows supporting him, and played the card he had been saving.

"It'd be a good idea to talk, Mrs. Fram. The city boys say it's only a matter of time before they catch up with Carson. Seems like they've found the woman he's been living with and they're watching the place like cats around a rat hole."

She twisted toward him, her face suddenly ugly. "You're just saying that to trick me! There's no woman!"

"A big blonde," Vaughan said, his voice gentle and a little mournful. "Good looking, they tell me. Works in a nightclub floor show. I wouldn't fool you, Mrs. Fram."

The woman had been rigid but now she collapsed. Her head went down on her chest, her legs sprawled in front of her on the steps, her shoulders sagged. The tears came and she made no attempt to hide them. Vaughan offered her his handkerchief, which she refused. After a moment she wiped her face with her hand and sat up straight again.

"I guess I was a fool to think he'd change," she said. "Why should I tell lies for him any more?"

"No reason to," Vaughan said. There was no triumph in his tone. "No reason at all."

"You had most of it right," she said. "Kit did it, all right. I was frying pork chops like I told you, only it was for Kit, not Sam. I thought Sam wouldn't be back for another hour. He saw us and got the gun and then there was a struggle out near the barn and Sam got shot."

"But you still say it was an accident?"

"Yes. Oh, yes. It just happened."

"I suppose," Vaughan mused, "after being married to Sam for over a year, this Kit fellow looked pretty good to you?"

"Not at first. Not when he first walked in. But he's a good talker, Kit is. He gets me all confused. It was always like that, he's always been able to twist me around, make me do anything he wanted."

Her voice was dry, the fires all burned out of it. Vaughan stood up and helped her to her feet, his hand resting lightly on her arm.

"Let's see," he said softly. "Sam had four thousand in insurance.

This place here's got some pretty good land if it was worked right. It'll bring maybe eight, ten thousand. No other heirs, so I guess it all would go to you."

She tried to pull away from him. He tightened his grip.

"I tell you what, Mrs. Fram," he said. "Every time you change your story you put a little more of the truth in it. Only one thing still bothers me—no, make it two. Why would this Carson fellow look you up? It could be because he was sweet on you, but it don't seem like that would be it, judging from his record. Besides, there's this blonde, and there seems to of been plenty of others between you and her. Only one thing'd make him come way out here and look you up, the way I see it. He knew how you felt about him and he figured if you was Sam's widow he could work it so's he'd get most of the money. That means he planned ahead of time to shoot Sam. That makes it first degree, and it means both of you are in lots of trouble."

"It was an accident!" she cried. "I swear it! They was fighting over the gun out near the barn and all of a sudden Sam was dead!"

Vaughan shook his head sadly.

"I don't know what to do with you," he said. "You keep telling me fibs, Mrs. Fram, and that ain't neighborly, is it? You know those crime-lab boys are pretty smart. They figured out Sam was shot from a distance of maybe five, six feet with the gun aimed level with his chest. That don't tie in with what you said. Besides, like I told you, Sam's prints weren't on the gun. And I know another thing you don't think I know—Sam wasn't shot out by the barn at all."

He let go his grasp and she took a step or two toward the porch railing. There was a rag hanging there and she picked it up and began polishing the worn wood.

"You was wondering what it was I noticed that first made me think you weren't giving me a straight story," he went on. "Well, I'll tell you. Last night, after we left here, I got to looking at Sam's clothes and there was grass stains on his overalls, the ones he put on fresh to go to town in, him being the kind of fellow who always liked things clean. They wasn't the kind of marks you'd get just sitting around, either. To me, those stains meant just one thing: after he was shot, he'd been dragged across the yard and then somebody'd taken a lot of trouble to clean up afterward so we wouldn't know it.

"Well, up until then I didn't have no real reason to suppose your story wasn't true as silk. The pieces didn't all fit together, maybe, but that's the way things usually are in a shooting and it didn't bother me.

I'm not a fellow that goes around looking for extra work. But when I seen those grass stains I knew Sam hadn't got shot out by the barn like you told us. I got to thinking that maybe if you hadn't told the truth there, it'd be worth some checking to see if you'd been fibbin' on some other stuff. That's when I talked old Keezey into calling those city experts in on it and then we started turning up stuff right and left that didn't fit into the story you'd told us.

"It hadn't been for those grass stains, though, I might of took your word for it, you being such a nice-looking young girl and all, and I'd be home today spading up the flower beds instead of having to arrest you as accessory to a murder."

The young woman's hands were still busy. Her whole body was concentrated on the task of polishing the worn railing. Her face, which had been defiant at first, then sullen, now wore a look of weary hopelessness.

"I'm tired," she said. "I'm too tired to lie any more." Then a little of her former manner returned. "I'm not answering anything else until I get a lawyer."

Vaughan nodded. "Guess that'd be smart," he said.

He scratched the back of his head, his eyes narrowed in thought.

"I got it pretty well figured out anyhow. Carson shot him. No doubt of that. Maybe you helped him plan it and maybe you just tried to cover up for him—that's something for the jury to figure out. Anyway, it must of happened here on the porch, because the city boys found a couple of fresh splinters stuck in Sam to go with the grass stains. The gun must of been aimed out away from the house or we'd of found the stray pellets. Probably Sam got shot as he was coming home for supper, maybe as he was smelling the pork chops you was frying and thinking how good they'd taste, maybe before he even knew Carson was here."

The woman stopped polishing the railing and faced him. He came over and put his hand on her shoulder.

"Don't know how I ever got mixed up in a job like this," he said. "Can't say as I enjoy it. I got a big bump of curiosity, though, when I get started and there's one thing I wish you'd tell me before we go see the sheriff. How come Carson didn't leave Sam where he fell? How come he hauled him out in the yard and got you mixed up on your story of what happened? If it hadn't been for that, your story might of held up."

"It was me," she said, looking into his face, her eyes dazed, wondering. "I dragged him. Kit shot him here on the porch but then he lost his nerve and run off, leaving me with the dirty work, like always. I dragged Sam to where you found him. I thought it'd be simpler if I just said that was where he was killed."

"Sam must of weighed close to one-ninety," Vaughan said. "How come you felt called on to do that?"

Her voice was earnest with the effort to make him understand. "Don't you see?" she said. "The porch. There was blood on the porch. I had to scrub it. I had to scrub it off right away or Sam would have run riot on me for real."

The First Moon Tourist

by Duffy Carpenter

When the legislature of my state decided to do something about the glut of cases clogging the Small Claims Court, they dreamed up an expansion of the referee system which allowed state-appointed non-lawyers to settle disputes below $1,000 in value. To qualify for this non-paying post, one had to have a background in business law, attend a series of lectures on procedure, and pass written and oral examinations.

The guiding principle, I was told in my classes, was the doctrine of the "reasonable man." Once I was actively hearing cases each Tuesday and Thursday night from 6:30 to 10:00 P.M., I wondered how far I was supposed to stretch being reasonable.

For the uninitiated, the legal definition of a "reasonable man" is a hypothetical being who exercises qualities of attention, knowledge, intelligence, and judgment. I do very well on attention because it would be impossible to fall asleep during the three-ring circus that these hearings are. I believe I also score well on the knowledge qualification, since I have a Masters in Business Administration and fifteen years of marketing experience. I even come up to snuff on intelligence, since I was smart enough to marry the prettiest girl this side of the Mississippi, have three bright children by her, and along the way managed to become a vice-president with a major corporation. So far, so good. But then we bump into judgment, and I think my first show of lunacy was becoming a referee in the first place. The second was allowing Minivich *vs.* Kripps to enter arbitration instead of alerting the local funny farm when they walked into my hearing room.

My initial reaction to the two contestants was that I had, through some magic, become the MC on "Let's Make a Deal." Minivich was a mustached man in his early thirties—at least I assumed that, because the visor on his space helmet blurred his features. Yes, space helmet, just like the astronauts wear. The rest of him was all denim. Jacket, jeans, shirt. This was set off by boots of silver. When he lifted the visor, I half expected him to say "Trick or treat." Instead, he said, "Minivich to Corbett, present for justice." I'm Corbett, so I nodded.

That was only half the walnut. Its counterpart, or more accurately, the defendant, Joe Kripps, was not to be outdone. He wore a long red smock and a white hardhat. So far, so bad, but atop the hat was a small revolving light. Red, blue, white, red, blue, white, etc. When Kripps turned to draw up a chair, I noted the lettering on his back in block letters: "Far Flung Travel, Go Go Go." He sat down with a broad smile on his pudgy face. "Kripps is on the pad, Mr. Corbett," he said.

I quickly remembered what the Chief Judge had told me about decorum, cleared my throat, and gave the spiel about their right to have the case heard before a judge and be able to appeal his decision. "Before a referee, the decision is binding, you both understand that?"

"Plaintiff to Corbett, A-O.K." Guess who said that?

"Binding and final, that's what I'm here for," Kripps said in cadence with his revolving light. Now it was white, blue and red, and I wondered how the hell he had reversed the sequence, because his hands were still on the table.

"Now, gentlemen, the subpoena states that this is a contest involving $550, which you, Mr. Minivich, claim is due you on a breach of contract by Mr. Kripps. Excuse me, Mr. Kripps, could I ask you to turn off your light? It's most disconcerting." I felt as if I were sitting in the old Aragon Ballroom.

"What time is it?" Kripps asked.

Dumbbell that I am, I told him. "It's 7:55."

"Eight o'clock it goes off, unequivocally."

"Inequivocally?"

"Right. After eight, there's no sense in transmitting signals."

"Well, I guess I can stand it for five more minutes. Now, Mr. Minivich, suppose you tell me your complaint."

"Roger. This crumb here . . ."

That did it. I slammed the table with the flat of my hand. "O.K., fellows! Let's cut the comedy. Take the screwy hats off. Now! Mr. Minivich, I expect more than shortwave responses from you. If you were in front of the bench, you would have been tossed out four minutes ago. Now let's get to it. What is your beef with Mr. Kripps?"

He took the space helmet off and cradled it in the crook of his arm. "No offense, Mr. Corbett," he said sheepishly, "I just wore this rig to point up my case."

"Apology accepted. Just what is your case?"

"I'm out five fifty bucks and he didn't get me on the moon. I want the dough back. No moon, no moola. No lunar trip, no lucre. That's my stand."

"Stand on what?" I turned to Kripps. "Mr. Kripps, will you turn that damned beacon off, please?" He did.

"That's why I brung in the space rig," Minivich went on, "'cause I knew he'd show up with some gimmick."

I was at the end of my patience. "What do you two think this is, a side show? Quick and easy, Mr. Minivich, state your problem!"

"Rog—sorry. Five years ago, I was the first person to sign up for Kripps Tour of the Moon. Five years, mind you—1825 days waiting around."

"One thousand eight hundred and twenty-six," Kripps put in. "Remember leap year."

"So there's an extra day. That's even worser. Right, Mr. Corbett?"

"I don't know what's going on, so how would I know what's right until you tell me? Just how was Mr. Kripps going to get you to the moon?"

"That's his problem. He just promised delivery of my bod' on the big blue cheese up there and there I ain't."

"May I inject a point of clarification?" Kripps asked.

"Clarification by all means," I said. "Maybe some sense too." Suddenly I knew how Margaret Dumont must have felt working with the Marx Brothers.

"I, sir, am the proprietor of the Far Flung Travel Agency. Several years ago, I offered a tour of the moon when and *if* the means of getting there was made available to tourists. As yet the means are not available. But Minivich's seat on the rocket is still reserved. Seat number one. We live up to our motto at Far Flung." He rose to his feet and recited: "Break your dull status quo, just tell Joe where you want to go." He resumed his seat like a senator who has just delivered a truly profound piece of insight.

"Mr. Kripps," I asked, "just what *means* were you referring to?"

"Commercial interstellar travel. The newspapers were full of it when the government said we would put a man on the moon back in the '60s. There were articles all over the place about folks someday being able to tour the moon, maybe even live there. I haven't put fifteen years in the travel agency game for nothing, so I started booking passages. I was saving that first seat for myself until Minivich here offered me a $200 premium over the $350 price to be number one. It's all here, signed and sealed in a contract."

He pushed the document across to me and I read it through. It had been legally drawn and spelled out the conditions and terms in plain language.

I looked at Minivich. He had a self-satisfied look on his face. Kripps was trying to erase it with some legal mumbo-jumbo. "My lawyer told me it is aleatory and still binding," he went on.

Minivich furrowed his brows and I explained as best I could.

"An aleatory contract, Mr. Minivich, is one where the performance of one party depends on the occurrence of some contingent event. The event here seems to be the availability of a means of space travel."

"*Commercial* space travel," Kripps put in. "Armstrong and Aldrin and those guys at NASA don't count."

"Yes, I'm aware of that, Mr. Kripps," I replied curtly. "The contract covers that. But the letter of the law is one thing and the color of the law is another. I think the issue here is the probability of such a contingency being fulfilled. It's a question of value."

"He got lots of value." Kripps tapped the table with his fingertips. "He got a swell plaque, real mahogany, and a brass plate saying C. A. Minivich was the number one passenger to the moon."

"Everybody got one of those," Minivich smirked. "How's it so valuable when almost a thousand people have one?"

"Not one that says they are the first, they don't."

"Aw, this is a bunch of bushwa anyway," Minivich said with disgust. "I've already been to the moon and it was a bummer trip and you had nothing to do with it so fork over the five fifty clams."

"You have been to the moon?" I said it slowly and clearly.

"Sure. That's why I'm here. I don't need his crummy contract any more."

"Ha, that's rich." Kripps shook his head. "You've been to the moon. Ha."

"Yeah, Kripps, and you had some nerve charging five fifty when I could get there for nothing."

"Just how did you accomplish this , , . ah . . . trip, Mr. Minivich?" I asked with some trepidation.

"UFOs is how."

Well, I couldn't say I hadn't asked for it. But madness, says the poet, has a contagion all its own, and I was definitely infected.

"Unidentified flying objects?"

"Right on the button, Mr. Corbett," Minivich assured me. "Hey, don't look at me like I'm a whackeroo, Kripps, lotsa people are getting free rides in space ships. Don't you read the papers, for crying out loud?" He then spun a rather ingenuous tale about a three-day trip to the moon aboard a space vehicle that sounded suspiciously like the *QE II*. Minivich's interplanetary hosts were called Zebtrobs and the head Zebtrob was called Hugo.

"How come I didn't read about your trip in the papers?" Kripps asked.

"Because Hugo told me to keep my trap shut. The only reason I'm bringing it up here is because my wife insists I get my money back. Hugo would understand that because his old lady is also a nag. Her name is Quilta and she's a drag."

While this exchange was going on, I found myself with the queasy feeling that if the local press got wind of this, I could become the biggest joke to hit the municipal building since the parking lot caved in. Of course, Minivich's story was a fabrication, or, at best, unprovable. The contract remained the real issue. Kripps must have been using ESP on me, because he brought up the proof aspect verbally.

"How can you prove you went to the moon? Did you bring back some rocks or something?"

"Hugo said no souvenirs."

"Huh," Kripps grunted. "At least you got a plaque from me."

"But no trip. Can I call a witness, Mr. Corbett?"

I warily looked around the room, half expecting Hugo and his Zebtrobian spouse to materialize.

"She's right outside in the hall," Minivich assured me.

"*Who* is out in the hall?" I asked.

"The old lady, my old lady." He got up and opened the door to admit what I might have assumed was Quilta had I not been told she was Mrs. Minivich. It was impossible to tell her age. Age! It was impossible to tell if she was female or even had a face under all the hair that sprang out of her scalp like straw and fell over her face, shoulders, and hips. Denim was a big item in the Minivich household, because she too was covered with the faded material, except that her outfit consisted of a long cape over a shapeless dress. I rose out of an instinct of courtesy— or maybe apprehension, because she was fumbling with something under her cape.

She came up to the table, whipped out a small twig, and waved it in front of me. "You are a just man," she intoned. "The spirits accept you." Then she sat down in the chair her husband had drawn up for her. "Did you get the dough?" she asked Minivich.

"Not yet, Giselle. Will you tell the court about my trip?"

"Wait a minute!" Kripps had his hand up like a traffic cop. "His wife can't testify."

"I ain't testifying *against* him," Giselle Minivich intoned. Her voice had the quality of a hammer striking an empty boiler.

"Let's hear what she has to say first, Mr. Kripps," I said.

"Well, she has to be under oath then."

Mrs. Minivich looked shocked. "A high priestess of the Subterranean Coven take an oath! Boy, the nerve of some people!"

I intervened. "Just tell us what you came to say, Mrs. Minivich."

"With pleasure," she said from inside the hair cover. "Kordo was gone for . . ."

"Kordo?" I asked. "Who's Kordo?"

"Him." She aimed a cocked thumb at her husband. "He used to be plain old Caesar Augustus Minivich until he went on that trip. Now he's Kordo, because that's what this Hugo Zebtrob called him."

"It's not Hugo Zebtrob, it's Hugo *the* Zebtrob," Minivich corrected her impatiently. "It's like calling me Kordo Earthling, for crying out loud. I'm Kordo *the* Earthling."

"O.K., O.K., don't get touchy." She looked at me mournfully. "He's been like that since this Hugo gave him a lift."

"You have met Hugo and Quilta?" I asked.

"Quilta?" She turned to her husband. "Who's Quilta?"

"Just one of the people on the ship."

"I thought she was Hugo's wife," I reminded him.

"Wife! You didn't say nothing about women being on the trip. Look here, Caesar Augustus Kordo Minivich, if you've been off in the clouds with some damned woman . . . you know how I feel about that jazz. You know what I'd do . . ."

The whole thing was going from the insane to the outer limits of credulity. Now I had three screwballs on my hands and a marital dispute as well. "Look, folks," I pleaded, "this is getting out of hand. Mrs. Minivich, answer yes or no. Did you see the space ship or this Hugo person?"

"No. I thought Caesar Augustus was laying in a ditch someplace for four days. I was wracked with worry, as they say. Then, thanks to the spirits of the deep, I made contact and they said he was O.K. Four whole days he's gone and then he comes back and tells me about his trip which turned out to be a bummer, or so he says. Was this Quilta one of those Amazon broads like in the movies?"

"Giselle, she was a drag."

"Well, I'm asking the spirits about that, don't you worry." She turned to me. "So he comes back and I tell him, 'Hell, Kripps got five fifty loaves of your bread and you got there free.' I told him to get the bread back 'cause we could use it for the Subterranean Coven. We're having a big membership push this fall."

"Oh, no you don't," Minivich said. "That money is going into space research."

That did it. As calmly as I could, I told them I would defer decision for two weeks to consider the merits of the case, and packed the lot of them out of there.

I sat in the blissful quiet of the hearing room and took a deep breath like a man who has just had a tour of Bedlam and needs to confirm his own sanity. Once I was properly assured that I still had all my marbles, I exercised my battered but unbowed facility to reason.

I was convinced of one point—Minivich took national honors for telling the biggest, most extravagant lie ever told to a wife to explain away an indiscretion. Many a guy has disappeared for a night or two and appeased the little woman's wrath with a fib or two. After fifteen years of dealing with salesmen, I thought I had heard the cream of the crop, but Minivich had outdone them all. I heard of guys who told their wives that they were on secret missions for the government. One very creative type had the moxie to concoct the canard that he had been held captive and was ransomed by his best pal, who backed up the tale. I am not suggesting that wives are gullible. There's an old backwoods saying that a smart goose only swallows what she knows will fit through her gullet.

I could find for Kripps on the basis of a seemingly binding contract, but I wanted the opinion of the Chief Judge. Maybe moon tourism would be available someday, but I doubted it would occur in Minivich's lifetime. No matter how big a liar he was, I couldn't see letting Kripps keep his $550 on a very nebulous future trip.

I made out a report starting quite honestly with, "Dear Judge Hopper: You won't believe this, but . . ." and dropped it off at his chambers before I left that evening.

Three days later, I was at my regular job at corporate headquarters dealing quite pleasurably with a staff of sane people, when a buzz on my intercom brought the world of Small Claims Court into my business life.

I told my secretary to show Lieutenant Bill Donnagan of the Detective Squad in. I've had dealings with this crusty policeman from time to time, and had casually suggested lunch to him several weeks ago. My assumption that he was there to take me up on breaking bread was in error; the call was official, *very* official, and his stern look proved it.

"Jeff," he said, taking a seat opposite me, "I don't know how you do it, but you are invariably involved in these things."

"What things?"

"You heard a case involving a guy named Minivich a couple of nights ago."

"Yes. It was a lulu."

"So I gather. Judge Hopper passed your report along to us when the case popped up."

"What case? Has something happened to Kripps? Or Minivich?"

"Yes, Minivich—something called murder—and I think you helped to bring it about."

"Now wait a minute, Lieutenant . . ."

"Jeff, take it easy," he said with a smile. "You didn't do it on purpose. Mrs. Minivich did her hubby in last night because he had been unfaithful to her. Of course, they were both a couple of kooks. She's a witch, or so she claims, and Minivich must have been a fruitcake himself."

"Oh, my Lord," I said when the truth hit me, "I mentioned the woman on the space ship and she killed him over that."

"That's what she says."

"She's confessed?"

"No, but she's given us a statement that's a beaut. Claims when she learned of her husband taking a trip with a space goddess, she decided to put a spell on him. She just wanted him to have a simple accident, but he ended up breaking his neck. He was pushed, or fell, from a ledge at the rear of their property. Of course all that garbage about space trips is nonsense. According to neighbors, they'd been fighting bitterly for two days, and it finally led to murder."

"And she says it was a spell that killed him."

"Yeah. Says she put too much power in it."

"Thank God I don't hear criminal cases. I'd hate to be the judge who sits on this one."

"That's why Judge Hopper brought your report to our attention. He thinks there's an insanity angle, and it will never come to trial."

"I feel awful," I said, and I did. If only I had kept my mouth shut. "Does she have an attorney?"

"The court will appoint one. She's in custody as a material witness at the moment. The D.A. says you might have to give a deposition to the psychiatrists, so I thought I'd give you some advance warning."

"Couldn't it have been an accident, Bill? Minivich could have fallen, you said."

"Sure, and it might have held up, except for the vicious fighting the neighbors overheard. She threatened to fix him. That's why she's taking this too-much-power-in-the-spell line and sticking to the story that he actually did go on a space ride. It's just another case of a guy who got caught playing around and got nailed. There's no wrath like a woman scorned, you know."

"Talk about a woman scorned, how about the other woman? He went *someplace* for four days, didn't he? Where was he? Who was he with? Couldn't that person have a motive?"

"Sure, we're sifting through the possibilities." He got to his feet and gave me a sarcastic smile. "Please, Jeff, if my wife ever asks you if I was with you when I've told her I was, don't blow the whistle on me."

"You're too old to play around."

"You're never too old, but you do have to be willing. See you, your honor."

I wasn't due back in Small Claims until Tuesday, and thank heaven the papers paid no attention to the case, including my part in it. Over the weekend, the thing gnawed at me. Was I responsible for Mrs. Minivich's act? I had to know, so when I got to the municipal building on Tuesday evening I stopped off in the police wing to see Donnagan.

"Well, I don't know if the D.A. would like it, Jeff," he said.

"I'm an Officer of the Court too, you know."

"Not the criminal division. But what the hell, I can see you're bugged, and it's probably my fault for rubbing it in last week in your office. Come on."

Giselle Minivich hadn't changed much since our last meeting. In fact, she hadn't changed a bit, not cloak nor denim dress nor whacked-out attitude. She looked at me through the bars and waved her hand in front of her.

"Corbett, you are a just man. The spirits tell me."

"Yes, of course," I said awkwardly. "Mrs. Minivich, I have to know something for my own peace of mind. If I hadn't mentioned this Quilta person, would you have put a spell on your husband? I mean, did it make you that jealous?"

"Not at first. But when she came back for him, I knew I had to use a spell."

"She came back for him? You saw her?"

"No, but I could see the lights of the ship every night. She was out there waiting for him, all right. I just used too strong a spell, that's all. I don't understand it, because I followed the incantation precisely."

"Well, I'm sorry for your trouble. Do you need anything?"

"They took away my wolfbane. Could you bring me some?"

"I'll try," I said, turning away from the cell, wondering where you could buy wolfbane.

Did you ever have an idea slug you? Not just happen in your head, I mean really slug you hard?

"Lights," I said, turning back to her. "You said you saw lights. Did you tell the police?"

"Those fools don't believe there ever was a space ship. They think my Caesar Augustus was having an affair, or was on a binge somewhere."

"What did the lights look like, Mrs. Minivich?"

"Very eerie."

"Were they flickering on and off? Red and blue and white?"

"Yeah. Then white, blue, and red. Caesar Augustus—I can't call him Kordo any more—he goes out to meet her in the dark and my spell got loused up and he fell off the ledge."

"Sure. Well, you sit tight, Mrs. Minivich. I've got an idea."

Ten minutes later, Lieutenant Donnagan was in his office showing me how irritable he could get.

"Jeff, this time you're going too far. What could Kripps have to gain by Minivich's death? He's not a looney like old Giselle in there. He's a promoter with some wild ideas, but he wouldn't kill somebody over $550."

"How about $350,000?"

"What $350,000?"

"It's right there in the report. Kripps sold Minivich the first seat at a $200 premium. So the other thousand or so places were sold for $350."

"So what, Jeff? People will buy anything. Hell, I've seen ads peddling deeds to one square inch of Texas, or cans of Alpine air. So Kripps had a great gimmick and made a killing on it."

"Made a killing over it, you mean. Don't you see, Bill? If I voided Minivich's contract, it would have made all the others questionable and challengeable. A referee doesn't set precedents at law, but remember, I took mine to the Chief Judge. And Kripps did have a flashing light."

"Anyone could have a flashing light, but we could investigate his movements on the night in question. I don't promise you anything, but I'll dig into it."

He must have dug very deep and very well, because three days later Kripps had taken Mrs. Minivich's place in jail. The police had only a circumstantial case going until a witness showed up to swear that Kripps had been lurking near the Minivich home on the night of the death. That disclosure softened the travel agent up and he told all. He had spent the space-flight money and feared that a finding for Minivich would start a series of suits which would bankrupt him. He was sure Minivich was crazy enough to believe that he was seeing a space ship and walk off the ledge in the dark.

"That's the one part I can't buy," I said to Donnagan a few days after the Kripps confession. "How could he be sure that Minivich would believe the lights were from a space ship?"

"It was worth a try, to his thinking. Minivich really believed in UFOs, you know. In a way, I'm getting to think they exist myself."

"You, a trusted police official?"

"Don't laugh. When we checked the other-woman angle, trying to find out where Minivich had been for the four days, we came up empty. There isn't a trace of _him_ being in this city during that time period, and no indication he left here by normal means of transportation. The guy just went poof for ninety-six hours."

"Sure, sure," I said.

"You never know, Jeff."

As I drove home that night, I watched the various lights in the sky—passing planes, the airport beacon off in the distance, headlights from cars up in the hills. Maybe, just maybe, I thought. I conjured up the image of a space Amazon. No, my wife wouldn't believe a word of it.

Quilta, I muttered to the skies, Quilta, stay away from my door.

The Long Arm of El Jefe

by Edward Wellen

Soon the presses of *Libertad* would roll and the blazing words of Juan Vallejo, leader in exile of all those opposing El Jefe, would bring new life to butchered trees. In his eagerness to stop the presses, Enrique Saenz made his fatal slip. He let Juan Vallejo see into his soul.

They had been talking about money and power. Vallejo had repeated to Saenz the theme of his lead editorial.

"The millions of dollars Uncle Sam pours out in foreign aid to our homeland go into the Dictator's pockets and those of his family and friends."

That was when Saenz burst out in raw self-interest. "Does that not tell you, Juan, it is well to be among El Jefe's friends?"

Vallejo looked at Saenz with the beginning of a smile, as though believing Saenz to be joking. The smile aborted. The tapping of typewriters and the stutter of the teletype in the crowded office outside Vallejo's swelled to meet the silence. Vallejo sank deeper in his chair as if an enormous weariness weighed upon him.

"So. It is painful to find out that someone I had thought my friend is my enemy's friend. Or do you deny it?"

Saenz shook his head. His throat tightened. He had not meant to admit the truth of Vallejo's charge just yet, but maybe it was just as well. It would never become less hard to soften Vallejo up and now he would not have to hint at the offer El Jefe had commissioned him to make. He stroked his silken beard.

"One million dollars in a secret Swiss or Bahamas account. You do not have to become a friend, merely cease to be an enemy. You do not have to support El Jefe, merely stop your attacks on him."

"Thank you, Enrique."

The sincerity in Vallejo's voice brought a cynical smile from Saenz.

"Yes, Enrique, it is worth a million to hear that. It tells me what I've been hoping all these years to hear—that your friend the Dictator is worried. He is right to worry. A change is in the wind."

Saenz's eyes fell to the polished rock paperweight on Vallejo's desk. Saenz knew the story of that rock. Vallejo had told him many times. The rock was all that remained to Vallejo of his homeland. In the days when Vallejo had printed his daily paper in the capital, someone in the up-and-coming party had flung it through the window of the composing room. Vallejo had polished it and put it to use as a paperweight. Shortly after, El Jefe had seized full control of the country and forced Vallejo to flee to New York. Now it was a symbol of the homeland, of Vallejo's own rocklike resolve to drive the Dictator from power.

Saenz pointed to the rock. "Juan, you are like that rock, a reminder of a lost cause. You have sentimental value, true, but otherwise you are worthless. What people want is bread, not a stone."

Vallejo sat taller.

"Freedom is bread for the spirit."

"Words! Freedom is a commodity like any other. Even the high-minded Juan Vallejo sells it, doesn't he? What else is this sheet of yours but—" Saenz picked up a desk copy of *Libertad* and weighed it in his hand "—two ounces of your brand of freedom?"

Vallejo's eyes narrowed. " 'Words,' you say. Let us try to use the words that fit this case. You have sold out to the man you call El Jefe. Or have you always been in his pay? Ah, I can see now! Your mission from the first has been to win me over, or at least to remove my sting. Go back to your Dictator and tell him you have failed. That is the worst punishment I can wish you, the best payment for your treachery. You have betrayed our friendship and you have abused my hospitality. I must ask you to leave. *Now*."

Saenz pulled together the tatters of his self-image. "Before I leave this sacred soil let me give you one word of warning. El Jefe's arm is long. It reaches far. The fingers of his hand will squeeze you lifeless—if you are lucky. If you are *un*lucky, his hand will snatch you back to the homeland, where you will find out for yourself whether there are indeed the torture cells you have written about."

Vallejo's finger poised over the intercom. "I too am a dictator. Before I dictate a new lead editorial is there anything you care to add? Any more threats? Or bribes? Both make very good copy."

Saenz filled with panic. Not only had he failed to neutralize Vallejo, he had provided Vallejo with more ammunition.

He picked up the rock.

Vallejo sat slumped forward, his face on the desk, his blood soaking through sheets of copy paper.

Saenz found himself foolishly wiping his hands on the paper instead of polishing the rock of fingerprints. But even that would have been useless. The only way out was through the editorial room and he would be the last to have been seen alive with Vallejo.

His only hope was to get out of the country before the police could arrest him. Once he set foot on his own soil he would turn from fugitive to hero. El Jefe might publicly deplore the killing of Juan Vallejo but privately he would reward Juan Vallejo's killer.

Saenz strode out through the editorial room. He held his pace down, though the urge to run was strong. Reporters and copy editors stopped what they were doing and stared at him. Had they heard the loud voices, the blow, the silence? Was there blood or its smell on him?

Their features and expressions were imprinted sharply on Saenz's mind, just as his were imprinted on theirs. They had seen him here often. They knew his name. When the alarm went out the police would have a make.

Once out in the corridor, he quickened his step. He punched the elevator button, but, remembering the old elevator's agonizing slowness, he took the stairs down to the street. A wise move. A hue and cry rose and swelled behind him.

Outside, he hailed a cab and gave his address. His heart beat faster and faster as the cab crawled the twenty blocks to his apartment. Every siren he heard spoke his name.

He had only to pick up his passport and his bank book, then draw out the balance El Jefe had fattened, but even this needed time, and the traffic was robbing him of time. Two blocks short of his address he told the cabby to stop, paid him, and got out.

Another wise move. Not only was it faster on foot, but when he stopped at his corner to scout the street ahead he spotted two men in plainclothes in a car across from his doorway. A stakeout.

Saenz hurried over to the next street and approached the apartment from the back. He could climb to his window by way of the fire escape. But the stakeout might include the apartment itself. Hugging the alley wall, he counted up to his window and kept his eyes on it. He watched for nearly five minutes, then he saw it. A curtain twitched, sending a chill through him.

Vallejo must have weighed more importantly than he had realized for the police to have moved so fast and so thoroughly. Had they sealed off the city as well? At the very least he had better get out of the neighborhood. He would have to go without his passport, but that would not matter at the other end and he would not need it at this end if he booked a seat on a flight to Puerto Rico. From there he could find passage by sea or air the rest of the way home. He had to leave his bank balance behind, but he had his credit cards . . .

He stopped short.

A credit economy worked fine—as long as you felt free to use the name on your credit card. But if the alarm had already gone out, if the clerks had his name on their list, if the police stood alert at all the terminals . . .

He could not flash his credit cards. He would need cash. But where could he borrow some?

He stopped again. He knew where to go.

Raquel kept her door on the chain. Her small face stared out at him. He did not like the look in her eyes. Or the tone of her voice.

"Don't give me 'darling.' You have some nerve coming here. I just now heard it on the radio."

He tried a smile. He had thought to borrow a razor from her to shave off the beard she had often told him lent machismo. He felt sure enough of himself without it, and without it he would be less likely to draw the notice of the police. But now he would be content to leave at once with whatever ready money Raquel could scrape together.

"Let me in. I don't know what you heard, but I'm sure I can explain."

Raquel's look softened, but she did not unchain the door.

"Are you going to keep me waiting out here?"

"Juan was a good man. I don't want to call the police, but I will if you don't go."

As he stepped back a pace to ram the door, it shut in his face. The dead bolt shot into place. He heard her walk away—and then silence. Suppose she were calling the police?

If Raquel's door closed to him, all other doors would be closed too. Cash was out. He would have to chance his credit.

He caught a cab to Kennedy Airport. Paying the cabby took the last of his folding money. He did not risk the ticket counters but joined the crowd watching the planes take off and land.

He looked surreptitiously for signs of unusual scrutinizing of passengers on their way to board flights. Just when he began to breathe easier he saw a pair of plainclothesmen examine the papers of a bearded man of his build.

He grimaced. Escape by plane was impossible. He would find the same barriers at bus and train terminals. He was trapped on alien soil.

Then it hit him—there was one place, in the heart of Manhattan, that offered sanctuary, promised asylum.

He mixed in with a group leaving the terminal building and enviously watched them board a chartered bus. He did not have enough change for the ride back, even on a regular bus. Not willing to run the risk of stiffing a cabdriver, he eyed the hazy glow in the west. It would be a long walk back to Manhattan.

He had to keep to the highway to avoid getting lost. The broken shoulders were hard on his feet. After a few miles he stopped at a diner for coffee. He lingered over the empty cup, finally forcing himself back out onto the expressway. Outside, his eyes lit on the cars in the parking area. He cased them, one by one, and finally found one with keys in the ignition. His heart racing, he pulled out into Manhattan-bound traffic.

After a few miles, he pulled over to see what else he had lucked into. In the glove compartment he found an electric shaver that plugged into the cigarette-lighter socket. Quickly he shaved off his beard.

Shortly after he crossed the bridge to Manhattan he ditched the car. Its number must be on the police band by now and it would be a fine thing to be picked up for driving a stolen car. He made a last-minute search of the car and found riches. In the corner under the dash a magnet held a coin container. He pocketed the three dollars' worth of quarters. Now, if the place had closed for the day, he had enough to see him safely through the night. All he needed now was a weapon in case someone should get in his way. He took a jackhandle out of the trunk and stuck it in his waistband under his jacket.

He would not have to wait till morning. As he approached the consulate its lights shone. Behind the windows figures hurried back and forth in a play of shadows.

The police would hardly dare cross that threshold uninvited, so the activity inside would not be a police search for Juan Vallejo's killer. Vallejo's death would no doubt be the catalyst but the activity would be strictly consular business. The information officer would be fielding reporters' questions about the slaying of El Jefe's foe and the communications officer would be handling messages between home, Washington, and the United Nations.

Saenz suddenly knew the assassin's glory, the feeling that he had changed history—whether for better or worse did not matter. He convinced himself that instead of striking out at Vallejo in panic he had struck out out of patriotism. The result was the same.

He looked and listened, then approached the consulate with caution. Voices in a hidden doorway froze him.

"Think that Saenz guy will show up here?"

"No, we're wasting our time. He'd be a fool to."

Saenz curled his lip. What arrogance! The police were the fools if they believed they could keep him from getting through to safe soil.

He backed up and went hunting. A lone policeman—one his size—patrolling a deserted area was his prey.

He walked eight blocks north and east before he saw a man of his slight build in uniform. Saenz approached him. Close to, the man proved to be an auxiliary policeman, a civilian who gave up a few of his nights to help man the streets. Saenz asked directions to an address uptown and when the man turned to point the way Saenz whipped out the jackhandle and cracked the man over the back of the head.

The door opened and the consulate guard stared at the uniform. Saenz tried to push inside before the men staked out in the street realized he was not one of them. The guard stopped him.

"I'm sorry, this is not U.S. territory. You can't come in."

"Yes I can, you idiot. I'm no Yanqui cop. Don't you know me?"

The guard's eyes flickered in uncertain recognition. A man appeared at the door behind him. "Who's there? What does he want?"

The guard stepped aside and Saenz moved in and shut the door. Safe!

The other man frowned at him. "Officer, I hope you realize your intrusion is most irregular. You are infringing on our sovereignty."

In the light Saenz remembered the man as an underling he had bypassed in his visits to the consulate for instructions from El Jefe. Saenz had even more importance now, and no time to waste giving explanations to this man.

"Take me to the consul."

"I am the consul now."

Saenz stared. El Jefe *could* be capricious at times, elevating or destroying a man on a whim. "I'm Enrique Saenz," he said. "I claim sanctuary. I wish to send a message to El Jefe."

The new consul's face turned to stone. "Saenz," he said. "Haven't you read the papers or listened to the news? You will have to deliver the message to El Jefe yourself—and El Jefe is dead. Your killing of Juan Vallejo set off the coup that has been so long in the making. This consulate, like the homeland, is in the hands of your enemies."

Death Sentence

by Stephen Wasylyk

The day was dark. Low fast-moving clouds brushed damp, disrespectful tendrils across the statue of the city's founding father atop City Hall.

The grey light filtered down to the elongated rectangular windows of the bastionlike row homes lining the narrow streets, and the man peering through the living room curtains of the three-story brownstone felt as though the gloominess of the day had permeated his soul until he smiled wryly, realizing that the source of his depression was not the day but the passenger descending from the cab that had just pulled up at the curb.

The man at the window was slight, his face shrunken by sixty years of never-easy living into a symmetrical assemblage of creased and wrinkled skin, prominent cheekbones and a too large nose. His hair was grey and sprouted in unruly tufts, his eyes surprisingly blue and gentle.

He wiped his hands thoughtfully on the laundry-worn, soft-collared shirt, hitched up his baggy trousers and turned to the woman standing with folded arms behind him, ignoring the disapproval etched into her face.

"He's here," he said.

"Damn him."

"Look," he said. "He is the old woman's nephew, her only living relative. If she wants to make her will in his favor, it is not our business."

"It *is* our business," she said. "We've watched over her and taken care of her for more than twenty years. She owes us something."

"There will be something for us," he said. "She told us so."

"Something," she said bitterly. "What? What could be left? It's not as though she has a million. What little there is would be just enough for us to live out our lives. A small part of it means nothing. Damn him and damn her."

"Hush," he said. "That's no way to talk."

"No way? Look at us." She spread her arms wide. "Look at me. This dress is ten years old. It is a wonder it still stays together. The shoes are so old the leather is cracked. Look at my face. She is eighty and I am sixty but I have as many wrinkles as she does and my hair is ugly." She brushed angrily at her eyes. "Ugly. What did twenty years of working for her get us except old?"

The doorbell rang.

"I'll let him in," said the man.

"Sure," she snapped. "Let him in. Let him take everything. We don't need it. We're both young and healthy enough to go out and get nice jobs, find a nice expensive apartment to live in." She folded her arms. "Let him in, you old fool, and then call the welfare office so that we will be prepared when she dies."

The man left the living room and walked into the foyer. Through the frosted glass of the door he could see the bulking shadow of the man from the cab.

She's right, he thought. We've worked twenty years for nothing.

He pulled back the double bolts on the heavy door, unfastened the chain, and swung the door open.

The shadow on the glass had indicated a big man but it had not shown that the bigness was soft, a protruding belly straining the expensive sport coat. The jowls of a round, fleshy face sagging. In his mid-forties, the man appeared successful and sure of himself, used to living well; but there was no pleasant, disarming smile when the door opened, only a flat look for expressionless eyes.

"Who are you?" he asked.

"You are Kimball Haworthy?" asked the old man.

"Who the hell do you think I am? A bill collector?"

"I'm Glinkos. I sent you the letter. Your aunt asked me to write it."

Haworthy pushed past him into the foyer, his eyes scanning the time-darkened interior of the house, seeing the once polished walnut trim, the scarred floors and the threadbare carpets.

"What a dump," he said. He stepped into the living room, eyes flicking from furniture to walls, from ceiling to floor, appraising and calculating and indicating they found nothing of value.

"This place is one step away from being an indoor junkyard," he said. "I've never seen so much crummy furniture in my life."

Resentment narrowed the woman's lips. "Never mind the furniture," she said.

Haworthy looked her up and down. "Who are you?"

"She is my wife," said Glinkos.

"That figures," said Haworthy.

Anger flickered in the woman's eyes. "Would you like to go up to see your aunt?" she asked tightly.

"What's the rush?"

"She is old and sick and looking forward to seeing you."

"Is she going to die within the next ten minutes?"

Mrs. Glinkos blinked.

"I just traveled a thousand miles and I need a drink," said Haworthy. "Is there anything in this dump?"

"There is an old bottle . . ." said Glinkos.

"Get it," said Haworthy. His mouth twisted in distaste as he looked around the room.

Glinkos brought a bottle of bourbon and a glass. Haworthy poured himself a drink, parted the curtains, peered outside and then turned to face Glinkos.

"I remember this place from forty years ago," he said. "I was five years old but I still remember. It was nice then."

Glinkos shrugged.

Haworthy downed the bourbon and laughed harshly. "That's what stayed with me. How nice it was. I thought of how much money it would be worth. I didn't expect this. Half the homes on the street are boarded up and the rest have been turned into rooming houses. There isn't a blade of grass left on any of the front lawns and there is more trash than shrubbery out there. The one thing you've got plenty of is graffiti. I've heard how the money people took off from some of these fashionable city neighborhoods but I never expected them to leave this one. This place can't be worth a dime. Your letter said she made me her heir. How much can she be worth, living in a place like this?"

Mrs. Glinkos leaned against the wall, her face impassive.

"Dumb," said Haworthy. "I'm just plain dumb. All I could think of was that she had all the money in the family, because my grandfather kicked my father out and left everything to her. Now it will all be mine, I thought, but from the looks of the place, she doesn't have a cent. Or maybe she still has it all because she never spent any of it. Is that it, Glinkos?"

He poured himself another drink and downed it. He placed the glass on the table. Mrs. Glinkos glided forward, lifted it quickly and wiped the polished top carefully.

"All right," said Haworthy. "I'll ask the old bat. Maybe she can tell me."

Mrs. Glinkos led him up the dark angled stairway and down a small hall to a bedroom door at the front of the house, tapped gently and pushed it open, motioning Haworthy into the room. He stepped through the door.

The bedroom was big but seemed crowded because of a huge canopied four-poster bed. The coverlet, the sheets and the woman in the bed were different shades of white; the woman's skin pale, almost transparent, hair snowy and sparse, lips colorless. The effect was relieved only by the dark eyes that fastened intently on Haworthy.

"You are Kimball," she said weakly.

Haworthy moved to the side of the bed. "You sent for me, Aunt Galatea," he said. "After forty years, why bother?"

"I wanted to see you."

"There was no need."

"You are my heir," she said. She waved a feeble hand. "Everything in the house will be yours."

"This junk?" asked Haworthy. "Is there anything besides this?"

"Only a little," she said.

"What happened to all of the money grandfather left?"

She sighed. "I don't know. The man at the bank talked about stocks and recession and inflation. I didn't understand any of it."

"So it's all gone?"

"Not all. There is still some left. He sends me money each week."

"How much?"

"Enough for us to live on. But there is still the house for you."

"Damn the house," said Haworthy. "Do you have anything worth money?"

The woman's eyes rolled upward and she gasped.

Mrs. Glinkos pulled savagely at Haworthy's arm. "Get out!"

Haworthy allowed himself to be pushed into the hall. Mrs. Glinkos closed the door behind him. He stared at the door resentfully, passed a hand over his face and went downstairs.

Glinkos watched him pour a big drink and down it. The young people had an expression, he thought. What was it? *A monkey on his back.* Something like that.

Mrs. Glinkos followed ten minutes later.

"Did she die?" asked Haworthy.

"No," said Mrs. Glinkos. "You had no right . . ."

"Never mind my rights," said Haworthy. "I didn't come here because of any love for that old hag upstairs. I came because I need money and I thought I could get it from her, an advance on the estate, something like that. Do you know what I do for a living? I'm a gambler. I bet on things. I play cards. Sometimes I win and sometimes I lose. The other night I was in a game with a very bad man. A *very* bad man. I should have had enough sense to stay away from him but I felt lucky. I thought I could take him but it didn't work that way. I lost. Twenty thousand dollars. And I gave him my marker. Do you know what a marker is? It's a promise to pay. Except that the marker is no good because I can't pay and he's going to be looking for me. Do you know what he'll do to me when he finds me?"

He poured another drink and gulped it down.

"I need that money," he said. "And I need it fast or I'm a dead man."

He moved toward the door.

"I have to talk to her again."

Mrs. Glinkos barred his way. "She's resting," she said. "I gave her one of her pills."

Haworthy looked down at her. "When can I see her?"

"She can't help you," said Mrs. Glinkos. "She made you her heir but there is no money here. She has no bank account."

"She said the bank sends her money each week."

"It is only a small trust fund," said Glinkos.

"She has no cash?"

"No cash," said Mrs. Glinkos.

"God," said Haworthy. "There must be something."

"There is nothing," said Mrs. Glinkos. "Why don't you go? Whatever the estate is worth, the lawyers will send it to you."

"Don't you understand?" Haworthy almost screamed. "I need it *now!*"

"It *can't* be now! If there was something, you couldn't have it until she is dead and the lawyers said it was all right for you to take it."

"There has to be something," said Haworthy, his eyes roving around the room as if he hoped to discover an object of value; but the furniture, though well polished, was old and the paintings on the wall seemed worth little.

"Go," said Mrs. Glinkos.

"No," he said harshly. "I won't go. I can't go. Get me something to eat."

"I am not your servant," she said.

He clenched a fist and held it up. "Listen, old woman. It wouldn't take much for me to smash you because I feel like hitting someone anyway. Now do as you're told. Get me something to eat."

"There is something to make a sandwich," said Glinkos quietly. "Will that do?"

"I wouldn't expect prime ribs in this place," said Haworthy.

He sprawled out in an overstuffed chair that protested with a weary sigh, his hands over his eyes.

The couple went into the kitchen.

Mrs. Glinkos pulled a loaf of bread and a small package of sliced meat from the refrigerator, slamming them down on the counter top.

"He's hungry," she said. "Hungry. I know what I'd like to feed him. Rat poison. That's what I'd like to feed him." She glared at her husband. "He was going to hit me and you did nothing."

"He's upset," said Glinkos. "You heard what he said about the money he owes."

"Do I care about that? That's his problem, not ours. He got himself into it. Let him get himself out. What do I care about him?"

She slapped a sandwich together, found a knife in the drawer and sliced it in half.

"Damn," she said. She drove the knife point violently down into the counter top and it stuck there, the handle swaying back and forth slowly.

"Now look what you've done," he said.

"It's only the counter top," she said. "I wish it was his heart."

"Wishing him dead means nothing," he said. "Wishing has never killed anyone yet. All you're doing is upsetting yourself for no good reason."

"There's good reason," she said. "I was thinking of the will. You know she explained it to us when we didn't know if the lawyers would find him or not. She said that if he was dead, we would get everything."

"But he isn't dead. He's alive."

"Suppose he was dead. Suppose we helped him to be dead."

Glinkos' face hardened. "I don't want to hear talk like that. We aren't much but we don't kill people for money like some bum slinking through the streets. There is too much of that in this city."

"Big man," she said. "Think of your future before being so righteous. Think of the opportunity we have to get rid of him."

"You talk as if it is something easy to do. You know that isn't so."

"Not for you. You have let people walk over you all your life. Whenever something has to be done in this family, I have to do it."

That really wasn't true, thought Glinkos. It was just that his methods weren't as direct as hers. She had always been brash and impulsive, quick to raise her voice, quick to move. Many people found her personality abrasive but he had learned to live with it and still love her because she could be kind and gentle, too, and no one could have taken care of the old woman better than she had.

"And then what would you do?" he asked. "How would you explain it? He would be dead and what would we do with the body? Do we bury him in the basement like they do in mystery stories? That is not the way in real life."

"Easy," she said. "I would stick the knife into him and dump him into the street after dark. In this neighborhood, it could happen to anyone stupid enough to walk alone, especially someone as well dressed as he is."

He shook his head. "And you think they would not come back to us? The lawyers knew he was coming here. They would ask questions. The police would ask questions. Do you think they are stupid? You are letting your emotions run away with you. You are not thinking. If you were, you would realize he is younger and stronger. Do you expect him to sit there and let you kill him?"

"Still . . ." she said, her fingers caressing the handle of the knife.

"Still nothing," he said. "We are caught. We worked for the old woman and thought she would take care of us but she decided to give everything to her nephew. That is her right. There were no promises made or promises broken. All we can do is care for her until she dies and then we will move on. We will find something."

"Yes," she said. She waved a hand. "The world is waiting for us. It can't wait until we get there. There will be a good job and plenty of money and a nice place to live."

He smiled. "You are a bitter old woman."

"And you are a fool."

He picked up the sandwich plate. "Yes," he said. "I am a fool because there were many roads I could have taken when I was younger but I took this one, so now I must live with what must be because I am too old to change anything."

He walked slowly into the living room with the plate in his hand. Haworthy wasn't there.

Glinkos heard a noise and followed it into the adjoining dining room.

Haworthy had found an old silver chest and was fingering through its contents.

"What are you doing?" asked Glinkos.

"This is silver, isn't it? It has to be worth something."

Glinkos put the plate down on the table. "I just told myself I was a fool but you are a greater fool than I."

Haworthy glared at him. "Watch your mouth."

"You said you owed the man twenty thousand dollars." Glinkos indicated the silver. "How much can that be worth? A few hundred? Do you think that will satisfy him?"

Haworthy let a set of forks clatter to the table and rubbed a hand across his face. "You're right. This stuff is chicken feed. It isn't going to help me at all."

"Eat your sandwich," said Glinkos.

"I can't believe that all her money is gone," said Haworthy. "I just can't believe it."

"You don't want to believe it," said Glinkos, "because you expected to walk in here and get twenty thousand dollars and now you see there is nothing here for you. Even if your aunt was still wealthy, if the house was worth a fortune, if she had a million dollars in securities, none of it would do you any good. First, you would have to wait until she dies. Then you would have to wait until the will is probated. It would take months before you received a penny. Like the rest of us, you are in the wrong place at the wrong time. Perhaps you would be better off somewhere else."

Haworthy's teeth tore at the sandwich, his eyes fixed on Glinkos. He swallowed and pointed a finger. "You and your wife seem very anxious to get me out of here for some reason. Why?"

"There is nothing here for you," said Glinkos. "There was always the thought that you might make your aunt's last days easier but that is not so. You are interested only in yourself. You have no feeling for her at all. You need money and there is none here. Why should you stay any longer?"

"I can't believe it," repeated Haworthy. He gulped down the rest of the sandwich and reached for the bottle. "She had plenty of money forty years ago. It couldn't all have disappeared."

"Forty years is a long time," said Glinkos. "Things happen. All stocks do not increase in value. Corporations go out of existence. Look at manufacturers of automobiles. How many are left? Look at the rail-roads. What has happened to their stocks? It takes great skill and good luck to increase your money. Your aunt is not a financial expert and the people she had advising her were incompetent. Then there is her illness and the medicine and the hospital bills and the doctor bills. She should really be in a hospital right now but she would be in a ward and she will not stand for that. There is also inflation. The money that was enough years ago is no longer sufficient. And there is more, per-haps the most important of all. Your aunt is old and dying now but once she was young and beautiful, yet you do not ask why she never married."

"Some women are like that. So are some men. You don't see me with a wife."

"Yet I am sure there was once a woman you were interested in."

Haworthy cursed. "Yeah. She took me for plenty before I found out about her."

"Your aunt had something similar happen. Perhaps it runs in the family. There was a man. She gave him money, almost two hundred and fifty thousand dollars over a period of time to help him in his busi-ness but he did not put the money into the business. He set it aside and when he felt there would be no more, he disappeared with another woman."

Haworthy stared at him. "Two hundred and fifty thousand?"

"She would listen to no one. She loved the man and trusted him."

"That's a lot of love and trust."

Glinkos shrugged. "It is too late to worry about it now. The lawyers wanted her to go to the police but she would not do that."

"Stupid old broad," said Haworthy.

"So you see, there is no help for you here. If you are in trouble, look elsewhere for relief."

Haworthy stood up, a hard gleam in his eyes. He drank deeply from the bottle. "No," he said. "I have nowhere else to go and I still think the money is here. I'm a gambler and no man is a good gambler unless he can sense when he has a winning hand. I want to talk to her again."

Mrs. Glinkos came in, her eyes flicking from the silverware to Haworthy, her mouth twisted in distaste.

"I see your friends are here," she said. "I suppose you'll ask them in but I'll tell you now, there is no more food or liquor."

Haworthy stiffened. "What friends?"

"Two men," she said. "They are outside. They do not belong in this neighborhood and they can only be friends of yours."

Haworthy half ran to the window and parted the curtains carefully. "Oh, God!" he said. "They've found me already."

Glinkos looked over his shoulder. Two men leaned against the shining big black car parked beneath the lifeless tree at the curb; incongruous in that neighborhood where most of the residents drove old cars, battered cars, cars pockmarked with body rot, cars that were transportation and no more than that. It was the kind of car that, if left there for any appreciable time, would either disappear or be stripped. Yet Glinkos knew no one who seeing the two men leaning against it would consider touching the car. One man was big, one was small, both dressed conservatively even though young, perhaps in their late twenties, and Glinkos was aware of an aura of menace surrounding them.

"Who are they?" he asked.

"The man I told you about," said Haworthy. "They are his collectors. He wants his money. They won't leave until they get it."

"How could they know where you went? How could they follow you to a place a thousand miles away? Did someone tell them?"

Haworthy let the curtain drop. "No one could have. I told no one where I was going and I took no luggage because I didn't want anyone who saw me to know I was leaving town." He slapped his forehead suddenly. "Your damned letter. I left it in my room. I should have known they would search it."

"Call the police if you are afraid of them," said Mrs. Glinkos.

"What can the police do? They have broken no laws." He took a deep breath. "Now I really have to get that money somehow. If I don't have it when I leave here, they'll kill me." He put the bottle aside, his voice low and resigned.

Glinkos looked at him. Haworthy's face was as white as the old woman's upstairs, perspiration beaded on his forehead and jowls, and Glinkos almost felt sorry for him.

Haworthy started for the door.

Mrs. Glinkos folded her arms and blocked his path. "You are not to go upstairs."

Exploding in a sudden fury, Haworthy pinioned her arms and threw her aside. She stumbled and almost fell. "Get out of my way and stay out of my way!"

He went up the stairs fast. Rubbing her arms, Mrs. Glinkos followed. Glinkos hesitated, then went after them.

Haworthy roughly pushed open the door to his aunt's room and strode to the bed, looking down at her. The old woman's eyes were closed and she breathed evenly.

Mrs. Glinkos pushed close to him. "Leave her alone!" she said fiercely.

Haworthy shoved her away and leaned over, shaking his aunt's shoulder. Her eyes opened, focused on nothing, dead pools that slowly became alive and found him.

"Can you hear me?" asked Haworthy.

Her head moved slightly.

"Then listen." Haworthy pointed toward the window. "Right now, out there, two men are waiting to kill me. Can you understand that?"

The head moved again.

"All I need to stay alive is a little money," said Haworthy. "Not after you die. Not next month, or the month after that or whenever your lawyers get through settling your estate, but *right now!* Is that clear to you?"

The woman nodded.

"Then help me," pleaded Haworthy. "I know you must have money. I know you must have something more than this old house and this old furniture. There was too much to begin with for it all to have gone. There has to be some left."

The woman's lips parted. "How much?" she whispered.

"Twenty thousand dollars," he said.

Her lips curled. "Money," she said. "Is that all men care about?"

Haworthy's hands clenched. Glinkos felt a touch of panic. Haworthy was a violent man balanced on the edge of disaster, frightened so badly his fear could be felt in the room. If he put those hands on the old woman, Glinkos would have to do something and Glinkos didn't know what to do.

"Listen," said Haworthy hoarsely. "I can kill you with one hand, old woman, and I'll do it if you don't help me. I don't care about your will or this house or anything else. I want what is due me *now!*"

The old woman sighed, the dark eyes fixed on the ceiling, the voice soft. "I don't like you. I had hoped you were something more than your father, but you are not. He was a weak man and you are a weak man. Still I should have helped him. I always felt guilty about that. I would like to help you now to make up for it but I have no money."

Haworthy's hands curled and reached out toward the old woman's throat. "Don't lie to me! You must have something!"

Mrs. Glinkos angrily pulled at his arm. "Leave her alone and get out!"

Haworthy whirled and slapped her, knocking her against the wall. The old woman in the bed tried to lift herself when she heard Mrs. Glinkos' sharp little cry, her eyes angry. Haworthy sprang back to her.

"Stop it!" said Glinkos sharply.

Haworthy turned to face him, breathing hard, and Glinkos felt a small touch of fear at the unreal light in his eyes.

Glinkos stepped forward. "Give him the jewels," he said to the old woman.

Mrs. Glinkos, her hand caressing her cheek, said, "No!"

The old woman's eyes fastened on Glinkos, studying him, then gradually softened, almost smiling. "Yes," she said. "Give him the jewels."

Mrs. Glinkos placed her hands on her hips defiantly. "You said you would never part with them as long as you lived."

"I do not need them now," said the old woman.

"Don't let him threaten you. They are yours until you die. Let him wait. We will call the police . . ."

"*Give him the jewels.*" The authority in the old woman's voice was unmistakable.

Mrs. Glinkos crossed the room to a high, multitiered dresser. She opened a door, reached inside, pulled out a large, old-fashioned jewel chest and carried it to Haworthy. She placed it on the bed and glared at her husband.

Haworthy drew his breath in, placed a trembling hand on the chest for a long moment as though he was afraid to open it, then snapped the catch. The front fell forward as the top rose, a series of black-velvet-lined trays fanning backward, exposing the contents. The trays held rings, bracelets, pendants, necklaces, all studded with stones that caught the light in the room, sparkling joyfully as if happy to be free of their dark prison.

Haworthy let his breath out. "I knew it," he whispered. "I knew there had to be something." He closed the chest quickly and glared at Mr. and Mrs. Glinkos. "You heard her," he said. "She gave them to me."

"You stole them," said Mrs. Glinkos. "You forced her to give them to you and that is stealing. You can't take them. I won't allow it."

Haworthy raised a fist. "Shut up! I've had enough of your big mouth!" He spun to face Glinkos, his jaw set, his eyes narrowed. "I'm taking these," he said. "Don't give me any trouble, old man."

"I wouldn't dream of it," said Glinkos.

Haworthy slid by him to the hall, the chest under one arm, seemingly half afraid that somehow the slight old man would take the chest from him. He reminded Glinkos of a starving animal slinking away with a morsel of food that meant the difference between life and death, ready to kill if someone made a move toward him.

Haworthy backed toward the stairs, then turned and ran. Glinkos moved to the front window and looked down into the street in time to see Haworthy run from the house. The two men stiffened, alert and deadly. Haworthy talked rapidly, holding the chest before him like some sort of offering. The three stepped into the car. Glinkos watched it go down the street and turn the corner, leaving tracks in the light rain that had started to coat the asphalt. He watched until the rain obliterated the tire marks and it was as though the car had never been there at all.

It is over, he thought.

He looked at the old woman in the bed. She had closed her eyes again, a slight smile on her face, and she was breathing evenly as if she had forgotten her nephew already. He motioned to his wife to follow him out of the room.

In the hall, his wife said, "I hope you're proud of yourself. If you hadn't told him about the jewels . . ."

"He would have killed somebody," said Glinkos. "He was crazy."

"I should have killed him. I told you I should have killed him before it went this far."

"And I told you," said Glinkos. "That was no solution."

"He hit me," she said angrily. "And you did nothing. You are an old fool and a coward."

"Well, I am an old fool," said Glinkos. "That much I admit. And if preventing someone from being killed is being a coward, then I am a coward. And it only appeared that I did nothing."

He went down the stairs, moving slowly, feeling tired. She followed. He went into the living room and sank into a chair, closing his eyes.

"What does that mean?" she asked. "It only appeared that you did nothing? What kind of fairy tale are you telling yourself?"

He opened his eyes and rubbed his prominent nose with a finger. "There was a time about a year ago," he said slowly, "when she first went into the hospital. You will remember that the lawyers called and I went to their offices. They told me there was no more money, that the trust fund had run out. What was there to do? Sell the house, they said. I said that wasn't very practical. It wouldn't bring much money and it would leave us no place to live. She needed someone with her and if it wasn't us, she would have to go to a home. She wouldn't do that. The house had to be kept so that you and I could take care of her. Sell the furniture, they said." He chuckled. "Can you imagine? Sell the furniture?"

"She wouldn't have allowed that," said Mrs. Glinkos. "She'd never let her precious antiques go. She spent too many years collecting them. A year ago she was still active, polishing and dusting them every day. The antiques were the children she never had. She would have noticed if just one piece was missing and it would have broken her heart."

"That fool Haworthy thought it was all junk," said Glinkos. "The lawyers didn't tell him so he didn't know."

"Still," she said bitterly. "What difference does it make now? It will all be his anyway. At least the money will be. It should have been ours. The furniture would bring just enough so that you and I would not have to worry any longer."

"You have forgotten the will," said Glinkos. "If he dies before the old woman, we are the heirs."

"That means nothing," she said. "You let him walk out. He is alive, thanks to you."

Glinkos shook his head. "Wait. I was telling you about the lawyers. She is a proud woman and stubborn, I told them, and there had to be a way to make her think the trust fund still had money so that she could live out her last days peacefully and quietly and happily. They were in favor of that, they said. All right, I said. It was impossible to sell the furniture so that she wouldn't know but there was one other thing. Something we could sell and pretend the money still came from the trust fund and she would never know." He leaned back, a smug look on his face.

Her eyes opened wide. "The only other thing she owned was the jewels," she said. "But the jewels were there. I don't know how many times I saw her examine them during the last year. I guess she liked to dream of when she was young and could wear them."

"Glass," said Glinkos. "Paste. We took the real stones while she was in the hospital and sold them and replaced them with worthless imitations. Haworthy may know nothing about jewels but even if he did, he didn't take time to look because he was so sure he had found what he had come for. When he gives them to that man, the man won't be so anxious. He'll examine them and I don't think he will be in any mood to listen to any explanations. I've heard of people like that. He will kill Haworthy for welshing on his debt and for trying to fool him. We will then be the heirs."

Anger came to her voice. "You never told me!"

"Blame the lawyers. They wanted no one to know because disposing of the old woman's property and concealing it is not exactly ethical, no matter how good the motive."

"And the old woman never knew?"

Glinkos pulled at his lower lip. "I didn't think so but her illness has affected her body, not her brain. She is a smart one and it is possible she realized what had happened and said nothing because she trusts us. The look she gave me . . ." He shook his head. "Yet I don't know if she could sentence her nephew to death."

"But you could, Mr. Self-righteous, after telling me in the kitchen that you are not the type to kill for money."

Glinkos left his chair to turn on an old floor lamp. The yellow light flooded the room, holding the greyness outside at bay, and the furniture was no longer dark and old-fashioned but handsome and gleaming. There was a warmth in the room that came from years of tranquil living, of understanding and of love.

"That's still true," he said. "When I suggested that he take those worthless jewels, the money never entered my thoughts."

"What other reason could you have, you old fool?"

Glinkos reached out and touched her lined cheek tenderly. "The man came in here, insulted us and threatened the old woman. Those things I could forgive because he had a problem, but then he struck you. That was when I made up my mind." Glinkos drew himself up. His voice was firm. "For that he had to be punished."

Kid Cardula

by Jack Ritchie

It's just about time for me to close down the gym for the night when this tall stranger comes up to me.

He wears a black hat, black suit, black shoes, black topcoat, and he carries a zipper bag.

His eyes are black too. "I understand that you manage boxers?"

I shrug. "I had a few good boys in my time."

Sure, I had a few good boys, but never *real* good. The best I ever done was with Chappie Strauss. He was listed as number ten in the lightweight division by *Ring Magazine*. Once. And I had to pick my fights careful to get him that far. Then he meets Galanio, which is a catastrophe, and he loses his next four fights too before I decide it's time to retire him.

"I would like you to manage me," the stranger says. "I plan to enter the fight ring."

I look him over. He seems well built and I put his weight at around one-ninety. Height maybe six foot one. But he looks pale, like his face hasn't seen the sun for some time. And there is also the question of his age. It's hard to pin-point, but he's no kid.

"How old are you?" I ask.

He shifts a little. "What is the ideal age for a boxer?"

"Mister," I say, "in this state it's illegal for any man over forty to even step into the ring."

"I'm thirty," he says fast. "I'll see that you get a birth certificate to verify that."

I smile a little. "Look, man, at thirty in this game, you're just about over the hill. Not starting."

His eyes glitter a little. "But I am strong. Incredibly strong."

I stretch the smile to a grin. "Like the poet says, you got the strength of ten because your heart is pure?"

He nods. "I do literally have the strength of ten, though not for that reason. As a matter of fact, realizing that I possessed this tremendous strength, it finally occurred to me that I might as well capitalize on it. Legitimately."

He puts down the zipper bag and walks over to where a set of barbells is laying on the mat and does a fast clean and jerk like he was handling a baby's rattle.

I don't know how many pounds is on that bar, weight lifting not being my field. But I remember seeing Wisniewski working with those weights a couple of hours ago and he grunts and sweats and Wisniewski is a heavyweight with a couple of state lifting titles to his credit.

I'm a little impressed, but still not interested. "So you're strong. Maybe I can give you the names of a few of the weightmen who work out here. They got some kind of a club."

He glares, at which he seems good. "There is no money in weight lifting and I need a great deal of money." He sighs. "The subject of money never really entered my mind until recently. I simply dipped into my capital when necessary and then suddenly I woke one evening to discover that I was broke."

I look him over again. His clothes look expensive, but a touch shabby, like they been worn too long and maybe slept in.

"I do read the newspapers," he says, "including the sports pages, and I see that there is a fortune to be made in the prize ring with a minimum of effort." He indicates the zipper bag. "Before I ran completely out of money, I bought boxing trunks and shoes. I will have to borrow the boxing gloves."

I raise an eyebrow. "You mean you want to step into the ring with somebody right now?"

"Precisely."

I look down the gym floor. By now the place is empty except for Alfie Bogan who's still working out on the heavy bag.

Alfie Bogan is a good kid and a hard worker. He's got a fair punch and high hopes for the ring. So far he's won all six of his fights, three by knockouts and three by decisions. But I can't see what's in his future. He just don't have enough to get to the top.

All right, I think to myself. Why not give the gentleman in black a tryout and get this over with so I can get to bed, which is a cot in my office.

I call Alfie over and say, "This here nice man wants to step into the ring with you for a couple of rounds."

It's O.K. with Alfie, so the stranger disappears into the locker room and comes back wearing black trunks.

I fit him with gloves and he and Alfie climb into the ring and go to opposite corners.

I take the wrapper off a new cigar, strike the gong, and start lighting up.

Alfie comes charging out of his corner, the way he always does, and meets the stranger three-quarters of the way across the ring. He throws a right and a left hook, which the stranger shrugs off. Then the stranger flicks out his left. You don't really see it, you just know it happened. It connects with Alfie's chin and Alfie hits the canvas on his back and stays there. I mean he's out.

I notice that my match is burning my fingers and quick blow it out. Then I climb into the ring to look at Alfie. He's still breathing, but he won't be awake for a while.

When you been in the fight game as long as I have, you don't need no long study to rate a fighter. Just that one left—and even the *sound* of it connecting—has got my heart beating a little faster.

I look around the gym for somebody to replace Alfie, but like I said before, it's empty. I lick my lips. "Kid, what about your right hand? Is it anywhere near as good as your left?"

"Actually my right hand is the better of the two."

I begin to sweat with the possibilities. "Kid, I'm impressed by your punch. I'll admit that. But the fight game is more than just punching. Can you *take* a punch too?"

He smiles thin—like a kid wearing new braces. "Of course. Please hit me."

Why not? I think. I might as well find out right now if he can take a punch. I take the glove off Alfie's right hand and slip into it.

In my day—which was thirty years ago—I had a pretty good right and I think I still got most of it. So I haul off and give it all I got. Right on the button of his chin.

And then I hop around the ring with tears in my eyes because I think I just busted my hand, but the stranger is still standing there with that narrow smile on his face and his hair not even mussed.

Alfie comes back into this world while I'm checking my hand and am relieved to discover that it ain't broken after all.

He groans and staggers to his feet, ready to start all over again. "A lucky punch." The boy is all heart, but no brains.

"No more tonight, Alfie," I say. "Some other time." I send him off to the showers and take the stranger into my office. "What's your name?"

"I am known as Cardula."

Cardula? Probably Puerto Rican, I guess. He's got a little accent. "All right," I say, "from now on you're Kid Cardula. Call me Manny." I light my cigar. "Kid, I just *may* be able to make something out of you. But first, let's get off on the right foot by making everything legal. First thing tomorrow morning we see my lawyer and he'll draw up papers which make us business associates."

Kid Cardula looks uneasy. "Unfortunately I can't make it tomorrow morning. Or the afternoon. For that matter, I can't make it *any* morning or afternoon."

I frown. "Why not?"

"I suffer from what may be termed photophobia."

"What the hell is photophobia?"

"I simply cannot endure sunlight."

"You break out in a rash or something?"

"Quite a bit more than a rash."

I chew my cigar. "Does this photophobia hurt your fighting any?"

"Not at all. Actually I regard it as responsible for my strength. However, all of my matches will have to be scheduled for evenings."

"Not much sweat there. Damn near all matches today are in the evening anyway." I think a little while. "Kid, I don't think we need to mention this photophobia to the State Medical Commission. I don't know how they stand on the subject and it's better we take no chances. This photophobia isn't catching, is it?"

"Not in the usual sense." He smiles wide this time, and I see why he's been smiling tight before. He's got these two outsize upper teeth, one on each side of his mouth. Personally, if I had teeth like that, I'd have them pulled, whether they got cavities or not.

He clears his throat. "Manny, would it be at all possible for me to get an advance on my future earnings?"

Ordinarily if anybody I just meet for the first time asks me for money, I tell him to go to hell. But with Kid Cardula and his future, I think I can make an exception. "Sure, Kid," I say. "I guess you're a little short on eating money?"

"I am not particularly concerned about eating money," the Kid says. "But my landlord threatens to evict me if I don't pay the rent."

The next morning at around eleven I get a phone call from Hanahan. It's about the McCardle-Jabloncic main event on Saturday night's card at the arena.

McCardle is Hanahan's pride and joy. He's a heavyweight, got some style and speed, and he's young. Hanahan is bringing him along careful, picking and choosing. Maybe McCardle isn't exactly championship material, but he should get in a few big money fights before it's time to retire.

"Manny," Hanahan says, "we got a little trouble with the Saturday night card. Jabloncic showed up at the weigh-ins with a virus, so he got scratched. I need somebody to fill in. You got anybody around there who'll fit the role?"

Jabloncic has 18 wins and 10 losses, which record don't look too bad on paper, except that it don't mention that he got six of them losses—all by knockouts—in a row after his eighteenth win. So I know exactly what type of fighter Hanahan wants as a substitute for Jabloncic.

I think a little. Off hand, there are three or four veterans who hang around the gym and could use the money and don't mind the beating.

And then I remember Kid Cardula.

Ordinarily when you got a new boy, you bring him up slow, like three-round preliminaries. But with Kid Cardula I feel I got something that can't wait and we might as well take some shortcuts.

I speak into the phone. "Well, off hand, Hanahan, I can't think of anybody except this new face that just come to me last night. Kid Cardula, I think he calls himself."

"Never heard of him. What's his win-lose?"

"I don't know. He's some kind of foreign fighter. Puerto Rico, I think. I don't have his records yet."

Hanahan is cautious. "You ever seen him fight?"

"Well, I put him in the ring here for just a few seconds to see if he has anything. His left is fair, but I never seen him use his right hand once. Don't even know if he has one."

Hanahan is interested. "Anything else?"

"He came in here wearing a shabby suit and gave me a sob story about being down and out. He's thirty-five if he's a day. I'll swear to that."

Hanahan is pleased. "Well, all right. But I don't want anybody *too* easy. Can he stand up for a couple of rounds?"

"Hanahan, I can't guarantee anything, but I'll try the best I can."

That evening, when Kid Cardula shows up at the gym, I quick rush him to my lawyer and then to the weigh-in and physical under the arena, where I also sign papers which gives us ten percent of the night's gross.

I provide Kid Cardula with a robe which has got no lettering on the back yet, but it's black, his favorite color, and we go out into the arena.

McCardle is a local boy, which means he's got a following. Half his neighborhood is at the arena and it ain't really a bad house. Not like the old days, but good enough.

We set up shop inside the ring and when the bell rings, McCardle makes the sign of the cross and dances out of his corner.

But Kid Cardula don't move an inch. He turns to me, and his face looks scared. "Does McCardle *have* to do that?"

"Do what?" I ask. "Now look, Kid, this is no time to get stage fright. Get out there and fight."

The Kid peeks back over his shoulder where the referee and McCardle are waiting for him in the center of the ring. Then he takes a deep breath, turns, and glides out of our corner.

His left whips out, makes the connection with McCardle's jaw, and it's all over. Just like that. McCardle is lying there in the same pose as Alfie Bogan last night.

Even the referee is stunned and wastes a few seconds getting around to the count, not that it really matters. The bout is wrapped up in nineteen seconds, including the count.

There's some booing. Not because anybody thinks that McCardle threw the fight, but because everything went so quick with the wrong man winning and the fans figure they didn't get enough time for the price of their tickets.

When we're back in the dressing room, the first person who comes storming in is Hanahan, his face beet red. He glares at Kid Cardula and then drags me to a corner. "What the hell are you doing to me, Manny?"

I am innocence. "Hanahan, I swear that was the luckiest punch I ever seen in my life."

"You're damn right it was a lucky punch. We'll have the re-match as soon as I can book the arena again."

"Re-match?" I rub my chin. "Maybe so, Hanahan, but in this event I feel that I got to protect the Kid's interests. It's like a sacred trust. So for the re-match, we make his cut of the gate sixty percent instead of ten, right?"

Hanahan is fit to explode, but he's got this black spot on his fighter's record and the sooner he gets it off, the better. So by the time we finish yelling at each other, we decide to split the purse fifty-fifty, which is about what I expect anyway.

A couple of nights later when I close up the gym and go to my office, I find the Kid sitting there watching the late show on my portable TV set. It's one of them Dracula pictures and he turns to another channel when I enter.

I nod. "Never could stand them vampire pictures myself either. Even in a movie, I like logic, and they ain't got no logic."

"No logic?"

"Right. Like when you start off with one vampire and he goes out and drinks somebody's blood and that turns his victim into a vampire too, right? So now there's *two* vampires. A week later, they both get hungry and go out and feed on two victims. Now you got *four* vampires. A week later them four vampires go out to feed and now you got *eight* vampires."

"Ah, yes," Kid Cardula says. "And at the end of twenty-one weeks, one would logically expect to have a total of 1,048,576 vampires?"

"About that. And at the end of thirty weeks or so, everybody on the face of the earth is a vampire, and a week later all of them starve to death because they got no food supply any more."

Kid Cardula smiles, showing them big teeth. "You've got a head on your shoulders, Manny. However, suppose that these fictitious vampires, realizing that draining *all* of the blood from their victims will turn them into vampires and thereby competitors, exercise a certain restraint instead? Suppose they simply take a sip, so to speak, from one person and a sip from the next, leaving their victims with just a slight anemia and lassitude for a few days, but otherwise none the worse for wear?"

I nod, turn down the TV volume, and get back to the fight business. "Now, Kid, I know that you'll be able to put McCardle away again in a few seconds, but we got to remember that fighting is also show biz. People don't pay good money for long to see twenty-second fights. We got to give the customers a performance that lasts awhile. So when we meet McCardle again, I want you to carry him for a few rounds. Don't hit too hard. Make the match look even until say the fifth round and *then* put him away."

I light a cigar. "If we look too good, Kid, we'll have trouble getting opponents later and we got to think about the future. A string of knockouts is fine, Kid, but don't make them look too easy."

In the weeks which follow while we're waiting for the McCardle rematch, I can't get the Kid to do any training at all—no road work and he won't even consider shadow boxing in front of a mirror.

So I leave it at that, not wanting to tamper with something that might be perfect. Also he won't give me his address. I suppose he's just got pride and don't want me to see the dump in which he lives. And he's got no phone. But he shows up at the gym every other night or so, just in case there's something concerning him.

The second McCardle fight comes and we take it in stride. The Kid carries McCardle for four rounds, but still making the bouts look good, and then in the fifth round he puts McCardle away with a short fast right.

In the days which follow, we don't have any particular trouble signing up more fights because we'll take any bout which comes our way. With Kid Cardula, I know I don't have to nurse him along. Also, we decide on the strategy of letting the Kid get himself knocked down two, maybe three, times per fight. With this maneuver, we establish that while the Kid can hit, he ain't so good at taking a punch. Consequently every manager who's got a pug with a punch figures that his boy has got a good chance of putting the Kid away.

We get seven bouts in the next year, all of which the Kid wins by knockouts, of course, and we're drawing attention from other parts of the country.

Now that some money is beginning to come in, I expect the Kid to brighten up a little, which he does for about six months, but then I notice that he's starting to brood about something. I try to get him to tell me about it, but he just shakes his head.

Also, now that he's getting publicity, he begins to attract the broads. They really go for his type. He's polite to them and all that, and even asks them their addresses, but as far as I know he never follows up or pays them a visit.

One morning after we'd just won our tenth fight—a nine-round knockout over Irv Watson, who was on the way down, but still a draw —and I am sitting in my office dreaming about the day soon when I sell the gym or at least hire somebody to manage it, when there's a knock at the door.

The dame which enters and stands there looking scared is about your average height and weight, with average looks, and wearing good clothes. She's got black hair and a nose that's more than it should be. In all, nothing to get excited about.

She swallows hard. "Is this where I can find Mr. Kid Cardula?"

"He drops in every now and then," I say. "But it's not a schedule. I never know when he'll turn up."

"Would you have his address?"

"No. He likes to keep that a secret."

She looks lost for a few seconds and then decides to tell me what brought her here. "About two weeks ago I drove out of state to see my aunt Harriet and when I came back, I got a late start and it got dark before I could make it home. I'm really not at all good with directions and it had been raining. I turned and turned, hoping that I'd find a road that looked familiar. Somehow I got on this muddy road and my car skidded right into a ditch. And I just couldn't get the car out. Finally I gave up and sat there, waiting for some car to pass, but there was no traffic at all. I couldn't even see a farmhouse light. I guess I finally fell asleep. I had the strangest dream, but I can't remember now exactly what it was, and when I woke, there was this tall distinguished-looking man standing beside the open door of my car and staring down at me. He gave me quite a start at first, but I recovered and asked him if he'd give me a lift to someplace where I could get to a phone and call my father and have him send someone out to pick me up. His car was parked on the road and he drove me to a crossroads where there was a gas station open."

I notice that she's got what look like two big mosquito bites on one side of her throat.

She goes on. "Anyway, while I was making the phone call, he drove away before I could thank him or get his name. But I kept thinking about . . ." She blushed. "Then last night while I was watching the late news, there were things about sports and a picture of Kid Cardula appeared on the TV screen, and immediately I knew that this must be the stranger who had driven me to the gas station. So I asked around and somebody told me that you were his manager and gave me the address of your gym. And I just thought I'd drop in and thank him in person."

I nod. "I'll pass the thanks on to the Kid the next time I see him."

She still stands there, thinking, and suddenly she brightens again. "Also I wanted to return something to him. A money clip. With one thousand dollars in it. It was found beside my car when the tow truck went to pull it out of the ditch."

Sure, I think. Some nice honest tow truck driver finds a thousand bucks on the ground and he doesn't put it in his own pocket. But I nod again. "So give me the thousand and I'll see that the Kid gets it."

She laughs a little. "Unfortunately I forgot to bring the money and the clip with me." She opens her purse and takes out a ball-point pen and some paper. "My name is Carrington. Daphne Carrington. I'll write the directions on how to get to our place. It's a bit complicated. We call it Carrington Eyrie. Perhaps you've heard of it? It was featured in *Stately Home and Formal Garden Magazine* last year. Mr. Cardula will have to come in person, of course. So that he can identify the clip."

When Kid Cardula drops in the next evening, I tell him about Daphne Carrington and give him the slip of paper she left.

The Kid frowns. "I didn't lose a thousand dollars. Besides, I never use a money clip."

I grin. "I thought not. But still she's willing to ante up a thousand bucks to meet you. Is any part of her story true?"

"Well . . . I *did* drive her to that filling station after I . . . after I found her asleep in the car."

"I didn't know you owned a car."

"I bought it last week. There are some places just too far to fly."

"What model is it?"

"A 1974 Volkswagen. The motor's in good condition, but the body needs a little work." He sits on the corner of my desk, his eyes thoughtful. "*She* was driving a Lincoln Continental."

"Don't worry about it, Kid. Pretty soon you'll be driving Lincoln Continentals too."

We begin spacing out our fights now. No bum-of-the-month stuff. Mostly because we're getting better quality opponents and also because it needs time and publicity to build up the interest and the big gates.

We win a couple more fights, which get television coverage, and the Kid should be happy, but he's still brooding.

And then one night he shows up in my office and he makes an announcement. "Manny, I'm getting married."

I'm a little astounded, but I see no threat. Lots of fighters are married. "Who's the lucky lady?"

"Daphne Carrington."

I think awhile before the name connects. "You mean *that* Daphne Carrington?"

He nods.

I stare at him. "I hope you don't take this wrong, Kid, but the dame ain't exactly Raquel Welch, even in the face department."

His chin gets stubborn. "She has a tremendous personality."

That I doubt too. "Kid," I say, "be honest with yourself. She just ain't your type."

"She soon will be."

Suddenly the nub of the situation seems to flash into my mind and I'm shocked. "Kid, you're not marrying this dame for her money, are you?"

He blushes, or looks like he tried to. "Why not? It's been done before."

"But, Kid, you don't *have* to marry anybody for their money. You're going to have money of your own soon. Big money. Millions."

He looks away. "Manny, I have been getting letters from my relatives and many concerned friends. But especially relatives. It seems that they have heard or been told about my ring appearances. And they all point out—rather strongly—that for a man with my background, it is unthinkable that I should be appearing in a prize ring."

He still didn't look at me. "I have been thinking this over for a long time, Manny, and I am afraid they are right. I shouldn't be a boxer. Certainly not a professional. All of my family and all of my friends strongly disapprove. And, Manny, one must have one's own self-respect and the approval of one's peers if one wants to achieve any happiness in this world."

"Peers?" I say. "You mean like royalty? You a count or something? You got blue blood in your veins?"

"Occasionally." He sighs. "My relatives have even begun a collection to save me from destitution. But I cannot accept charity from relatives."

"But you don't mind marrying a dame for her money?"

"My dear Manny," he says. "Marrying a woman for her money is as good a reason as any. Besides, it will enable me to quit the fight game."

We argue and argue and I beg him to think it over for a while, telling him what all that ring money could mean to him—and me.

Finally he seems to give in a little, and when he leaves, he at least promises to think it over for a while.

About a week passes. I don't hear from him and I'm a nervous wreck. Finally, at around ten-thirty one evening, Alfie Bogan comes into my office with an envelope.

Right away I get the feeling that the envelope should have a black border. My fingers tremble when I open it and read the note from Kid Cardula.

> Dear Manny:
>   I sincerely regret the way things have turned out, but I am determined to quit the ring. I know that you pinned a great deal of hope on my future and I am certain that, under

different circumstances, we would have made those millions you talked about.

But goodbye and good luck. I have, however, decided not to leave you empty handed.

Best wishes,
Kid Cardula.

Not leave me empty handed? Did he enclose a nice little check? I shake the envelope, but nothing comes out. What the hell did he mean he wouldn't leave me empty handed?

I glare at Alfie Bogan, who's still standing there.

He grins. "Hit me."

I stare. Somehow Alfie looks different. He has these two big mosquito bites on his throat and these two long upper teeth, which I swear I never seen before.

"Hit me," he says again.

Maybe I shouldn't do it, but it's been a long hard week of disappointments. So I let him have it with all I got.

And break my hand.

But I'm smiling when the doc puts on the cast.

I got me a replacement for Kid Cardula.

Invisible Clue

by Jeffry Scott

Normally reticent to the point of rudeness, my friend Morlock does rather plume himself on the Leander affair.

And with good reason. After all, Major Colin Morlock, former soldier and retired colonial policeman, is not a detective. Yet he cut to the heart of the Leander case without setting eyes on either of the men involved.

That is a feat any professional criminal-investigation operative must respect. Even more startling is the fact that it was done by means of a clue which could not be seen. If it had been visible, it would have been no clue at all—or so Morlock explained teasingly.

"Like Conan Doyle's dog, whose significance lay in *not* barking?" I suggested, trying to sound intelligent.

"Not a bit like, laddie," Major Morlock snorted.

He is dapper and saturnine, somehow out of his spiritual era with his starched collars and painstakingly buffed handmade shoes. The sight of him used to put me in mind of wicker chairs, Burmese cheroots, sundowners, and jungle-surrounded tennis courts. Then I realized that Morlock was a character seeking the proper Somerset Maugham story while enduring a long distasteful exile in modern London.

Deny it as he will, Morlock cultivates that aura. It leads people to dismiss him as a harmless relic. But he still plays murderous squash and will be doing press-ups on the changing-room floor long after I have collapsed in a puddle of sweat.

Morlock calls himself a personal security consultant—it sounds dull and respectable and, well, reassuring. What he sells is reassurance itself, for Major Colin Morlock is a bodyguard—among the best dozen of them in the world, some would say.

"I'm like an old football player" is his own modest assessment. "I can't dash about, but I can jolly well read the game. It's a matter of recognizing patterns, having a good set of trouble muscles, and then *walk-*

ing in a rapid but unflurried manner so as to be in the correct spot at the best time."

Trouble muscles? According to Morlock, his back aches like a pregnant woman's in the presence of danger to himself or a client.

Having heard about the invisible clue, I pestered him for the story.

"The case hasn't come to trial yet and I dare say it will be heard in camera," he warned. "I'll change the names on that account. I'll also deny any knowledge, if you quote me. But it's all true, my word on that, laddie . . ."

The story started in Major Morlock's office suite near St. Paul's Cathedral, as half the pigeons and public clocks in London made a fearful racket to signal that another day's business ought to be launched.

Those offices! He got the place cheap when a pop record company went bankrupt. The decor was ten years out of date, marking the worst and wildest excesses of psychedelic decorations. Each door, and there were many, was a different clashing color. Walls and filing cabinets and desks were unlikely shades of tangerine, yellow, purple, and green, all of which did not suit Morlock. The rent, however, did.

After the best part of a week out of town, he was listening to a tape recorder.

From it rattled the voice of Linda, his secretary. "I've handled all the routine stuff, sir. Only one mildly interesting item. Squadron Leader Alex Leander telephoned for you this afternoon. I've never heard of him, but there was a definite you-must-have-heard-of-me note in his voice."

Major Morlock smiled wryly. He was being made to feel his age.

Alex Leander had been a brilliant fighter pilot during the Battle of Britain. But that was a long time ago—his secretary's parents had been teenagers themselves when it was fought out above their heads.

I've never heard of him. Morlock, lost in a reverie, had to stop the tape and wind back. After World War Two, Leander had emigrated to Africa, going in for farming and stockbreeding on the grand scale. Less happily, Squadron Leader Leander had become involved in emergent-nation politics, respected by black nationalist leaders and looked at askance by his own kind.

Morlock pressed the Start key again.

Linda was saying: "He sounds nice—but scared, edgy-like. He must have pots of money because he's got a permanent service flatlet in Maybury Towers, that huge place in Mayfair, although he only comes to London once a year, if that. He wants you to contact him as soon as possible. Says he got plenty of sleep on the plane over here, but he won't be able to stay alert for more than 24 hours. That gives him about eight hours to go, by the time you get back."

Linda burst in while her final recorded words were still emerging from the machine. She listened sheepishly. "Ever so sorry, Major—I meant to scrub that tape last night, but my feller called for me and I clean forgot."

"Why on earth scrub it?"

"It's all off," said Linda blithely. "He popped in just before I shut up shop yesterday evening—Squadron Leader Leander, I mean. Full of apologies, changed his mind. Nice old boy—well, not *old* old. About your age." She blushed and shook her head.

With lethal patience, Morlock suggested, "Drop the silken courtesy and the diplomatic touch, they don't suit you. Facts, if you please!"

Linda gave him a glance blending irritation and reproach. "No need to get shirty. He paid fifty pounds as a cancellation fee. Insisted on it. If you ask me, he was ashamed of getting in a tizzy and shouting for help, and wanted it all smoothed over and forgotten quick."

Major Morlock frowned and started massaging the small of his back. Alex Leander might have changed in thirty years or more, but Battle of Britain aces, as a breed, are not notorious for getting in tizzies and issuing needless SOS messages.

Also, Morlock had a knack for picking up scraps of information bearing on his own line of business. Recently he had escorted a Nairobi businessman who was in London to exchange diamonds for cash, and wanted to lose neither. Alex Leander's name had cropped up during one of the endless hotel-bedroom waiting periods, and the name was connected with at least two assassination attempts.

"No reply," Morlock grunted. He had looked up Squadron Leader Leander's telephone number at Maybury Towers. The place was a Twentieth Century cliff-dwelling—a thousand or more air-conditioned centrally heated caves looming above Hyde Park.

Rather subdued now, Linda handed him a cup of coffee. "Well, he's cancelled. Probably out for the day. He won't thank you for chasing him."

"Maybe." Major Morlock brooded over the coffee. He looked up sharply, catching her eye. "Tell me everything you can remember about his visit."

Linda shrugged and pulled a face. "What's to tell? He was a bit, you know, embarrassed. Dropped his money on the carpet when he was paying me the fifty pounds."

She snapped her fingers and giggled. "Tell you what, Major, he's color blind. Couldn't wait to get out once he'd explained about canceling. Walked straight into the lavatory. I told him it was the green door, but no, he went steaming through the red one, and that's just the broom cupboard. So he sort of swore under his breath. I kept saying, 'The *green* door, sir.' Bless my soul if he didn't try the pink one, to the fire escape. Ever so embarrassing for both of us—I had to scoot over from behind the desk and sort of lead him to the exit."

But Linda was talking to Major Morlock's back. He had whirled to the phone. Within ninety seconds he was talking to Superintendent Blaikie of Scotland Yard's Special Branch.

"Morlock here. Trouble, laddie, probably serious. Certainly urgent. Squadron Leader Leander—yes, the Africa chap. He is or was at 524 East, Maybury Towers. Somebody's out to kill him. I'll join you there."

When Blaikie and his men kicked down the door at Maybury Towers they found Alex Leander sprawled in the tiny bedroom, in a coma after what appeared to be an attempt to commit suicide with barbiturates.

After treatment in the Intensive Care Unit of a nearby hospital, Leander explained that he had indeed taken a drug overdose. His visitor had given him the choice of that or a bullet through the head. Leander had opted for almost-certain death rather than the absolutely certain variety.

It must have been a bizarre and quietly evil scene: the man with the gun sitting nurselike beside the bed as Leander's color changed and his breathing grew ever slower and more labored . . .

"As soon as it became obvious that the Leander who called at my office was an imposter, then the most likely reason for the masquerade was to make sure that I wouldn't go looking for the real Leander," Major Morlock lectured me.

"Now then, if the assassin heard Leander phoning me, which must have been the case, it meant that he had bugged the phone or was using a listening device from a flat adjacent to Leander's. Superintendent Blaikie's chaps checked the phone and it wasn't bugged, so they looked for holes in the walls—and found one leading them to 523, next door. Prints all over it. The man had a record and they caught him at the airport."

Morlock seemed to take it for granted that I understood what had alerted him. I could follow his early doubts, when Leander asked for and then rejected a bodyguard. But somewhere along the track, he had lost me, I said as much. Major Morlock looked genuinely surprised.

"But my dear chap! Wake up, laddie. The man who canceled my services was color blind. Ergo, he could not be Squadron Leader Leander. You simply aren't allowed to become an R.A.F. pilot if you're color blind!"

Accidental Widow

by Nedra Tyre

The gun in Millie's right hand fired.

Si didn't even have time to look surprised.

He fell dead at her feet.

"Damn," Millie said softly. It wasn't fair that she had lost another husband.

She hadn't wanted the silly gun to begin with. She'd begged Si not to give it to her—his name was Simon but he liked for people to call him Si. Protests were brushed aside. Si had insisted she must learn to shoot. He was the bossiest and most stubborn of all her husbands. He had put his foot down. Millie had to know how to handle a gun expertly so that she could defend herself. Si's job kept him out of town on business more and more and it wasn't safe for Millie (whose real name was Millicent) to be alone in their country place unless she had ample protection, which meant she had to be able to shoot an intruder.

Millie's dread of guns, revolvers, pistols—whatever they were called—was phobic. Rather than have a pistol in the house she begged Si to let her travel with him so she could have his continuous protection. Si wouldn't think of it. He wouldn't let Millie sacrifice her pleasant life to trail along with him.

So, in spite of anything that Millie could do, Si had bought the gun or pistol or revolver or whatever it was and proceeded to give her her first lesson.

"Look, darling," he had said, "this is the way you release the catch," and he had done it with considerable grace and had handed the gun to her to repeat his action. The instant Millie touched the gun it went off.

Poor dear Archibald—he wanted people to call him Arch—had had an equally abrupt demise. He was crazy about the water. Her Uncle Adam said Arch should have been born with fins—or was it gills?—he was so foolish about water.

Millie was terrified of water. She had few fears. Lightning didn't frighten her and she thought that mice were cute. She was even fond of snakes. But she didn't like water. That is, she didn't like wide expanses of it. Swimming in small enclosed pools was pleasant enough. She would never have ventured outside the United States if she'd lived in a time when one had to travel by ship. Arch doted on water, and Millie encouraged him to spend as much of his leisure as he liked at the lake. She just requested politely that he not ask her to join him in his boat—she would gladly sit on the shore and watch him row and wave at him.

But that wasn't enough for Arch. He was determined to cure her of her fear of the water and rationalized it so that her fear and her love for him were somehow the same, and if she didn't get in the boat with him it meant she didn't love him. When he put it like that, what could she do?

So she had gingerly climbed into the boat and even as they edged away from the dock she begged and pleaded with Arch to take her back. She was literally out of her mind from fear. Arch laughed at her, and her fear became so great that she had decided to leap into the water and to drown herself to kill her fear. She had stood up and Arch had risen and was reaching toward her and she pushed him away.

Suddenly there was a splash, and she was alone and began to scream.

People nearby heard and rowed toward her and she told them about Arch and they dived and summoned other help.

But nothing helped Arch. It took four hours for them to find his body.

Jonathan was the next one. At least as Millie recalled it he was the one she had married after Arch. Jonathan wanted people to call him Jon, and spell it J-o-n. He got very peeved with Millie's mother because she always wrote of him or to him as John. He said that Millie's mother was the most wonderful mother-in-law a man could wish for, but why did she insist on spelling his name John instead of Jon? Poor lamb, there wasn't much time left to him in which Millie's mother could misspell his name.

Jon was mad for picnics. But of a very primitive sort. Millie agreed that picnics had their place. She loved it when you took a folding table and chairs and a small tent and cushions and silver and napkins and a feast of chicken breasts and ham accompanied by plenty of iced champagne. Um.

But Jon was all for living off the land. A picnic was no picnic, he claimed, unless you gathered what you ate. It was the way you showed your mettle.

On their last picnic he had gone fishing while he left it up to Millie to gather the mushrooms and wild strawberries for the rest of the meal. She didn't know beans about selecting mushrooms and told him so, and he explained very carefully what she must look for and what she must avoid. She tried to obey his instructions, but she hadn't brought her glasses. Jon disliked it when she wore glasses. He acted as if it were some fashionable whim of hers to wear glasses and that she didn't need them at all. So without her glasses she had done the best she could in picking mushrooms and strawberries.

Jon had come back flourishing the fish he had caught, and he and Millie had settled down to drinking bourbon straight from the bottle as an appetizer. They did not spare themselves and in a little while became as giggly and exuberant as children. They discovered they were ravenously hungry and had rushed about gathering wood for a fire and had buried the fish near the embers and Jon had begun to eat the mushrooms. Millie didn't like raw vegetables and had deadened her appetite with some of the wild strawberries, and Jon had kept dipping into the mushrooms while the fish took its time about being cooked.

Most of the mushrooms had been good, but enough of them had been poisonous to end Jon's short and (Millie was sure) happy life.

Then there was Pen—short for Pendleton. Millie could cry her eyes out when she thought about what had happened to him. If only Pen had stood a bare inch—or even a fraction of an inch to the right or left, forward or backward—the bust would not have struck him in the exact spot on his skull which had proved fatal.

Pen had wanted to be an interior designer, but his father had put his foot down, and instead Pen had worked in a bank. After he had married Millie his flair for design had erupted all over the house, especially in the main hall. He had no sooner completed the hall in regency style than he wanted it Victorian or modern, and then his most ambitious scheme was to make it classical and have the theme extend all the way upstairs and across the balustrade on the landing, where he proposed to set half a dozen busts of various Roman emperors to complement another half dozen set on pedestals in the lower hall. His sketch of the completed design which he presented for Millie's approval looked impressive if somewhat forbidding. Soon various deliverymen staggered in beneath monstrously heavy busts which they deployed according to Pen's directions.

Then one doom-laden night not long afterward, Millie had gone upstairs and Pen had called to her from directly below the landing to ask her to put on her blue satin nightgown and she had leaned over to blow him a kiss and to say all right, darling, and had somehow sent Gaius Julius Caesar tumbling from his perch.

Her parents, as always, were wonderful and sympathetic and stood by Millie faithfully, though when her poor mother learned of Pen's mishap with the bust of Gaius Julius Caesar she tactfully explained a somewhat awkward development.

"Millie, dear," her mother said, "I'm just as embarrassed as I can be, and I don't want to sound inhospitable—it breaks my heart to have to mention it—but there's simply no room for Pen in the family plot. You see, darling, your Uncle Adam and Aunt Bess, your grandfather, and daddy and I—and of course you, baby—have got to be buried there, and though we've been more than happy to accommodate your husbands up to now, there's just no space for Pen."

So at the last minute Millie had to bustle about buying a cemetery lot and the only one available was way across the river.

After the service was over she felt so bad about leaving Pen out there all alone.

As it happened he did not have to wait very long for company.

Al, whose name was Aloysius, was just as bullheaded that she play softball as Jon had been that they picnic off the food they gathered.

Al was a sports enthusiast. Millie didn't like sports. Oh, she thought it was nice enough to watch tennis if she had a seat in the shade, and she had been to lots of high school and college football games—twice she'd been homecoming queen. But she didn't like to participate in sports. She blistered too quickly and sprained too easily and she was too nearsighted to see a ball until it had almost struck her in the face. Al paid no attention to her protests and he listed their names as a participating husband-and-wife couple for a softball game at the club.

And there Millie was, standing at bat, completely a fish out of water, and Al was behind her saying, "Strike it, sweetheart. Give a big strong swing. Come on." And she had swung with all her might, and with such a display of force that she had pivoted before she could stop herself and had struck Al. He had collapsed in a dead heap.

Not that anything really good came of that awful afternoon, but at least Millie hadn't struck Joe Moore who had been playing catch or whatever you call the person standing behind the batter. Joe had been playing at that position until Al had asked to take his place while Millie was at bat. Just suppose Joe had still been there when Millie had tried to strike the ball! Mary Moore would never have forgiven Millie if she had killed Joe.

Of course it was all just a terrible accident and Millie had only been trying to please Al when she hit him instead of the ball.

So Al went to join Pen in the new cemetery lot.

Lucky for Millie, other men didn't seem to lose heart—at least up to now. She heard her grandfather mutter about fortune hunters swarming around Millie like flies around a sugar bowl. But that really wasn't very kind of Grandpa, for even though it was true that none of the men she had married had any money to speak of, they were attractive and loving and had good jobs. It turned out that they had left her tidy sums after all, as her father had seen to it when he approved their engagements that they carried sizable amounts of life insurance, and accidental deaths paid double. And you didn't have to pay inheritance tax on insurance. So if her husbands had been hunting fortunes, she had been the one who had actually found them.

Her next husband was Gar—his real name was Beauregard.

Gar was the most affectionate man Millie had ever known. There was always a glint in Gar's eye, whatever the season—not that she had him for many seasons. While he was relatively composed when he drank scotch, bourbon or vodka, he could sometimes be a bit of a handful when he had gin. So Millie purposely did not buy gin when she shopped for liquor, except when she gave a big party and there were others besides Gar to drink it.

One afternoon her Uncle Adam came out to visit and he brought gin because he said martinis were the world's most civilized drink and he hadn't seen them served in Millie's house since she had married Gar. Uncle Adam stood by admiringly as Millie mixed martinis exactly to his specification. He was almost her favorite relative and his visit seemed much too short. She begged him to take his bottle of gin when he left, but he wouldn't hear of it.

Gar arrived from work as Millie lingered at the door saying goodbye to Uncle Adam and by the time her uncle had departed Gar had fastened upon the gin with rabid enthusiasm.

Hoping that food would deflect Gar, Millie had dashed into the kitchen and asked the cook and butler to serve dinner early, and they had gladly obliged, but for every ounce of beef that Gar consumed he took two ounces of gin.

The glint in Gar's eyes was at its most glinted.

Good gracious, Millie was still in her street clothes and eager for dessert—apple dumpling made from her Aunt Bess's recipe—and as soon as she had finished eating she intended to watch the evening news.

Her plans were in jeopardy.

Millie hadn't seen such fervor in Gar since their wedding night or at least since the last time Gar had drunk lavishly of gin. He ignored his apple dumpling. Millie was halfway through hers and intent on eating Gar's if he didn't settle down and behave himself. Gar splashed more gin into a glass and then ran upstairs to the sitting room, and called out for her to follow him onto the balcony to look at the full moon.

Like a pirate Millie grabbed and gobbled Gar's apple dumpling and then went upstairs to the balcony where Gar was standing, gesturing dramatically toward the full moon. Some of the gin spilled from his glass to the bed of verbena below. With a damn or two he regretted the loss of the gin and rushed downstairs to replenish his drink.

That part of the balcony on which Millie was standing was curtained from the moonlight by heavy vines, and she turned to watch Gar reenter the sitting room. The almost empty bottle of gin was in his hand. He started to pour the gin into his glass, and then instead he leaned his head back and drank from the bottle, and with a yell of pleasure threw the empty bottle through the open door. The bottle arched past Millie and she waited for it to crash on the paved patio, but there was only a thud. Its fall had been muffled by the shrubbery and the bed of verbena.

"Where's my girl?" Gar asked. "Where's my darling girl?"

He sounded so sweet, so pleading, and it wasn't his fault that Uncle Adam had left the bottle of gin. And he probably had had a hard day at the office and needed to unwind and, for heaven's sake, what was wrong with a little horseplay? Husbands had to be cherished and encouraged. Their moods must be pampered.

Millie giggled and said, "I'm here but you can't find me."

Sure enough, Gar couldn't find her, so she darted out from the shadows to tease him, and he tried to grab her but she escaped to the other side of the balcony. Then Gar dashed after her, and somehow or other he crashed over the slender iron railing.

Fate was not as kind to Gar as it had been to the empty gin bottle. Neither the shrubbery nor the verbena bed deterred his fall. Gar fell directly onto the patio pavement.

And so Millie's life proceeded while all around her men were losing theirs.

Some of her marriages had lasted only a few months.

Her marriage to Adelbert—or Bert as he liked to be called—had lasted a year. As in the case of each of her marriages, she would have been content for it to last throughout eternity. And if it hadn't been for the pills, Bert would be beside her at that very moment.

Bert was as silly as Gar—no, it wasn't Gar. Gar had loved her glasses —but Bert and one of the others whose name she couldn't remember at the moment hated it that she had to wear glasses to see anything clearly at all. Bert was so stern. He said she was perfect, that she mustn't mar her lovely face by wearing glasses, and she did her best to please him, just as she did her best to please all her husbands, though she thought it was silly of Bert not to let her wear glasses in his presence. She'd read that half the people in the United States wore glasses, and why shouldn't she?

So in a way what happened to Bert served him right.

No, that was too awful a way to put it.

Anyhow, Bert really did dramatize his illness—everyone, including his own mother and Millie's mother, said so.

Why he'd had a heart attack in the first place was unaccountable. No man only 26 years old had any business having a serious heart attack. Bert had been released from intensive care in the hospital to bedrest at home, and Millie had taken over nursing him. During his convalescence he acted like a spoiled brat—that was the only adequate term for his behavior. He made Millie cater to him day and night.

Late one afternoon she had fallen asleep exhausted as she sat beside him, and he waked her by jabbing at her and screaming that he had to have his pills. She hadn't had her glasses and had fumbled in the drawer and had given him the pillbox right in front, and it turned out they weren't the pills he should have taken.

As far as Millie could tell, the doctor didn't even realize what had happened. He comforted her by saying that a man in Bert's condition could die at any moment.

In that lapse of time after Bert died, Millie had an interval to think of everything that had happened to her and her husbands.

She got her husbands confused, she must admit, no matter how conscientiously she tried to keep them separate and distinct. She recalled that she had sent a large contribution to the alumni fund of Tech in honor of Gar, when she remembered too late that it was Bert who had gone to Tech. Not that it mattered to Tech—they kept the contribution and wrote a warm if somewhat vague acknowledgment. Once she had made a sizable donation to the ASPCA to mark Jon's birthday, only to recall that Jon didn't care at all for animals—it was Arch who had been the animal lover: during the brief extent of their marriage the size of their menagerie vied with that of the city zoo. Besides, it hadn't been Jon's birthday but Al's.

And she would attribute in memory some exquisite nuance of love-making to Si only to have to contradict herself later that it had actually been Pen. She would recollect the transports she had experienced in Paris with Gar, when she had never been to Paris with any of them but Arch, and she mooned in retrospect over Venice with Jon when in fact she had been with Al when she had fed all those pigeons in St. Mark's Square.

Never mind. She meant no disrespect to any of them because she couldn't keep track of what had happened to her with whom. She had cherished them all. It wasn't her fault that she had ended up with so many. From the time she was a little girl and had learned about hus-bands and weddings she had dreamed of celebrating her golden anni-versary with her one and only predestined mate.

But life hadn't worked out that way.

Millie was years short of being 30 and she had had—well, exactly how many husbands was it?

She ticked them off.

Thumb, left hand—Bert.

First finger—Jon.

Second finger—Arch.

Third finger—Gar.

Little finger—Si.

Thumb, right hand—Pen.

Six—not that she had them in the right order. Six husbands! Only think of it. Why, it boggled the mind!

But just a minute. What did she mean—six husbands? She had for-gotten Al. How could Al have slipped her mind? He was one of her fa-vorites.

Al. First finger, right hand.

Al made seven.

Darling men, all of them. That was the only possible way she could describe them. She had been the luckiest woman in the whole world.

And the unluckiest.

What now?

Life had ended for her, she felt it in her bones. She was positive that no man would ever approach her again in a romantic way. Anybody who knew her story would think twice before he came courting, no matter what her Grandpa had said about her fortune being like a sugar bowl to attract flies.

She longed to speak of her doubts and misgivings with someone. If only she could discuss her anxieties. But the more often she had married, and the more often her husbands had died, the less her family and friends had seemed inclined to talk about Millie's unusual situation. It was almost as if they were embarrassed by what had happened to her, as if it were too indelicate to mention. They were the soul of tact, hovering over her with love and sympathy but ignoring her pressing and acute problem—which was the necessity to talk with someone about all her tragic losses.

The prolonged ringing of the doorbell interrupted her self-pity.

Her caller was a handsome, very tall man. And he was old. He must have been forty, at least. Her husbands had all been her own age, give or take a year. So this couldn't be anyone intent on matrimony.

"Mrs. Raymond?"

He had come to the wrong place.

"Mrs. Raymond?" He repeated it as if Millie hadn't understood him.

"Mrs. Raymond?" he said for the third time.

The last repetition brought Millie to her senses.

Good gracious, one of her husbands had the last name of Raymond. Of course! It was Bert, poor darling. His last name was Raymond.

The last name of her last husband was Raymond, so of course it was her last last name. She had had so many last names. How could she be expected to keep up with them all?

Millie nodded to the man.

"My name is Williams. May I come in?"

Millie nodded again.

Williams did not give his first name. Or his profession. Or his rank.

He was the lieutenant in charge of the Queenborough Homicide Squad. He purposely did not divulge any information about himself. Nothing about this visit must get back to headquarters just yet. He had wanted to make a routine aboveboard investigation. For some time he had longed to bring Millicent Raymond to account for her crimes. After the third accidental death he had approached the chief, who waved him aside. The chief knew Millicent Raymond's grandfather and father intimately. There wasn't a finer family in the South—in the world if it came to that, he said—and Millicent was the pride of the family.

After the fifth accidental death Williams made another attempt to get an investigation under way and the chief's blood really did boil. What was eating Williams anyway? He must stop his foolish suspicions and get down to punishing the real criminals. Weren't there enough murderers loose on the streets of Queenborough to satisfy him? How dare he think of accusing an innocent girl?

What was eating Williams then and what had kept eating Williams was a very healthy sense of justice. What was eating Williams was honest outrage that a clever murderess was free to decimate the young manhood of Queenborough.

Well, seven murders were enough, and he would put a stop to it.

So there Williams was at Millicent Raymond's front door. He really hadn't known what to expect—perhaps someone whose guilt would be apparent at first glance—but Millicent Raymond's lovely face was unmarred by guilt. There were no circles under her eyes and he was sure she slept like a baby. Her tiny hands impressed him. Those dainty, delicate little fingers had short rounded nails like a child's, and yet they had sent seven good men to their deaths. He wondered if she had portraits and snapshots of her husbands. It would take a trophy room, and a big one at that, to accommodate photographs of them all.

She was beautiful, he would admit, and seemingly unconscious of her charm. It was easy to understand how all those poor bastards had fallen in love with her.

Williams was positive she would betray herself, and with the lapse of every moment in her presence he became more positive. Words tumbled out of her mouth as if she had too long repressed her terrible crimes. She seemed grateful to be at last able to talk freely about her husbands. No doubt assailed him, he was sure he would have her confession before the afternoon was over.

Millie was very much won over by her unexpected caller.

This was what she had been longing for, someone to whom she could unburden herself. What truly touched her was all the information Mr. Williams had about her husbands. Why, it was uncanny. Even she—much less her parents and Grandpa and Uncle Adam and Aunt Bess—couldn't keep her husbands in proper sequence. Mr. Williams had no trouble at all. He even contradicted her when she put Al before Si or whoever it was. He seemed almost to cling to every word she said, and every now and then he took out a notebook and jotted something in it.

And he was so interested in the house—not that that was unusual since it was old and famous and people swarmed to it every time it was open for a benefit or for the spring and Christmas garden tours.

Mr. Williams showed marked curiosity in exactly who had died where, and yet he seemed wary. He leaped back when he had stood in the front hall beneath the balustrade as if what had happened to poor darling Pen might happen to him, though all those Roman emperors had been donated to the museum in Pen's memory two days after his funeral.

Mr. Williams was timid, too, about going out on the balcony from which poor darling Gar, absolutely loaded with gin, had plunged. He apparently thought that he, too, might accidentally fall.

A thunderstorm had been in the making since a short while after lunch and the house grew darker and darker. Millie turned on the lamps. Strong gusts made the outside shutters beat against the house and Millie excused herself to go close the shutters and windows. Mr. Williams gallantly offered to help, but he kept his distance from Millie, always cannily gauging where she was before he turned his back on her and leaned out a window to draw in and latch the blinds.

Lightning struck nearby and the lights went out. There was no telling when they would come back on. It didn't matter. Millie loved candlelight. Sometimes she thought the house was at its prettiest and most romantic when it was lit by candles. She handed a candlestick to Mr. Williams and lighted a candle for herself and they continued their rounds of closing shutters and windows against the storm.

When Millie and Mr. Williams went down the back stairs they were both offended by a strong smell of gas.

"It's from the basement," Millie said. "The wind must have blown out the flame for the water heater."

Williams snuffed his candle and ordered Millie to blow out hers. "Stay out of the way," he said, "and keep the door to the basement open."

Then he groped down the dark, narrow steps.

Mr. Williams was so masterful, so completely in command, barking orders like a drill sergeant. He sent little thrills up and down Millie's spine.

Blow out that candle! Stay out of the way! Keep the door to the basement open!

Just for a second Millie imagined that he had been overcome by fumes and she had rushed to his rescue, leaning over him giving him mouth-to-mouth resuscitation.

It was all so romantic—like a Gothic novel, really—an old historic mansion far, far out in the country besieged by a storm, a mysterious stranger alone with the trusting heroine. And she was the heroine. Goodness, how thrilling.

A sharp noise ended her fantasy.

Mr. Williams must not have got to the heater on time. Something had set off the escaping gas and there had been an explosion. All was lost. The house would burn to the ground, leaving only the chimneys standing to make a pathetic yet wonderfully romantic landscape.

Then she realized that there hadn't been an explosion. A gust from the basement had slammed the door shut at the head of the stairwell outside the kitchen. Millie was neglecting her duties—Mr. Williams had ordered her to keep that door open.

She dashed to the door and hurled it open with all her might.

What happened in that instant was something that couldn't possibly have happened in a million years. Yet it did happen. Just as Millie swung the door back Mr. Williams had sprinted to the top of the stairs to do the same thing and the door struck him a brutal and savage blow.

He fell backward, down, down, down the steep steps and died instantly when his head smashed against the brick floor of the basement.

Millie was devastated.

What a terrible, terrible thing to happen to such a nice man. But in a manner of speaking something like this had happened to her so often that she knew exactly what to do. In the case of an accidental death she must summon the authorities and touch nothing.

As she hurried to the telephone she thought how strange it was that she didn't know Mr. Williams' full name. And he had known every single one of hers, one right after the other.

Element of Surprise

by Bruce M. Fisher

He was strictly a break-and-entry man, he told himself, but he had done what was necessary to make the murder look like the work of a sex maniac. Three ravaged female bodies had been found during the past year. One more might spur the police to catch that lunatic strangler. But his main reason had been to direct suspicion away from his own particular line. He didn't even feel like a murderer, so complete was his assurance that another would be blamed.

It was a large estate. From the busy highway a broad black-topped driveway led to the big copper-roofed stone house in the restricted building area five miles from town. The grounds were beautifully landscaped—shade trees, flowers, the whole bit. Behind the house, a narrow pathway wound through a hardwood grove, over a hill and down a gentle slope to this hut and the manmade lake nearby. His panel truck was hidden in a tiny lane off the gravel road beyond the lake.

An hour ago, in the dusk, he had skirted the lake and strode confidently up the pathway, empty suitcases giving him respectability, a plausible lie ready on his lips. Neither the back doorbell nor the brass knocker in front had brought the whisper of a footfall in answer. He had expected as much, having studied the house and its occupants carefully.

The man, woman and their teenage daughter invariably went out on Friday evenings and didn't return until midnight or later. They had a daytime gardener to keep the place in trim but no servants. The house was in darkness. There was a feeling of emptiness about it, and this, though it was not always a reliable guide, convinced him that he was alone on the premises.

Locked doors were no proof against him. He entered and set the suitcases down, eager with gloves and flashlight to explore for the richest and most compact articles. Then the lights came on blindingly.

He had to marvel at his coolness. He neither whirled in surprise nor leaped to the nearest window for escape. He turned slowly, smiling his pleasant, innocent smile, and, seeing nothing more dangerous than a sleepy fifteen-year-old girl in a blue dressing-gown, he had pulled an envelope from his pocket. She must not live to relay his description to the police.

"Perhaps you can help me, Miss," he said, as if he had every right to be there, as if he were an old but somewhat puzzled friend of the family. "I find that I—but here, read for yourself." And while his left hand extended the letter, his right fist drove upward with smashing force.

So much for the element of surprise. And so much for the house. Its contents must wait for another time. He must get away from it and mingle in bright busy places . . .

He thought he had killed her with his fist back in the house and his first impulse had been to dump her in the lake and cloud the reason for her death, but the warmth of her body over his shoulder, the flapping of her dressing-gown, and the sudden thrashing of her legs as he hurried down the pathway had inspired other ideas. He had carried her into the hut.

He grinned in the darkness. She had put up quite a fight, but she hadn't had a chance against his weight and strength. He'd had to strangle her afterward to shift the suspicion from him. He must never wear this brown sweater or the grey pants again. Some fibres might be caught in her fingernails.

He mopped his face with his sleeve and placed a cigarette between his lips. He reached for his lighter and rubbed his thumb over the embossed initials of his name. He had got this expensive item on a previous job, though it bore different and engraved initials then. In this line, you had to be everything from silversmith to wood refinisher.

He caught himself and tapped the lighter on the table in self-reproach. Stale smoke or cigarette ash might contradict the evidence he had set up if the real sex criminal was thought to be a non-smoker.

He flicked his flashlight on for a last look around, glanced at the huddled form of the dead girl, then opened the door of the hut and stared out into the star-relieved darkness. He could not see the house because of the trees and the intervening hill. Swiftly, grasping the empty suitcases, he glided through the grove, skirted the lake, and found his truck.

He put the gloves and flashlight into the glove compartment, started the engine, and backed onto the gravel road before switching on the headlights. He pushed the cigarette lighter in, turned on the radio, lit his cigarette and inhaled luxuriously. The night was a loss, but that happened sometimes, and other nights would make up for it. He drove toward town, in a hurry to be seen in reliable company.

He parked on a side street and went to the nearest theater, to chat with the cashier, but the booth was closed for the evening. At his favorite poolroom, he found all the tables busy and made do with casual nods to acquaintances. The bowling alley was also crowded. He had a sandwich and a cup of coffee in a dingy restaurant and insulted the waitress there, just to be remembered, but she was used to insults and ignored him. The brisk woman at the cash register took his money and shoved a book of paper matches back with his change without looking up. He used one of the matches to light another cigarette and strode out.

Not one of those people, he knew, would actually remember him. He looked down at his shoes and decided they were due for half soling. A little ruckus about poor workmanship would settle the issue in his mind. Greg's Shoe Repair remained open until eleven o'clock on Friday nights.

His shoes went through a tiny opening in the grille over the scarred counter and disappeared into a back room where a solitary stitcher yammered. A ticket was shoved at him and a heavy voice slurred, "Fi'mints-avaseat."

He sat on the one bench beside a bespectacled middle-aged gentleman with a pleasant face and quiet manner, the kind you hardly noticed unless he spoke to you. This one made conversation. "They must take in quite a bundle here."

"Yes, I suppose they do."

"I always wanted to be a cobbler," the man said. "Not a shoe salesman or a shoe rebuilder, a cobbler. Shoes nowadays are built on universal lasts, turned out wholesale, as if each man's foot was the same shape and bone structure as the next man's."

"I don't know what you mean exactly."

"You don't! My dear young friend, in the old days shoes were *built* in much the same way that a harness-maker builds a horse collar. He measured with care and precision, and determined the exact shape and slope before even thinking of laying awl to leather. Yes, a true cobbler built a shoe or boot of great comfort and durability—"

"Cobbler?" Half listening, he placed a cigarette in his mouth and extended the pack. "Smoke, sir?"

The gentleman's hand rose in protest. "Thank you, no. I never indulge. Sorry."

"That's all right." He reached for his lighter, stopped, and leaned forward to accept a light from the wooden match that the gentleman struck for him. He puffed, and said, "Thanks."

"Sorry if I bored you," the gentleman said, rising. "I often forget myself thinking of old times. But I must be off home now or Ethel will be furious." He bowed slightly with old-fashioned courtliness and departed.

His shoes were ready. The instant he paid, the wicket was closed. No sooner had he tied his shoelaces than he was ushered quickly out into the warm summer night. He rocked on the new soles to make them flexible.

His cigarette had gone out.

He reached for his lighter. It wasn't in his pocket.

He patted his pockets in a frenzy. His wallet was there but not the lighter. Cold sweat broke out on his brow. Where had he had it last?

The hut! He distinctly remembered tapping the table in the hut with his lighter because he had nearly made the mistake of smoking there. He hadn't handled it since!

He was not superstitious but it suddenly seemed as if the Fates were pitted against him. The cigarette lighter in his truck, the matches in the restaurant, the match in the shoe repair shop. He could accept the first incident, even the second, but the third, on this particular night, was beyond the bounds of coincidence. His initials on that lighter would hang him!

He sped down the street to his truck, leaped in, and tore out of town, down the gravel road to the lake. He ran through the grove, stopped, remembered his flashlight in the glove compartment, and ran on without it. He knew exactly where the lighter was, on the corner of the trestled table.

He yanked open the door of the hut and began feeling around in the darkness. He felt over the table top and along the benches, the breath rasping in his throat, his heart pounding in his ears.

He was down on his knees, scrabbling about the floor, when they found him, the two policemen and the anxious father whose home-checking phone call had gone unanswered—the deadly calm father whose piercing eyes detected a tuft of brown wool between his daughter's death-clenched fingers. Under the glare of their powerful flashlights, he knew the game was up for all time.

Several miles away, a quiet little man examined a silver-plated cigarette lighter and smiled to think that he had not lost his touch. It was
all a matter of being ahead of the quarry. To refuse a cigarette in order
to have a match ready to forestall a damning search for a lighter was
being ahead. If that stupid young man hadn't had his wallet under his
hand in his left trouser pocket, he'd have got that too.

Looking for Milliken Street

by Joyce Harrington

Caroline picked up the telephone.

"Hello?"

"Hello. Can you talk to me?"

"Who is this?"

"Can you help me?"

Caroline tried to place the voice. It sounded very young. "What's the matter?" she asked.

"What's your name?" the voice asked in return.

"Caroline Anderson. Are you in trouble?"

"That's a pretty name. Where's your little girl?"

"I haven't got a little girl." Not yet.

"I have a sister. She's littler than me. She's a cry-face. I hit her and she fell down the stairs and now she's crying and we have to eat lunch and go back to school."

"Where's your mother?" Caroline asked, beginning to be alarmed.

"Working. If Michele doesn't get up pretty soon and stop crying I'm going to hit her again. She makes me sick."

"Wait a minute. Maybe Michele is hurt. Isn't there any neighbor you can call? Where do you live?"

"Oh, I have to go now—the soup's spilling all over the stove!"

Caroline returned to her own lunch, leftover macaroni and cheese, reheated and grown cold again. What an odd phone call; she'd heard of people getting obscene calls and nuisance calls, but this was something different. This was a child in trouble. Two children in trouble, from the sound of it. Caroline stared at the congealed mess on her plate, wishing there were something she could do, some way she could reach them. She rose heavily from the table and scraped her unappetizing lunch into the disposal. Criminal, she brooded, the way some people leave their children alone. She looked down at her swelling stomach. Never, never in a million years will I ever leave you alone like that.

Over the rush of water in the sink and the slurping grind of the disposal, the telephone burred. Caroline ran clumsily, hands dripping, to snatch it up.

"Yes?"

"Is that you?" The same voice, but this time whispering.

"This is Mrs. Anderson." Play it cool, Caroline told herself. No pressure. Maybe she could find out who the child was—and where she lived.

"Michele is O.K. now."

"That's good. How about you?"

"I'm O.K. Michele is mad at me. I made her wash her face and she threw the towel in the toilet and it went down and the water's all over the floor and Mommy's gonna be mad at me." The whispering young voice seemed on the edge of tears. Be firm, Caroline warned herself. Be matter-of-fact. Get the situation under control and then try to find out who this poor kid is.

"Now listen. Don't flush the toilet anymore. Got that?"

"Yes."

"Then mop up the water. Use a mop or some old rags."

"Michele did it. Michele should mop it up."

"Both of you mop it up. Then wash your hands."

"I'll mop it up with Mommy's tablecloth. I'll mop it up with Daddy's underwear. I'll mop it up with Michele's new dress and her Chatty Cathy and her tricycle and her pillow and her snuggle bear and—" The voice was loud now, punctuated with giggles and excited, vengeful breathing.

"Hold on. What's your name?"

"Emily."

"What's your last name, Emily?"

"Not gonna tell."

"Well, I told you *my* last name. How can we be friends if you won't tell me yours?"

"I'll tell you, but I'm not sure which one is right."

"What do you mean?"

"Sometimes it's Cranford and sometimes it's Frank."

"Which one is it now?"

"I don't know." A wail. "My daddy went away and then my mommy got a new daddy and we came to live here and then he went away too."

"All right, Emily. It doesn't matter. Either one is fine. Now tell me where you live. If it's not too far I can come over and help you."

"I don't know." A silence in which Caroline thought, Good grief, what have I gotten myself into? This kind of trouble I don't need. The reedy voice continued. "I can't tell the name of the street. It's a hard name and I can't say it. It sounds like 'moocow.' "

"All right. Never mind that for now. What's Michele doing?"

"Oh, she's eating her soup. She eats like a pig." The voice drifted away from the phone, chanting, "Pig, pig, piggy piggy pig." An enraged cry and a clatter followed, and then Emily was back on the line.

"She's an awful cry-face. And she threw her spoon at me."

Caroline decided to try one more time to find out where this little scene was being played. Emily sounded like a little bully, but she probably had too much responsibility for a child her age.

"Emily, how old are you?"

"Seven and a half. Michele's five, but boy is she dumb. She can't even tie her shoes."

"You sound like a pretty big girl for seven and a half. Where does your mommy work?"

"In a store. She says it's a big store. She bought Michele's Chatty Cathy from there, but she didn't bring me anything."

Try another tack. "What's your phone number, Emily?"

"What time is it? We have to go back to school when the little hand is near the one and the big hand is on the nine."

"It's twenty to one now. You have five minutes. You'd better get ready."

"O.K. Can I call you tomorrow?"

"Well, all right. But I may be out." The obvious question flared in Caroline's mind. "Emily, where did you get my phone number?"

"It's a pretty number. Goodbye."

"Emily, be sure and tell your mother about the towel in the toilet." Caroline realized she was talking to a dead phone and hung up. She gazed at the number on the face of the dial. What was there about it that would seem pretty to a child? It was just a group of numbers, neither pretty nor ugly, whose sole function was to cause this particular telephone out of millions to ring and bring Caroline Anderson running to answer it.

"The area code! Oh, dear!" Caroline had assumed that Emily and Michele were squabbling and slopping soup somewhere in the city. Now she was staggered by the realization that they could be calling anywhere from Alaska to Florida. How could she hope to find them?

Why should she *want* to find them? In no way were they her responsibility. She'd done the best she could to help them—and if she did find them, what could she do? Would their mother welcome a meddling stranger telling her she shouldn't leave two little girls alone? The questions rose one after another. Why didn't they take their lunch to school? What school did they attend? Surely Emily would have told her that if she'd thought to ask. Where did they go after school? Who looked after them then? Questions. Questions that increased her uneasiness about the two girls and provided an answer of sorts to the overriding question of why she should want to find them. She'd seen too many of them, the Emilys and the Micheles, the Tommys and the Marks, in her work as a remedial reading teacher. Key children with old eyes in tiny pinched faces, their house keys slung on grimy bits of string around their necks, their minds and bodies irretrievably undernourished. She had wanted to save them all, to fill them with good food and the joy of learning, and with the cherishing that so many of them seemed to lack.

"Caroline Anderson, you are a dope," she announced to the sunny afternoon. "You miss your job and you're a sucker for a sob story."

As she trundled her cumbersome body through the afternoon's chores, she thought back over the eight years she'd spent in the city's schools. Eight years of small victories and enormous frustrations. Eight years of precious equipment destroyed by vandalism, of even more precious ideas blocked by rigid school-board bureaucracy, and through it all the saving reward of witnessing the dawn of comprehension in young eyes, the satisfaction of guiding at least one child out of twenty to the notion that reading was not only necessary but could be fun.

Eight years, too, of Ted urging her to quit when the disappointments became too great and she would come home from school drained and exhausted, full of bitterness against a system that could be so immune to the needs of the young lives entrusted to its care. Still, she had hung on, certain that on the next day or the next some small breakthrough would make it all worthwhile. Eight years of promising Ted that the instant she became pregnant she would give it all up and happily stay home and lavish on her own child the concern and love she'd tried to dole out to the hundreds of children who'd passed through her reading lab. Had she been a dedicated teacher, or simply a young woman with a strong mothering instinct and a love of reading that she tried to foist onto the unwilling minds that came within her scope?

Well, whatever, it was all in the past now. In two more months all that mothering instinct would have a definite object. Caroline complacently laid her two hands on the high mound of her stomach and immediately felt the inner shifting that was one of the pleasures of pregnancy. No, this child would never need to call strangers on the telephone. Not if she could help it.

"It could be a joke. Just a bad practical joke."

"Oh, Ted. You wouldn't say that if you'd heard her. Anyway, I don't think children that young are capable of complicated telephone jokes."

Caroline dawdled over her ice cream and coffee. Ted had finished his, and she knew he was eager to relax into his comfortable chair with the evening paper.

"If it bothers you, you should report it to the phone company. I don't want you getting upset over some kid who uses the phone as a babysitter."

"I'm not upset. Just concerned. And what could the phone company do? Millie Bernstein had a breather once. He used to call her every night and just breathe into the phone. She reported it, and all the phone company told her was to hang up on him and suggested that she get an unlisted number."

"Do you want to get an unlisted number?"

"No, Ted, that's not the point. The point is that there are two little girls somewhere who are being left alone every day. Neglected. And I'm the only one who knows it."

Ted crumpled his paper napkin and came around the table. He stood behind her and gently massaged her shoulders. "Don't flatter yourself. You're not the only one who knows it. Their mother knows. Their father probably knows. They have neighbors and they go to school. Somebody knows. You don't have to do anything about it."

"I guess you're right." Caroline sighed and laid her cheek on the hand that tenderly pressed the stiffness and worry out of her tense shoulders. "Still, the whole world could know about it and not *do* anything. Oh, Ted, it seems so cruel and unfair."

"Do you know what's really cruel and unfair? You haven't asked me yet how things went at the office today. You're neglecting your one and only husband. I guess I'll just have to start calling beautiful blonde phone numbers to get the sympathy and understanding that's lacking in my home."

"Ted, you idiot. How *did* things go at the office today?" Caroline struggled out of her chair and began clearing the table.

"Fine. Just fine. We clipped two poodles, spayed three cats, gave twelve rabies injections, saw one hip displacement, two cases of ear mites, set a broken leg and the star boarder is back again. I don't know why that woman keeps a dog. He spends more time with us than he does at home."

"Would you say he was neglected?"

Ted laughed and followed her into the kitchen with the coffee cups. "Point taken. But at least she sees that her precious Baron is well taken care of. She doesn't go off and leave him to fend for himself."

The next morning Caroline devoted to working on the nursery. It was a tiny room next to their bedroom, not much bigger than a walk-in closet. It had been freshly painted and the new crib installed. There was just enough room left for a chest of drawers and a small flat-topped dressing table. The chest was one they'd had for years, crammed full of the odds and ends of their life together—photographs, souvenirs of vacation trips, Ted's baby book faithfully kept up by his mother until he was five or six and passed on to Caroline early in the marriage in the glowing hope that she would soon be keeping one herself.

They hadn't wanted a child right away, not while Ted was still working for his D.V.M. And Caroline was teaching. Then, when Ted had gone into partnership with old Dr. Crouch and they'd decided it was time to start a family, nothing had happened. Eight years of waiting and hoping, of medical tests that showed no reason for infertility, of repeated advice to be patient and keep trying. Until last spring. Caroline, leafing through the mementos of those eight years of waiting and being patient, remembered the excitement of that windy March afternoon when the obstetrician had confirmed what she was almost afraid to believe and gave her a sample package of vitamin pills. She and Ted had celebrated that evening and she'd downed the first of the pills with a glass of champagne, solemnly toasting the event. This had to be the most wanted baby ever conceived. Only two more months to go.

Caroline sorted the contents of the drawers. At the back of one of them, she found a street map of the city.

"So that's where that's been hiding."

With an hour before she was due at the doctor's office for her checkup, Caroline unfolded the street map on top of the chest of drawers.

"Moocow Street," she murmured. "Moocow Avenue. Moocow Lane."

She scanned the configuration of the city, found their own street and Ted's animal clinic half a mile away. No Moocow Street. Her eyes drifted to the bottom of the map where the streets were listed alphabetically with their location guides. Her finger traveled down the list of M's.

"M, M, M. MacKenzie. Madison. Malkover Lane. Markham? Mascoulie Drive?"

She carried the map to the kitchen table and settled down with pencil and paper. She'd make a list of possible Moocows. Not that she would ever do anything with it, but maybe if Emily called again she would recognize a street name that sounded like "Moocow."

Caroline soon had a list that ranged from MacKenzie to Murchison and a fair idea where each was located. Fifteen streets, a couple in suburban areas, one downtown thoroughfare that was obviously out, the rest scattered throughout the city's residential areas, some familiar, others that she knew only by reputation, and still others about which she knew nothing at all.

Time to go.

The doctor's office was crowded. The nurse announced that he'd had an early morning delivery and there would be a slight delay. The waiting ladies smiled at each other in patient complicity and settled down with magazines and quiet chat. Caroline had brought along a romantic paperback, trivial and undemanding. Just as her body fidgeted under the weight she carried, so her mind veered away from heavy reading.

At last her turn came. After the usual weighing in, the palpating of her protuberant stomach, listening to the fetal heartbeat, the repeated caution not to gain too much weight, the calm reassurance that all was well and the suggestion that it might be wise to pack her hospital case and keep it ready, Caroline hurried home.

It was one-thirty by the time she reached the apartment. Too late for phone calls from Emily. The girls were probably safely back in school. She made some lunch and ate it from a tray in the living room, her feet propped up on a hassock, the final chapter of her novel for companionship. When youth, beauty and virtue finally triumphed at the last possible moment, Caroline yawned. She would take a little nap, and after that she would begin repainting the chest of drawers for the nursery.

The bedside telephone jolted her out of a dream in which her baby, her own little girl, was crying somewhere in the apartment, but although Caroline scoured all the rooms, rummaged in all the drawers and closets, even looked inside the dishwasher, she couldn't find the crying infant. As she rose muzzily out of sleep, she realized that the crying in her dream was the sound of the telephone. She glanced at the alarm clock on Ted's night stand and saw that it was almost three-thirty.

"Hello?"

"I called and I called but you weren't there," the voice accused.

"Emily?" Still groggy from sleep and from the awful anxiety of her dream, Caroline felt a wave of guilt at the accusation.

"Where were you? You said I could call again today."

"I had to go to . . ." Caroline caught herself just in time. She was simply not going to explain herself to this demanding child. "I was out. I told you I might not be here."

"Guess what? Michele ran away."

Caroline heard the smug, self-satisfied tone of the announcement, but ignored it in her panicky concern.

"Emily! Did you tell anyone else? Someone should be out looking for her! The police . . ."

"Oh, she's O.K. She came back after school. I told her I was gonna make her eat monkey meat for lunch, so she ran away and hid. Isn't she dumb?"

"Oh, Emily, that was a terrible thing to do." Caroline was uncertain whether the terrible thing was the tormenting of Michele or the ease with which Emily evoked her own fears. "Are you sure she's all right?"

"Sure. Do you want to talk to her? I'll get her." Caroline heard Emily's voice shrieking away from the phone. "Hey, Michele. Come here. The lady wants to talk to you. Come on, or I'll kick you."

Caroline waited, listening to the scuffles and cries at the other end of the line. "Why don't I just hang up?" she asked herself. "Because she'll just call back again. Besides, there's something so wrong going on there, I've got to find out who they are and where they live."

Presently another voice came over the wire, younger-sounding and lisping. " 'Lo."

"Michele?"

"Emily's bad. I hate her "

"Michele, listen to me. What school do you go to?"

"Kindergarten. We have gerbils. Emily says gerbils eat noses."

"Where do you live, Michele?"

"Right here. I don't want to talk anymore."

The phone clattered down but the connection remained unbroken. Caroline listened, straining to hear what fresh indignities Emily might be visiting upon the hapless Michele. Only silence. Suddenly Emily was back.

"You see how dumb she is? Mommy likes her best. She beats me, but she never beats Michele."

"Now listen, Emily. You're a big girl, and I'm sure you're doing a good job of looking after yourself and your sister. But I'd like to come over and help you out a little. Can you tell me the number of your house?"

"Sure. That's easy. It's 1825. It's in big gold numbers over the front door. We live on the third floor."

"That's fine. Now what about the street?"

Emily sighed.

"Emily," Caroline continued, "yesterday you said it sounded like 'Moocow.' Can you hold on a minute and I'll read you some street names and you tell me if any of them sound right."

"O.K." Emily sounded dubious. "I looked at the street sign today. It starts with an 'M,' but then all the letters get mixed up and I can't read it."

"Hold on, Emily. I'll be right back."

Caroline dashed to the kitchen and returned, breathing heavily, with the map and the list of street names.

"Emily? Are you still there? Now listen carefully." She began reading from the list. Each name brought a negative from Emily. Some were definitely not right, some sounded almost right but not quite, two evoked giggles. None of the fifteen names on Caroline's list was the right one.

Emily, obviously wanting to be helpful and enjoying the game, said, "I think it has an 'l' in it, and a 'k.' K-l-m," she chanted, "M-l-k."

"M-l-k," repeated Caroline. "K-l-m. Klamath? M-l-k, milk?"

"That's right!" shouted Emily. "It sounds like milk."

Caroline consulted her street map for names that hadn't made it onto her list.

"Sounds like milk. How about Milliken?"

"That's it! That's it! Milkilen. Mikkilen."

Caroline's excitement grew, but she managed to keep her voice calm. "1825 Milliken Street. All right, Emily. You and Michele stay right there. I'll be over just as soon as I can."

"Oh, Mrs. Anderson, don't come. Please don't come. Mommy'll be home from work soon, and she won't like it."

"That's all right, Emily. I'd like to talk to your mommy too. See you in a little while."

Caroline ran a comb through her hair, slipped into a jacket and snatched up purse, street map and car keys. As she locked the apartment door, she heard the phone jangling inside. She hesitated for a moment. Should she go back inside and answer it? It might be Ted. Should she tell him of her success in locating the girls? No, if she did she would have to tell him of her plan to go and see them and he would tell her not to get involved. She would tell him this evening, after she'd seen the girls and done what she could for them. Caroline moved away from the apartment door and down to the elevator. The phone continued its distant ringing until the elevator came and bore her away to the basement garage.

She was uncomfortable behind the wheel of the small car. Even with the seat pushed back as far as it would go, there wasn't much leeway. The seat belt was adjusted to capacity and sat absurdly on top of her bulging stomach. As she drove along the familiar crosstown streets, she wondered what she would find when she got to her destination. She was prepared for anything. Milliken Street was in an area she'd never visited and knew nothing about. Would she find a grimy tenement with flaking paint and scurrying roaches? Or would it be a prim row of genteel boardinghouses, lace curtains and snake plants in the windows? For all she knew, it might be a mammoth housing project or a faceless new condominium.

What would she do when she got there? Well, she'd figure that out once she saw the girls. At the very least, she might be able to persuade their mother to enroll them in a day-care center after school. Emily sounded as if she could use a little therapy, but there might be too much resistance for that. She'd play it by ear and put them in touch with Family Service. That's really all she could do. Then at least she'd know they wouldn't have to be left alone anymore.

After crossing a bridge, with a quick glance down at the sprawling network of railroad tracks beneath, Caroline found herself in strange territory. She pulled over to the curb to check the map. Milliken Street wasn't far. According to the map, it angled off from the street she was on and meandered crookedly into a tangle of short crowded streets and alleys bunched together into a spider web. It seemed to bisect the web and come to a halt at the far side where a superhighway was indicated by a double red line.

Caroline drove on slowly, counting blocks and watching street signs. The street was a busy one. Impatient cars honked and passed her. She crawled along in the exhaust of a bus that stopped at every corner. The sidewalks were lined with small shops whose grimy windows displayed everything from wedding photographs and color televisions to limp vegetables wilting in splintered crates. People surged in and out of the shops. Children played in littered doorways. In front of certain store fronts whose window glass had been painted an anonymous dark green, men sat on boxes and dilapidated kitchen chairs and watched. Occasional bands of three or four tall elegant young men swaggered down the street, their bright clothes a marked counterpoint to the prevailing grey weariness, their frothy natural hair topped off by huge caps of black, red and green or by immaculate white Borsalino hats. After one of these youths stared insolently at her through the car window, Caroline clicked down all the lock buttons. She wasn't frightened, but she knew she was out of place here and there was no sense in taking chances.

She came upon Milliken Street suddenly. The bus creaked on its way, its passage revealing a street sign that tilted crazily upward atop its post. Caroline turned gratefully off the busy street and drove for several blocks. A small brick house with green shutters proclaimed itself to be No. 262. Still a long way to go—but as Caroline drove along Milliken Street, she was heartened by its apparent respectability. Back on the swarming shopping street she had been tempted to turn back, and, when Emily called again, to tell her there was nothing that she could do for her and to please stop calling. Now that she was here on Milliken Street, her resolution returned, bolstered by the rows of neat small houses interspersed here and there by a four- or five-story apartment building.

Milliken Street twisted and turned, and the occasional passerby paid no attention to the small blue car that traveled its length, slowing now and then for the driver to check her progress. A drugstore on this corner, a newsstand and tobacconist on the opposite, a dry cleaner and launderette side by side across the street, all served to allay Caroline's apprehensions and she drove on.

Abruptly, the rows of neat houses gave way to blank-fronted loft buildings. Battered signs announced apparently defunct commercial enterprises. Some line of demarcation had been crossed and Caroline hesitated. She peered down the remainder of Milliken Street which seemed to end in a large hulking dark mass several blocks away. Still, she'd come this far. If the girls lived at this end of Milliken Street, among these deserted warehouses, they really needed help. She drove on.

If she didn't see any more houses in the next block, she'd turn back, she told herself—but there were houses. Three grey houses with tattered curtains and sagging stoops leaned against each other as if for companionship against the surrounding blight. Overflowing garbage cans and a grinning dog at an open second-story window were definite signs of life. Caroline's apprehensions returned. The girls couldn't possibly live in this disaster area!

All right. One more block and then I get out of here, Caroline told herself. One more block brought her face to face with the massive black end of Milliken Street. Gaping double doors, wide and high enough to admit a truck, slanted backward into a deeper blackness. The building stretched across the end of the street and continued in both directions, empty and threatening. End of the line. Caroline stopped the car in mid-block and scanned both sides of the street in search of numbers. Where was 1825? Across the street a single small house crouched forlornly, its windows decorated with tall white X's. On either side, boarded-up warehouses loomed morosely. None of the buildings were numbered. There were no other cars on the street. No other people.

Caroline was about to swing into a U-turn and go back the way she had come when a woman lurched out of the doorway of the house across the street. It was impossible to tell her age. She was painfully thin and her clothes flapped loosely on her body. Her pallor was unhealthy and was accentuated by the lank red hair that hung in greasy strands to her shoulders. She leaned wearily in the doorway and seemed not to notice Caroline in her shiny blue car across the street.

Caroline stared for a moment, wondering if this could be the girls' mother. Then she rolled down the window and called across to her. "Hi. I'm looking for number 1825. Do you know where it is?"

The woman raised her head but made no reply.

Caroline called again. "1825 Milliken Street. Is it near here?"

The woman muttered something and gestured toward the end of the street. Caroline couldn't hear what she said. The woman turned to go back indoors.

Caroline scrambled out of the car and hurried across the street. "Wait! Please wait! I couldn't hear you. I'm looking for 1825 Milliken Street."

The woman faced Caroline with something like annoyance in her glance. When she spoke again Caroline saw that several of her teeth were missing.

"I said maybe it's around the corner. The street, you know, it turns a lot."

Caroline continued. "I'm looking for two little girls who live there. Do you know of any children in the neighborhood?"

The woman took in Caroline's swollen body and suddenly turned loquacious.

"No kids around here. Nobody around here. Just me. It's all gonna come down and then there won't even be me. But I'm staying until they throw me out. Got no heat and got no lights, but I'm staying. Urban Renewal they call it. I call it shoving me around." The woman trembled as she spoke, either with rage or illness. She mumbled over her problem for a moment, then suddenly shifted back to Caroline's quest. "No kids around here. You're gonna have a kid. You shouldn't be hanging around down here. What are you hanging around for?"

"I'm looking for two little girls," Caroline explained again. "They live at 1825 Milliken Street. I've got to find them."

Disinterest clouded the woman's face. "I dunno. Maybe around the corner." She waved a shaky hand toward the end of the street.

Caroline felt eyes follow her as she marched purposefully to the corner. She wondered if the woman were seriously ill. She might be an alcoholic or a drug addict. Caroline quickened her pace, she looped the strap of her pocketbook over her shoulder and tucked the bag securely under her arm.

Long shadows lay across the street and a chill wind pasted scraps of paper to her ankles. Caroline shivered and scanned the building fronts, looking for numbers that could connect this wasteland with the officially recognizable world that offered shelter and safety. She reached the corner and peered around it.

Caroline felt as if she'd suddenly been transported to a movie set. The row of buildings ended abruptly like a false-fronted western town, and behind them stretched a nightmare landscape of rubble and twisted girders. Here and there a wall stood alone, grey sky luminous through staring window slots. The wreckers had begun their work. Across the way, the deserted factory staggered off into the infinity of late afternoon. From behind it there came a subdued hissing roar from the superhighway. People were on their way home from work. Time she went home too. Out of the corner of her eye, as she took one final look around, Caroline caught a hint of movement within the gaping doors of the deserted factory, a shadow that quickly faded back into deeper shadow. Nonsense, she told herself, there's nobody there. You're imagining things. She stared into the gloom for a long moment, scalp prickling and each breath sharp and shallow. Then she turned and started back up the street to the haven of her little blue car, a distant half block away. The red-haired woman was no longer watching from her doorway. There wasn't another soul in sight.

She tried to run, but all she could manage was a fast shuffle. Why had Emily lied to her? Told her she lived in this desolate, condemned wilderness? Maybe it was a mistake. Emily could have mistaken Milliken Street for some other street that sounded similar. It was Caroline's own fault for pressing the issue. Maybe there was another Milliken Street in some other town. She had assumed that this was the right one and ignored the possibility of Emily's burning up the long-distance wires. Her thoughts skittered wildly as she hurried toward the car. Her legs felt tired and heavy as if she were plodding through clinging mud.

The afternoon sun slanted yellow light against the building fronts, turning the remaining top-floor windows into pitiless golden eyes. In the street, Caroline struggled through the deepening twilight. An interminable length of cracked and littered sidewalk still stretched between her and the car. Where was the red-haired woman? Had she gone back inside her wreck of a house? Even her presence would relieve the dreadful emptiness of this nightmare wasteland. The silence was broken only by Caroline's hurrying footsteps and the distant roar of the highway. Time hung vacant and unmoving in the heavy afternoon.

Behind her a furtive pattering invaded the stillness. Had there really been someone hiding in the shadows of the deserted factory? Was he following her now? Without stopping, Caroline glanced back over her shoulder. The pattering noise stopped and the street was empty behind her. Was he hiding in a doorway? Or was it just the wind blowing bits of trash through the littered gutters? Scarcely breathing, head pounding, a tinny taste of fear in her mouth, Caroline ran. The car was just a few yards away.

The brick came from nowhere, a crumbled piece of the pervading desolation lying in her path. Caroline saw it a split second too late. She tried to avoid it, but her foot was already upon it. With a grating wrench, her ankle twisted. She felt herself toppling heavily to the sidewalk. She tried to break her fall, but there was nothing to cling to. She tried to twist her body to protect its precious burden, but only succeeded in knocking her head against a fire hydrant. A brief flash of pain, and then she felt nothing.

She didn't see the red-haired woman dash from her doorway. She didn't hear the harsh voice nor feel the rough hands trying to shake her into consciousness. She lay insensible on the sidewalk as the woman took a dime from her pocketbook and ran off up the street to the nearest telephone. She didn't feel the first grinding birth contraction, nor any of the ones that followed. She never knew that the red-haired woman returned and pillowed her bleeding head in her lap until the first sirens screeched down Milliken Street and policemen and white-coated attendants gathered around her.

Ten days later, Caroline Anderson entered her apartment. Ted hovered protectively behind her. High on her forehead, almost concealed by her hair, she wore a small bandage. She walked slowly, her slender body slightly bent, her arms hanging limp at her sides.

"I should get down to the office. Will you be all right?" Ted had spent several days and most nights at her hospital bedside.

"Yes." The monosyllable came grudgingly from her lips.

"Is there anything I can get you before I go?"

"No."

"I wish you'd perk up, Caroline. There's no sense in brooding. We'll have another chance. All we can do is look to the future."

"Yes. You go along now." Caroline dropped into an armchair and turned her head slightly so that his kiss fell on her jaw.

She watched him go out the door. Poor Ted. He didn't understand, and she couldn't explain it to him. He thought it was losing the baby that had her down, but it wasn't that, although that was bad enough. It was the betrayal, the double betrayal. Emily's for leading her to that awful place, and her own gambling with her baby's life. How could she have been so selfish? Tears lurked behind Caroline's eyelids. She lurched out of her chair and wandered moodily to the doorway of the empty nursery. The crib occupied one corner, bare and white. The chest of drawers stood amid the clutter of its contents, unpainted. Caroline contemplated the tiny silent room and wondered how she would live with this room accusing her daily.

The telephone rang. She seemed not to hear. It rang again and again. At last she moved wearily to the bedroom extension and picked up the receiver.

"Hello?"

"Oh, Mrs. Anderson. Have you been away? I called and called every day. I wanted to explain."

"Emily?" Caroline's voice was a barely audible whisper.

"Well, yes. Except that Emily isn't really my name. Remember the afternoon you were going to come over? Well, I called you back right away to tell you the truth, but I guess you'd left already. You never found Emily and Michele, did you?"

"No. I never found them." Caroline wondered about the voice on the phone. It seemed older somehow, not a bit childish.

"Well, I'm sorry about that. It was really dumb to give you a made-up address. But you kept asking me. I had to tell you something."

"Why? Why did you call in the first place?"

"Oh, Mrs. Anderson, I hope you're not mad at me. I just had to talk to someone. But I couldn't talk to anyone I knew. I couldn't tell the truth or let anyone know who I was, because of my mother. I mean, she might have lost her job if anyone found out. I mean about her drinking and all the rest of it. And then I remembered how really nice you were when I was in your reading group in fifth grade. You were the only nice teacher I ever had. First I called the school but they said you weren't there anymore. I called a lot of Andersons before I found you. I remembered your voice right away. You helped me a lot when I was little. I thought maybe you could help me again. But I couldn't even tell you. So I started pretending all that stuff about Emily and Michele. And then I couldn't stop."

The voice babbled on. Caroline listened, only half aware of the flood of words. In her mind, she was back on that gloomy, desolate street, the vacant buildings pressing in on all sides, the indefinable menace behind her. Would she ever be able to forget? Would it help to let Emily know what she had done? Emily?

"What *is* your name?" Caroline asked. "How old are you?"

"I won't tell you my name," the voice replied. "I'm fourteen. I'll be fifteen in January. And everything's going to be all right now. My father came back to live with us. That part of it was true. And Mommy joined A.A. so she'll be getting better. Everything's going to be all right."

"I see." Caroline's face flushed hot with resentment. Everything might be all right for the person she knew as Emily, but would anything ever be all right for herself? "You really told a convincing story. What about Michele?"

"There isn't any Michele. I never had a sister. That was me too.

Anyway, I wanted to thank you for listening to me. I really would have told you the truth from the beginning, but I was so ashamed. And I'm sorry if you went on a wild-goose chase. I hope you're not mad at me."

Caroline laid the receiver in her lap for a moment and thought of all the things she could say to this incredible child. She could blame her for the accident. She could tell her about the loss of the baby, call her a murderer. But what would that solve? Would it relieve her own anguish and guilt? She herself had been naive and impulsive, rushing headlong into danger on the strength of those phone calls. How would she ever rid herself of blame for her own gullibility? She heard the phone clucking in her lap and with a tight smile she picked it up.

"I'm not mad at you, Emily. And I'm glad everything's working out for you. But please don't ever call me again."

"Oh, I won't. I just wanted to be sure you understood. I feel so much better now. Goodbye. And thanks a lot."

"Goodbye, Emily."

Caroline sat quietly beside the phone for a few moments. Then she got up and walked calmly to the nursery and sat on the floor beside the chest of drawers. If she remembered correctly, the bottom drawer held all of her old school records. How lucky that she'd kept them. "Emily" had given her the clue. It shouldn't be too difficult to figure out which year she had taught her. And from that year, she ought to be able to determine which of the girls was the right girl. All she had to do was think back and remember. The voice and the year were all she had to go on, and the voice was seared into her brain.

She opened the bottom drawer and slowly pulled out the stacks of looseleaf folders. Once she'd located the girl it would only be a matter of time and patience, of waiting and watching for the right opportunity. Traffic accidents happened every day. Children died tragically in swimming pools and on playing fields. They fell under buses and off bridges. This time, she would find "Emily," and then . . .

Caroline knew all about waiting and being patient. Page by page, she began leafing through the record books.

Judgment Postponed

by Robert Edward Eckels

As a mark of how important a matter he thought it, Slingerland himself came down from the front office to introduce our new branch chief, calling those of us on the staff together into a group and making quite a little speech about how lucky we were to get a man as well qualified as Edgar Wilson to lead us. Slingerland didn't elaborate on those qualifications, and I presumed it was because Wilson's entire background was in Operations and not in Fiscal Control, which was our branch's area of responsibility. That was an uncharitable thought, I knew, but under the circumstances—my circumstances at least—not an unnatural one. I'd spent over twenty years in Fiscal Control, the last eight as Number Two man.

Afterwards, as the rest of the staff were filing out, Slingerland touched my arm, stopping me. "I think you deserve a personal introduction, Oren," he said. "Ed—" he turned to Wilson "—this is Oren Anderson. You've heard me speak about him."

Wilson nodded, his eyes full on mine and appraising. He was an inch or two shorter than Slingerland, which made him about my height. He was about my age too—although you'd never tell it to look at him. There wasn't a line in his face and the deep even tan bespoke a good many hours spent under the sun, or a sunlamp.

"Oren was Lew Benton's right-hand man when Lew was branch chief," Slingerland continued, "and he's been sort of holding down the fort since Lew retired. How long has it been, Oren? Six months? Seven? Bet you're glad to get the load off your shoulders."

Wilson's mouth twisted into a slight and, I thought, sardonic smile. "I'm sure he is," he murmured. Then the smile faded. "I'll be talking to you later, Oren," he said.

"Yes, sir," I said and, recognizing a dismissal when I heard it, left.

I was conscious of a number of eyes following me as I crossed the office floor to my desk, but nobody said anything. Then George Leduc sauntered over. He is a tall gangling man, only slightly junior to me in the branch. "It was a rotten deal, Oren," he said, "getting passed over like that."

My face felt very tight and uncomfortable. "Perhaps," I said, swallowing hard, "but these things happen. And to tell you the truth, I never really expected to get the job."

Not at first anyway. Benton had as good as told me I wouldn't just before he retired. "I've recommended you, Oren," he had said, "but there's some feeling in the front office that we need new blood and that the place to bring it in is at the top. It's not fair, but—" He hadn't finished the sentence but I'd known what he meant: It's the way things are.

And I'd accepted it—until the months dragged by and the job still hadn't been filled, obviously because the front office was having difficulty finding a qualified candidate. Under the circumstances, it had been impossible not to hope and in time even convince myself that in the end the company would turn to me.

But, of course, it hadn't worked out that way.

"Well," Leduc said now, "I just wanted you to know how I felt. And I'm not the only one. A lot of us around here are sorry it wasn't you."

Perhaps, but on the other hand there were some who had reason to be glad. One of these was Sally Brennan, the younger of the two stenos who did our typing and clerical work. She was a snip of a girl I'd clashed with several times about tying up the phone with personal calls and the length of her skirts.

Wilson hadn't been on the job three weeks when he appointed Sally his personal secretary at a substantial increase in pay.

I kept my personal misgivings to myself, but I felt it my duty to report to Wilson that this had upset the other steno—who was senior in service as well as age. He shrugged it off. "There are too many people around here hiding behind their seniority," he said.

I suppose I should have recognized that as a warning that my own time to be shaken up was coming. But I didn't and I was completely unprepared the next time he called me into his office.

He kept me standing before his desk like a penitent schoolboy. "Why are you still approving these things, Oren?" he said, tapping the payment voucher form on the desk before him. "Isn't that my responsibility as branch chief?"

"Well," I said, "technically, yes. But Benton never wanted to be bothered with details, so he left it up to me. I just assumed you'd want to operate the same way."

"I see," Wilson said. He paused for a moment and studied the form thoughtfully. "How many vouchers did you approve last week?"

I shrugged. "I don't know," I said. "They come in from the various divisions at odd times, but we average about twenty or thirty a week."

"I see," Wilson said again. He gave the form one final tap, then leaned back in his chair. "All right," he said briskly. "Let's see if we can't make some order out of chaos. Ask Sally to set up a control and hold the week's receipts until Friday. Then send the whole batch in to me at one time for approval."

"It'll mean slower payment," I said.

"Not that much slower," Wilson said. "And on the plus side it'll give us a better idea of what we're doing around here."

"Whatever you say," I said. I turned on my heel and went out to tell Sally what the new arrangements were.

Only, as I'd known all along, they didn't work out the way Mr. Order-out-of-Chaos Wilson expected. Early the next week he called me back into his office. This time a whole sheaf of payment vouchers lay spread out on his desk.

"All right, Oren," he said resignedly. "Tell me why these were all returned stamped Unable to Process."

I picked up the vouchers and leafed through them, although I really didn't need to. "It's very simple," I said. "The girls just forgot to add the proper accounting number. They frequently do that unless you remind them."

"Well then," Wilson said, "why in heaven's name didn't you remind them? And follow up to make sure they had before you sent the vouchers to me?"

"Because I never saw these vouchers," I said. "When you said you wanted to approve all vouchers yourself I assumed you meant just that and had these sent directly to you."

"Oren, Oren," Wilson said. "All I wanted was to set up a control. You can't expect me to know every little detail of how the forms should be completed. Not at first anyway."

Obviously not, I thought, but remained standing silently.

"Look, Oren," Wilson went on, "I want to work with you and I want to be fair. But you make it hard. Not only do you pull stupid little tricks like this but you're continually trying to undercut me with the staff."

"That's not true."

"I'm sorry," Wilson said flatly, "but I have reason to believe it is."

"Then I suppose there's nothing I can do or say that will change your mind," I said. "But you aren't the only one to have grievances, you know. I spent over six months doing two jobs and what did I get for it? Absolutely nothing. At the very least, I should have gotten a bonus or a raise."

Wilson regarded me soberly. "That would be up to the front office to decide, wouldn't it?"

"All they need is a reminder," I said. I hated myself but the truth was that I had overextended myself in anticipation of getting the branch chief's job and I needed the money badly.

"I'm not so sure about that," Wilson said. "I didn't want to tell you this, but the reason this job was left vacant so long was to give you a chance to prove you could do it. And you failed, Oren. So I really don't think a bonus would be in order even if I were inclined to recommend it. Which I'm not. In fact, about the only thing I'd consider recommending you for is early retirement." He leaned back in his swivel chair and folded his arms across his chest. "You might give that some thought," he added grimly, "and be guided accordingly."

"Yes, sir," I said.

Back at my desk I sat with my fists clenched on the blotter before me, stung by the unfairness of it all. Thinking back, I was convinced I had gone out of my way to support Wilson. After all, hadn't I told Leduc that I hadn't expected the job? And there were other occasions too when I could have been critical and wasn't. As for the vouchers—well, all I had done was follow orders. It wasn't my fault the orders were foolish.

I didn't believe that about the job being left vacant to test me either. That was just an excuse to keep me from getting what the company owed me. And I had a good mind to go over Wilson's head to Slingerland to demand it.

But then I realized with a sudden sense of deflation that whatever his personal feelings, Slingerland would never overrule a branch chief. And there wasn't a thing I could do about it.

I was just sitting there staring at my hands when Sally came over with a stack of returned vouchers. "Mr. Wilson said to have you put the accounting numbers on these and then give them back to me to send over for reprocessing." She paused and looked down her nose at me. "He said to tell you he was holding you personally responsible for their not coming back again," she added.

I sighed. "All right, Sally," I said. "Just leave them."

I continued to sit there for another moment or two, then reached for my ballpoint to begin the mechanical job of entering the accounting numbers. As I did so, my eye fell on Wilson's initials on the "approved" line. Like so many VIPs he apparently considered careful calligraphy obsolete and his signature had deteriorated to a stylized squiggle. His ENW was barely recognizable as the initials the letters were intended to represent. I'd seen that signature literally dozens of times since he had come into the branch—but what hadn't struck me until now was how easy it would be to copy.

Pushing the vouchers to one side I got out a sheet of scratch paper and began to try. My first attempts were well off the mark, but within a matter of minutes I had it down well enough to know that with more practice I would have no trouble duplicating it exactly. I crumpled the paper and tossed it in my wastebasket. The plan that would get me the money I needed was already formed in my head and ready for execution whenever I was ready.

But only when I was ready. I did nothing more now except complete the rejected vouchers and take them over to Sally, who stuffed them into an envelope without looking at them.

I cleared my throat. "From now on," I said, "let me see the vouchers when they come in and then again after Mr. Wilson approves them."

She looked at me curiously, "*After* he approves them?"

I nodded. I'd anticipated the question and it was a difficult one to answer. But I had to see the vouchers a second time. Once approved, they were never questioned except on format and that I could control. What I couldn't control was Wilson questioning one before approval. "If I'm going to be personally responsible," I said, "I think I'm entitled to double check."

I knew that made me sound like a prig, but maybe that was all to the good. Sally just gave me a scornful look, then shrugged, accepting the reason. And that was that. So far so good.

I knew, though, that I couldn't send vouchers through in my own name or risk having them mailed to my home. So at noon I skipped lunch and set about establishing the existence of a non-existent firm, the Acme General Supply Company. Actually, that's easier than you might think, requiring only a mailing address—accomplished by renting a P.O. box—and a bank account. Also, despite the banker's vaunted reputation, accomplished quite easily. The chink in their armor is that they never question anybody who *deposits* money with them. And once a depositor has the account established, all he's got to do is deposit a check, give it time to clear, and then withdraw the amount, using the signature card on file as his only identification.

Well satisfied with what I'd accomplished, I went back to the office only a few minutes later than usual and put in the rest of the day working. At quitting time, I carried out a supply of bank voucher forms rolled up in my newspaper.

Later that evening I practiced Wilson's initials until they rolled off the tip of my ballpoint easily, effortlessly, and flawlessly. Then, using my old portable, I filled in one of the voucher forms, picking $197.50 as an amount neither too large nor too small to excite any suspicion. I double-checked each entry to make sure no oversight tripped me up. Satisfied, I picked up my pen again, hesitated only a fraction of a second, then dashed off Wilson's signature on the "approved" line. I compared it to Wilson's real signature and, try as I might, I couldn't distinguish between them. Smiling, I locked the voucher in my desk and got ready for bed.

Friday afternoon Sally laid the week's batch of vouchers, approved and bearing Wilson's initials, on my desk. She didn't speak, but her expression said clearly enough that she thought me an old woman. If only you knew, I thought as she walked away.

I made a pretense of going through the vouchers again. Then, when I was sure no one was paying any attention to me, I slipped the false one safely in the middle. To be perfectly safe, I waited another five or six minutes before taking them back to Sally. "All correct," I said.

"Dandy," she said and set them carelessly to one side of her desk.

That startled me, because I'd expected her to seal them immediately in an envelope where they would be safe from prying eyes. I stood hesitating by her desk. "Was there anything else?" she asked.

"No," I said and went back to my own desk. But I couldn't keep my eyes from sliding across to that exposed pile of vouchers. I was seriously considering getting them back on some pretext or another when the in-office messenger came in on his rounds and Sally hastily stuffed them into an envelope and handed it to him. I heaved a sigh of relief and sagged back in my chair.

The relief was short-lived. Despite my years with the company, I had no idea how long it took to process a check once the voucher was approved. And I spent the next week and a half literally on the edge of my chair, approaching the post office each day with a mixture of anticipation and dread. Until at last there it was—a slim brown envelope with the name Acme General Supply peeking through the address box. It had worked and I was home free . . .

My original intention was to stop as soon as I'd collected enough to pay off my debts. Perhaps if I had done that everything would have turned out all right. But the plan was working so well that it seemed foolish to give it up. Until, of course, Wilson called me into his office and showed me the pile of vouchers spread out on his desk. Then it seemed foolish to have ever started.

"What ever possessed you to do it, Oren?" he said. "Even if Sally hadn't noticed that we were consistently sending out more vouchers than we received, the auditors were bound to find you out."

I looked at him blankly. "I didn't know about any auditors."

"Of course not," Wilson said. "Only Sally and I knew in the branch. But a man with your background and experience must have realized that when expenses started running significantly and unexplainably too high, the company would take steps to find out why."

It was only later that the real significance of what he'd said came through to me. Right now I was too overwhelmed by the enormity of being caught to take it in.

Wilson looked at me disgustedly. "But apparently you didn't, did you?" He shook his head. "It's almost against my better judgment," he went on, "but I guess we do owe you something for all the years you've put in. So I'll give you a week to make 'voluntary' restitution before I pass what I know on to the front office. If you can do that I'll recommend there be no prosecution."

I stood up slowly. "Thank you," I said, and turned to leave.

Wilson stopped me. "Of course," he said, "there can be no question of your staying on here. I'll explain to the staff—until the news breaks—that you're on vacation. But leave your office keys with Sally."

I nodded and went the rest of the way out.

Sally accepted the keys gravely. "You may not believe this," she said, "but I really am sorry. I didn't have any choice though."

"No," I said, "you didn't."

I turned away, thinking at least I had a week and that was *something*.

Something, perhaps. But as you know, if you've ever tried to raise a large amount of money under pressure, not enough. Still, judgment postponed once might be postponed again. And that hope sent me to Wilson's home the night before his deadline ran out.

He lived at the end of a secluded street in the western suburbs. I shivered in the wind as I stood on his step, pushing the door buzzer. I could hear the chimes sounding faintly from within but otherwise the house was silent. I pressed harder, half panicked that he might not be home and that my time would run out by default. But then suddenly the door was jerked open and Wilson glared out at me. "For God's sake, Oren," he said. "What are you doing here?"

"I have to talk to you," I said. "And I didn't want it to be at the office."

He hesitated, glancing back into the house. For a moment I was afraid he was going to slam the door in my face, but then he shrugged and moved aside to let me enter. "All right," he said.

"You'll have to excuse the clutter," he went on loudly, leading me down the hall, "but my wife's visiting her sister and I've been batching it the last week and a half."

He opened a door at the end of the hallway and ushered me into a pleasant paneled room furnished as a study and warmed by a gas log blazing in a stone fireplace. A door to the left of the fireplace led deeper back into the house and stood slightly ajar.

One other thing struck my eye immediately—two glasses standing side by side on a low table, both partially full and one unmistakably edged with lipstick. So that was why Wilson had been so long answering the door and why he had spoken so boomingly. He had a woman here with him—and not his wife.

Wilson frowned when he caught the direction of my gaze. "All right, Oren," he said irritably, "what was it you wanted to talk about?"

"I need more time to raise the money," I said. "Another week—"

Wilson shook his head. "No," he said. "If you don't have the money now, you won't have it in another week."

"Yes, I will," I said. I plunged on breathlessly. "I have some property. The sale's all arranged but the man needs some time to get the money together." That was a lie, but a week was a week no matter how it was gained. And in that time I might be able to find out more about the woman Wilson was seeing and use it as a lever to force him to drop the charges altogether.

Now he took a cigar from his breast pocket and held it lightly between his fingers, chest high. "How much would you net?" he said.

"Six thousand," I said eagerly. "Enough to cover the vouchers and even leave—"

"Leave what?" Wilson cut in. "Six thousand dollars isn't a tenth of what you stole."

"That's not true," I protested. "Tally up the Acme vouchers. They come to just over $3,000."

"I'm sure they do," Wilson said. "But add in Calvert Associates, Jefferson-Leeds, and all the other phony companies you invented and the grand total comes nearer $75,000."

I just looked at him. "No," I said finally, and my voice sounded weak even to me. "I don't know anything about any of those other companies."

"Oh, come on, Oren," Wilson said. "You don't really expect anybody to believe that, do you?"

Suddenly everything clicked into place and my temper flared. "No," I cried, "and you don't expect anybody to believe it either, do you? My God, I should have realized that I hadn't stolen enough for it to be noticed! I was careful to keep the amounts low for just that reason!

"But *you* didn't have to be careful, did you? Because you'd set me up as the perfect scapegoat. That's why you gave me the week's grace. You thought I'd run, leaving you free to tell whatever story you liked. Well, it's not going to work that way. I'm going to see that everybody knows the truth."

"That's enough!" Wilson said sharply. "I really don't know what you hope to gain by trying to smear me with wild accusations you couldn't possibly back up in a thousand years. But let me tell you this—the net effect is to kill any hope you ever had of mercy from me." He made a short emphatic gesture with his cigar. "You say you'll have $6,000 in a week? Good. You'll need it for a lawyer." And with that he turned abruptly to stick the cigar in his mouth and strike a match on the stone of the fireplace.

That sent me completely over the edge. I grabbed up the nearest object to hand—a heavy glass ashtray—and smashed it down against the back of his head. Wilson lurched forward against the fireplace, then crumpled up and lay motionless on the floor.

For a long moment I just stared at him. Then I bent, pulled him away from the fire and felt for his heartbeat. There wasn't any. I'd killed him. I gave in to panic then and fled.

Somehow I drove more or less sanely back to my apartment, but I remember none of it. My first coherent recollection is of standing just inside my apartment door, breathing hard and trying to think what to do next. And realizing that there was nothing I could do. Even if I hadn't left my fingerprints smeared over everything, that hidden woman had heard the whole argument—and possibly even seen me. She'd send the police straight to me and there would be no escape—except one.

Without taking off my coat I walked to the bathroom, opened the medicine cabinet, and took out the bottle of sleeping pills I kept there. It was almost full. I shook two out into my hand, washed them down with a glass of water, then shook out two more. And stood staring at them, unable to raise my hand to my mouth a second time.

Finally I put them back in the bottle and went into my bedroom. I lay down still clothed and eventually the two pills I had taken took hold and I slept.

The phone woke me the next morning. Feeling utterly defeated, I dragged myself out of bed to answer it. But it wasn't the police as I expected, it was Slingerland.

"Oren," he said, "thank God you're home. Something terrible has happened and we need you back at the office right now. I hate to ask you to cut your vacation short, but—well, frankly, Wilson's dead and we're not sure whether it was an accident or suicide. He had a gas fire in his study and somehow or other the gas was on but not lit and then he struck a match or something. There was a hell of an explosion and we'll probably never know for sure what *did* happen."

His voice trailed off, then picked up again. "You're bound to know sooner or later, Oren, so I might as well tell you. Wilson was approving false vouchers to nonexistent companies. He was aware that we were calling in auditors and knew he was bound to be caught, so it looks as though he took the easy way out."

I started to tremble, remembering how close I'd come to taking that way myself.

"Can we count on you, Oren?" Slingerland persisted.

"Yes," I managed to say. "Of course."

"Fine. And, Oren, I think we're going to reconsider our position on you as branch chief. You may not be the world's greatest administrator, but at least you're honest. And there's a lot to be said for that."

"Yes," I said. I put the phone down. I was almost afraid to let myself believe it had really happened. But it had. Incredible as it might seem, that gas fire *had* exploded, obliterating the evidence of what had really happened, and I was free to tell any story I liked about the vouchers.

But why hadn't Wilson's girl friend gone to the police? It stopped me for a minute, then I realized she was probably married herself and afraid of scandal. Whatever her reason, she hadn't come forth and because of that my world was suddenly a brighter place. I went to shower and dress with a mental reservation to keep it that way. No more fooling with vouchers—if for no other reason than because I could never be so lucky again.

I was just tying my tie when the door buzzer sounded. I finished the knot, pulled it straight, then went to answer the door.

Sally stood smiling cryptically and dangling a set of keys from her upraised finger—the keys I'd given her when Wilson had fired me. "You'll be needing these now that you're coming back to the office," she said. "I thought I'd bring them over and save you the trouble of asking for them."

She put the keys in my hand and moved past me into the room.

"Really, Oren," she said, her smile fading, "for a man who's supposed to be smart, you certainly behaved stupidly last night. Running off and leaving him lying there like that!"

I had the presence of mind to slam the door and lock it. "You," I said. "You were the woman at Wilson's last night."

"That's right," she said. "And damn lucky for you I was too. If I hadn't been there to blow out that fire and then set up a kitchen timer to strike a spark half an hour later you'd be in handcuffs now instead of sitting on top of the world."

"But why?" I said.

"Because it wasn't Ed who set up those other false vouchers, lover, it was me. It took me about three weeks to figure out what you were up to, then—well, what you could do I could do. In perfect safety too, because any time I needed to I could just point the finger at you and you couldn't prove you hadn't done the whole thing yourself.

"Of course, now that he's dead, poor old Ed makes an even better scapegoat." She sighed. "Although in one way it is a pity. His signature was so absurdly easy to forge.

"Still," she went on, "now that you're going to be branch chief, that won't be a problem at all. Will it?"

The Window

by William Bankier

The dental building was in a respectable part of Montreal, but it was old. The antique elevator was a mahogany coffin standing on end. Years ago when Gerry Lunsford took his first ride in it, the door closed and the box remained motionless for seconds before it began lurching upward a few inches at a time. He almost panicked. Lunsford's claustrophobia could drive him off a crowded bus or even out of his company's board room if he allowed himself to think about the closed door.

His appointment today was going to be an ordeal but not because of the scheduled root-canal work. He could bear pain. It was the feeling of being trapped in the chair with his mouth jammed full of appliances, unable to move while the animal inside him insisted on moving *now*; that was the torment he would have to live with for the next hour.

He ignored the waiting elevator and started climbing the first of six flights of stairs, taking them lightly, the change bouncing in the pockets of his suit. He was in shape, he exercised every morning before breakfast. Bernice had walked in once and reeled back in genuine fright, seeing him spread-eagled on the carpet, thinking he had passed out. When he tightened his stomach muscles and raised his legs, they both laughed. That was years ago when they were still laughing.

Lunsford slowed his pace. He could thank his lucky stars for the considerate Dr. Telling. It had only been necessary to mention the panicky feeling to him once.

"I feel very stupid, Michael. But I get this urge to climb out of the chair. It's claustrophobia; I have to move, I have to run."

Michael Telling's ruddy face had looked down at him with an expression of simple interest in the small blue eyes. "That's O.K. You just tell me and you can get up any time you want. No problem."

Then, as he fitted a rubber dam across Lunsford's mouth, he fixed it so that it covered only a part of the opening. "I'm leaving you a hole you can climb out of," he said, grinning.

What an understanding man! Bernice had found a beauty when she came up with Michael Telling.

Lunsford's heart was pounding and his shirt was sticking to his chest when he reached the sixth-floor landing. He stood for a minute outside the door, running a comb through his closely trimmed grey hair. He wanted to look his best because Margo Mantro would be there and he intended to ask her to come with him and have a drink.

This chance of socializing with the dental assistant was the reason why Lunsford would accept appointments only at the end of the afternoon. Bernice said he was crazy; Michael got tired like anybody else and would not be as efficient late in the day. But Lunsford liked being the last patient, then hanging around for a few minutes and latching onto Margo as she came out of the building.

One time, Telling came out on Margo's heels and saw Lunsford holding her arm and flagging a taxi. "I'm going to squeal on you two," he said.

"You can't talk," Margo said, "the way you and Mrs. Lunsford carry on."

Lunsford remembered this remark later and spent some time wondering if there was anything in it. There had been a time when his feelings of jealousy were as strong as any man's. When Colleen was a baby and Bernice was home looking after her, Lunsford, away at the office all day and sometimes into the evening, would torture himself with suspicion. Not any more, however. He must be getting old.

He opened the waiting room door and stepped into an area of white walls with magazines scattered over a number of low tables. FM radio played through a concealed speaker. The room was empty. Usually there would be a mother waiting for a child, or a couple of patients would be ahead of him, but not today. He had the place to himself.

Before he could sit down, Margo Mantro stepped out of the inner office. "Good afternoon."

Lunsford had long ago ceased trying to figure out why Miss Mantro was so appealing to him. Almost all of her features could be faulted; almond-shaped eyes slightly heavy in the lid, teeth protruding behind full lips, her smooth black hair cut short with no particular styling—but she had a vibrancy about her, a sense of supreme confidence in her femininity.

"Hello, Margo. This place is a tomb today."

"There was some confusion. Michael got his calendar mixed up so he put off some people he shouldn't have."

"Bloody morgue around here."

Michael Telling appeared in the doorway of his surgery. He filled it, stooping his shoulders, carrying the bristling red head forward. "I could set my watch by you, Gerry. Come on in."

The dentist went into the small office beside the surgery, leaving Lunsford and Margo alone in the reception room.

"Can we have our drink afterward?" Lunsford asked her.

"You won't feel like it. He has a lot of work to do on you this afternoon."

"I'll feel like it. Meet me at the Empire?"

"I should go home. I have things to do before the weekend."

"What things?"

"Washing my hair. Packing some things. I'm going up to the Laurentians."

"Oh, come on and have a drink."

"Just more talk, Gerry?"

"I have to talk. These are bad days for me, Margo. Something has to happen."

Telling's voice issued from the office. "Margo, honey, you've got to stop hiding that X-ray file."

"Coming!" She looked straight into Lunsford's eyes. Rising on her toes, she slipped an arm around his neck and kissed him on the mouth. She smelled of cinnamon.

Margo hurried into the office and Lunsford walked into the surgery. He stood by the open window and looked past the billowing curtains to the courtyard, six floors below. The backs of deserted buildings, broken windowpanes, a fractured rain barrel met his eyes. Faintly, from the office, came the busy voices of Margo and Dr. Telling.

With the excitement of his contact with the girl diminishing, Lunsford found himself slipping back into the cold, grey pool of depression he had been struggling through these past weeks. How quickly one kiss from her had lifted him out of it. He remembered how Bernice had been able to do this to him twenty years ago with her boldly erotic behavior in the park, on a crowded bus, anywhere.

Nothing was happening these days. If their feet touched before they went to sleep, they excused themselves. How very courteous they were in bed—but nowhere else in the apartment.

"The agent says houses are going to go up. Now is the time to buy." He saw her sitting wedged in at the end of the kitchen table, coffee mug poised below her upturned chin, the place mat littered with crumbs from the slice of toast she had destroyed before eating part of it.

"Fifty-five thousand dollars," Lunsford said.

"We have fifteen in cash to put down. Without touching the mutual funds."

"A forty-thousand-dollar mortgage loan. That's forever."

"Pay it off sooner. Use your bonuses at Christmas."

"That's vacation money. Don't you want to go back to England? We said we'd make it a month next time. See Dover again, maybe go on to France."

"We can do that and buy a house, too."

Lunsford tried to explain how he felt. "For me, being locked into a mortgage would be like being buried alive."

"It's called security. A place of our own instead of always paying rent to a landlord. Dammit, Gerry, we're the only people I know who make what you make and still live in an apartment."

"I didn't think you'd understand."

He heard the sound of water running in the sink. Dr. Telling was washing his hands. Lunsford turned from the window and forced himself to sit in the chair. He leaned back and raised his feet.

Telling stood over him, drying his hands on a towel. A slight frown creased his eyes. "Are you all right?"

"You know me, Mike. The old anxiety."

"Listen, I'm going to make this as easy on you as I can." Telling handed Lunsford a couple of capsules and swished some water into a plastic cup. "Swallow these. As we go along, you'll start to feel out of it. But I guarantee you won't feel anxious."

"What are they?"

"Very powerful tranquilizers. Drink 'em down and we'll start with the easy part."

Lunsford swallowed the capsules.

Margo came into the room and stood at Telling's shoulder. Her presence helped Lunsford relax. He lay back and stared into the reflecting light above his face. He read the manufacturer's name over and over. He read it backwards. He counted the ripples in the corrugated glass reflector. The dentist's hands were busy with the needle, but they were deft and gentle. He barely felt the pressure as the local anesthetic was applied. While it took effect, they left him alone for a few minutes.

He lay there waiting for the panic of claustrophobia to overtake him. It was early for that, of course. It usually began when his mouth was full of metal and the dentist was engaged in the trickiest part of the work—but maybe not this time. The capsules were taking effect; he felt a warm sensation of tranquility.

Telling returned, said something reassuring and went to work. Margo handed him the instruments he needed, opened drawers, closed them, left the room. Did she come back? Lunsford could not tell. He heard sounds only faintly, as from a great distance.

The session which he had dreaded so much for days was, in fact, anticlimactic. It was all over while he was still waiting for it to begin. Telling said something to him which he barely grasped, grinned cheerfully and left the room. Margo cranked him up in the chair, unfastened the bib from around his neck, lowered the upholstered arm and set him free.

"That was a piece of cake," he said to Telling, sticking his head inside the office where the dentist was turning the pages of his calendar.

"Watch yourself," the dentist said, "you're still a little high."

"Can I have a drink?"

Telling winked at Margo over Lunsford's shoulder. "As long as you have a qualified nurse in attendance."

Lunsford left the old building delighted at how well he was feeling. His jaw was stiff on the right side, but apart from that he felt no ill effects. He walked three blocks to the Empire Hotel. The Candlelight Bar was busy on Friday afternoon, the happy hour about to begin, but their table, the small one behind the piano, was unoccupied. He slipped into a deep leather chair and ordered a double Scotch and water and a gin and tonic for Margo.

She showed up as soon as the drinks did.

"That was fast," he said.

"You're under heavy medication," she said. "I'm not supposed to leave the patient on his own."

"Bless your heart, Margo." They raised their glasses and drank. Then he said, "No, not bless your heart. I'm through saying trivial things to you."

"Not bless my heart? What, then?"

"I love you, Margo. That's what."

She laughed, but when he extended a hand toward her cheek, she brushed her lips across his fingers. "What was in those capsules?" she asked.

"Truth, maybe. Come away with me. Let's go somewhere and not come back."

"Be careful, Gerry."

"It's so simple, I should have suggested it before. Let's go to England and find a place in London. We'll spend years walking down different streets."

"You've got a wife, Gerry. And a daughter."

"Colleen is twenty-one. And she's got the right idea; she's hardly ever home. Spends all her time with her friend Steve. They're not talking about mortgages and pensions and getting the furniture recovered in gold thread."

"And Bernice?"

"We ran out of our relationship years ago. She'll fall down on her knees and thank me."

Margo smiled into her drink. "I'll believe that when it happens."

"Never mind her. This is between you and me." He put the back of his hand under her chin and raised her eyes to his. "I'm dying," he said. He saw her blink. "I mean nothing else is going to happen in my life unless I make it happen."

"I want to come with you, but it isn't that easy."

"What's the problem?"

"My job."

"Mike? He's a pussycat. Tell him what we're doing. If anybody would understand people wanting to get away, Michael Telling will."

"You, maybe, but not me. He doesn't like anybody interfering with what is his."

"You don't belong to him, you only work for him."

"You don't know him as well as I do." She finished her drink and Lunsford caught the waiter's eye. "Two years ago," she continued, "I was working for another dentist, a very nice old man named Willibroad. Dr. Telling came to have some work done; haven't you ever wondered what dentists do when they have a toothache? Anyway, from that one meeting, Michael decided he wanted me to work for him. He took me to lunch and made me a very flattering offer, a lot more money and extra holidays. When I told Dr. Willibroad, he raised my salary because he wanted to keep me."

"That's what I would have done."

"So I got back to Michael and he sounded kind of cold on the telephone. Then the next thing I knew, Dr. Willibroad came in one morning and told me I'd better accept Telling's offer. Told me to never mind working out my notice, just to go. I couldn't get him to level with me. But a few weeks later, when I was working for Michael, he took me to lunch again. Do you know what he'd done?"

"Tell me."

"He hired two hoodlums and sent them around to Dr. Willibroad's house to talk to him. They said they were from my family and they wanted me to take this other job. I don't know what else they said but they must have scared the blazes out of him."

Lunsford was appalled. "I wouldn't have believed it."

"To tell the truth, I was pleased that Michael wanted me so badly he'd go to those ends to have me. But I've begun to understand him. He's that way about anything he sets his mind on." She tried her new drink, pouring into it the dregs of the first one. "So I don't think he'll be wild about my taking off with you."

Lunsford said, "O.K. That's a problem to be solved. Will you let me talk to him?"

"With pleasure."

"I'll call him at home." He looked at his watch. "Would he be there by seven?"

She laughed. His enthusiasm was getting to her. "Eager beaver," she said.

"If we delay, it will never happen. All I needed was your approval, and I think I have that."

"What will we live on?"

"Sweetie, money is the least of our problems. I have all we'll need for the foreseeable future. I'm talking about the next three years. Anybody who plans beyond that these days is an idiot. The days of the peaceful retirement and comfortable old age are gone forever, if they ever existed. We live now. Right?"

They squeezed hands. Her face was radiant. "Right, I suppose. Why not?"

There was a flight to London leaving at 11:15 that night. Lunsford called from the bar, using his clout with the travel agency that handled all his company's business. When they were confirmed, he delivered Margo home and told her he would pick her up at 8:30. Then he powered his car aggressively through rush-hour traffic to his apartment building. Telling's capsules were still affecting him. He felt light-headed and bursting with euphoria.

Bernice met him at the door and followed him into the bedroom. She said, "You're under a full head of steam tonight."

"Feeling very fine."

"I telephoned Michael. He said it went well."

"One of the world's great dentists, and a gentleman through and through." He fished his two suitcases from under the bed. "That reminds me, I have to call Michael in a few minutes. Do we have his home number?"

"Yes. It's in my book." She paused. "What's wrong?"

"Nothing. Just have to tell him something."

He was opening bureau drawers and transferring neatly folded garments into the suitcases. Bernice was sitting on the corner of the bed. From time to time he glanced at her. Her sturdy legs were crossed, her back straight as a board.

"Why two bags?" she asked. "You ordinarily make do with one."

"It isn't a business trip, love. I'm going away."

She did not speak for quite a while. A lot of useless dialogue was being edited in her sensible mind. "Is somebody going with you?"

"Margo."

She laughed abruptly. "Michael's Margo? That little tartar!"

"I wouldn't expect you to see what I see in her."

"On the contrary. If one enjoys making love to animals, I should imagine she'd do very well."

"It'll be a refreshing change from making love to a statue."

"I've never been called that before."

"It's what you've become."

"It's what you've turned me into."

Lunsford stopped and stood erect, feeling a loss of breath. The freezing was coming out of his jaw; a thin sliver of pain worked its way between his clenched teeth. This was crazy. He was leaving this woman forever; why argue with her? "Would you get Michael's home number for me? I'm in a hurry." He snapped shut the first bag.

She arose, opened a drawer in the bedside table and took out a small blue leather book. She found a page and laid the book down face up. "There it is."

"Thank you."

"Have you told poor Margo what a baby you are?"

"If I'm a baby, she'll find out."

"I pity her."

"Don't. When I left her a little while ago, she looked remarkably happy."

"I pity both of you. You've got a life here, Gerry. You're established, you've got status and position. And you're about to throw it all away."

"I've got nothing. My life is over if I stay here. Everything is all taken care of. Fifteen more laps around the track at the agency and then retirement, if I'm still alive. With a pension that won't be worth anything when I get it."

"Nothing to worry about, then," she said.

He turned to her, absorbing the dangerous effect of her withering smile. "The money won't stop because I'm gone. I'll see that you have plenty." He went to her and took her hand. The fingers were clenched in a hard fist. He put an arm around her and drew her to him, kissing her cool forehead, but her folded arms were between them, preventing his body from touching hers. He felt he had attended to a formality.

He returned to his packing. "I won't need any supper," he said.

"You never do when you've been drinking." She went back to her perch on the end of the bed. "What about Colleen? This isn't just you and me."

"If Colleen were still a child, there might be something to consider."

"She's coming over later with Steve. What shall I tell her?"

Lunsford went to his bureau and wrote swiftly on a pad of paper.

"Colleen the Queen," he wrote, using their latest intimate salutation, "now hear this. The old man is up, up, and away like Supermensch as of tonight. Much to explain and would have words with you face to face. Or face to face to face if that lout Steve is with you. Am departing for London on Air Canada at 11:15. Please come out to Dorval and see me off. Will explain all then. Luv, Daddyo."

He tore the sheet from the pad and placed it on the table near the bedroom door. "There," he said, "you don't have to tell her anything." He went back to his packing and completed it quickly. Then he went to the telephone and dialed Michael Telling's home number. Bernice absorbed each twist of the dial.

"Hello?" The familiar, hearty voice.

"Michael, this is Gerry Lunsford."

"Uh-oh. How are the teeth?"

"Nothing wrong there at all, Mike. Your usual super job. No, this is something else. Have you got a minute?"

"Shoot."

"Well, I'm getting set to go away, to London as a matter of fact. Flying out tonight."

"Lucky dog. You advertising guys have all the fun."

"It isn't business. Actually, I'm going away for good."

"Sounds like a sudden decision. Did you know this afternoon?"

"It was in the back of my mind, and then it all came together. Anyway, Bernice is staying here; she can explain more to you next time you see her, but right now there's a particular thing I have to tell you."

"Yes?"

"I'm taking Margo with me."

"My Margo?"

"She wants to come, but she told me you might be a little upset at losing her. I hope it doesn't hang you up too much."

Telling's reply came without hesitation. "It hangs me up a hell of a lot. You can't just pull her out like that."

"I know it's sudden, but that's how these things are. The feeling takes you and you have to do it. Now or never."

"I don't know what the hell's come over you, Gerry. But you'd better think again."

"I don't have to. I've done my thinking."

"And it's all wrong. Don't do it, my friend. I'm not kidding."

"I *am* doing it. We're getting on that plane tonight and we'll be in London in the morning. We didn't even have to tell you. This is a courtesy call. If you don't appreciate it, I'm sorry."

"I don't appreciate it at all. I went to a lot of trouble to get that girl in my office."

"Yes, I heard about that."

"Then you'd better believe I don't want her stolen from me."

"Nobody's stealing anybody. She's a free woman and she's decided to come away with me."

"You won't get away with this, Lunsford."

"You can't stop me." Lunsford slammed down the telephone and turned to close the second bag. His hands were trembling. Bernice was smiling at him. He said, "Michael Telling is out of his mind."

"You're the one who's out of his mind. I've been watching you. You've been coming apart for the past six months."

"Maybe I have. But now I'm back together."

"Like hell. You're just transporting the disaster. You're going to fall apart in London. Alone, with nobody to support you."

"I won't be alone," he said. "I'll have Margo with me."

"Michael isn't going to like that." She got up and took one of the bags, helping him to the front door.

"Michael will have to live with it."

"You don't know Michael."

Lunsford turned, with the vague idea that he would kiss his wife of twenty-five years for the last time, but she was on the other side of the luggage and there seemed to be no expectation of affection in her. He opened the door, stooped over and hefted the bags. "Good-bye, Bernice."

There was a thoughtful look on her face. "What is it you're really after, Gerry? Adventure?"

"I suppose that's what it is. I want to put in a few events between me and the end of my life."

"Well, in that case, good luck."

There was an elevator waiting. He stepped into it and the door closed, cutting him off forever from his old life. He fell sixteen floors to whatever was waiting for him.

It was too early to pick up Margo—she needed time to pack—so Lunsford drove around, then selected a bar at random. He liked walking into a place where he was a stranger. The bartender and customers knew nothing of his weaknesses and past failures. That meant Lunsford was able to pretend for a while that he was a success.

Back at his old hangout, the Rainbow, this was not the case. Dallas had poured him many a whisky, noting his glazed eyes, picking up on the continuing saga of his failed existence.

"You all right, Mr. Lunsford?"

"I should be. I make $35,000 a year."

Dallas, with a sheepish grin, said, "That's a lot more than I make."

"I have a beautiful daughter who's almost twenty-one, and she's not pregnant."

"A lot of guys would like to be able to say that."

"My wife is forty-three, almost as old as I am. She looks fifteen years younger."

"I've seen her. Mrs. Lunsford is a great-looking lady."

"Apart from the flu once a year and a couple of bad teeth, I've never been sick a day in my life."

"You're a lucky man, Mr. Lunsford."

"Then tell me, Dallas. Why do I feel as if a car just hit me?"

Dallas never had a proper answer to this question. What was more important, the bartender Lunsford was now approaching would not even have to be asked. Lunsford was up. He was sky-high.

"Rye," he said, "with some plain water and a little ice. Make it a double."

The anxiety he had felt in saying good-bye to Bernice was gone. In the manner of a man dragging himself free of a bog, he felt light-footed, capable of great speed and distance.

Michael Telling's anger on the phone, disturbing at the time because it came as a surprise, now seemed like the petulant discontent of a child not able to have his own way. Well, let him find himself a new nurse.

Lunsford's drink came and he swallowed almost half of it at the first draught. Was he being a rat in this affair, serving himself at the expense of those around him? If so, he wasn't the only one. The people he worked with showed him all kinds of imperfections every day. They were prepared, most of them, to live and let live.

As he went outside and got back into his car, the idea of live and let live echoed in his mind, bouncing off the stern image of Dr. Michael Telling. Would the dentist be prepared to forgive and forget? What could he do, call in the Mounties? Or give Bernice substandard dental care? Fat chance of that with the way those two got on.

Lunsford parked outside Margo's place. He entered the vestibule, gave the bell labeled Mantro two long rings. Almost immediately the inner door lock buzzed and he went in.

A door opened at the end of the ground-floor corridor. He entered and closed the door behind him. Margo was in the livingroom, sitting on the edge of the chesterfield, her back turned to him, her hands over her face.

"What is it?"

"He was here. He just left."

"Who?"

"Michael. He said you called him." Her voice was crushed.

Lunsford went to Margo and lifted her up. She was trembling. He drew her hands away from her face and saw the residue of terror in her eyes. Her cheeks were wet. She was wearing a nylon gown. The drawstring neckline was torn. She drew it together with one hand, staring at him apprehensively.

"Did he do that?"

"He didn't hurt me. He just tore my robe."

"I'll kill him."

"No, Gerry. Don't do anything. He's gone."

"Did he say where he was going?"

"It doesn't matter. I'm not hurt." He was turning toward the door and she held his shoulders, bringing him back. "He sounded crazy. If you get involved with him now, we'll never get away."

"He put his hands on you. I'll kill him."

"I'm not hurt, Gerry. Stay with me." The damaged robe slipped down over her shoulders. "If you go after him, we'll miss the plane, we'll never get away."

His rage caused his hands to tremble as he lifted the torn material. "There's a mark on your shoulder."

"It's nothing." She closed her eyes.

He drew her to him, kissing her lips, lifting her in his arms so that she hung heavily against him. He carried her back to the sofa and sat down—she was laughing now, not crying.

"You're going to be something of a delight to live with."

"I think we'll manage."

He helped her finish packing. They had to hurry to make the check-in at Dorval. She was sure she was forgetting a million things and she made frantic tours of the apartment, opening and closing drawers, writing a note for her girlfriend who was going to move in and use up the last three months of her lease.

She was dressed in a grey traveling suit with chunky wine-colored shoes on her feet and she looked unbearably cute, her movements alive with the energy of a child. As he opened her front door and she stood beside him, her hand on the light switch, she said, "Did you feel a pang saying good-bye?"

"Very minor."

"I don't feel a thing. I suppose I'll feel sad later."

They drove swiftly to the airport, past the low shapes of manufacturing plants, some of them Lunsford's clients at the agency. What would they say when the word got around that he had bailed out? They would have to envy him, those who were honest with themselves, have to wish they had the guts to try something similar.

The radio was on and Mancini strings and piano made the glowing interior of the car into their own corner of the world. Margo's hand was on his thigh, resting gently. He was running away from what he had assumed were his permanent responsibilities. Where were the problems? Why was he feeling no guilt?

They checked in at the airline counter to find their flight delayed. There was time for a drink or two before takeoff. He was guiding Margo into the lounge when he heard his daughter's voice.

"Dad!"

There she was, a tall figure in jeans and khaki jacket, breaking away from her escort, Steve. She ran across the concourse and stopped in front of him, her face stern and mischievous at the same time. She was excited. "What's this I hear about your cracking up?"

"Am I acting crazy? What's your opinion?"

"Well, I guess you only live once." Colleen glanced over his shoulder at Margo waiting in the doorway of the lounge.

Lunsford called Steve over. Past the black beard and the heavy glasses, he could make out an interested face. "Steve, that's Miss Mantro over there. Go into the lounge and find a table for four. We'll be right with you."

He took Colleen's hand and they walked slowly down the marble corridor. She was almost as tall as he, and her pace matched his in easy strides.

The best part of his earlier days, the part he remembered now, used to be the hour after supper when he took his daughter for a walk and bought her an ice-cream cone. He would hold her on one arm outside the apartment building as the sky darkened and the air turned cool, their faces side by side.

Now this tall young woman strolling beside him said, "Is she the reason, Dad?"

"Margo? I'm happy she's coming with me. It means I won't be lonely. But it didn't start with her."

"Is it Mom?"

"Not really. Your mother and I were good for each other for a long time. Mom is O.K., you're O.K., Steve is O.K. I'm the one who needs a change."

"You think Steve is O.K.?"

"Why, don't you?"

"He's all right to drink beer with, but I wouldn't want to wake up beside him for the rest of my life."

They stopped walking and faced each other. Lunsford said, "If you have any doubts, kiss him off. Don't make a mistake you'll regret for the rest of your life."

Colleen grinned. "My generation doesn't do that. That was your generation." She kept smiling at him. "I was hoping I could get on that plane with you tonight."

Lunsford felt embarrassed. "Three's a crowd, honey."

"I didn't mean to buy another ticket. You said you were only taking her so you wouldn't be lonely. If I came instead, you wouldn't be lonely."

"There's more to it than that."

"Well, at last you've admitted it." Her hands were fists in her pockets. "You're getting old and you want to try convincing yourself you're still young by going to bed with that fat nurse."

"Is this what you came here to tell me?"

"No. And I'm sorry I said it."

"Don't be sorry. The truth sets us free." Lunsford strolled on and she followed him. "And your old Dad is now free as a bird."

When they went into the lounge, Colleen refused to sit down. She took Steve's hand and drew him to his feet. With her other hand, she patted Margo's shoulder. "Good luck, young lovers," she said. "Keep looking over your shoulder in London. If you see somebody following you, it could be me and Steverino."

Lunsford took out some money and pushed it at the boy. "Let me get these drinks," he said.

"Not on your life, Mr. Lunsford. Drink all four of them and have a great trip."

The drinks Steve had ordered proved to be doubles. When their flight was called, they were feeling quite high and the mood of exhilaration was back. In the lineup at the boarding gate, Lunsford was standing close against Margo's back when he felt her body stiffen.

"What?"

She half-turned and frowned toward a news agent's booth. "He's here."

"Who's he?"

"Michael. He was watching us."

Lunsford felt a cold steel spring compress inside his stomach. The warming effects of the alcohol vanished instantly and left him with a grainy feeling in his eyes. He craned his neck to scan the concourse but saw no sign of the dentist.

"Are you sure it was him?"

She moved so unsteadily that he took her arm and guided her toward the airplane.

"God help us," she said. "If you could have seen the look on his face."

"What time is your appointment?" Margo called from the bedroom.

"Ten-thirty." Lunsford was still getting used to the dim lighting in the mews house bathroom. It had low-wattage fluorescent tubes concealed behind either edge of the huge, gloomy mirror. To shave the left side of his face, he had to walk from the sink to the other side of the mirror and lean partway over the black bathtub.

The macabre tub had some value; Margo looked good in it.

He finished shaving, splashed on some of the new lotion she had bought him the day they arrived, and went into the bedroom to finish dressing.

"You are one strange man," Margo said. She was propped up against two pillows with a sheet across her bare body. At nine-thirty, in July, the room was pleasantly cool. Through the open window came sounds of industry from the auto repair shops down the lane. The stone walls and cobbled paving of the mews acted as an echo chamber, making sleep impossible when the pub closed or when one particularly throaty set of neighbors drove home and bayed behind their open windows.

"How am I strange?" he asked. He leaned against her, letting her massage his scalp. The inflated, floating feeling was back. Every once in a while he tuned out, lost track of what was happening. If it kept up, he would have to call somebody.

"I'm talking about the interview. Before we left Montreal, you said there was lots of money."

"There is."

"All right. We're two weeks in England and here you are, about to lock yourself into another job."

"Because I want to, not because I have to. There's a difference."

"If you say."

"And the money won't hurt. Sooner or later we'll need it."

She saw him close his eyes. "Are you all right? Are those teeth bothering you again?"

"A little bit." The throbbing in his jaw was just enough to bear. It came and it went. He said nothing about the light-headedness. He didn't want anything to spoil the precious mood they had achieved.

Margo stroked his jaw. "If it doesn't stop soon, I'm going to find a dentist for you."

"O.K. But let's give it a day or two."

She saw him away at the front door, her kiss tasting of toothpaste. "Tell me again where we're meeting," she said, pretending to be scatterbrained.

"The National Portrait Gallery. In front of Robert Louis Stevenson. At 2:30."

He looked back and she was standing in the doorway with one hand raised, a yellow-flowered figurine framed in white woodwork. The garage mechanics raised their heads from the workings of the MG's and Porsches, looked at her, looked at him.

"Good morning, gentlemen," he said and they responded with perfunctory good cheer as he whistled down the lane.

It was a fifteen-minute walk to Oakley's Advertising and he was in no hurry, so he stopped at a greengrocer's to buy an apple which he ate along the way, chewing carefully on the good side of his jaw.

Sternthal, the creative director at Oakley's, had been very positive during the first interview earlier in the week. He was a New Yorker and was happy to see an experienced "American" after having to tolerate a stuff of low-pressure Englishmen who didn't understand selling. Lunsford did not bother pointing out that he was a Canadian. He knew what Sternthal was getting at.

"Sell," Sternthal had crowed, "they don't even like to use the word." He was a short, compact man with wiry white hair and a Will Rogers squint. He was in his shirt sleeves. "Tell you what I mean. Went into a food store the other day and asked for kitty litter. Girl said, 'We don't do kitty litter.' She meant they didn't *sell* it, but she couldn't say the dirty word. Nobody does around here."

Today's discussion was to be a formality as Lunsford understood it. They would probably dicker over money, but he was in good shape. He could accept whatever Oakley's wanted to offer.

The first indication that all was not well came from Sternthal's secretary. The other day she had been effusively courteous. This morning she seemed preoccupied. She showed him into the inner office with a minimum of fanfare and then got the hell out.

Sternthal was busy with papers on his desk. "Sit down, Gerry," he said. He used the mandatory North American first-name salutation, but he did not look up. Bad news.

Lunsford sat down and tried to relax. So what if the verdict was no? His life did not hang on the outcome of this meeting. Finally the grizzly head tipped back and Lunsford was allowed to see one of Sternthal's wrinkled grins.

"O.K., Gerry, how's it going?"

It was a funny opener. The man could not really expect to hear a news report. "It's going fine, Len. How are things at Oakley's?" That was about as quickly as he could return the ball to Sternthal's side of the net.

"Not so good on this end. I wish you'd have given me the full story the other day, Gerry. I went to my managing director in good faith."

"What full story?"

"I told him I'd found the guy we were looking for, and now I learn what happened with you. I wish you'd have leveled with me. This is no way to start a relationship."

The ache from Lunsford's jaw flowed up into his forehead. He wanted not to close his eyes in Sternthal's face, but he had to do it. "I'm not with you, Len. What have you heard?"

"About the way you left Montreal. A wife abandoned. The company left in the lurch without any notice at all. This is not the way I like to see a man operate. I've never operated that way."

"Neither have I."

"You mean it isn't true?"

"It's a corruption of the truth. Not the whole picture."

Sternthal picked up a piece of paper, frowned at it, set it down again. "Well . . ."

Lunsford said quietly, "How did you get hold of this information, Len?"

"We were told. I hoped you'd be able to say it was false, Gerry."

"Who told you?"

"If it's true, I don't see that it makes any difference."

"I'd like to know. If somebody is making defamatory phone calls about me . . ."

"I'd never listen to a phone call. Man came in and sat right where you're sitting."

Lunsford looked down at the arms of the chair, seemed to sense them moving up to take hold of him, to make him a prisoner. He sat forward and the arms relaxed. "What was his name?"

"Said his name was Templeton."

"I don't know any Templeton." Lunsford got up. He looked out Sternthal's window at a sea of roofs and chimney pots.

"I'm sorry about this, Gerry. I suggest you level with the next person you see. Get it right out on the table."

"What did Templeton look like?"

Sternthal had a good eye and a writer's command of words. As Lunsford listened with mounting anguish, the American adman gave an exact description of Michael Telling.

Back on the pavement, Lunsford walked along Praed Street, passing several pubs until he came to one that seemed right. He went in and paid for a pint of bitter and took it to a table in the corner. The idea that Telling would cross three thousand miles of ocean to pursue him and spoil his life was shocking. It was such a vindictive thing to do, the sort of evil performance one would expect from a madman.

Somewhere along the line Margo would have to be told, but Lunsford decided to say nothing until after the fact. First he would find
some way to deal with Michael, to get him out of here and back to
Montreal.

Lunsford bought another pint of bitter at the bar and brought it back
to the table. His jaw was beginning to ache again, and the feeling of
light-headedness was back with a vengeance. A conviction arose in his
mind suddenly: Michael Telling was poisoning him. The dentist had
planted a slow-working but ultimately fatal substance in the root canal,
covering it with a filling. The poison was seeping into Lunsford's system, causing the heady feelings of the past weeks. Eventually it would
kill him, either in his sleep or by causing him to black out at the wheel
of a car or while crossing a busy street.

Then he thought, I'm becoming paranoid. If I go on like this, I'll be
as mad as Michael.

By leaning back in his chair, Lunsford was able to touch the back of
his head against the wall. Closing his eyes, he achieved a slight relief
from the inflated feeling inside his head. If it continued, he would have
somebody lift the fillings and test the packing underneath. Hell, he had
not quit his job and left his family and traveled all this distance to die
in England.

Somebody had Lunsford by the shoulders. He had trouble opening
his eyes. He did at last and saw strong, bare forearms. He was confused
—he imagined Michael Telling had hold of him and his heart lurched
inside his chest. Then he saw the pub surroundings, almost empty now.
The barman was standing over him. "Are you all right, sir?"

"Wow." He managed to sit up. They had cleared away his table.

"Thought you were going to drop out of the chair."

"No, I'm O.K. I guess I fell asleep."

He was lucky to find a taxi outside the pub. As they entered Lei-
cester Square, Lunsford saw a small center of activity on the sidewalk;
somebody was shining shoes. This was a rarity in London and Lunsford liked to have his shoes shined. The National Portrait Gallery was
only a couple of blocks away so he asked the driver to let him out on
the corner.

The shoeshine experience turned into a major embarrassment. He
began to lose his balance, standing with one foot raised on the metal
pedestal. It wasn't the ale, it was just this shattered head of his, but
how could he explain that to the people looking on? As Lunsford's shoe

slipped off the pedestal for the third time, the man wielding the brush asked, "You all right, gov?"

It was all anybody said to him any more. Two young boys left the watching crowd and held him in place, one on either side.

He was fine once he started walking again, and he made his way quickly to the main entrance of the Portrait Gallery. Years ago, vacationing with Bernice, Lunsford's feeling had been that he could take art galleries or leave them, but once inside and standing before the portraits, those giant windows into the past, he was won over completely. The portrait that had moved them most deeply was a head and shoulders of Robert Louis Stevenson. He was young and handsome and, according to the dates beneath the painting, dead at forty-two. This discovery shook Lunsford. He was already three years past Stevenson's age. It gave him an uneasy feeling of being on borrowed time.

The guards inside the main entrance looked him over as he drifted by. They were stationed there to search handbags for bombs, but a drunk among those priceless works might be just as dangerous. He made a strong effort to move with control and they turned away.

Lunsford went to Stevenson's portrait on the second floor and found the area deserted. He looked at his watch; he was ten minutes late, but he had shiny shoes.

Margo, always punctual, had probably gone off on a circuit of one of the other rooms. His best bet was to stay put until she returned. He stared at the poet's benign face, the moustache, the long hair, the gentle smile. A fragment of the poet's work came into Lunsford's mind: "Bright is the ring of words/ When the right man rings them,/ Fair the fall of songs/ When the singer sings them . . ."

He must have spoken aloud because a voice behind him carried on: "Still they are carolled and said—/ On wings they are carried—/ After the singer is dead/ And the maker buried."

He turned around and there was Michael Telling. The dentist was smiling.

"I took Stevenson in school, too," he said.

"Where's Margo?"

"I imagine she's almost packed by now. I told her to be ready to leave in an hour."

"What the hell are you talking about?"

"You've caused me a lot of trouble and expense, Gerry. I really should fix you for that, but I think you've fixed yourself enough."

"Margo is staying with me."

"No, she's not. She's coming back to Montreal. I wish I could tell you she took a lot of persuading, but I'm afraid it was easy."

"I won't let you take her."

"There's nothing you can do about it. Wake up, Gerry, you're such a terrible loser. Don't you see that? I'm not taking Margo. I'm just providing the opportunity for her to get back to where she was. She's been a bad girl but she regrets her mistake. No hard feelings."

"Hard feelings? I'll kill you, you arrogant—"

Telling loomed over Lunsford. The big, bristly head was like a malignant balloon. "You're some threat, Gerry. Look at you, you're on your last legs."

Lunsford balanced himself against the wall with one hand. His head was pounding. "You've poisoned me. You've done something to me."

"Go prove it." The dentist had a pleased grin on his face. He was talking in whispers. "You're a dead man, Lunsford. Fall down."

In the vaulted room, crowded with framed portraits, Lunsford was losing his sense of perspective. He was having trouble distinguishing his enemy among a crowd of shapes from the past. "I'm going to get you, Michael. If I have to kill you to get some peace, I'll do it, you can believe it."

The answer came from a distance. "Some chance."

When he opened his eyes, people were looking at him across their shoulders. There was no sign of Michael Telling; had he been there in the first place?

Lunsford went outside and found another taxi. He gave his address and fell into the back seat. As the taxi turned onto Charing Cross Road and stopped in traffic, he saw Michael unlocking the door of a blue sedan parked at the curb. The dentist stepped to the side of the taxi and spoke through the open window.

"Attaboy, Gerry," he said. "If you hurry, you'll have time to apologize to Margo before she leaves."

Lunsford left the taxi at the end of the mews and ran down the sloping alleyway, his shoes slipping on the oily cobbles.

One of the mechanics he had greeted so blithely that morning was sitting on the running board of an antique sedan with a packet of sandwiches open on his lap and a pint of milk in his hand. "Don't break a leg," he said. "She wouldn't appreciate that."

The parking space in front of the house was empty. Had Telling been and gone? Lunsford doubted it. He let himself in and found

Margo sitting at the rosewood table in the dining area. Her suitcases were on the floor at her side. She was drinking a cup of tea.

"Then it's true." He closed the door.

"He showed up just after you left." She looked into her teacup. "He made me tell him where I was meeting you."

"Did he twist your arm while you packed both of those bags?"

"I should never have come with you. It was a mistake."

"The only mistake we're making is letting him push us around. How can he do that? He's only one person." Lunsford took one of the bags to the foot of the stairs. "You're not going with him."

"Yes I am. He'll hurt you. He'll hurt me."

"How can he hurt us? There are policemen out in the street. We can dial 999 and have cops here in a minute. We're free to do what we want."

"Not with somebody like Michael. He's a psychopath. He doesn't care what he does."

"I'm beginning not to care either." Lunsford came back, pushed the swinging door and walked into the tiny kitchen. He found a heavy iron rod used for sharpening knives. He brought it back with him. "When he shows up, I'm going to persuade him to go home and leave us alone."

She got up and took the iron bar from Lunsford's hand. Like everything else about him today, his grip was weak. "That's no good, Gerry. Even if you got rid of him now, he'd just follow us around."

The room had grown dark. A spattering of rain swept across the front windows. One of the windows was cranked open and the white curtain billowed in as drops of rain hit the parquet floor. A car was approaching along the lane, throttling down.

"I'm going to stop him," Lunsford said.

"How? You'd have to be as wicked as he is."

"I don't understand you, Margo. If the man is so evil, how can you pack up and go with him?"

She got up and went to the foot of the stairs where she picked up her suitcase and brought it back to its place beside the other one. "I'm doing what's best in the long run."

A car door slammed outside.

Lunsford took Margo by the shoulders. Her face looked different; she had touched her cheeks and eyelids with makeup. "This morning we were so close," he said.

"This morning he wasn't here."

A heavy knock sounded at the door. Margo broke away, went to the door and opened it. Michael Telling stepped inside, brushing rain from the shoulders of his black coat. It was buttoned to the neck, the collar turned up, his head a bulging orange gourd above it.

"Change in the weather," he said. "I hope it won't spoil our drive down to Dover." He glanced around the room and grinned at the packed suitcases. "I've decided to give Margo a little treat. We're driving down to Dover, getting on a channel boat and catching a train at Calais. We'll be in Paris tonight."

Margo was looking at Lunsford. "Will you be all right?"

"Not if you walk out on me."

"Go back home. Call Bernice and tell her you're coming home."

"Margo, I'm sick. He did something to me in the chair when he filled those teeth. He poisoned me, I think."

She turned to Telling, who raised his shoulders and made the little blue eyes wide. "The poor guy is delirious."

"If I'm delirious, I need my nurse." Lunsford extended his hand. Margo took it, but her fingers were cold and stiff.

"I have to go with him, Gerry. If I don't, this will just go on and on."

Telling picked up the suitcases and carried them into the lane. Margo followed him, standing in the open doorway to keep clear of the rain. When Telling had the trunk of the car open and was stowing the bags inside, Lunsford pushed past Margo, grabbed the back of the black raincoat and pulled the big dentist erect. He swung hard and caught Telling with a right-hand punch on the side of the head. Telling slipped and went to one knee in a puddle of oily rainwater. Over his shoulder, Lunsford could see the mechanic standing in his garage doorway, milk bottle poised halfway to his lips, watching the action.

Margo yelled from the doorway, "Michael, don't hurt him! I'm coming with you." She stepped out and opened the front door of the car. She was getting in.

Telling said, "I really think I should break your head, Gerry." He got up and came on fast, bulling Lunsford back through the open doorway of the house. Their momentum carried them across the room so that Lunsford was bent across the table with Telling leaning over him. The dentist's huge hands were clamped about his throat. Lunsford tried to break the grip. He seized Telling's wrists, clawing at them, feeling his fingernails digging in, breaking the skin.

The grip tightened. His focus of vision was narrowing as though he were looking down a tunnel at Telling's twisted mouth and squinting blue eyes. The man was in the process of killing him. He was seconds away from death.

Lunsford must have blacked out because he opened his eyes to find himself sitting on the floor with the garage mechanic kneeling beside him.

"Bloody strong one," the mechanic said. "Took me and the lady to pull him off of you."

A car engine was retreating down the lane. Lunsford tried to struggle to his feet.

"You'd better lie still and try to collect yourself. That's the way."

He lay back flat on the carpet and looked at the ceiling. The rain shower had been brief. Now the sun was out again and an elongated rectangle of light approximated the shape of the window on the white plaster above him.

The mechanic brought a glass of water and stood over him with it. Sunlight concentrated in the bottom of the glass so that it glared in Lunsford's eyes, reminding him vaguely of the light above Telling's dental chair. He drank the water and then said he was all right. He wanted to be left alone. The mechanic combed his hair in front of the glass in the bookcase and went away.

Lunsford kept his place on the floor, half-asleep. He was not sure how much time had passed when he heard a car approach down the lane, stopping outside his front door. He struggled to his knees, hoping Margo had changed her mind but not really believing it. Before he could get to his feet he heard his daughter's voice.

"Daddy, are you all right?"

He felt strong hands under his arms as Steve steadied him and guided him onto a chair beside the rosewood table. Colleen was a blur before his eyes; they were both indistinct images.

"I'm O.K. Listen, I have to tell you something."

He must have blacked out again because he was next aware of hot tea being spooned past his lips.

"He needs a shot of brandy," Steve said.

"Not if he's bombed already." Colleen's tone was a mixture of anxiety and irritation.

"I'm not drunk. Thank God you're here. You can help me."

"That's why we came. Mom is worried. You wrote just once giving us this address and then you never answered her letter. She had a terrible feeling something had happened to you."

"Good old Bernice. Bless her heart. She knows me, she's right here inside of me." He was crying but he couldn't help it. "You can't rule out twenty-five years."

"So Steve and I hopped on a plane. We planned to visit you soon anyway, but Mom insisted we come now."

"I can use you. If ever the old man needed help, this is the time. You've got wheels?"

"A rental," Steve said.

"O.K. We're going for a drive."

Between sips of unwanted tea, Lunsford told his story. The suspected poisoning, Telling's interference with the job interview, his abduction of Margo, the fight in the lane, their departure for Dover.

"And that's where we're going," Lunsford said. "He's not going to get away with it."

Colleen seemed unconvinced. "Dad, are you sure? I mean she's a grown-up woman. If she went with him . . ."

Lunsford stood up and reeled toward the front door. "Where's the car?"

He heard Steve's subdued mutter, "Let's go along with him, Colly."

The drive took place without much awareness on Lunsford's part. He must have slept, slumped half over in the back seat. When he opened his eyes and sat up, he saw they were near the top of a hill. The channel was below them, the harbor filled with ships, and the hazy roofs of Dover. Ahead, on a grassy plateau in the middle distance, was a large castle, a mass of stone walls, turrets and streaming flags. The declining rays of the sun in early evening painted the castle gold on one face, deep blue on the others. In Lunsford's eyes, it appeared as a ghost castle, the misty frontispiece from an adventure book he had read in his childhood.

"You feeling O.K.?" Colleen asked, turning her worried face over the front seat.

"Must have slept," Lunsford said. "That'll put me on my feet." But he felt as bad as before; throbbing jaw, light, airy head.

"What do we do now?" Steve asked. He was crouched behind the wheel, wild-haired, bearded; a Canadian bear driving a small British car. "How do we find them?"

"We keep our eyes open and hope we get lucky. I'm due for some luck."

A blue sedan was parked on the grass a hundred yards ahead beside an ice-cream truck. Two familiar figures stood at the counter accepting cones from the vendor.

"And how about that?" Lunsford said.

"Is that her?" Steve asked.

"And him."

"Daddy, don't get in any more trouble."

"Don't worry, I'm only going to talk to him," Lunsford assured her, but he knew what he was going to do and where he would do it. "Park here, Steve."

The dentist and Margo seemed hardly surprised to see him.

"Well, you're here with reinforcements," Michael said. "Hi there, Colleen. Everybody have an ice on me."

Margo raised a hand. "Hello, Steve. Colleen, honey, take care of your father."

Colleen did not look at Margo. "Somebody has to," she said.

"No ice cream for me, thanks," Lunsford said. He made his voice cheerful and was surprised to hear it working better than it had in days. "You know something, Mike? You and I have to get sensible. We have to straighten this thing out. Will you come and talk?"

"Sure, Gerry. That's all I wanted to do in the first place. But you said everything was settled."

"Then was then and now is now." He took Michael's arm and led him up the slope.

Colleen called after her father. "Where are you going?"

"A little stroll. Enjoy your ice cream. Watch the channel boats. See you soon."

He found himself able to chat easily with Michael as they climbed the grassy slope and emerged finally on the crest above the chalk cliffs. Here they sat with their backs to the sun, their eyes squinting into the wind off the water, looking down at a squat car ferry slowing down and bouncing in the chop as it approached the breakwater.

"O.K.," Lunsford said. "Getting right to the point, I have been a middle-aged damn fool."

"Don't be hard on yourself, Gerry."

"It's true. I must have gone out of my mind. There was a lot of pressure at the office these past few months. I talked myself into believing I could run away and start over." Lunsford pried a lump of chalk from the edge of the grass, stood up and threw it far out into the air. It spun away fast, disappearing against the mottled backdrop of the water.

"Anyway, I'm going to pack it in and go home. If Bernice will take me back."

Telling stood up, too.

"She'll take you back. With open arms."

"Sorry I made all this upset."

"Don't apologize. Hell, Margo and I are going to make a holiday of it." He turned. They were out of sight of the cars and the ice-cream truck. "That's how you should think of it, too."

"I suppose I will one day. Wow, look at those arms. Did my fingernails do that?"

Telling looked at the deep scratches. "Who could blame you? With what I was doing to you."

They walked toward the path leading back down the slope. Lunsford pointed to a rusty aperture in the face of an outcropping of chalk. "Look," he said, "an old World War II gun emplacement. Ever been inside one?"

Telling's eyes lit up. "No. That's where they sat waiting for the Nazis. Only they never came."

"Come on. Bernice and I were here a few years ago. It's fascinating, once you get used to the smell."

There was a strong latrine odor inside the gloomy cave. Their footsteps echoed on the rocky floor. Steel bulkheads were scrawled in rough chalk with hundreds of names and dates. "Don't trip over those rails," Lunsford said. "They used to run the ammo up in trucks."

Michael Telling stood in the actual gun turret, staring out through a rectangular slot in the rusted metal. Lunsford stood behind him.

"Hey," the dentist said, "this is just like all those war films," and Lunsford swung hard with the sharp rock in his right hand, crushing the back of Telling's red-thatched skull.

Colleen and Steve and Margo had finished eating their ice cream. They were leaning on the side of the blue sedan, staring up at the walls of Dover Castle, shrouded now in near darkness. The sky was cobalt blue, pricked with a few silver stars in the east. Lunsford walked up behind them.

"Ladies and gentleman," he said, "we are free to go."

Margo looked past him, frowning. "Where's Michael?"

"Michael has listened to reason. I knew he was a good guy underneath."

"Where is he?"

"He took the shortcut down the cliff to get to the city. He's catching a train back to London and a plane back home."

"Without saying good-bye?" Margo said.

Colleen asked, "Is this true, Dad?"

"Of course it is. He sent you all his love, and he even gave me the keys to his car. With all sorts of apologies for making a pest of himself."

Lunsford opened the door of the blue sedan and held it for Margo. "Climb in, luv," he said. "And as for you two kids, have a nice vacation. And when you get home, tell your mother I'll write soon."

He drove away with Colleen's puzzled face centered in the rear-view mirror till it dwindled away.

For some time Margo was silent. Then she said, "You killed him."

"Don't be silly."

"I know Michael. There's no way he'd walk out of this scene."

Lunsford was driving into a small village. There was an ancient church at a curve in the road. The walls were of flint, the square Norman tower decorated with a frieze of bizarre faces.

"You *thought* you knew Michael. You *think* you know me." He slowed down and drove the car onto the grassy verge below the churchyard. He turned the key and the engine died. "I thought I knew you. Nobody knows anybody any more." His light-headedness, gone during the action in the gun turret, was back now, worse than ever.

Margo got out of the car. He climbed out after her. She was walking away. "I'm not driving any farther with you."

"Where do you think you're going?"

"To the police. How did I let myself get into this mess? You're worse now than Michael ever was."

"Come and talk, Margo. Don't walk off. It's getting dark, there's nothing open around here."

"I'll find a phone."

"Margo, don't leave me. I need you now more than ever." He sat down on a fallen gravestone. "Margo," he called, and his voice broke.

She came back and stood beside him. "What is it?"

"The poison. My head feels full of it. I can hardly think."

"That's crazy. Nobody's poisoned you, Gerry. You're out of your mind."

She turned and he caught her by the ankle, tripping her. Her head struck a stone sarcophagus as she fell, leaving a white scuff mark in the dark green moss. She lay still. He crouched over her, listening for a heartbeat. There seemed to be none, but he lifted a heavy slab of granite and dropped it on her anyway.

Then he staggered to the car and drove for some distance along winding roads until a passing car veered, flashed its lights and sounded its horn. Then he switched on his own lights and drove more slowly.

He was a long time finding his way back to London although he had driven these roads with Bernice two years ago. Throughout the long drive, he was consumed with panic; he was alone now. Without Margo, he would never have had the nerve to leave his wife. Now Margo was dead, and where was he to go from here?

He parked the car at the head of the mews and went into the Rose and Crown. There was half an hour of pub time left and he could not face the empty house without something to drink.

He ordered two double whiskies and took them to his favorite table. The red plush chair opposite him where Bernice had sat two years ago and, more recently, Margo, was empty now, angled accusingly in the room. He drank the first double at a draft and held the second one close to his pounding heart.

What was left for him now? A month ago life was solid and secure, apart from his struggle with job boredom and a running argument with his wife. Didn't all of that make him the average North American man?

Well, he had changed his situation in a few short weeks. He was average no longer.

The publican's voice rang out, calling for final orders. Lunsford drank his second double whisky and went back for a refill. The carpet undulated beneath his feet.

He was back on his bench when he saw a black raincoat and an orange head disappearing through the door to the men's room. He knocked the small table over getting up. Inside the men's room was another door leading to the alley. He opened it and saw the familiar figure dart around the corner into the mews. There was a patch of white bandage on the orange head.

"Are you all right, sir?" The publican was at his shoulder.

Lunsford would have to reassure yet another stranger. "Yes. I'm all right."

Outside in the mews, he was not the least bit surprised to find the blue sedan missing. Naturally, Telling had a spare set of keys—but how had he survived the blow on the head? And how had he made it back to London so quickly?

Of course he himself had stopped off in the churchyard with Margo.

Blindly, Lunsford skidded down the slippery cobbled lane toward the house. The repair shops were all bolted shut, the mews echoed with emptiness. He unlocked his front door and let himself into the silent house. He turned on the kitchen light and sat on a stool beside the counter, wondering what to do. Michael had him where he wanted him now. Assault with a deadly weapon. Attempted murder. All he had to do was show up with a police officer to win the game once and for all. They'd ask about Margo's absence and sooner or later they would find her.

How had the whole thing turned around on him? It was a nightmare.

He decided to call Bernice. There was nothing else he could do. He checked his watch; it would be around 6:15 P.M. in Montreal. He dialed the call direct and was lucky with the circuits. The phone buzzed twice in the house on the other side of the ocean, and there was Bernice.

"Hello?"

"It's me."

"Gerry, where are you?"

"Still in England. But I'm in trouble."

"Then come home if you're in trouble."

"I was afraid you wouldn't have me."

"Oh, sweetie, we help each other when we need it. Don't ever be afraid to come to me." Her voice was warm. Lunsford felt tears of relief in his eyes.

"I should never have left. Everything has fallen apart, just like you said."

"Never mind what I said. You just get on a plane and come home and it'll be all right. Everything will be just like it was."

"No, never again. I've done terrible things over here."

"What things?"

"There's been violence. Killing. The police will be coming for me."

Bernice's voice barely hesitated. "Whatever it is, the thing is for you to get home. Once you're home, everything will be all right."

"O.K., then. I'm coming home."

He took a taxi to the airport. He drank in the lounge until his departure was called. The time passed in hazy, disjointed segments and so did the flight itself. Before Lunsford knew it, he was getting off the plane in Dorval, blinking in the sunlight, his head throbbing, the pressure in his aching jaw increasing by the minute.

Then he found himself in a taxi outside the front door of his house and Bernice was coming down the walk to help him with his bags.

"Are you all right?" the taxi driver inquired.

Inside the house, he stood with his hands on her shoulders, looking into her face, trying to begin telling his wife what had happened to him.

"I don't want to hear. Not now. You're going to sleep and then, when you wake up, we'll decide what to do."

She helped him upstairs and into their bedroom where the spread was turned down. He collapsed on the bed and she moved about, straightening his legs, adjusting the pillow under his head, drawing the drapes to darken the room.

He closed his eyes.

Sometime later he heard a voice outside the door, a male voice, talking on the telephone.

". . . not a thing to worry about. I told you, it can't go wrong. He's helpless." It was Michael Telling's voice. The maniac had followed him across the ocean! He was in the house. He must have killed Bernice and now he was coming in to finish him off!

"Don't call me here again." The dentist sounded tense. "Just sit tight. I'll get rid of him and I'll call you later."

Who was he talking to? Margo? But Margo was dead in an English churchyard.

Lunsford tried to open his eyes; the room was bright. The light dazzled him. Hadn't Bernice drawn the drapes? He had to get up and get to the window. Telling was in the hallway outside the bedroom. If he could get through the window onto the balcony, he could escape into Colleen's room. He had to get through the window.

"O.K., Gerry." Michael's voice was right beside his ear. Strong hands were fastened on Lunsford's arms. He opened his eyes and saw the stark white walls of the dental surgery, the green leather chair from which he had just been lifted, the billowing white curtains at the wide-open window.

Lunsford tried to cry out but his mouth was stiff with anesthetic, his brain numb with heavy sedation.

"As we say in the trade," Telling grunted, forcing Lunsford's leg up over the window frame, "this will only hurt for a second."

Then Lunsford was through the window, in the air, half-turning as he fell six floors to the empty courtyard.

The police inspector was satisfied. He thanked Mrs. Lunsford for coming down to say what she could about her husband's recent depression. Then he told the shattered dentist not to blame himself. It could have happened to anybody.

"I shouldn't have left him alone." Dr. Telling drove his fist into his palm, stood up and walked to the window. He reached up and slammed the frame down so hard the glass rattled. Too late; the horse was gone. "I knew how anxious he was. Hell," the dentist turned to the inspector, his eyes wide with agony, "I probably shouldn't have given him those tranquilizers. They must have depressed him even further."

"You were trying to help the man."

Bernice Lunsford agreed. She took a deep breath. "He's right, Dr. Telling. The claustrophobia . . . Gerry used to go wild in the chair. We both know that."

The dentist nodded slowly, but he was not convinced. On the way out of the building, the inspector said to the ambulance driver, about to leave for the morgue, "We should board up that window or you may have another customer. That dentist up there is inconsolable."

The driver was a cynic. "He's upset because he won't be able to send the widow his bill."

Bernice Lunsford, wild with elation, tried to kiss Michael Telling. He shrugged her off, rolling his eyes toward the adjoining office where Margo Mantro was sitting behind the desk, her face turned to the wall. Telling mouthed, "Call you tonight." Then he saw Bernice to the door and let her out with a mumbled apology.

"Please," Bernice said in a clear voice, "don't blame yourself." She winked and blew a kiss.

Dr. Telling stood in the office doorway. He stared at Margo for a few minutes and she stared back at him, a slight frown between her eyes.

"Something troubling you, Margo?"

The nurse shook her head. "No," she said. "I was just thinking, if you hadn't sent me across the road to the lab with those inlays, I might have been able to grab poor Gerry before he jumped."

"That's wishful thinking," Telling said. "It doesn't help. Now you go on home and try to get over this. It'll be hard, but we'll both have to try."

He went to the sink and ran the water to wash his hands. Margo stared at the livid scratches on his forearms.

"Harder for you than for me," Margo said.

She telephoned the police inspector the next morning after a nearly sleepless night. She said she had been thinking about Lunsford's death and it just didn't seem right to her. The inspector said a few doubts had crossed his mind, too, but did she have anything specific?

"Yes. There were long, bloody scratches on Dr. Telling's forearms yesterday afternoon which were not there earlier. Suppose you check under Mr. Lunsford's fingernails. If you find tissue there, and it compares with Dr. Telling's scratches, would that be something to do on?"

The inspector told her it would, indeed, be something to go on. He thanked her and said he would be talking again at much greater length to her and to Dr. Michael Telling.

Margo put down the phone and went into her kitchen to put on the kettle. Usually on Saturday mornings she had tea instead of coffee, but today she set the kettle aside unfilled and poured herself a whisky instead. It was Gerry's drink, and she drank it to him. He was a nice, harmless guy who was too shy ever to do more than invite her once in a while to the Empire on a Friday afternoon. Until yesterday, when he acted as if he was about to open up with her.

Now she'd never know what was on his mind.